"An exotic a... ...an outsider's perspe... ...crafted, suspenseful tale of the bygone era before Florida came to the mountains." —Sharyn McCrumb, *New York Times* bestselling author of *St. Dale*

"Vicki Lane captured my ear on the first page. Her dialect is right on the money. Her characters live and breathe and hold their secrets close—heart-wrenching secrets that pulled me in and kept me reading. . . . Add to all this a beautifully told tale with a great unexpected twist and you've got one of the best mystery books I've read in a long time."
—Sheila Kay Adams, author of *My Old True Love*

"One can't live in the Appalachians without hearing the stories rising from them. Vicki Lane is one of those rare storytellers who transports the mysteries and tales and characters of her beloved mountains into the greater world with dignity and sympathy and intelligence."
—Tony Earley, author of *Jim the Boy*

"*Signs in the Blood* warmed me and kept me engaged until the last page. . . . Ms. Lane's understanding of mountain language, history, and culture, combined with a wonderful ability to tell a story made for an absolutely great read."
—Rob Amberg

"What makes Vicki Lane's novel so enveloping is the honest and convincing portrayal of the Appalachian neighbors with whom her main character finds herself emotionally involved. . . . A true and fascinating picture of the area that lends a palpable tension to the underlying and complicated mystery of this novel."
—Jeanne McDonald, co-author, with Fred Brown, of *The Serpent Handlers: Three Families and Their Faith*

SIGNS

IN THE

BLOOD

VICKI LANE

A DELL BOOK

SIGNS IN THE BLOOD
A Dell Book / June 2005

Published by Bantam Dell
A Division of Random House, Inc.
New York, New York

Lyrics on page 84 from "San Francisco (Be Sure to Wear Some Flowers in Your Hair)," written by John Phillips, performed by Scott McKenzie, MCA Music, 1967.

Lyrics from the traditional ballads "Wagoner's Lad" (p. 43) and "Little Mathey Groves" (p. 168–169), Granny Dell Records, 1990, reprinted with the permission of Sheila Kay Adams.

Excerpt on page 301 from "Invictus," by William Ernst Henley, 1875.

Excerpt on page 313 from "The Second Coming," by William Butler Yeats, 1921.

This is a work of fiction. Names, characters, places, and incidents either are the product of the author's imagination or are used fictitiously. Any resemblance to actual persons, living or dead, events, or locales is entirely coincidental.

Dell is a registered trademark of Random House, Inc., and the colophon is a trademark of Random House, Inc.

ISBN 0-440-24208-8

Printed in the United States of America
Published simultaneously in Canada
www.bantamdell.com

OPM 10 9 8 7 6 5 4 3 2 1

For Karol and Madelon,
who started it and kept it going.
And for John, who has had to live with it.

ACKNOWLEDGMENTS

First of all I owe heartfelt thanks to my agent, the indefatigable Ann Collette, and to my splendid editor, Kate Miciak, who wanted more. What unparalleled good fortune to work with these women! And thanks too to Connie Munro, eagle-eyed copy editor, who patiently worked with my outmoded punctuation and caught some outrageous errors, and to Anna Forgione, my managing editor, and unsung hero of production.

And many, many thanks are due to all those who helped in so many ways, most especially: Paul and Grace Henderson, Mearl Davis, Eileen Kulp, Margaret Payne, Retha Ward, and the late Clifford and Louise Freeman for friendship and knowledge of the old ways. Thanks to Connie Buckner and Virginia Norton for enthusiastic support and use of the library; to Sallie Bissell and Sharyn McCrumb for valuable insights into the world of the novelist; and to Sheila Kay Adams for musical and literary inspiration. Malcolm Owen gave me the tale that led to Little Sylvie, and the late Vickie Owen introduced me to these mountains and told me the story that opens the book. Thanks also to Justin Skemp for anthropological and philosophic insights; Cory Barlow for technical support; Wily DuVall for historical knowledge; Greg Higby for pharmacological guidance; and Bill Brooks, for invaluable advice about doilies. ("Get rid of them," he said.)

Three books were extremely useful to me. *The Serpent Handlers* by Fred Brown and Jeanne McDonald (Winston Salem, North Carolina, John F. Blair, 2000) and *Salvation on Sand Mountain* by Dennis Covington (Reading, Massachusetts, Addison-Wesley Publishing Company, 1995) gave me an in-depth look at the signs-following religion. And Wilma Dykeman's classic *The French Broad* (New York, Holt, Rinehart and Winston, 1955) deepened my understanding of the region in which my story is set.

I must express my great appreciation and love for the beautiful county I have called home for the past thirty years. It would be useless to deny the similarities that exist between it and Elizabeth's Marshall County. I must, however, say that, to my knowledge, we have no right-wing militia, no commune of star children, and no painting evangelist.

And finally, thanks to Caitlin Alexander for her diligence and good humor.

SIGNS

IN THE

BLOOD

CHAPTER 1
You Just Got to Have Faith
(Monday)

WHEN DESSIE MILLER LAY DYING AT HOME, her family overflowed the little house in a bittersweet reunion. Food was on the table at all hours of the day and of the night, continually replenished as newcomers arrived with their contributions. "This here's the tater salad that Mommy always loved" accompanied an aluminum dishpan heaped with a pale yellow mound of potatoes, chopped pickles, and hard-boiled eggs, all glistening with mayonnaise. A gaunt chain-smoking woman, just off her factory shift, set down a cardboard tub of fried chicken with a dismissive wave of her cigarette: "It ain't but Colonel Sanders but I reckon someone kin worry it down." A grizzled farmer in clean overalls handed a covered bowl to one of the daughters. "Them greasy cut-short beans is some Ollie canned; she cain't come 'cause she's down in the back, but she cooked 'em up fer you 'uns." The Ridley Branch Freewill Baptist choir sang "O Come, Angel Band" in the living room and two teenage grandchildren got saved in the kitchen.

Elizabeth Goodweather sat quietly at one end of the plastic-upholstered sofa. The heat in the crowded house was stifling but she couldn't step out to the porch, not yet, not while Pastor Briggs was praying aloud for Dessie and for all the "miserable sinners" gathered there. He went on and on in the hypnotic chant that was the way of so many old-time mountain preachers, his voice rising and falling, a loud inhalation at the end of each phrase keeping his message from ever coming to a full stop.

The sonorous words rolled out, almost in an auctioneer's chant: "Yes, it's the hour of decision, brothers and sisters, the time when you make your choice . . . you make your choice between the fire below . . . and it's a hot fire . . . and it's an eternal fire . . ."

I hate the emphasis on damnation, thought Elizabeth, *but I know it's what these folks expect out of a sermon.* Across the room she saw Miss Birdie Gentry, one of her longtime neighbor friends. Birdie and her middle-aged son, Cletus, lived in a tiny log house down by the paved road that ran beside Ridley Branch. Cletus was what people called "simple," but he and Miss Birdie took care of each other and scratched out a living from their tobacco patch and garden. Miss Birdie's eyes were fixed on the preacher and her lips were silently moving.

". . . but there's a lifeline . . . and it's a heavenly lifeline . . . and Jesus, he'll pull you out of the pit . . ."

Many of those in the little room were swaying and nodding now; some of the women held up their open-palmed hands in an almost ecstatic surrender. "Thank you, Jesus," someone murmured. A few cigarette-hungry men shuffled uneasily by the door, held in place by sharp glances from their wives.

Elizabeth bowed her head, hoping fervently that she would not be noticed there on her corner of the sofa. She had come to say good-bye to Dessie, the old woman who, some twenty years ago, had first welcomed her and

Sam to Ridley Branch, here in the mountains of North Carolina. Dessie had been in her midsixties then, sturdy and vigorous. She could hoe tobacco for hours on end or dart up the steep mountain trails after a wandering milk cow. Dessie and her husband, Odus, had taken Sam and Elizabeth under their wing, helping the newcomers to adapt to country life and teaching them how to do the myriad tasks that were part of life on a small mountain farm.

From planting potatoes to plowing with a mule, from milking a cow to butchering a hog, Dessie and Odus had taught the young couple, delighted to be passing on their knowledge of the old-time ways. From them, Elizabeth and Sam had learned the vocabulary of the mountains, had learned that a small creek was called a branch and a bag was called a poke, had learned to say "holler" for hollow, "mater" for tomato and "baccer" for tobacco. "It's about communication," Sam had said when Elizabeth's inner English major winced at these pronunciations. Now, of course, with the passage of years, the mountain dialect had flavored and enriched her own speech and she could appreciate its unique music.

Odus has been gone, it must be almost fifteen years, thought Elizabeth. Dessie had carried on with the help of her children, but time had taken its toll. She had still tended a big garden every year, but with each season she grew frailer. Every spring, as the garden patch was being plowed under her critical eye, she would say that this was her last year to put out so much corn, so many rows of beans and tomatoes. Now, it seemed, that time had come. There was no garden this year. After an unsuccessful operation—"Hit was everywhere; they said she was plum eat up with it"—and a brief stay in the hospital, Dessie had been brought home, where she could be tended by hospice volunteers and by her numerous loving family.

At last the prayer was ended and the preacher was being escorted back to Dessie's bedside for a farewell blessing. Louvanda, the youngest of Dessie's four daughters, leaned down to Elizabeth and whispered, "Soon as Preacher gets done, she wants to see you. She asked for you particular."

"Thanks, Louvanda," Elizabeth said. "I'll wait out on the front porch if you don't mind; I need to cool off a bit."

"Lord, don't I know," agreed Louvanda, fanning her own reddened face. "Seems like I ain't never goin' to get through the change."

The porch was empty except for Dessie's half-blind old cow dog. Patsy thumped her tail and lifted her head to acknowledge Elizabeth's presence, but stayed curled up on her scrap of faded carpet. Sinking gratefully into a weathered oak rocker, Elizabeth stretched out her long legs, propping up her sneaker-clad feet on a milk crate, and looked across the road to new-plowed tobacco fields. The red dirt lay in furrows, heavy clods thrown to the side and dotted with streaming tufts of deep green barley, the remains of a winter cover crop. Beyond the tobacco fields and just out of sight behind a small ridge lay her land—more fields and pastures, barns and outbuildings. And above them all rose the tree-clad peak that was Pinnacle Mountain—her home. Elizabeth's eyes traveled lovingly up the slope, relishing the vibrant yellow-greens of new foliage merging with the deeper emeralds of pine and fir. At the top of the mountain, a slash of pasture gleamed like polished jade amid the trees.

I will lift up mine eyes unto the hills. The verse sprang into her mind, a relic of her churchgoing childhood. *They do give me strength, even if I don't have the same kind of faith my neighbors do.* She thought of the women inside with their uplifted hands and radiant faces. *It would be so comforting, so relaxing, just to believe and not think. I had that kind of faith when I was young.* A bitter inner voice sounded mockingly: *Didn't you used to believe in a lot of things— Santa Claus, the Easter Bunny, and happily ever after?*

Elizabeth sighed, looking at the western sky beyond the mountain. Four in the afternoon and the sun was still high over her farm. She had welcomed the lengthening days of spring, and now that May was here, with its profusion of flowers and garden work to be done, she hoped that the joyless cloud that had so unexpectedly settled on her last fall would finally lift. There would be time to work in the garden before supper. Time to hoe or dig till exhaustion forced her inside, and then a quick supper, a soak in a hot bath, and she could fall, bone-weary, into bed and sleep without thinking about the empty space beside her.

Sam's death, almost five years before, had shattered her world, but she had forced herself to carry on. She had told herself that there would be time to mourn later: later, after her girls, Rosemary and Laurel, were established in their lives; later, after she had proven to herself that she could keep the farm going. Pressing needs on every side—the farm, the girls, the business—had forced her to hide her grief in some unvisited corner of her mind. Four years had gone by and her friends and family had marveled at her strength, her cheerfulness, and her acceptance. *But last October, when Laurel moved to Asheville, I just crashed,* she thought.

Laurel, her younger daughter, was a self-described "struggling artist" whose large semiabstract acrylics were beginning to attract the attention of a few galleries. She was fiercely independent and extremely competent. *And she's twenty-four years old and certainly capable of being on her own,* thought Elizabeth. *But as sophisticated and swaggering as she comes across, there's a core of . . . of naïveté. I still feel like I have to watch out for her. Or is this just the old empty-nest syndrome hitting with a vengeance?*

Elizabeth had spent the winter in a kind of wounded numbness, suddenly mired in loss. She felt in need of comfort but didn't know where to find it, having been unwilling to tell her two daughters—or indeed any-one—that she missed Sam now even more than she had at the time of the accident that had taken him from her.

"Well, Lizzie Beth." Miss Birdie came out, closing the screen door carefully behind her. "Hit's good to see you. I know Dessie'll be proud you come." She wiped her eyes and Elizabeth suddenly realized that Miss Birdie, once an energetic and bustling little butterball, had lost weight and seemed frail and old. Her face was thin and haggard and she was using a cane. *A cane—when did this start?* Elizabeth wondered.

"Why don't you sit out here with me for a while, Miss Birdie?" Elizabeth suggested, pulling a rocking chair over near her own. "This must be awfully hard on you. You and Dessie have been friends since you were little girls, haven't you?"

"That we have, Lizzie Beth, honey. But when the Lord calls, I reckon we have to answer." The little woman leaned heavily on her cane and brushed her hand across her eyes. "I'm sorry I can't stay and visit with you, Lizzie Beth, but I'm lookin' for Cletus to be home today. He'll be wantin' something hot for supper after bein' back in them woods a couple of weeks." Miss Birdie shook her head. "He's right bad to loafer but he always comes home when it's gettin' time to hoe the baccer. And they's a big tent revival next week up on the bypass and that boy does purely love a tent revival. Hit's some preacher from away called John the Baptizer is what Pastor Briggs done told us."

Miss Birdie went slowly and carefully down the steps and out to her ancient pickup truck, pausing to call back, "You come see us, now."

Once again, the screen door opened and Louvanda and Pastor Briggs stepped onto the porch. "Thank you for coming today, Pastor," said Louvanda. She wrapped her arms across her chest and stood silent for a minute. Her face was wet with tears as she began again, "The home health nurse said Mommy's sinkin' fast; it was a true blessing to have you to pray with her before the end."

Pastor Briggs pulled a folded white handkerchief from the back pocket of his shiny black trousers and wiped his face. "Preaching's hard work, but I'm glad if I could be of comfort to Sister Miller and bring a few more souls to Jesus."

His dark eyes flicked toward Elizabeth, taking in her blue jeans and faded work shirt with disfavor. Louvanda followed his gaze and said, "This here is Miz Good-weather. She lives over yon, almost to the top of Pinnacle, you know, the old Baker place. Miz Goodweather's been a good neighbor to Mommy ever since her and her man moved here. Mommy wants to see you now, 'Lizbeth," she continued. "Just go straight on through. She's still awake but she just had some more of the pain medicine and she'll likely drop off pretty soon."

Stepping back into the claustrophobic heat of the house, Elizabeth saw that most of the crowd of family and friends were filling plates from the laden kitchen table and settling in chairs all around the living room to eat, to gossip, and to reminisce. She knew many of the members of Dessie's large family, and nodded and smiled her way through the throng back to the bedroom where her old friend lay.

Kylie Sue, Dessie's oldest daughter, was standing guard at the door. Her weatherworn face looked tired but serene, and she smiled sweetly at the sight of Elizabeth.

" 'Lizbeth, you come right in. She's gettin' sleepy but she was set on talkin' to you. She was askin' for you this mornin', but then the preacher come." Kylie Sue rolled her shoulders and stretched her arms. "Lordy, I been set-tin' there with her I don't know how long. I'm stiff all over. If you don't care, 'Lizbeth, would you stay with her till she falls asleep? I need to go get me some coffee."

The old woman lay in the dim light of the little bed-room, a tiny wasted shape under the softly glowing blues and reds of a Delectable Mountains patchwork quilt. Her eyes were closed but her thin fingers picked at the black cover of the worn Bible that was resting on her chest. Elizabeth hesitated. Then she said softly, "Hey, Dessie."

The eyes slowly opened and Dessie squinted up at Elizabeth. Her toothless mouth formed a smile. "Hey yoreself, Lizzie Beth." She stretched out a bony hand and Elizabeth took it. "Get you a chair, Lizzie Beth; I got something to say to you. Seems like it's been just a-goin' round and round in my head and I'll not be easy till I tell you."

Still holding Dessie's hand, Elizabeth sat in the ladder-back chair that was pulled up to the side of the bed. "What is it, Dessie? Is there something I can do for you?"

Dessie looked at the younger woman fondly. "Lizzie Beth, you been a good neighbor to me all these years but there ain't a thing you can do for me now. Preacher's prayed over me and I've had a word with all the young uns. They even brought all the least uns in to say good-bye to Mamaw. I'm content in my heart. But I been studyin' about you, Lizzie Beth. All winter long you ain't been yoreself, worser even than right after yore Sam was took. Now, I know you ain't one to talk about yore troubles, but I could see it just the same. You have a great sorrow on yore heart, a hurt that ain't a-healin'."

Elizabeth started to protest but Dessie squeezed her hand with surprising strength. "Honey, I don't want you to say nothing. But I got to tell you, I seen that things is gonna be different; like the old hymn they sung this mornin' says, they's a glory side to the cloud . . ."

Her eyes drifted shut but she continued to talk, her voice growing fainter with each word. "I seen it in a dream and the Lord laid it on my heart to tell you. Lizzie Beth, there's more trials ahead but you'll make it through. You just got to have faith . . ." Her voice was a wandering whisper. "I keep a-dreaming dreams. I dreamt of Little Sylvie, that wild girl who used to live up to your place. She was afore my time but my mamaw done told me of her and I seen her just now as plain as anything. She was a-laying in death, a-laying in the dirt with her babe in her arms and a gold locket round her neck . . ."

The dying woman tossed restlessly on her pillows. "How come I to see her like that? Mamaw said that Little Sylvie run off and left her poor baby to starve. I can't make it out." Dessie's words faltered and at last trailed off into a low snore. Elizabeth sat quietly and watched her old friend sleep.

"She's been talking about that Little Sylvie since she woke up this morning," said a voice from the doorway. Kylie Sue had returned and was looking down at her sleeping mother with great affection. "She woke up this morning and said she'd had a dream about you and Little Sylvie. She said she'd not go home till she spoke to you."

Kylie Sue's tired smile illuminated her face. "I believe, 'Lizabeth, that with her time so near, why, she's plumb full of the Spirit right now. I reckon she just had to share it with you."

As her jeep ground its way up the steep gravel road to her farmhouse, Elizabeth found herself wondering about the dying woman's message. *How did Dessie know that I was so unhappy? No one else noticed.* Indeed, she had done her best to present her usual cheerful front. Her daughters certainly had no idea. Laurel was engrossed with her upcoming show at a well-known art gallery, as well as her "day job," tending bar at a trendy nightspot in Asheville. And Rosemary, busy with her assistant professorship of English at Chapel Hill, was home only for the occasional weekend. Even Ben, her nephew and partner in the herb and flower farm, even Ben, who saw her every day, had no idea of her current state of mind. *But Dessie knew. And she saw something else coming.*

The sight of her house, perched on the mountainside and surrounded by tiers of gardens, lifted her spirits as it always did. She and Sam had built it to look like the old mountain houses—board and batten, metal-roofed, with a long front porch. Over the years various additions had been made, but it was still a modest farmhouse of unpainted, weathered wood. Only the bright periwinkle-blue doors, the attached greenhouse, and the solar collector on the roof gave notice that this was not an absolutely typical mountain dwelling.

Elizabeth's dogs greeted her joyfully, each vying to see who would be first to go through the door with her. Once inside, they ignored her and headed for the denim-covered sofas while Elizabeth started into the kitchen to fix a glass of iced tea. Passing a mirror that hung near the kitchen door, she paused to examine her reflection. *What did Dessie see that told her how unhappy I've been?*

The face that looked back at her seemed little changed from the previous summer—the long straight nose and high cheekbones a little more prominent, the thick braid of dark hair a little grayer. Her deep blue eyes were clear, but there were violet shadows under them that she hadn't noticed before. *What do you expect?* she asked her reflection. *You're fifty-two. Like that card you got on your fiftieth birthday said, "Remember the glass isn't half empty; it's one-third full!"*

"Aunt E?" A deep voice echoed through the house, causing the dogs to bark wildly even as they ran, tails wagging exuberantly, to greet the tall young man coming up the basement stairs two at a time.

"In here, Ben," she responded. "I'm making some tea. Would you like a glass?"

"No, thanks, Aunt E. I just came to tell you that Miss Birdie called while you were gone," her nephew said, and stood there shifting uneasily from foot to foot.

"I just saw her over at Dessie's," Elizabeth said, puzzled. Then, with an ominous feeling growing as Ben's sun-browned face held its somber expression, she asked quickly, "What's wrong?"

"It's Cletus, Aunt E. Miss Birdie says something's happened to Cletus. He's not home but she's sure something's happened to him. She sounds real upset and she wants you to come right over."

CHAPTER 2
WHAT WENT WITH CLETUS?
(MONDAY)

A S SHE DROVE THE FEW MILES TO BIRDIE AND Cletus's house, Elizabeth wondered what had happened so suddenly to make Miss Birdie worry about her son. The little widow was used to her Cletus's ways. When his work was done and the crop laid by, he would wander through the woods for days, camping out in all weathers and living off the hard-baked cornbread he carried with him, now and then shooting and cooking a rabbit or squirrel. Eventually he would fetch up at some remote cabin where the inhabitants would give him a meal and call Miss Birdie to come get him.

"He's a good boy and he never goes off lessen we've got a full woodpile and the big chores is done," Birdie had once told Elizabeth. "But seems like he has to wander some, just like an old hound. You know, you can keep a hound tied up for just so long, then if it can't run the woods, it'll break its heart. Cletus is just the same."

Elizabeth swung the jeep off the road and rattled across the plank bridge that spanned Ridley Branch in front of Birdie's cabin. Miss Birdie was standing out in the yard holding one end of a length of clothesline, while an excited black-and-white mongrel danced and tugged at the other end. Miss Birdie's wrinkled face was anxious and she pulled the dog along with her as she hurried over to the car.

"Lizzie Beth, I thank you for comin' so quick. I think we had ort to call the sheriff but I want you to do the talkin' for me."

"What's happened, Miss Birdie?" Elizabeth asked as she climbed out of her car. "Ben said it was something about Cletus."

"Look over yonder at what Pup brung home." Miss Birdie pointed a gnarled finger at a filthy camouflage knapsack lying beneath a big rhododendron.

"Do you think that's—?" Elizabeth began, but Miss Birdie cut her short.

"I know that's the poke I fixed for Cletus. I sewed that there patch on the pocket after hit got tore up with him crawlin' under some bobwire fence back of this."

Elizabeth pushed aside the heavy pink blooms of the rhododendron and grabbed the knapsack by one of its shoulder straps. Across the yard Pup yelped and leapt at the end of the clothesline. As she lifted the muddy canvas bag, she realized that it had a very unpleasant smell and an equally unpleasant soggy heft to it. *Oh, shit,* she thought, *this is going to be something awful.*

Holding the knapsack at arm's length, she gingerly undid the buckles. The smell intensified as she pulled back the flap. Inside lay the decomposing bodies of six squirrels. The slimy forms were hairless but for a few tufts of red fur clinging to their sides. The interior of the knapsack was alive with maggots.

"You see," Miss Birdie demanded as Elizabeth hastily lowered the bag to the ground out of reach of the urgently whining dog. "Somethin' must have happened to

Cletus. Else how come Pup to bring that bag home? We got to call the high sheriff and get them to go out and find my boy. Cletus may be layin' up some'ers with a broke leg . . . or worse," she said grimly. "I'm gonna tie up this dog and bury that nasty bag. Washin' won't never get that smell out. You go on up to the house, Lizzie Beth, and call the sheriff for me." Miss Birdie stumped off toward a doghouse surrounded by hard-packed dirt, towing the still agitated Pup.

"Wait, Miss Birdie," said Elizabeth. "Where should I tell the sheriff to start looking for Cletus? Where does he usually go?"

Miss Birdie paused. "Be still, Pup!" she admonished the unruly dog, who was deeply intent on getting back to the knapsack and its reeking contents. Her face was troubled as she said, "Lordy, Lizzie Beth, I can't rightly say. He took off up Pinnacle but he'd a hit the ridge and started walkin'. Ain't no tellin' where he might of come down. One time he ended up almost to Tennessee. They's a world of deep coves all along there."

As Birdie went to find a shovel, Elizabeth delicately opened the smaller pocket of the knapsack. Inside were several shriveled plants, dried black forest soil still clumped about their fleshy roots.

"Miss Birdie," she called. "There's ginseng in here too. Where would Cletus go to hunt ginseng?"

From the lower part of the barn Miss Birdie's voice called back, "Lizzie Beth, honey, ain't no sang hunter ever told nobody where he gets his sang."

Elizabeth found a little stick in Miss Birdie's woodpile and knelt to poke at the knapsack's repulsive contents. *Maybe there's something else in here that would give us some clue as to where Cletus could be,* she thought, breathing through her mouth and trying to ignore the rank odor of the rotting squirrels. *Nothing but maggots and carrion there,* she decided, and turned her attention to the smaller pocket. A glint of yellow caught her eye, and she pushed aside the dirt and ginseng plants to reveal a small, intricately folded origami crane. She stared at the fragile little thing, wondering how Cletus had come by such an exotic creation out in the backwoods of Appalachia.

"I done dug us a hole, Lizzie Beth. Let's go drop that nasty thing in and cover it up good." Miss Birdie was at her side, holding out her hand for the knapsack.

"Look at this, Miss Birdie." Elizabeth teased the little yellow crane out of the pocket with the stick. "Does Cletus know how to fold paper into shapes like this?"

Miss Birdie regarded the crane with disapproval. "Naw, I wouldn't think so. Though he's a right good hand to make a paper aeroplane. No tellin' where'bouts he might of picked that up. That boy's like a crow, purely loves bright things." She sniffed, wrinkling up her face in disgust. "Let's get that poke in the ground. That smell's like to make me vomick."

Elizabeth said nothing but continued to work at the paper crane with the stick, carefully unfolding it. A few black marks were visible on the paper, and she hoped there might be writing that would give some clue as to the origin of the thing. But as the last fold was opened out, only a few wavy lines were revealed. She peered closely at the paper. It seemed to be a copy, not an original, and there was no writing at all. Just the wavy lines and, down in one corner, something that might be a sketch of a hand.

"You know what, Miss Birdie?" she said, aware of her friend's impatience. "I think we ought not to bury the knapsack. The sheriff might want to see it for evidence."

Miss Birdie's mouth set in a thin line. "Hit'll be evidence Cletus was huntin' out of season. How come him to do that anyhow? Now, I don't say that boy wouldn't take one or two squirrels if he was wantin' some meat, but what for would he shoot six? Hit ain't like Cletus to do that way. I tell you, Lizzie Beth, there's something quare goin' on."

The sheriff was not disposed to take the tale of the returned dog and knapsack very seriously. He had known Miss Birdie and her son for years and was confident that Cletus would return home soon. "That dog of Cletus's, it's a right young one, isn't it? I reckon it just got to playin' and grabbed the knapsack. Then Cletus prob'ly hollered at it and it took off for home. Cletus'll turn up directly. Let me speak to Miss Birdie."

When Miss Birdie put down the receiver ten minutes later, tears brimmed in her eyes. "He don't think nothing's wrong," she told Elizabeth. "But he said they'd start askin' around and if Cletus ain't showed up by tomorrow, they'll get a search party goin'." She sat down heavily on a kitchen chair. "Ay law, I got a bad feelin' about this. What went with that boy?"

Later that evening, Elizabeth was finishing up her supper dishes and thinking about her neighbor. Birdie had sent her home with a promise to call if Cletus returned. "But he ain't a-goin' to, Lizzie Beth; I'm right sure of it."

Giving the countertop a final swipe with her dish towel, Elizabeth poured a mug of rich dark coffee and flipped off the kitchen light. She was heading for the front porch and a peaceful rocking chair when the phone rang.

"Is this Ms. Goodweather?" asked a polite male voice.

"Yes, it is," Elizabeth answered warily, being generally suspicious of calls from unknown people. Such calls were never to tell her that she'd won a sweepstakes or was the recipient of an unexpected inheritance; no, usually it was someone trying to convince her to change her long-distance carrier.

"This is Phillip Hawkins . . ." The deep gravelly voice hesitated.

For a brief moment the name meant nothing to her and she was about to hang up, thinking that this was just another annoying telemarketer. Then she remembered. Phillip Hawkins had been a friend of Sam's from his days in the navy. The two men had kept in touch; indeed, had met and traveled together to some sort of reunion just before the plane crash that had ended Sam's life. Hawkins lived somewhere on the North Carolina coast, she remembered, and Sam had mentioned several times that he had even invited him to the farm. But Hawkins's job— *What was he, a police detective or something like that?*—had forced him to cancel plans several times. So Phillip Hawkins had never visited them and she had never met him, at least not till after Sam's death.

Wondering why he should be calling, she said, "Phillip Hawkins, yes. I remember you."

She could picture him now, a burly brown bear of a man. Hawkins had come to Sam's memorial service and introduced himself to her after the simple and mercifully brief ceremony. He had started to say something about Sam and had become abruptly inarticulate with grief. She still remembered the almost painful handclasp and his hasty departure. Later he had written her a very moving letter about how much Sam had meant to him.

"Ms. Goodweather," the voice sounded tentative, "I found some old pictures of Sam and I wondered if you'd like to have them. Back from when we were in training together."

The lump rising in her throat annoyed Elizabeth and she breathed deeply before replying. "Thank you, that would be really nice. Sam didn't keep many pictures from his time in the navy. It would be particularly nice for the girls to see them." When there was no reply at the other end she went on, "Do you need my address to send them to me?"

"Fact is . . ." Hawkins stopped as if at a loss for words. "Fact is, Ms. Goodweather, I'm in Asheville visiting my daughter."

"Your daughter?" Elizabeth repeated, making polite conversation. "That's nice. Are you on vacation?"

"You could call it a vacation," Hawkins replied. "I'm on an extended leave—family problems. I have an aunt out in Marshall County, lives back of beyond at a place called Shut In. Anyway, she's pretty much all alone and getting on in years. I've got to check on her living situation and see if she can continue to manage. And then there's my daughter Janie. She's in her junior year at University of North Carolina-Asheville and she's having trouble with her classes and her boyfriend. The boyfriend was the whole reason she came to UNCA in the first place. I tried to talk her into transferring back to East Carolina where her brother is, but no way. Janie says she loves Asheville; says it's her 'spiritual home.' So I thought I'd come visit and see what was up," he concluded.

"How long are you here for?" asked Elizabeth, continuing to wonder what this had to do with her. She took a small, silent sip of her coffee.

"Not sure," was the reply. "I've got a year's sabbatical. I haven't taken a vacation since I don't know when, and the leave time has mounted up. I've talked to some folks at the community college here, what's it called?—AB Tech?—about teaching in their criminal justice program, and they have an opening next semester. I think I'd like to get an apartment and stay around for a while, at least till Janie gets straightened out. She seems to like the idea that I'd be in Asheville, believe it or not."

Elizabeth remembered Sam telling her that Hawkins was divorced and that his wife had long since remarried. *Not many men would, even if they could, take time out to deal with the problems of a college-age daughter,* she thought. *He must be pretty nice. I wonder why he and his wife got divorced.*

"That sounds like it'll be good for you and for your daughter," she said politely. "Have you started looking for an apartment?"

"Well, actually," he said cautiously, "that's another reason I'm calling. I thought that maybe you and I could get together and I could give you those pictures and, at the same time, I could find out more about the area from you. I mean, you've lived here for quite a while—"

"I don't know that I would be that much help; I really don't spend a lot of time in Asheville." As the words left her mouth, Elizabeth realized how unfriendly she sounded. *Good grief, Elizabeth, give the poor guy a break.* "But I'd be glad to tell you what little I do know," she amended hastily, and then wished she hadn't.

Hawkins ignored her lack of enthusiasm and plowed on. "I was thinking maybe I could take you to dinner and kind of find out about the Asheville area. I'm staying in downtown Asheville but I could pick you up, and we could go to dinner out in Ransom some night."

"I don't know . . ." began Elizabeth.

"I'd really appreciate it, Ms. Goodweather. I don't know anyone around here over twenty except my ancient aunt at Shut In. And she goes to bed when the sun sets."

Elizabeth stood in her darkening kitchen, holding the phone to her ear and looking out the window at the fading pinks and lavenders tinting the mountaintops across the valley. She thought about how much Sam had liked this Phillip Hawkins, and how often he had talked about their friendship. She remembered the ravaged look on Hawkins's face after Sam's memorial service, and at last she heard herself say, "Why don't you come out here to lunch one day this weekend? There's not much of anywhere to eat dinner in Ransom."

Hawkins objected at first, saying that it was too much trouble for her, but quickly allowed himself to be persuaded. He took down her detailed directions and they agreed on the coming Sunday.

"Bring your daughter, if you don't think she'd be bored," offered Elizabeth. "My nephew Ben is usually here for lunch. He's probably a few years older than she, but they might find something to talk about."

"That's really nice of you but Janie's got some big paper due next week and I expect she'll be hard at work all day Sunday. But I'll be there. It'll be nice to see you again . . . under different circumstances." Hawkins had sounded so enthusiastic about the invitation to lunch that Elizabeth unexpectedly found herself beginning to look forward to seeing him again.

Humming to herself, she dumped out her now cold coffee, poured a fresh cup, and went to sit on the front porch and watch the stars come out. A chorus of spring peepers in her goldfish pond provided the music and a few early lightning bugs rose out of the grass to punctuate the night's darkness. She sat and rocked and thought about what she would fix for lunch on Sunday.

Elizabeth was in bed by nine. *Not quite as bad as Hawkins's aunt,* she thought, *and anyway, I'm not going to sleep; I'm going to read a while.* She reached for one of the *New Yorkers* from a pile by her bed and, after enjoying the cartoons a second time, settled down to a funny piece by Calvin Trillin, always a favorite of hers. That finished, she turned, still smiling, to the featured short story and began to read. It was an odd bit of fiction, well written, of course, or it wouldn't be in the *New Yorker,* she reminded herself, but somehow . . .

She realized that she was resting her eyes, closing them for just a minute before continuing the undoubtedly fascinating piece that, when she had read a little more of it, she would surely appreciate . . .

Zen reading, that's what Sam used to call it, she thought drowsily as the open magazine slowly settled across her chest. As she sank down into blissful sleep, she seemed to see the slender form of a young girl, wearing the homespun floor-length skirts of an earlier time. The girl's long brown hair framed a beautiful face that was bowed to smile down at the infant cradled in her arms. Her feet were bare and around her neck was a thin gold chain from which dangled a little golden heart.

The sharp buzz of the phone beside her bed startled Elizabeth awake and she picked it up on the second ring.

The bedside light was still on and the little clock beneath it said nine-thirty. The caller was Louvanda, Dessie's daughter, and Elizabeth already knew what she had to say.

" 'Lizbeth, I'm sorry to be callin' so late but I wanted you to know that Mommy's gone home to Jesus. It was right at supper time . . . she just slept away so sweet and peaceful." Louvanda's voice was composed as she continued. "They'll be a viewing Thursday at the funeral home in Ransom and Friday we'll have the buryin' here."

Elizabeth pictured the little family cemetery on a hilltop behind Dessie's house. Dessie had always mowed and trimmed it weekly during the growing season, adorning the graves with bright plastic flowers—yellow, pink, and blue on Decoration Day, then replacing them with plastic poinsettias in December. Odus rested there, as well as an infant son and daughter of his and Dessie's. "I'll be there, Louvanda," Elizabeth promised, her throat suddenly tight as she realized that her old friend was indeed gone. "Can I do anything to help?"

"No, 'Lizbeth, we'll make out just fine. Besides, I just talked to Miss Birdie and she says she's aiming to get you to help her hunt for Cletus tomorrow, if the sheriff ain't found him. Reckon she wants you to take her in that jeep of yours up some of them steep back roads her truck can't climb."

But in the end, they didn't have to hunt for Birdie's missing son. Early the next morning a kayaker on the French Broad found a body in the river a few hundred yards beyond a train trestle. It was Cletus.

CHAPTER 3

THE HOLINESS CHURCH OF JESUS
LOVE ANOINTED WITH SIGNS FOLLOWING
(SATURDAY NIGHT)

S ALEMMA LOCAMA, SALEMMA LOCAMA, ASONAMATEE maleeko . . ." Aunt Belvy Guthrie's voice was hoarse and beginning to crack but it rose above the ragged sound of the guitar and the insistent jingle of the tambourines. The prophetess of the Holiness Church of Jesus Love Anointed with Signs Following had made her way to the front of the sanctuary and was speaking in tongues.

"Praise God," someone called out, and most of the congregation began to pray aloud, not the same prayer but individual outpourings of emotion. Men and women standing, kneeling, swaying, sobbing, rejoicing—each one speaking directly to God in fervent, personal tones of praise and supplication. The clamor of voices and music rose in a crescendo and Aunt Belvy's long white hair began to shed hairpins and escape from its knot as the old woman's head swung in ecstatic circles. Miss Birdie punched Elizabeth in the ribs with her elbow and whispered excitedly, "She's gettin' close!"

Five short days had passed since Dessie Miller's death and the discovery of Cletus's body on the rocks of the French Broad River. Only yesterday Dessie had been laid to rest in the little hilltop graveyard, but Cletus's remains were still in the Asheville morgue, awaiting the autopsy mandated by the state for "unattended" deaths.

Miss Birdie had appeared on Elizabeth's front porch early Saturday morning, flushed and exhausted from the hike up the steep road that her battered old truck couldn't climb. "Why didn't you call me?" Elizabeth had demanded. "I would have come over."

"I know you would of, honey. But I just took me a notion to walk while I still can. Let me just set here in this rockin' chair and get my breath." Finally, after a glass of water and the usual mountain courtesy of small talk before asking a favor, Miss Birdie had come to the point.

"Sheriff says hit were likely an accident," she informed Elizabeth. "He thinks Cletus was a-crossin' that trestle at night and done lost his balance. But, Lizzie Beth"—the little woman had balled up her frail fist and banged it down on the flat arm of the wooden rocker—"there weren't no way Cletus would of gone out on that railroad bridge. That boy was just naturally afeared of heights! Why, he'd get all swimmie-headed just going up a ladder. He'd even unch way down in the truck when I had to drive us across the big bridge over the river. There ain't no way anybody can tell me Cletus went to cross that high up old trestle where you can look down between yore feet and see the river and the rocks." Birdie's voice was urgent and her wrinkled face had been deeply troubled. "Lizzie Beth, honey, I got to know what *really* happened."

Then she had paused, as if to collect herself, and had looked out across the valley where the morning mists were rising up from the river toward the warmth of the sun. "Ay law, hit's purty up here, Lizzie Beth. Makes a body see why you put up with that steep old road."

The little woman had slumped back in her rocker and seemed to look inward. Her face was sad but after a moment she smiled weakly and gestured toward Ben's cabin. "You know, hit was right over yon where Little Sylvie lived."

Elizabeth followed her gaze. The one-room cabin was said to be about a hundred and fifty years old—the oldest on the branch. Hastily constructed of small logs that one man could lift, it had nevertheless been in continuous use up to the 1950s. Its dry-laid stone chimney still stood square and true, and Ben had rechinked the gaps between the logs. A gnarled apple tree and an overgrown mass of orange daylilies beside an old-fashioned deep pink shrub rose gave evidence of past occupants. The cabin had been built just uphill of a huge flat rock that reached head-high next to the cabin and sloped to waist height at the front. Elizabeth remembered lying on that rock with Sam beside her on a warm August night, watching the Perseid meteor shower trace glowing trails across the deep black velvet of the summer sky.

"You know, Lizzie Beth, I'd plumb forgot that ol' story till poor ol' Dessie started in to talkin' about hit when I sat with her that last day. Wanderin' in her thoughts she was, like they sometimes do." Wiping her eyes on her sleeve, Birdie added, "Ay law, I do miss Dessie. Seems hard to lose her and my boy all to once."

Hoping to distract Miss Birdie from her grief, Elizabeth had replied, "I don't know the story about Little Sylvie. Dessie just said she was a wild girl."

"She was a shameless huzzy, leastways that's how I heared it. Her folks was the Bakerses, lived in a big old two-story log house down there where yore rent house is. That log house burnt up back in, let me see, I believe it was '52. Anyhow, they say Little Sylvie married a rich man, a Mr. Tomlin from Tennessee. He must have been a good somebody; it was him give the money to build the church down on the branch. Him and Little Sylvie lived for a time in that cabin right over yon, but they say he was aimin' to build a big fine house down by the river."

Miss Birdie was, like so many of the older generation in these mountains, a born storyteller. For the moment, her losses seemed forgotten, and she spoke of a time she had never known as if it were personal experience.

"Why, Little Sylvie's husband worshipped the ground she walked on—wouldn't hardly let that girl out of his sight. When Little Sylvie had a baby, that man was the proudest daddy around though hit weren't but a girl-child. And when that child was still but a titty baby, Sylvie, she up and run off with some feller and never come back. Some folks said that her and her new man stayed up on the mountain, like wild Indians. (I believe hit was a Johnson boy whose family lived over to Walter and Ollie's old place that she took up with. Seems like his given name was Levy or some such.)

"Howsomever, the way they tell it, for a time him and Sylvie lived in a cave partways up the mountain. Course there ain't no caves on Pinnacle, but I believe they must have been namin' that place up from yore house where them big rocks leans together. I know my boy sheltered there one time when he was a-huntin', and Cletus he said it was as dry as ary house but hit gave him bad dreams and he swore he'd not go back."

"I never knew there was anyplace like that up the mountain, Miss Birdie. I can't believe my girls didn't discover it, as much as they liked to roam around."

"Ay law, Lizzie Beth, Cletus said he wouldn't have known about it iffen hit weren't for Pup, no, hit was afore Pup's time; hit would have been old Rover that chased a rabbit or some such varmint into it. Cletus called and old Rover didn't come out so Cletus went atter him. That boy allus was plumb foolish over his dogs. Cletus said he had to get down and squinch under a big ledge for a ways but then he got to a place like a nice room, most big enough to stand up in. He reckoned the Indians might of used it way back for he saw they'd been a fire in there and that they was bones scattered around. I told him not to say nothing about it for fear yore girls would try to go in there and get snakebit."

Miss Birdie had smiled sadly at this memory of her lost son, then resumed her tale. "Now, the way they tell hit, atter a time, whilst they was livin' in this cave, Little Sylvie took a notion to see her baby and she come back to the cabin but her husband wouldn't let her in—slammed the door in her face. So she clumb up on that big rock out front of the cabin, thinkin' to see the baby through the window. Now, Little Sylvie weren't but a little bitty thing and the window too high. So she'd jump up and catch at the windowsill and hang there a-lookin' in but then she'd lose her grip and kindly slide down the logs. Mamaw said that she had seen the scratch marks on the logs where Little Sylvie had clung, a-tryin' to see her little one. Mamaw allus said that hit was a sight to break yore heart."

"But how does the story end, Miss Birdie?" Elizabeth had asked.

"They say Little Sylvie and Levy Johnson run off, never to be seen again. They say she stole her daddy's shotgun and her husband's gold. And I think that the little baby died." Miss Birdie frowned. "But that story

don't sound right, do it? Hit's always puzzled me some—
what for would she go off when she wanted to see her
baby so bad that she left scratch marks in the logs? And
why didn't no one ever blame her husband for not lettin'
her in to feed that baby?" The old woman shook her
head. "Ay law, they tell these stories, but I reckon sometimes they don't get 'em just right. One'll say one thing
and another'll have it to be different. But hit was a hundred year ago and I guess hit don't matter to no one anymore."

Miss Birdie had rocked in silence for a moment and
then had said, "Lizzie Beth, I need for you to do something for me."

"I'd be glad to," Elizabeth had replied, happy for any
chance to help her friend. "Do you want me to talk to
the sheriff for you, Miss Birdie? I could tell him about
Cletus and how he was afraid of bridges."

"Honey, I done told him that. He just don't want to
pay no mind. No, Lizzie Beth, I got another thing to ask
of you. If you don't care, I want you to go with me
to that Holiness church over there in Cocke County,
Tennessee. They's a woman I know over there named
Belvy; they call her Aunt Belvy, and she's a prophetess in
the church. When she gets the spirit on her, she can see
things that's hid. She's found lost things for people back
of this. I want her to tell me what went with Cletus's
shotgun."

"His shotgun?" Elizabeth had asked in bewilderment.

"Yes, his shotgun. They didn't never find it in the
river nor up on that trestle neither. Cletus may of been
slow, but whiles he was livin', he would of held on to
that there gun. He was so proud of it . . . cleaned it all
the time . . ." Miss Birdie's voice had faltered and she had
looked away before continuing. "What I think, Lizzie

Beth, is that somebody knocked my boy on the head and then threw him in the river. And if Belvy can tell us where that shotgun is, we'll be closer to findin' out who done it. They're holdin' a meetin' tonight and I'm askin' you to drive me over there 'cause I can't drive that far after dark and 'cause I know you ain't afraid of snakes."

Snakes. The two plywood boxes that sat beneath a table at the front of the room were an ominous presence. So far no one had touched the boxes or even alluded to them, but Elizabeth was constantly aware of their squat brown shapes, pierced with air holes in cross-shaped designs. The boxes seemed to exist within their own quiet circle of menace, untouched by the praying and singing that filled the church.

"How do you know about this Aunt Belvy?" Elizabeth had questioned Birdie as they drove the winding road over the mountain and down into Cocke County with its rolling farmland stretching out before them, warm gold in the mellow light of the late afternoon.

"Law, honey, Belvy used to live on Ridley Branch, up there where those McHenrys are now. Her and me been friends since we was young uns. Now, she was always real big in the church—there ever time they cracked the door. But then her and her man quit the Freewill Baptist church and took to going to a Holiness church they used to be over on Rocky Fork. Her husband and both her growed boys got to preachin' and to handlin' them snakes. And then, atter a while, Belvy got the gift of prophecy. Some says hit's the devil, not the Holy Spirit workin' on those folks, but I don't believe that. I've knowed right along that Belvy is a good woman. Howsomever, when one of their members got snakebit and died of it, the law shut that church down. Well, Belvy and her family and a whole bunch of them Holiness people just up and moved to Tennessee and opened them another church.

"They don't handle ever time," Miss Birdie had told her. "I called Belvy to ask could she help about Cletus and she said I'd have to come to church and see did she get an anointin' of the Spirit. She said she couldn't tell nothing without an anointin', just like wouldn't no one handle a serpent without the Spirit was on them."

Well, it sure looks like the Spirit or something's *on a bunch of them right now,* decided Elizabeth, watching the small congregation on that Saturday night. The cacophony of prayer had died down and the worshippers had resumed their seats, but three women still stood, arms uplifted, eyes closed, and tears streaming down their shining faces. Aunt Belvy alone continued to speak, but the incomprehensible syllables of the gift of tongues suddenly segued into recognizable language.

"Seek and ye shall find, yea, there's one here who seeks an answer." Like a stately ship, Aunt Belvy made her way through the parting throng of worshippers to the back of the church where Elizabeth and Miss Birdie sat. Birdie was gazing openmouthed, her eyes fixed with rapt attention on the prophetess.

Aunt Belvy was a big woman, tall and powerfully built. In spite of her age—*She must be in her eighties,* thought Elizabeth—she stood straight and moved gracefully. Her flowing white hair, now completely freed from its knot, was bone straight and fell to the waist of her ankle-length print dress. She had high cheekbones and dark eyes, and Elizabeth found herself wondering if there was Cherokee blood in this alarming but undeniably impressive personage.

"Lift up yore eyes unto the hills from whence cometh yore help." Birdie rose unbidden, as if lifted by invisible strings, and stood looking up at her old friend. Aunt Belvy rested her two big hands on the smaller woman's shoulders and continued. "In the dens and in the rocks of the mountains they try to hide. But the righteous will seek them out and the truth will be known." Aunt Belvy's eyes were closed now and her head was thrown back. "The sanctuary in the wilderness is red with blood, and the wicked rejoice. But a day will come when the veil is lifted and the truth is shown." The sibyl's eyelids fluttered open, revealing only white. She turned her head and Elizabeth felt the sightless eyes stare down at her. A feeling akin to panic rose in her as the old woman declaimed, "Woe to the sinner for she shall ride with death. Death and corruption wait within her gate and her child shall weep in the wilderness."

Aunt Belvy raised her hand and pointed heavenward, then swayed and at once two men were there to catch her when she fell. Elizabeth felt stunned—*Was she talking to me?*—and glanced at Miss Birdie to see what her reaction had been. Birdie's head was bowed; she was smiling peacefully as her lips moved in prayer.

A tall man in black trousers and a pale blue longsleeved shirt made his way to the front of the room. He was broad shouldered and slim hipped, with a wide, unexpectedly sensual smile that flashed white against the rich tan of his face. His dark, hooded eyes swept the little congregation and there was an expectant hush as people settled back on their benches. It seemed to Elizabeth that his gaze rested on her briefly, summed her up, found her wanting, and moved on. She noticed two young women

sitting together in a pew near the front nudging each
other and blushing as the man at the pulpit nodded and
smiled at them. *He'd be good-looking if he didn't use so much
hair goop,* Elizabeth thought. *A preacher with bedroom eyes,
how odd.*

"Thank you, Lord, for layin' your hand on Sister
Belvy." The tall man held up a Bible with an odd mottled
binding. "It's in His Word, ain't it?"

"Preach it, brother!" called out a man on the front row.

"First Corinthians, book twelve, verses eight through
ten tells us 'For to one is given by the Spirit the word of
wisdom; to another the word of knowledge by the same
Spirit; to another the working of miracles; to another
prophecy; to another discerning of spirits; to another di-
vers kinds of tongues; to another the interpretation of
tongues.' " He was speaking from memory, the Bible still
unopened. " 'They shall speak with new tongues,' it says
in Mark."

The sermon, if it was a sermon, continued. Aunt
Belvy, now recovered, sat up straight near the front,
fanning herself vigorously and calling out an occasional
amen. Miss Birdie had resumed her seat and was leaning
back with her eyes closed, breathing heavily. Elizabeth
relaxed slightly, keeping an eye on the as yet untouched
serpent boxes, and surreptitiously began again to study
her surroundings.

The little congregation, no more than twenty people,
sat on simply made wooden benches. The white-painted
walls of the concrete block building were unadorned except for a faded reproduction of Leonardo's *Last Supper* on
the wall behind the pulpit, beside a plaque bearing the
verses which defined this "signs-following" group of believers.

And these signs shall follow them that believe;
In my name shall they cast out devils;
they shall speak with new tongues;
they shall take up serpents;
and if they drink any deadly thing, it shall not hurt them.
Mark 16:17–18

The windows on either side of the room were filled with plain frosted glass. A low platform held a lectern, a table with paper cups, a plastic jug of water, and the serpent boxes. To one side of the platform sat a man with a guitar and a woman and a teenage girl, each with a tambourine. Elizabeth had noticed that the girl had managed, in the way of teenagers everywhere, to look bored, even as she had rattled her tambourine all through the frenetic praying and speaking in tongues.

In general, the men and women of the church had the look of the hardworking rural folk of Appalachia. The women all wore dresses, most with long sleeves even on this warm evening. All had long hair and many let it fall unconfined down their backs. None wore jewelry, not even a wedding band. A few sleepy children leaned against their mothers. The men wore jeans or slacks and long-sleeved shirts buttoned to the neck. Their hair was uniformly short and there was not a beard or a mustache to be seen. One or two of the younger men sported modest sideburns, trimmed a careful inch or two below the ear top.

The sermon appeared to be winding down now. The guitar began again and, with a final song, the service was over and men and women began to make their way out of the little building. Elizabeth waited in her place while Miss Birdie went forward to speak with Aunt Belvy. The man who had been preaching tucked his Bible under his arm and picked up both of the serpent boxes. He stepped down off the platform and stood chatting casually with two other men. One jerked his head in Elizabeth's direction and said something. There was a low laugh from the other two men.

Miss Birdie and Aunt Belvy appeared to be catching up on several years' worth of talk. Elizabeth put her hand in the pocket of her denim skirt and fingered her car keys. *Come on, Birdie! It must be nearly eleven and we've got an hour's worth of twisty roads ahead of us,* she thought, then relaxed. *Who knows, maybe Aunt Belvy's explaining her prophecy to Birdie. Maybe she's even telling her what happened to Cletus.*

The tall preacher with the serpent boxes left the other two men and started for the door at the back of the room. A dark-haired young woman, one of the pair who had blushed when the preacher nodded to them, came toward him from the pew where she had been waiting, but he brushed past her with a polite word and continued down the aisle. Elizabeth saw the look of puzzled hurt on the girl's face change to anger as the preacher came nearer. He stopped in front of Elizabeth and, leaning down to set the boxes on the bench, said softly, "I don't believe I know who you are."

Elizabeth couldn't take her eyes off the Bible under his arm. The binding was snakeskin, the distinctive diamond pattern of the rattlesnake. Following her gaze, he suddenly thrust the book under her nose. "*That* what you come to see?"

Jerking back involuntarily, Elizabeth was instantly annoyed with herself for letting this oddly intense man startle her. She put out her right hand and answered evenly, "I'm Elizabeth Goodweather, Miss Birdie's neighbor.

Aunt Belvy invited her to come to church and since Miss Birdie can't drive at night she asked me to bring her."

Ignoring her outstretched hand, he asked, "Do you read your Bible? Do you know what it says in First Peter?"

She hesitated, tempted to compose some answer along the lines of *Yes, I have read the Bible; no, I have no idea what it says in First Peter, and why are you asking me anyway?* Without waiting for her response, however, he shook his Bible under her nose and continued, ". . . ye were not redeemed with corruptible things, as silver and gold." The snakeskin binding brushed near her left ear, lightly touching her little gold hoop earring, and she had to repress a second backward movement.

"I can tell you ain't no Holiness woman." He laughed briefly, then his dark eyes bored into hers. He seemed to consider for a moment. Then, as if the words were forced from him, he said, "You read your Bible and come back another time. You might could get hit with the Holiness gun." Sticking the snakeskin-covered Bible back under his arm, he picked up the serpent boxes. "Too bad didn't no one get an anointin' to handle tonight. You'd'a seen what this is really all about, Elizabeth Goodweather."

He raised one of the flat brown boxes up to Elizabeth's face and held it there, swinging slightly from its hinged handle. A thick, musky smell oozed toward her, filling her nostrils with some perilous message. She could see a slight movement through the air holes and hear a dry rustle as the big snake shifted defensively against the tilt of the box. Willing herself not to draw back again, Elizabeth tried to hide the chill that was lifting the hairs on her arms. "I'd like to see that," she told the tall preacher, realizing with some surprise that she really would.

As they drove back to North Carolina, over the mountains, through Hot Springs and back toward Ridley Branch, Miss Birdie was full of ideas about what Aunt Belvy's words might have meant. "She said to look to the hills for help and that the wicked was hidin' in the dens and the rocks of the mountains. We got to look for the answer there, not in the river like Sheriff said. I reckon that sanctuary in the wilderness that's red with blood is where Cletus got killed, so that's what we got to find."

"Miss Birdie," Elizabeth interposed gently, "you know, I don't think the sheriff's going to pay much attention to what Aunt Belvy said tonight."

Miss Birdie looked at her in amazement. "Law, Lizzie Beth, I know that. That's why you're a-goin' to have to help me search in them hollers where Cletus used to go wanderin'. Like Belvy done said, 'The righteous will seek and the truth will be known.'"

LITTLE SYLVIE'S STORY

I–APRIL 1901

I weren't but thirteen years of age when Daddy sold me to a stranger man for a shotgun and five hundred dollars. I didn't know that was what he done, but he done it all the same. Mister Tomlin was a rich man from over to Tennessee. He rode a handsome bay single-footin geldin named Nebuchadnezzar for some king in the Bible and he was travelin through our country buyin up standin timber. They said he was lookin out for a place by the river where he could build him a sawmill and float the lumber down to Newport. Mister Tomlin was an old man, something over fifty. They said he'd buried two wives and had grown children livin over to Greeneville, but he was most as stout as a young man and his hair was still as black as a crow's wing.

Me and Clytie was up on the hillside lookin for guinea nestes when we seen that fine horse a-comin up our road. Hit was nigh dinnertime and Clytie looked at me and said Lo and behold, here comes a stranger man and what do we have in the house to give him to eat? She knowed as well as I did that there weren't nothing but some cold biscuits from breakfast. We hadn't laid out to cook no dinner for Daddy had gone off to Ransom early that morning and we didn't look to see him back till dark. Maybe not till morning for Daddy was bad to drink when he went into town. He'd not abide nare drop of likker in the house, but when he went to Ransom, more often than not he'd get him a bottle of whisky. Then he'd have to drink it all up for he wouldn't bring it home. Romarie said that he'd solemn promised our Mommy when she was a-dyin not to have no likker in the house.

Mommy died birthin me. I was her seventh. The first one was Romarie, who was a great grown girl when I was born. She was twenty-eight years old when I married Mister Tomlin, an old maid and like to stay one with the sharp tongue and mean ways she has. Romarie says hit was havin to raise up all us young uns atter Mommy died made her so ill-natured but Aetha, who's twenty-two and married to the Worley boy down the branch, says Romarie always was mean as a snake. They was three boys born too, between Aetha and Clytie, but they ever one died afore they was a year old. They're up in the graveyard on the hill, just three little stones in a line along side of the big white rock Daddy hauled on a sled to mark where Mommy lies.

Aetha says she can remember when Daddy used to be different, back afore all the boys died. Said he was allus laughin and whistlin and grabbin Mommy round the waist a-wantin her to dance. Aetha says that it seems like with every boy child that died, some of the spirit went out of him and then when Mommy was took he turned into the hard, scowlin Daddy he is now. Course I know hit's been hard on him, tryin to work a farm without no sons. He's taught us girls to do a man's work though and he sometimes hires help from the Johnson boys over to t'other side of Pinnacle. And I will say that though he is right strict with us girls, Daddy ain't never lifted a hand to hit a one of us. The worst he ever done is to call us turdhead iffen we're careless in our hoein and chop down a young baccer plant.

The stranger man kept a-comin up the road and I knowed he had to be makin for our place for they ain't no one else livin in this lonesome cove. Used to be Mommy's brother lived in the little cabin at the upper place but three years back of this, he married Widder Caldwell and moved to her place over on Bear Tree Creek.

I looked and seen Clytie hightailin it for the house, pullin off her sunbonnet whilst she ran. I figured she wanted to be there to greet the stranger man and that she was goin to try to primp a little first. Clytie is sixteen and like a she-cat in season when she sees a man. She says if-fen she don't marry afore she's twenty, she'll throw herself in the river sooner than slave for Daddy the rest of her borned days. Myself, I don't see that it makes no difference one way or t'other who you slave for.

The stranger man reined up his horse and rested there in his saddle by the foot log that spans the branch runnin in front of our house. He didn't make no move to light, just set there a-gazin round at the barns and the house and the big bottom where we'd soon be plantin corn. I looked for him to hello the house and waited to see if Clytie would have had time to shift her rags and put on her Sunday dress. Then I seen Daddy a-comin up the road on old Bell. What on earth? I thinks to myself. What's he doin back so soon? I lit out down the hill for I knowed Daddy'd be wantin his dinner and bein as Romarie had left out early and gone down the branch to tend to Miz Phelps who was havin her fourth, hit was on me and Clytie to get the victuals.

I hit the back porch and went to the bin and began to bolt some meal for cornbread. I hollered to Clytie to build up the fire and in just a few minutes here she come, prissin along in her Sunday dress. She was bitin at her lips to make them red and I believe she had put powder on her face. I knowed she had some for I seen it in the box where she keeps her plunder.

I'll make the cornbread and biscuits, Sylvie, Clytie says. You build up the fire and go out to the meathouse and get some sidemeat. And pull some of them lamb's quarters. We can cook them up quick for a sallet.

I done what she said and got some taters out of the root cellar too. They was beginnin to swivel up a little and was sproutin some, but I pulled off the sprouts and set in to peelin. I could hear the sound of boots on the front porch and the creak of the hickory bark–bottomed chairs as Daddy and the stranger man set down. Daddy hollered out, You girls best step lively; we got company to dinner.

Hit'll be ready soon, Daddy, I called back. I could hear them talkin and laughin and Daddy said, They's three to choose from, all of them good hands to cook and ever one of em raised to work hard. I could tell he'd been drinkin for his voice was louder than usual and he was a-laughin.

Afore long we had it all ready and set it on the table. Clytie like to break a leg tryin to be the one to go to the door and call them in. I just let her go and busied myself

*fillin the drinkin mugs with cold buttermilk I'd fetched from
the springhouse.*

Daddy and the stranger man come in and Daddy cut his
eyes all round the room. Where's Romarie at? he asked real
sharp-like. When we told him she was over to Phelpses, he
just snorted and said that maybe that was just as well. We
all set down to the table and Daddy says, Girls, this here's
Mister Tomlin. Him and me has struck a little deal. He's
needin lodging whilst he's in this country and I done told
him we had plenty of room and plenty of gals to do the
cookin and washin. Then he asked Mister Tomlin would
he return thanks and Mister Tomlin begun to pray like one
thing. I had my head bowed and my eyes most shut but I
was a-lookin at him while he prayed.

His eyes was squinched tight but his head was rared
back like he was sendin his words straight up to Heaven
and you could tell from the way he talked that he was right
certain Jesus was a-listenin. Mister Tomlin had black
whiskers with some gray coming into them, but they was
trimmed close and neat and the black hair on his head was
sleek and shiny. His clothes looked to be all store-bought
and near bout new, though dusty with travelin. They was
a gold watch-chain stretched against his vest front and on
the little finger of his left hand he had a golden finger-ring
with a bright red stone in it that I thought was the prettiest
thing I ever seen. Hit put me in mind of the sun just
a-glancin off a redbird's wing. I peeped around to where
Clytie was settin there next to me and seen that she was
a-watchin him and lookin at that finger-ring too.

All the while we was eatin, Daddy was a-braggin on
our cookin and promisin Mister Tomlin that another day

we'd really show him what we could do. I got me a taste for some fried chicken, girls, he said, and I believe you could find a mess of early peas. We just said yessir, for Daddy don't hold with us talkin too much at table, especially when they's company, but I could see Clytie smilin and figgered she was thinkin about makin one of her ginger and dried apple stack cakes too.

So Mister Tomlin came to stay with us as a boarder. Like Daddy said, we had a plenty of room for our house was a big log house with a box stair and rooms above. Downstairs was the big room with the fireplace where we done all our cookin and a pie safe and the table and benches and chairs. Daddy's big old bed with the feather tick was over to one corner. Us girls all slept upstairs where there was two big rooms. Daddy had fixed hit thataway back when him and Mommy thought that they'd have a big family. But now there was just me and Clytie in the one room and Romarie in t'other. There was one more room in the house, a little small room downstairs, built right next to the chimbly. It was meant to be a bornin room or a place if someone was sick and needed to keep extry warm, but since Mommy had died in there, it hadn't been used none.

Daddy set us to cleanin that room and Mister Tomlin took the saddlebags off his fine horse and brung them in. He also brung in a fine long double-barreled shotgun and stood hit in the corner of his room. I heard Mister Tomlin tell Daddy hit was of English make and the best of hits kind that there was. When Daddy looked at that shotgun his eyes got all hungry—like me a-lookin at that red stone finger-ring.

CHAPTER 4
LUNCH AT FULL CIRCLE FARM
(SUNDAY)

"O-oh, hard is the fortune of all womankind.
She's always contro-olled; she's always confined.
Controlled by her pa-a-rents, until she's a wife.
A slave to her husband the rest of her life."

ELIZABETH SANG THE OLD BALLAD LOUDLY AND NOT very tunefully as she ambled down to her garden on Sunday morning to pick lettuce for the sandwiches. As she sang, she did a mental run-through of her lunch plans. The turkey breast was roasting in the oven, well seasoned with garlic slivers, lemon juice, *herbes de Provence,* and crazy salt. A bottle of white wine was in the refrigerator, as well as some St. Pauli Girl beer and a pitcher of unsweetened iced tea. *I don't know what he'd like to drink so I'll have several choices . . . oh, and pick some of the Blue Balsam mint for the tea,* she reminded herself, carefully breaking off the crisp outer leaves of the young lettuces. There was her homemade sourdough bread to be warmed at the last minute and those decadently good rosemary-and-olive-oil potato chips from the Fresh Market. *And cut-up strawberries and mangoes for dessert. That should do it.*

As she climbed the steps back to her porch, Elizabeth's thoughts returned to the problem of Miss Birdie. After the "prophesies" of the night before, Birdie was adamant in her belief that Cletus had been murdered somewhere back in the mountains before he had been thrown into the river. And Elizabeth was reasonably sure that Miss Birdie would not be satisfied till her son's missing shotgun had been found, no matter what the sheriff said. *And that's going to mean going up in a bunch of those deep hollers "where the sun don't never shine," like they say.*

She paused at the top of the steps as a tiny shudder shook her body. *Gramma would have said that was a rabbit running over my grave,* Elizabeth thought, but the idea of the deep dark hollers continued to nag at her. *They tell stories about some rough folks in this county, but everyone I've met has been pretty nice, at least once you get to know them. It'll be interesting,* she told herself, *seeing some of these places that are just down the other side of the mountain. Cletus rambled all around the area—*

She stopped in mid-thought, pushing away the unspoken *and look what happened to him.* "I'd better get this lettuce washed," she said aloud. As she went inside she reassured herself, *Maybe I'll call the sheriff tomorrow and see if they've looked for the shotgun at all. Birdie was so sure that Cletus would have kept it with him no matter what . . . it's probably in the river and just hasn't been found.*

The kitchen clock told her that it was a quarter to eleven. Forty-five minutes till she was to meet Phillip Hawkins down at the lower barn. She'd warned him not to attempt the last steep quarter-mile of her road in his car. "It's not just the steepness," she had explained, "it's the water breaks." These were five deep trenches across the road, used to carry off water from a heavy rain. While a car with four-wheel drive could creep slowly over a water break, an ordinary car, needing a fair amount of speed to pull the steep grade, would hit each trench hard, sometimes with appalling results for the undercarriage.

She glanced at the dining table there against the row of windows that looked across the valley to the distant Blue Ridge Mountains. She'd already set the table with her cobalt pottery plates and the indigo-and-white batik napkins. A creamy old ironstone pitcher held three clusters of crimson rhododendron blooms and several spikes of Siberian iris, their deep purple petals looking like a flight of exotic butterflies above the lush rhododendrons.

"So who is this Hawkins guy?" Ben called from the little office where he was updating farm records on the computer. "Someone you and Sam used to know?"

"I told you, Ben, he was in the navy with Sam. I never met him till he came to the memorial service. He's moving to Asheville and he has some pictures of Sam for me. And he just wanted some information about the area."

"Oh, right, I remember now." Ben wandered into the room, twisting his long sun-bleached hair into a ponytail and eyeing the table. "Looks nice, Aunt E; what're we having for lunch?"

Elizabeth looked at her tall, handsome nephew, and thought, as she often did, how lucky she was that Ben had wanted to come to live at Full Circle Farm. Two years ago Ben Hamilton had finished college with a degree in philosophy and a desire for what he called "the simple life." Though he had grown up in Florida, where his mother, Elizabeth's sister, still lived, he'd often spent the summer with Sam and Elizabeth and their girls, reveling in the freedom of exploring the mountain's woods and pastures with his two cousins.

When Sam had died four years ago in the crash of a friend's small plane, Elizabeth had been determined to carry on the herb and flower business they had built up together. Although she was financially secure in a modest way, due to the unexpectedly generous insurance settlement after Sam's death, she had welcomed the endless physical toil in the fields and drying sheds. The exhaustion she felt at day's end, as well as the sense of duties fulfilled, dulled the pain of her loss and made it easier to fall asleep in the lonely bed at night. But as time passed and her daughters became ever more involved in their own careers, she began to find the work, even with hired help, increasingly difficult. And then last year, Ben had come to her, asking to learn the business. He had set about becoming knowledgeable in every aspect of growing and marketing the herbs and dried flowers that the farm produced, and had moved into the old log cabin across the creek from Elizabeth's house. *Little Sylvie's cabin,* she thought with a sudden memory of the story Birdie had told.

"By the way, Aunt E," Ben said, having satisfied his curiosity about the menu by a look around the kitchen, "Julio wants to rent the old house down by the workshop. He's bringing his wife and family up from Mexico."

Elizabeth smiled. Between Ben and Julio, most of the actual work of the business and the farm had been taken out of her hands. She constructed the elegant driedflower-and-herb wreaths that were the farm's signature product and that fetched such surprising prices in a few upscale shops, but the backbreaking field work was no longer her job. She maintained her own vegetable garden and her flowers, as well as doing huge amounts of weedeating in the summer, but she had more free time now than at any other point in her life on the farm.

And that's given me time to miss Sam, she thought ruefully. *But it also means I'll have plenty of time to help Birdie discover what happened to that shotgun . . . and to settle her mind about Cletus. I wonder what Sam would have thought about this—was it an accident or . . .* The word "murder" formed in her mind but she rejected it. *And you're not here to help me find out, are you, Sam? I'm on my own. Again.*

Elizabeth arrived at the big red barn on the lower part of her property a few minutes before eleven-thirty. This was where she had told Hawkins that she would meet him and there was an unfamiliar gray car parked over to one side, but no Hawkins. Then she saw him out in the field bending down to examine a gray-green row of fragrant lavender. He straightened up and came walking briskly toward her, his olive-skinned face alight with pleasure.

"Mr. Hawkins, I'm glad you made it. I hope my directions were fairly clear."

"Perfect," he said with a grin. He was as she remembered him: a compact and burly man, just slightly taller than herself. The black hair rimming a tanned bald scalp showed a little more gray, but otherwise he was unchanged. "I'd allowed some time for getting lost and I got here early. But could we just make it Phillip?"

"Sure," she answered after a small hesitation, "and I'm Elizabeth."

After lunch was finished, Ben excused himself to go back to his computer and Elizabeth and Phillip took their coffee out to the front porch. "You and Ben have answered a lot of my questions already," he said, settling comfortably into one of the rocking chairs. "From what you've told me, I think I'll start by looking for a place in Weaverville; that's plenty close to Asheville." A lean red hound with luminous black-rimmed yellow eyes nudged at his knee and he leaned down to scratch behind her ears. "Aren't you a beautiful girl!" He looked up at Elizabeth. "What's her name?"

"That's Molly, and the shaggy black one asleep over there is Ursa, and the small brown one is James." James, clearly the result of an ill-advised union between a dachshund and a Chihuahua, rolled on his back and bared his teeth ingratiatingly.

Phillip scratched James's stomach gently, then, as Ursa roused and pushed her way forward, began to massage the big black dog's ears. She pressed even closer and buried her shaggy head in his lap. Hawkins chuckled. "I've wished I could have a dog, but living alone and with the weird hours I used to have to keep, it just wouldn't have been fair to the dog. Maybe when I finally do retire . . ." His voice trailed off.

Without even realizing she'd done so, Elizabeth made up her mind. "Mr. Hawkins—Phillip—you're a police detective, aren't you?"

"For the past, ah, twenty-two years." He raised his thick black eyebrows quizzically.

"Well, I'd like to ask your advice about something. You see, I have this neighbor . . ."

It took refills on the coffee to get all the way through the story of Miss Birdie, her dead son, and the prophetess of the Holiness church. "The thing is, the sheriff says it was an accident, but Miss Birdie is convinced Cletus was killed somewhere else and then dumped in the river," Elizabeth explained. "She's asked me to help her—"

"What did the autopsy show?" Hawkins broke in. "Was this Cletus drowned or not?"

Elizabeth put her coffee mug on the porch railing before replying. "I have to admit I didn't think to ask. But that would clear it up nicely, wouldn't it? If Cletus was drowned, then Birdie would have to accept the fact that he died in the river, not back on the mountain."

She paused, thinking rapidly, then went on, "Of course, he could have been killed by the fall onto the rocks. The river's pretty shallow a lot of the time. I'll call the sheriff tomorrow; I'll tell him Miss Birdie's not satisfied they've got it right and find out what the autopsy showed." She paused again, feeling a sudden pang of guilt. "I should have done it earlier; I'm afraid the sheriff doesn't take Miss Birdie very seriously."

"You say they found him last week?" Hawkins asked. "If the sheriff thinks it was just an accident, it could be several weeks before the autopsy gets done—at least, back in Beaufort that's how it would be. Medical examiners' offices are usually overloaded. Maybe it's different up here." He shrugged and, standing, leaned on the railing to watch a pair of red-tailed hawks circling in the distance. He stood in silence, eyes fixed on the wheeling birds, then said slowly, "You know, I thought that since I've lived on the coast most of my life I'd miss the water when I moved here." His eyes followed the hawks as they disappeared behind a ridge. "But in a place like this you still get that same feeling, that feeling of . . . I guess you'd call it spaciousness."

He looked down at the open deck below the porch and at the little goldfish pool nestled in the green and gold and silver evergreens. The filmy-tailed fish swam in lazy circles and a patterned snake slid off the rocks edging the pond into the clear water. "Whoa! That looked like a copperhead!"

"No, that's a northern water snake. They do look a lot like copperheads—that is, till you see the real thing. The water snakes don't have that triangular viper head, but they get killed for copperheads just the same."

"It doesn't bother you to have snakes so close?" Hawkins watched intently as the snake emerged from the pool, followed by a second smaller one. The two reptiles coiled themselves elegantly on a flat rock in the sun. "A lot of people can't stand to be around snakes of any kind. Like that church service you told me about with the serpent boxes." He grinned and shook his head. "I know quite a few folks who wouldn't have set foot in that church if there was even a chance of snakes being there, boxes or not."

"They don't bother me as long as I know what they are. I like to watch them, and they keep the goldfish population under control. And they always go and hide when I have to reach into the pond to get at the filter to clean it."

Hawkins continued to stare at the little pond. Then he asked abruptly, "Could we walk around and you show me some more of the place? Sam was so proud of what you two had accomplished, called it 'an earthly paradise.'" He waved an arm toward the tiered garden and the masses of blooming shrubs. "Didn't he say that this was originally a tobacco field and you two did all this landscaping? Amazing!"

Leaning over the railing he peered at a drooping fir dotted with bright coral cones. "You've got a lot of plants and things I don't recognize, but some I do remember from my aunt's place. Did I tell you I used to spend summers up here? My mother's people are from Shut In, and I stayed with Aunt Omie every summer till I turned sixteen." He was silent, evidently remembering those long-ago summers, then he continued, "Do you know Shut In?"

"Actually, Miss Birdie and I passed near there last night on our way over the mountain to the church in Tennessee. Shut In's almost an hour from here," she explained.

"It was a great place for a kid." Hawkins's eyes were dreamy. "I had a little hideout under this big bush by the front porch—it was like those bushes with pink flowers there where you parked the car. Aunt Omie called them old pink flower. Or 'flahr,' as she would have said. What's their real name?"

"Weigela," said Elizabeth. "Those were just tiny sticks when I planted them about twenty years ago. Now they're eight feet tall and I have to prune at them every year to keep them from taking over."

"So you two really planted all of this?" Hawkins asked as Elizabeth led the way off the porch down to her gardens.

"Yes, this had all been a hillside tobacco field. We had a bulldozer make a flat place for the house and two smaller flat places below for a yard. It was really just so the girls would have a place to play, but over the years we got into planting more and more flowers and shrubs. At first everything came from friends who'd give me cuttings or divisions from the plants they had in their yards, like the iris and forsythia, the mock orange and the daylilies. But now . . ." She shrugged. "Now I really like to find unusual plants and probably spend more than I should on new flowers and shrubs."

They were standing by a waist-high rock wall bordering the driveway. Soft gray thymes and golden yellow sedums cascaded over its flat top, while above it spiky clumps of purple irises and cushions of deep pink dianthus bloomed. Elizabeth absently pulled out a few encroaching weeds while Hawkins moved forward.

"What about this wall?" he asked. "It looks like it's been here forever."

"It does, doesn't it? Actually, Ben just finished it last year. It's made from rocks picked out of the pastures. Ben started work on it back when he just spent summers with us. As a matter of fact, it was Cletus who taught him how to build walls, and they worked on it together." She rested one hand on a huge capstone, remembering the gentle ways of Cletus. He had never been able to learn to read, but he could construct a dry-laid stone wall that was as solid as if he'd used mortar. Miss Birdie's son had possessed an intuitive genius for finding just the right rock from a heap of miscellaneous fieldstone to fit any given space. He and Ben had spent many weekends constructing the long wall, working side by side with very little conversation. But when they were finished, Ben had told her that he had learned more from Cletus than from many of his college professors.

She brushed the sun-warmed rock with her fingertips, thinking of this lost friend. *Another loss . . . like Sam. And just as senseless.* Suddenly she knew that she was out of small talk. She realized that she felt uneasy around Hawkins, and began to wish she hadn't invited him to the farm. *You hardly know this person, Elizabeth,* she thought. *Just because he was a friend of Sam's doesn't mean—*

But Hawkins was bounding up the set of rock steps that led to a lush planting of pink peonies and deep red rhododendrons. She followed reluctantly as he made his way along the uneven stepping-stones to the blue bench under the apple tree. Here he stopped and flung out his arms as if to encompass the whole mountainside. "This is incredible, Ms. Good—Elizabeth. Just beautiful!"

Hawkins dropped onto the long blue bench and gazed appreciatively at his surroundings. With an inward sigh, Elizabeth resigned herself to being sociable a little longer and sat down on the other end of the bench. Hawkins said nothing but continued to look around in obvious admiration. And, as often happened, Elizabeth found herself seeing her house and her garden as if through the eyes of her visitor, delighting anew in the beauty that she—*and Sam*—*and Ben and Cletus*—had created.

It is beautiful, she agreed silently. Below the driveway the tiered vegetable garden lay in orderly rows. Pea vines covered their trellises like lacy green shawls stretched out to dry. In the raised beds, dark green parsley, golden oregano, and purple-leafed sage crowded one another, while the bright chartreuse and deep burgundy of loose-leaf lettuces scrolled in bold patterns. Elizabeth had discovered long ago that dividing each rectangular bed into three triangles and then planting contrasting colors and textures within each division would produce a kind of cut-rate formal garden—at least till all the lettuce was harvested.

Behind the blue bench her most recently acquired rhododendron—a "Gomer Waterer"—was thick with blooms. The creamy blossoms were tinged with gold and pink—*just like a sunrise*—*and just like the catalogue promised*.

"So, we must be facing due east." Hawkins broke into her reverie. "You've got the ideal location—east-facing,

southern exposure"—He motioned toward the vista before them—"and then there's the view. . . ."

The ranks of gently rounded mountains marched into
a smoky blue distance. Their slopes were covered with
the bright greens of the new-leafed poplars and oaks
and maples, punctuated with dark evergreens. Here and
there the trees gave way to an emerald swath of pasture
or the raw dark red of a fresh-turned tobacco field. The
sun glinted from a bright metal roof in a newly cleared
area, and Elizabeth remembered that only two roofs had
been visible twenty-some years ago. Now there were
seven, counting this one. *At least they're so far away we can
just barely see them. Our nearer neighbors we don't see at all
from here.*

Hawkins was saying something more about the house's
perfect location and her thoughts turned unwillingly to
Sam—Sam who had insisted on the due east alignment
and southern exposure for the greenhouse—Sam, who
had *husbanded,* in the excellent old agricultural sense, the
land. *So now we're both widows*—she thought with a rush
of bitterness—*me and the land.* She dug her thumbnail
hard into the soft flesh at her wrist in an attempt to escape her thoughts. *Goddammit, Sam. Goddammit.*

At last the early afternoon heat drove them back to the
shade of the porch. Elizabeth brought tall glasses of iced
tea and once again Hawkins stood at the railing, silent
and gazing off into space. She sat in a rocking chair and
sipped her tea, waiting for him to signal that he was ready
to leave. Finally he drained his glass and, without turning, said, "I'd like it if you'd come into Asheville and
have dinner with me sometime, Elizabeth. Maybe go to

a movie. Or when I get a place rented I could fix dinner for you—"

"Would you like some more tea?" Elizabeth interrupted, standing up so hastily that her rocker banged against the porch wall, startling the three dogs out of their sleep. James, as was his wont, began to bark mindlessly, while Molly and Ursa stalked down the steps to the yard with offended backward looks.

"No thanks, no more," Hawkins replied quietly as she collected his empty glass and headed for the kitchen. "I'd better get going—you've probably got things to do."

"Oh, no, not today," Elizabeth called back from the kitchen where she was furiously rinsing the glasses and coffee mugs. "But if you need to get back, I'll take you down to your car."

Ben, who was sitting at the kitchen table with a second cup of coffee and a gardening magazine, lifted a quizzical eyebrow and silently mouthed, *What's your problem?*

Ignoring her nephew, Elizabeth set the mugs and glasses in the dish drainer and returned to the porch. Hawkins put out his hand and said, "Thank you for everything, Ms. Goodweather. Lunch was delicious and I really enjoyed seeing this place. Sam told me so much about it and about you that almost all of it seemed familiar." The handclasp was polite and brief. His thoughtful brown eyes rested on her momentarily and he said evenly, "You don't need to drive me down; I'd enjoy the walk."

You were unforgivably rude, Elizabeth told herself as she watched Hawkins's stocky form moving purposefully down the road. *No wonder he didn't want a ride.* As Hawkins rounded the barn and disappeared, the familiar sense of loss that was her heart's constant core seemed to swell, constricting her throat and forcing tears into her eyes.

CHAPTER 5
MISS BIRDIE INSISTS
(SUNDAY AND MONDAY)

ELIZABETH WAS STILL WATCHING THE EMPTY ROAD when the screen door banged and Ben came out onto the porch.

"What the hell got into you, Aunt E? A nice guy asks you for a date and you act like he's a serial killer or something. It sounded like you two had a lot to talk about—you know you like it when people want to look at your flowers—but all of a sudden, boom, you're in doing the dishes. He just asked you out to dinner, for God's sake. Even if you're not interested in him as a date, he might have helped you out some with this Cletus thing."

"Oh, I know, Ben. It was just . . . I guess I wasn't expecting . . . I don't think that I . . ." She sank down heavily in the nearest rocker. "He was nice, Ben," she explained carefully, "but I don't feel like getting involved with anyone. I just—"

"Involved? Since when is going to dinner and a movie with someone 'getting involved'? You know what, Aunt E?" Ben hitched himself up to sit on the wide porch railing and she realized that she was in for a lecture. *At what point,* she wondered, *did the roles reverse? Just about when I really began to try very hard not to interfere in the lives of my children, then they, and Ben as well, decided to fill the gap by taking an interest in mine. The girls tell me what I should or rather, shouldn't wear, and now Ben . . .*

". . . do you good to have some social life," he was saying. "Sam's been gone almost five years now and you've hunkered down like Queen Victoria mourning Prince Albert." Elizabeth's eyebrows shot up in surprise and he went on. "You know, like in that movie you got from the library—*Mrs. Brown* or whatever it was."

He continued hurriedly; having once broached the topic he appeared determined to have his say. "I mean, everyone knows how you carried on with the farm and the business and no one ever even saw you cry. You were really brave and all. But, my god, since last fall it seems like you've been in a blue funk; instead of getting back to some sort of a normal life, it was like Sam had just died and you were sadder than ever."

Ben stopped in some confusion, but when Elizabeth said nothing, he renewed the attack. "Aunt E, don't you see . . . the girls and I have been really worried, but you're so . . . what do they call it? . . . such a private person that no one wanted to say anything." He shook his head. "You know, when Rosemary was home for Christmas, she told me that, in her opinion, you might be clinically depressed. She thought that maybe we should try to get you to talk to a doctor about medication. Laurel's even been thinking that maybe she should move back, but I told them I thought you'd snap out of it before long. I was really hopeful today, seeing you enjoying this guy Hawkins's company. It's time you had some social life."

Elizabeth stiffened in her chair. Now she felt indignant to think that while she had believed that no one had noticed her sorrow, Ben and her girls had been discussing her and, even worse, pitying her. "I appreciate your concern," she said formally as she got to her feet, "but I'm fine and I don't really want a social life."

The screen door slammed behind her and she headed upstairs to her workroom in search of something useful to do, something to erase the memory of Hawkins's cool manner as he said good-bye and started down the road. Behind her she could hear Ben saying dryly, "Sorry, Aunt E. I guess it's none of my business." *At least you got that right, Benjamin,* she thought, as she climbed the steps to the airy room that served as her sewing room, junk repository, and general sanctuary.

A stack of patchwork squares waited by the sewing machine, an unfinished piece of embroidery lay in its hoop by her ratty but supremely comfortable chair, and a small pile of shirts reproached her from the ironing board. She ignored them all and scrabbled through a closet filled with the odds and ends of her life. At last she found it—a topographical map of Marshall County. Spreading it out on the desk beneath the window, she began to make notes on a yellow legal pad. At the top she wrote, in bold letters, WHERE WAS CLETUS???

An hour later she had a plan. She would get in touch with the sheriff tomorrow and find out if the autopsy had been done. If it had, and if it was clear that Cletus had drowned, maybe Miss Birdie would accept the findings and agree with the sheriff that Cletus had fallen accidentally from the trestle while foolishly trying to cross it in the dark. But just in case Birdie still wanted to search the nearby hollows for any evidence of where Cletus had been before he died . . . Birdie had said that Cletus started out up Pinnacle Mountain, the three-thousand-foot peak that rose above Elizabeth's house. *He would probably have gone up the old logging road that runs along our southern line,* mused Elizabeth, tracing the road along the ridgeline on the map. *Once at the top, would he have gone down the other side immediately? or along Pinnacle Ridge? And which way?*

The ridge ran roughly north and south and was furrowed with numerous coves and hollows. A century ago, much of this land had been open pasture and fields, and every hollow had supported one or more large families. The ridgelines had served as highways for travel by foot or horse, and a young man would think nothing of working in the fields all day and then walking miles over the mountain to attend a "singin'," to play baseball, or to go courting. *Like Little Sylvie's lover,* Elizabeth realized, tracing with her finger the short distance between her cove and the cove just on the other side of the mountain. *Birdie said his name was Johnson, and there are Johnsons still living over there.*

The ridge runners had traveled these high trails till after the Second World War, when improved roads and affordable cars had made horse and foot travel obsolete. Now most of the fields and pastures were covered with second-growth timber and the insidious multiflora rose. Subsistence farming had given way to jobs in the city, and many old mountain farms had been abandoned. The sturdy log tobacco barns still stood, though, their rusting metal roofs incongruous amid the encroaching trees.

Elizabeth noted down the nearest hollows on the other side of the mountain; many were named on the map by the branch or creek that ran through them—Little Branch, Devil's Branch, Sweet Water Creek—but others had names taken from some long-forgotten event—Lonesome, Turkey Feather, Hog Run, Buckscrape. She could imagine the early settlers naming these places: "You mind that ole holler where them big bucks clean the velvet offen their antlers—we call it the Buck-scrape?" She had been in a few of these "hollers" years before when she and Sam had tracked some of their cows that had gotten out through the old barbed-wire fence at the top of the mountain. But most of the hollers, though only a few miles away, were totally unknown to her. To get to them by car she would have to go down Ridley Branch to the bridge and then up the road that ran by Bear Tree Creek for four or five miles. *I'll talk to Birdie about it tomorrow, after I find out about the autopsy. If we have to go hunting, Birdie can suggest the likely places to start.*

Early Monday morning, Elizabeth fed her chickens and walked through her vegetable garden, trying to decide which chores should take precedence. The tomato plants that she had started in a cold frame were too small to set out yet. The potatoes were pushing up through their thick blanket of hay and needed no attention. She could hoe around the young broccoli and collards, or she could do some weed-eating. *But first you call the sheriff,* she reminded herself.

The deputy who took her call was vague as to the sheriff's whereabouts but reasonably sure that Cletus Gentry's autopsy had not yet taken place. He suggested that she call back toward the end of the week. No, there was still no reason to regard this as anything other than an accident.

"Well, hell," said Elizabeth, hanging up the phone. It startled her by ringing immediately. *It's going to be Birdie, and you can probably forget about getting that weed-eating done,* she told herself as she picked it back up.

"I'm ready, Lizzie Beth." The old woman's voice was

quavering but steely with determination. "I done packed us some sausage biscuits and some applesauce biscuits and a jar of buttermilk and I'm just a-settin' here waiting for you. Reckon we could start by goin' up Lonesome Holler."

As they drove the narrow road that wound its way up Bear Tree Creek, Elizabeth glanced over at Miss Birdie, who was clearly enjoying herself. She had something to say about each farm or house they passed. "They must of got their baccer set right before that last big rain; hit looks real purty . . . *That* old place was like to fall down, then some Florida people bought it and fixed it up good as new. . . . Look-a there, they done set their mailbox up on an old bull-tongue plow."

Elizabeth had been somewhat surprised at Birdie's calm acceptance of the fact of Cletus's death. Birdie had not shed a tear, to Elizabeth's knowledge; instead, she had resolutely concentrated her emotion on the question of how Cletus had met his end. The old woman was just commenting on a cow in a pasture by the road—". . . puts me in mind of that old Jersey we used to have, old Polly. She poured the milk but was awful bad to kick. Cletus, he wouldn't have nothin' to do with her, though he was usual a right good hand to milk"—when she broke off abruptly and looked at Elizabeth, as if she'd read the latter's mind.

"Reckon I don't sound like a natural mother, just a-goin' on like that and my boy dead and not even in the ground yet. But, Lizzie Beth, I tell you how it is. Cletus has gone to be with Jesus and I know he's safe now. . . . These last few years, I been studyin' what would happen to him when I was gone. I'll be eighty-two in October and him just forty-one." Miss Birdie's eyes were misty now. "He was the onliest one of our babies what lived. We had five afore him and they was all born dead or died afore they could walk. I thought I wouldn't have no more, then he come along and me thinkin' I was havin' the change. Me and Luther was so happy, and even when we knowed he was simple, why hit didn't hardly matter; he was a good help on the farm and as sweet as the day is long. He couldn't never learn to read, but . . ."

She wiped her eyes and blurted out, "When Luther died ten years ago, some lady from the county come out and talked to me about Cletus, said maybe he would do better in one of them special homes. I run her off right quick, but I knowed that if something was to happen to me, they'd take and put him in one of those places and, Lizzie Beth, he couldn't of stood it. So I guess maybe the Lord knowed that, too, and that's why He called my boy afore me."

Elizabeth started to speak but Birdie went on, her voice stern now, "But that don't mean I don't want to find whoever it was knocked my boy on the head and throwed him in the river like a bag of garbage."

Lonesome Holler was aptly named. A narrow dirt and gravel road ran between two freshly plowed and harrowed tobacco fields and up a densely wooded mountainside. Next to the road a swift-moving stream hurtled down over huge mossy boulders. Ancient dark green rhododendrons loomed above the road, bathing it in deep shadows.

"I thought we'd best start here 'cause it's the clostest place he mighta gone," Miss Birdie explained, holding on with both hands as the jeep crawled over the rutted road. "This here's where Walter and Ollie Johnson live; do you know them? It was Walter brought them beans over to Dessie's that last day."

"I know who they are. . . . Sam and I were over here years ago, looking for some of our cows that had gotten out. I think I remember . . . there was a beautiful little pool at one place in the woods, under a big oak tree in a clearing. . . ." With a sharp pang she remembered the day: hot and sweaty from the long hike up and then partway down Pinnacle, they had come upon this perfect bathing spot hidden away in the woods. They had quickly stripped and immersed themselves in its four-foot depth, delighted at this rare find so high up a mountain. They had emerged and dressed just as quickly, huddling their clothes onto still-wet bodies, when they heard voices and realized that there must be a house nearby. "Do they live in a pretty little log house—two rooms with a dogtrot down the middle—almost to the top of Pinnacle?"

"Used to they did," Birdie said. "That is, till their childern got the notion Mommy and Daddy was too old to live up there so far from the hard road and without no phone nor 'lectricity."

They had reached a clearing where a small barn and a newish white single-wide mobile home sat on a bulldozed cut in the side of the slope. A shed-roofed porch attached to the front of the trailer was lined with plastic lawn chairs. As Elizabeth pulled the jeep to a stop beside a rusted Ford truck, the door of the trailer opened and Walter and Ollie Johnson came out and sat down, ready to receive company. Ollie, a large, comfortable-looking woman with fluffy white hair, urged them, "Get you uns a chair," and flapped her apron to shoo a yellow cat off the porch.

Once they were all seated, Miss Birdie began. "You

uns know Lizzie Beth. She lives right down the other side of the mountain from you—the old Baker place."

Walter, a wisp of a man in faded overalls, leaned slowly forward to peer at Elizabeth. He was about to speak when his wife said, "Why, yes, we know who she is. You remember, Walter, her and her man come huntin' their cows, back when we was livin' up on the mountain, must have been ten, twelve years ago. I believe hit was in June and they was just soaked with sweat. They found them cows, too, in the pasture with old Pet."

She smiled widely at Elizabeth. "Hit's good to see you again, Miz Goodweather." Then she lowered her voice and leaned toward Birdie. "Birdie, honey, Burlen done told us about your Cletus. I hate it for you but I know he's singin' with the angel band right now." She touched Birdie's arm consolingly.

"I thank you, Ollie. I was just tellin' Lizzie Beth that my Cletus is safe with Jesus. But I still want to know how come him to end up in the river when I seen him goin' the other way, headin' up Pinnacle. I was wonderin' if he'd come this way—hit would have been about three weeks back of this."

Again Walter Johnson leaned forward, shifting his chewing tobacco into his cheek, but once again Ollie spoke first. "Why, no, honey, we didn't see him. And iffen he'd come this way, he surely would of stopped in. Cletus did love my biscuits and many's the time he come this way and stayed with us. But we ain't seed him since back in March. I know because I always write it on the calendar when people come by and when Burlen told me about Cletus, I went and looked to see when it was he was last here. March twenty-seven, hit was."

"Do you reckon he might of gone to your old place?" Birdie asked earnestly. "Lizzie Beth could take me up the road in her jeep. I'm a-lookin' for Cletus's shotgun what he had with him. Hit weren't there . . . where they found him."

"Law, honey, you can't get nary a vehicle up to the old place no more. That big ice storm last winter blowed over nineteen big trees right acrost the road. They's a big poplar down right around the curve. No, the onliest way is to walk. Me and Walter ain't been up to the old place since last fall. That old arthuritis won't let neither of us clamber over them big trees."

Walter raised a finger and began, "That preacher—"

"That's right," Ollie continued. "They's a preacher man from outside of here been stayin' up there since the beginning of March. He's one of these travelin' evangelists—Burlen knows him from some'ers. Burlen said this Brother Slagle was lookin' for a quiet place to be alone and pray between his travels and asked could he use our old cabin."

"Lizzie Beth," Birdie explained, "that Burlen she's namin' is Pastor Briggs, the one was over to Dessie's that last day we was there. Burlen Briggs is Ollie's baby brother."

"I reckon that preacher's found hit quiet enough; we ain't seen but very little of him," Ollie continued. "He did pass by just yesterday and stopped to visit. Iffen he'd seen Cletus, reckon he'd of said something to us." She darted a look at Walter, who was noisily clearing his throat and added, "That preacher man's a-settin' up his tent on the bypass now, gettin' ready for a big revival startin' next week. They call him John the Baptizer."

Walter slowly hoisted himself out of his chair and, shuffling forward, spat a thin stream of tobacco juice into the weeds below. A bit of the amber liquid caught the edge of the porch and Ollie exclaimed, "Walter, why can't you use that spit can I fixed for you? Let me get a rag and wipe that off." She bustled into the trailer, still fussing vociferously at her husband.

As Walter made his unhurried way back to his seat, he caught Birdie's eye and wheezed, "Reckon you ought to go ask them hippies up on Hog Run did they see Cletus."

II–APRIL 1901

Romarie took on like one thing when she come home from Phelpses and found out that we was a-goin to have a boarder. Daddy and Mister Tomlin had gone off down to the river to look at a piece of land Daddy knowed of and Romarie just let loose. You mean to tell me, she hollered, we got us another man to feed and do for? But when we told her about the gold watch chain and the red stone finger-ring she quieted down some and asked what age of a man Mister Tomlin was.

By the time him and Daddy come back for supper, Romarie had fixed her hair up in a big pompadour like what the schoolteacher has, and had got out some of the jelly and pickles that she puts up special for when the preacher comes to dinner. I believe that she had got into Clytie's powder too.

Daddy looked close at Romarie as she got the supper on the table. She was askin me and Clytie will you and why don't you just as sweet as if she'd never in her life offered to slap us twist-legged if we didn't hurry up with that wood-splittin. When we was all at the table and Mister Tomlin had said another one of his great long prayers, she com-

menced to askin after his family. When she learnt that he were a widder-man, she had a time to keep from grinnin outright. But she acted all sorrowful-like and ast Mister Tomlin iffen he wouldn't try some more of her blackberry jam.

I could see right off that hit weren't no use, for though Mister Tomlin was a gentleman and answered her polite, I could feel him a-drawin back from her. Ol Rom never was pretty even when she was a girl and her hair and eyes is kindly no color atall so that she looks like she don't have no eyebrows nor lashes neither. She's always been sickly lookin though they ain't a thing wrong with her but that she is eat up with meanness.

Me and Clytie take atter Mommy. At least that's what Aetha says. We have dark brown hair and bright blue eyes. Clytie has hips and bosoms like any grown woman, but I'm still flat front and back. Hit don't bother me none. But hit did surprise me when I seed that Mr. Tomlin was treatin me like I was growed up—askin me would I walk to church with him on Sunday. I didn't know what to say and I looked at Daddy. He just nodded his head yes and went on spoonin up his soup beans.

That like to killed Romarie. She jumped up from the table so fast that her chair banged over and she started to clearin the dishes though Mister Tomlin was yet butterin a biscuit. And I could see Clytie's lower lip a-startin to pooch out like hit does when she don't get her way. Well, thinks I. Well.

When Sunday morning come, Romarie stayed in the bed and left it for me and Clytie to do all the work. She let on *that she was taken bad with her time of the month but I had seen her washin her clouts two weeks back and knowed she didn't have her period on her. I allowed as how she just didn't want to be there when I come a-walkin up to the church house with Mister Tomlin.*

Howsomever, I done the milkin and fed the chickens whilst Clytie fixed breakfast. Daddy had said to fix fried chicken for dinner. We didn't have no extry chickens for a coon had killed the young cockerels I was fattenin. Well, girl, Daddy had said, you kill one of them young pullets. And just you take my shotgun up to the chicken house tonight and lay in wait for that coon.

I caught one of the young pullets and wrung her head off. I was settin on the back porch, pluckin off the feathers and puttin them in the feather basket when Clytie hollered out that the food was on the table. I could smell the sausage and my mouth fairly watered to think of biscuits and sausage gravy. But I had yet to gut and wash the pullet and put her to cool in the springhouse.

By the time I got that done and washed the blood and feathers and that nasty chicken smell offen myself, they was all finished with breakfast. Daddy and Mister Tomlin was settin on the front porch a-smokin some long black cigars that Mister Tomlin had brung with him. There weren't no sausage left but Clytie had saved back some gravy and biscuits. I et it standin while Clytie done up the dishes. She was already wearin her blue Sunday dress and had her hair pulled up all puffy like Romarie had taken to doin since Mister Tomlin come to stay.

Little Sylvie, Daddy called out, you stir yore stumps and get ready for church. Yessir, Daddy, I said, and took off up the stairs. I had some biscuit for Romarie but she just let out a big groan and turned her face to the wall when she seen me. I left the plate there on the floor by her bed and made for me and Clytie's room, a-pullin off my old work rags as fast as I could.

My Sunday dress was one what Aetha had made for Clytie but Clytie had got too big for it with those bosoms of hern afore she could wear it out. Hit was a pretty pink calico with a fancy ruffle going from each shoulder down to the waist in a big vee like flyin geese. Aetha's a good hand to sew and her man got her one of them sewin machines soon atter they was wed. I hope to have me a sewin machine for my own someday. I do like to work that treadle.

I unplaited my hair and brushed hit out. I wisht that Clytie would come upstairs and show me how to fix hit like hern but I knowed that she wouldn't. So I just let hit hang. Hit reaches past my waist to where I can sit on hit. I was just about to look in Clytie's box for that powder when Daddy hollered up the stairs, You, Little Sylvie, get on down here. I don't want to miss the preachin.

We walked down our road, Daddy and Clytie in front and me and Mister Tomlin behind. Clytie was a-switchin her bottom like one thing and oncet we had to all stop and wait while she pulled off a briar that was caught in her dress hem. She lifted up her skirt and twisted hit thisaway and that till she made sure Mister Tomlin could see them narrow ankles of hern she's so proud of.

When we reached the little road that runs up the hill to the graveyard, Daddy said, You uns walk on and me and

Clytie'll go up and visit Mama for a minute. I wondered at this, seein he had been in such a hurry to get to the preachin but I just said, Don't you want me to come too, Daddy?

He give me one of them sharp looks and said, Didn't you hear me right, girl? I said walk on.

Down on the road that runs along Ridley Branch, I could see a whole gang of them Gentrys a-walkin toward the church house. I quickened my step, thinkin to catch up with them and walk along in company for I was kindly shy of bein alone with Mister Tomlin. But he pulled up and said, Now, Little Sylvie, let's just bide here for a spell so as we don't get too far ahead of your pa.

They was a big flat rock over to one side of the road and Mister Tomlin he took my hand and led me over to it. He pulled out a white pocket handkerchief and spread it on the rock for me to set on. Now, Little Sylvie, says he. I want to tell you how I'm situated. And he stood there before me, one hand deep in his pocket a-jinglin of the gold coins that was always in there, and he begun to talk. He told me how he was a lonely widder-man in need of a helpmeet to brighten his days. He talked of how much money and property he had and how, oncet that he got his sawmill built, he would build a big house and his wife would be able to take her ease.

I spoke up and said that it seemed to me a big house would just make for more work and he laughed and patted me on the hand and said, Why, Little Sylvie, I'm well able to hire a servant to do the work. My wife wouldn't have to do a thing in this world but wear pretty dresses and sit on a tuffet and sew a fine seam. His hand rested there on mine and hit seemed like the sun struck sparks offen that ruby in his finger-ring. I knowed now that was the right name for that blood red stone for Clytie had asked him.

I don't rightly know what is a tuffet, I said, but I do like to sew. Aetha done learned me to use her machine and I can do right good with it.

Just then Daddy and Clytie come along and Mister Tomlin put out his hand to help me up. We'll talk more about this in a while, he said. But I believe that we can come to an understanding.

All during the preachin I was thinkin on what Mister Tomlin had said. Hit seemed queer-like but hit appeared that he was a-makin up to me and wanted me for his wife. I looked acrost the church house to the men's side where him and Daddy was settin and seen that Mister Tomlin was a-lookin back at me. My face got hot and I quick looked up at the preacher. Brother Gosnell was goin on about how our church house was too small and in need of a new roof and he was askin the Lord to move the hearts of men to help to build us a new church house. He prayed and carried on and talked of Baby Jesus with no place to lay his head and at last he come right out and asked for folks to stand and say what they would give toward a new church house. If the Spirit moves you, children, he said. Listen if you don't hear the Spirit a-callin on you to do yore part.

Well, ain't no one round here got much but first one and then another stood and said that he would give so many days of work toward the buildin. One allowed as how him and his ox team could haul rocks for a foundation and the Gentry boys said they'd give so many logs offen their place, but no one offered any cash money. All of a sudden up jumps Mister Tomlin. Most folks knowed who he was for he'd been all up and down the creek offerin to buy timber and they knowed he was namin to buy the old Freeman place down by the river. Most knowed but on the bench in back of me I heared nosy old Granny Plemmons whisper to her daughter, Who is that fine-lookin man?

Mister Tomlin stood there and looked around the church house. Then he spoke to the preacher. Brother Gosnell, says he, I thank the Lord for bringin me into this country. On Ridley Branch, I believe that I've found all that I was seekin. You good people have made me welcome and quick as I get my mill built, first boards I saw will go to build your new church. I'll undertake to supply all the lumber you need and, what's more, I'll pay for a first-class metal roof.

Brother Gosnell threw up his hands and hollered Praise the Lord and all of a sudden the men was ever one comin and pumpin on Mister Tomlin's hand. The women was all a-whisperin and Clytie give me the queerest look.

When preachin broke, we all walked home together, us and the Gentrys. Daddy and Mister Tomlin and Mister Gentry was talkin about the new sawmill and the Gentry girls and Clytie was all actin the fool to see could they get Mister Tomlin to look at them. Billy Gentry kept tryin to pester me and would pull at my hair till I hollered at him to leave off. Him and me had set together the last time we had dinner on the grounds at the church and I had thought he was right good-lookin then but now his face was all spotty, most like he'd gotten into poison oak, and hit seemed like his ears stuck out more than they had used to. I run him *off, then his sisters Retha and Margaret come wantin to know was Mister Tomlin married and was it true he had brung a bag of gold double eagles with him from Tennessee.*

Hit was but three days later that Daddy come out to the barn while I was doin the evening milkin. Ol Poll was actin ill; first off she wouldn't let her milk down though I washed her tits off with warm water and butted her ol bag with my fist like as if I was her calf. She danced around and almost got her nasty foot in the bucket. I had to put her out some more corn afore she would settle and even then, oncet the milk was a-singin into the bucket, what does she do but wrap her dirty ol tail around my head and slap my face.

You ol huzzy, I said, I wisht I could be shed of you and your ways. Just then I looked up to see a dark shape there against the evening light. At first I thought hit might be Mister Tomlin, come to talk to me some more, but then I seen hit was Daddy. He leaned against the big logs there in the barn hallway but didn't say nothing for the longest time. When at last I had stripped ol Poll dry and turned her back out to the pasture, Daddy said, Little Sylvie, Mister Tomlin wants you for his wedded wife. I didn't answer him right off, for though I had thought some about hit, I couldn't rightly say how I felt. Well, girl, Daddy said, wouldn't that be a fine thing? Romarie and Clytie has both told me that hit ain't fair, him a-sparkin you and you the least un, but yore the one he wants. And I'll tell you what's the truth, Little Sylvie, a chancet like this'll not come yore way again.

I stood there in my old ragged work dress that had be-
longed to Clytie and to Aetha before her. I thought of what
Mister Tomlin had said about his wife not having to lift a
finger. My face stung where Poll's tail had whipped me,
and atter a while I said, I reckon I just as soon.

CHAPTER 6
HIPPIES ON HOG RUN
(MONDAY)

AFTER ANOTHER FORTY-FIVE MINUTES OF VISIT-
ing with the Johnsons, Elizabeth had heard
enough about whose taters were growing
good and which cousin had a brand-new
tractor. The hint about hippies on Hog Run tantalized
her—could Cletus have been up there recently? But
mountain manners required that they stay at least an
hour, and Birdie was obviously relishing her visit. The
talk ranged on: from Dessie's funeral to the weather and
back to the state of their gardens and who would have
the first ripe maters. Walter had refused to say anything
more about the hippies and Ollie too had been strangely
silent, on that subject at least. *Relax, Elizabeth*, she told
herself, *there's time; this is what you're doing now.* She
leaned back and let the quiet talk flow around her.

She watched Walter and Ollie: the one, taciturn, the
other, talkative, but each completely attuned to the
other. *They're the two parts that make a whole*, she thought
enviously. *Sam and I were like that. And we were going to
grow old together, die on the same day, and be buried in the
same grave. Oh, Sam!*

Elizabeth took a deep breath and resolutely turned her

mind to other things. *Walter would be kin to the Johnson fellow that Little Sylvie ran off with,* she thought. *I wonder what he could tell me about them? That is, if Ollie would let him. It's a sad story—if the baby died of neglect, I wonder how Little Sylvie and her lover could have been happy with each other.*

But at last Miss Birdie was pulling herself up from her chair and the standard mountain exchange of parting courtesies was beginning. "Go home with us!" Birdie said, and "Stay all night!" Ollie answered. Elizabeth, wondering if anyone ever acted on these routine invitations, waved a good-bye to the Johnsons as she and Birdie climbed into the car.

Birdie started to buckle her seat belt, then stopped. "Lizzie Beth, honey, I done left my walking stick on the porch by my chair. Let me just—"

"I'll get it, Miss Birdie," Elizabeth said hastily. "You wait here." She hopped out of the car and hurried back to the trailer's porch. Walter and Ollie had gone inside and as Elizabeth bent down to retrieve the cane, she could hear Ollie's voice.

"Walter Johnson, you know it ain't right. We got to stop her. I'll speak to Burlen—"

"I'm just getting Miss Birdie's cane," Elizabeth called out, embarrassed to be eavesdropping, however inadvertently. Immediately Ollie's head peered round the door. She glanced at the car where Birdie was waiting, then whispered fiercely to Elizabeth, "It ain't goin' to do a bit of good you and her pokin' into things. They's a sight of mean folks back in some of these hollers. You best leave things be!"

The change in Ollie's demeanor was startling. She

watched unsmilingly as Elizabeth stammered something and retreated back down the steps. Then she turned and disappeared into the trailer once again.

"Ay law, honey," Birdie said as the jeep jolted its way down the steep road back onto the pavement. "I sure am proud we got to see Walter and Ollie. I don't know how long it's been since I seen Ollie; anymore, they don't hardly leave their place. Walter don't like to drive only to the grocery or to the doctor. But they know a-plenty about what's goin' on and if they didn't see Cletus, I reckon he must of gone some other way. Reckon we ort to go up Hog Run next, like Walter said. I mind Cletus talkin' bout them hippies; he said they was right peculiar folks, but that they was allus good to him."

Squirming uncomfortably in her seat, she continued, "If you don't care, Lizzie Beth, maybe we could pull off the road up here and eat our dinner. That bumpy road done something to my back. Hit's like fire runnin' up and down my vertables."

They parked under a spreading black walnut that grew beside Bear Tree Creek to eat their lunch. "I'll just rinse this mason jar out in the branch," said Miss Birdie when they had eaten the biscuits and drunk the buttermilk. "Hit'll feel good to walk a mite and kindly unjangle my vertables."

Elizabeth was studying the map she'd brought with her, noting just how many coves and hollows there were that Cletus could easily have hiked to from the top of Pinnacle. Suddenly she heard a barely suppressed cry of anguish. Birdie was standing on the pebble-strewn creek bank, bent almost double, one hand pressed to her side. Her face was pale with pain.

"What is it, Miss Birdie?" Elizabeth called anxiously as she ran to help the old woman.

"Oh, Lizzie Beth, honey, I done stepped wrong and wrenched my back. Hit's happened afore and hit'll pass off, but I got to get back home and lay down."

Elizabeth delivered Miss Birdie to her house, found her an aspirin to take, and settled her in the big recliner chair that faced the television. When Birdie seemed to be more comfortable, Elizabeth asked gently, "Miss Birdie, do you want me to go on back to Hog Run and see what I can find out? Or do you want me to wait till another day when you can go with me?"

The old woman thought briefly then said, "Lizzie Beth, honey, if you don't care, I reckon hit'd be best was you to go on without me. Hit may be a week afore my back feels better. I'd take it mighty kindly was you to go on and ask about Cletus everwhere you can."

Elizabeth left Birdie watching a soap opera. "Law, honey, the things these folks gets up to, hit's a scandal." Her eyes were glued to the screen as she said, "Now you call me iffen you find out anything." As she left the little house Elizabeth could hear the words, "Brad, I don't think you realize what Cynthia has been through."

Back on Bear Tree Creek, Elizabeth turned her jeep up the rutted tracks marked by a green sign that read HOG RUN ROAD. At the base of the road were weedy pastures and overgrown fields, which gave way to second-growth timber. After about a quarter of a mile she came to a large clearing where four broken-down house trailers were propped up on blocks. All but one seemed to be occupied: drying clothes flapped from makeshift clotheslines; grimy, half-naked children played on the packed dirt around the trailers. An ancient claw-footed tub was a center of activity as squealing youngsters climbed in and out, splashing water at each other. Two little boys were struggling toward the tub with a red plastic bucket filled with muddy water from the branch. Just upstream from the spot where the children had dipped their bucket, murky water swirled around the rotting head of a deer.

Elizabeth slowed as she saw a little girl hauling on a rope attached to what at first she took to be a large dog. As the pair came closer she saw that it was actually a goat wearing a ragged pair of men's pajamas. By the side of a ramshackle tobacco barn, a dark-haired man was skinning some small animal. Drying hides of many different sizes and colors were nailed to the silver-gray planks of the barn. The man looked up from his work, squinted at Elizabeth's car, then spat to one side. Elizabeth increased her speed slightly. As she left the clearing behind, she caught sight of two more men tipping a filthy green sofa onto a small fire of worn-out car tires.

My god, she thought, *it's the Trailer Park of the Damned. It's like a modern Brueghel or Hieronymous Bosch.* Such squalor was unusual in the mountains. Most people's places, whether mobile homes, ancient cabins, or new brick ranch houses, were kept painfully tidy, mowed and weed-eaten at least weekly. More than once Elizabeth had been thankful that her farm was not visible from the main road so that her somewhat relaxed standards of lawn care would not be apparent to her neighbors.

"I can allus tell when Lizzie Beth's been weed-eatin' down along the hard road," Dessie had said with a laugh years ago. "She won't mow down a weed iffen hit's got a purty flower." So Elizabeth's roadside boasted untidy clumps of blue chicory, red clover, yellow hawkweed, and the delicate white umbrellas of Queen Anne's lace.

As did the roadside ahead of her, she realized. The straggling dusty grasses of the unmown verge had given way to a close-clipped tidiness punctuated with wildflowers. A wooden gate, artfully constructed of peeled rhododendron limbs, lay open before her. Hanging from the gate, a carved sign read STARSHINE COMMUNITY. The letters were picked out with gold paint, and small golden stars were scattered on the deep blue background. Beyond the gate, the road forked. Another carved sign set in a clump of orange daylilies said VISITORS and pointed down the right fork.

The narrow road ran past thick woods on the left and steep sloped pastures on the right. A six-strand electric fence bordered the field, which was home to a large flock of droopy-eared Nubian goats, most munching industriously on the huge multiflora rosebushes that dotted the mountainside. Elizabeth stopped her car and leaned out her window for a closer look at a beautiful long-eared doe that was cropping weeds near the fence. The goat raised her head and regarded Elizabeth appraisingly through her odd slit-pupiled eyes, then went back serenely to her browsing.

"She was hoping you might, like, have some goat feed with you. They're all pretty spoiled."

The voice startled Elizabeth, and she turned her head to find a sweet-faced young man with long blond dreadlocks speaking to her through the open window on the passenger side of her car. "Were you, like, looking for someone?" he asked.

"Well, yes, in a way," Elizabeth answered. "Maybe you read about the man they found in the river about a week ago?"

The young man looked at her blankly for a moment, then replied, "We stay out of the world's doings as much as possible. No newspapers, no radio, no TV. It's Polaris's rule."

Okay. And Polaris would be . . . ? Elizabeth thought, finding herself feeling unaccountably annoyed by the beatific little smile on the young man's face.

Polaris, she learned, was the founder of Starshine Community. He and three others had bought the hundred-and-sixty-acre property a few years ago, and it was he who decided who could come to live in the community. "We all, like, take star names when we evolve," the young man informed her. "I'm Rigel."

Rigel listened serenely, his forearms propped on the open window, as Elizabeth introduced herself and then told him about Cletus and the missing shotgun. Finally he had said, "You'd better talk to Polaris. He would know if your friend's son had been here recently. We always, like, take visitors, especially earth parents, to him."

"Earth parents?" Elizabeth asked, wondering if she had heard correctly.

"Once we join the community we acknowledge that we are children of the cosmos," Rigel explained solemnly. "We're supposed to share with our earth parents about how we've, like, evolved beyond them. But some people who come here, they've, you know, run away from bad situations. And sometimes their earth parents come looking for them."

Finally Rigel had directed her to follow the right fork to a big dome. "Polaris is usually there after the day-star meal, like, meditating and stuff. He'll be able to help you for sure; he's the most evolved of any of us." The young man straightened and stood back from the car, indicating with a wave of his arm which way she should go.

As she continued up the road, Elizabeth glanced in her rearview mirror and saw Rigel pull what looked like a cell phone from one of the pockets of the baggy sun-bleached overalls that seemed to be his only garment. He put it to his ear as he disappeared back into the wooded area between the two forks. *I wonder if he's a watchman or something,* Elizabeth thought half seriously. *He could be reporting on me to, what was his name? Polaris?*

The road ran through a gentle little hollow that showed the remains of a once extensive apple orchard. Here and there small, newly built log cabins were scattered, interspersed with an occasional felt-covered yurt. Elizabeth smiled nostalgically, remembering when these shelters—originally the portable dwellings favored by central Asian nomads—had been embraced by counterculture types back in the seventies. *The* Whole Earth Catalog *lives!* she thought with a grin.

Beneath one of the largest of the apple trees lounged a group of young women, all very pregnant. They were wearing gauzy white robes; some of them had wreaths of flowers on their heads. They glanced without curiosity at Elizabeth's car and one or two gave a perfunctory wave. *And the flower children, too.* She nodded at the picturesque group and drove on, humming, *"If you're going to Saan Fraan-ciso, / Be sure to wear some flowers in your hair. . . ."*

A little beyond the old orchard was a geodesic dome of the type popularized by Buckminster Fuller. *More seventies stuff,* she thought, smiling broadly. *I have obviously driven right into a time warp.*

Composed of large triangular panels, the dome rose huge and sparkling white in the sun, an imposing and unlikely sight in this ancient mountain cove. Triangular windows were set in vertical rows over its surface, and two tall purple-painted doors stood open at the end of a quarry-stone path. Elizabeth parked in the neat gravel parking area, marked with more of the hand-carved signs.

Polaris, Algol, Altair, and Canopus each rated a private spot, while the eight remaining slots were all labeled "Visitor." As she crunched her way through the thick gravel toward the dome, she noted that Polaris had a very new white Range Rover, while Algol and Canopus made do with silver Navigators. Altair was not there and there were no visitors besides herself.

It took a moment for her eyes to adjust as she stepped from the bright sunlight into the cool dim open interior of the dome, the heavy doors automatically and silently swinging shut behind her. The sensation was very different from that of entering an ordinary building. Somehow, there was a feeling of vastness—as if the interior of the dome was bigger than the outdoors. She felt the urge to call out *Hellooo,* as one might in a cave, certain that there would be an echo.

How big is *this thing?* Elizabeth wondered. *A hundred feet across? More?* A small sign inked in elaborate calligraphy requested that shoes be removed. Simple racks on either side of the door provided space for many shoes but were empty except for one pair of men's sandals.

Elizabeth hesitated at the entrance, peering around her. The only light was that which poured in shafts through the triangular skylights set in the upper curve of the structure. The floor beyond the tiled entryway was covered in rich blue carpeting. A circular dais, also covered with the blue carpet, occupied the dome's center. In the dimness, Elizabeth didn't at first notice the figure on the dais. Then a sudden shaft of light—a cloud passing away from the sun's face?—illuminated the white-bearded man who sat there with crossed legs and folded hands, eyes closed but obviously fully aware of her.

"Come in, daughter." The low, resonant tones seemed, oddly enough, to come from all around her rather than from the seated figure. Elizabeth toed off her sneakers and put them on the rack by the door. Then, feeling faintly ridiculous, she approached the white-bearded figure. *Like a child at the mall going to sit in Santa's lap,* she told herself. *Or Dorothy approaching the Wizard.* The man continued to sit motionless, eyes shut, till Elizabeth had reached the edge of the dais.

Restraining the impulse to begin by saying, "O great Oz," she cleared her throat and said, "I'm sorry to bother you, but—"

"We know of the transition of Cletus, Elizabeth Goodweather, and we grieve with you. He was a gentle spirit."

So it was a cell phone, Elizabeth thought. *Or a walkie-talkie. But maybe he really did see Cletus here.* Aloud, she asked, "Are you, uh, Polaris? Someone named Rigel told me to look for you here. I'm trying to find out where Cletus Gentry was two or three weeks ago. He was a small man, about five four, in his forties, short dark hair, and he would have had a shotgun—"

Polaris opened his eyes and turned their brilliant turquoise gaze full on her. *Those have got to be tinted contacts,* she thought, as Polaris said, "We knew Cletus well, Elizabeth Goodweather. Many times has he shared our evening-star meal. We knew him well and we cherished his simple wisdom. But he has not graced our table since the winter's solstice. And now we shall not see him for many circuits of the heavens."

Polaris closed his eyes again. He began to hum, almost inaudibly at first, but then growing in volume till the sound seemed to fill the entire dome. Elizabeth stood transfixed as the unearthly tones swirled around her. *How does he do that? A hidden microphone or what?* Suddenly the humming ceased. Tiny echoes seemed to chase each other around the curving walls.

Abruptly Polaris rose to his feet and stretched extravagantly. Then he jumped lightly from the low dais to stand in front of Elizabeth, crossing his hands on his chest and bowing slightly. Only then did she realize that he must be much younger than the white hair and beard would suggest. His slim, muscular body, clad in loose trousers and a tunic of thin white silk, was that of an athlete in his early thirties. The pale, smooth skin around his eyes could have belonged to an even younger man.

"My meditation time is accomplished. How may I help you, Elizabeth Goodweather?"

Once again she began to explain, getting as far as ". . . and he headed up Pinnacle Ridge, right along my property line. My farm is on Ridley Branch—" Polaris smiled gently and held up both hands, palms outward.

"I know your farm, daughter, as I know all these coves and hollows, all the folds and hidden places of our dear foster-mother Earth. Many times have I journeyed in my astral body, gliding along the mountaintops, cherishing the sweet valleys and rivers, before voyaging outward to the stars. The creatures of these hills, the trees, the streams, the very rocks, all inform me as I travel, each one singing its own part in creation's many-voiced song."

The full force of the turquoise eyes swept over her and Elizabeth stood there, mouth agape, for once, utterly and completely, dumbfounded.

CHAPTER 7
THE RUNAWAY STAR
(MONDAY)

YOU'RE A BLEEDING NUTCASE, THOUGHT ELIZAbeth, the quote—*Was it Monty Python? Douglas Adams?*—rising unbidden in her mind. Immediately the voice of political correctness within countered, *Now, Elizabeth, don't be so cynical. 'There are more things in heaven and earth, Horatio, than are dreamt of in your philosophies,' or however it goes.* But aloud, she said only, "Then maybe you would have some idea of which way Cletus might have gone."

Polaris shook his head slowly and his eyes darted to a slim, expensive-looking watch on his right wrist. "Each spirit must walk its own path, Elizabeth Goodweather. Be not troubled for the spirit that was Cletus; it has evolved into a higher sphere."

Elizabeth doggedly persevered. "Cletus's mother wants me to try to find out what happened to the shotgun he had with him. I wonder if you could ask—"

Polaris smiled disdainfully and spread out his open hands in a priestly gesture, "We have nothing to do with the futile weapons of this world, my daughter. They have no power here in this sacred place. Yet, if you wish, I shall make inquiries. But now . . ."

Behind her, Elizabeth heard a rustle and murmur. She turned: Seven young women were removing their sandals at the door. Polaris continued, "But now I have a cluster to orient. Please return by the same way you entered our community; the area beyond is private. If you would like more information about Starshine Community, you may visit our Web site." The young women, all wearing light sleeveless robes in shades ranging from creamy yellow to deep orange, were approaching with measured steps. Their heads were bowed and their hands were crossed on their breasts. Polaris bowed slightly, then turned and sprang back onto the dais. Elizabeth had been dismissed.

She returned to the door and contrived to stuff her feet back into her sneakers without untying the laces. The young women circled three times around the dais where Polaris stood, then sank gracefully to the carpet to kneel facing the tall white figure. *Like stars wheeling around the North Star,* Elizabeth thought as the dark purple doors closed quietly behind her. The picture of the yellow and orange robes puddled on the deep blue carpet stayed with her. *It's unreal,* she decided. *Everything here is so beautiful, like one of those movies where each frame could be a painting.*

Driving back toward the gate, she wondered about Polaris. *How could someone with pure white hair look so young? Daughter, indeed! I could be his mother! Maybe he's an albino? His skin was certainly pale. But his eyes weren't pink, though that wild turquoise was probably courtesy of contacts . . . And what in the world, or out of it, are these people up to? I'd heard there was a "hippie commune" up here, but I sure didn't expect anything this organized. Someone's spent a lot of money here. Hippie communes are usually raggedy-ass poor, at least they used to be.*

The women under the apple tree were gone now, and there was no sign of life in any of the little cabins or the yurts. It was like a fantasy village, tended by invisible gardeners and unspoiled by human squalor. She continued on down the road toward the entrance. The goats had moved higher up in the pasture to the shade of a grove of locust trees. Elizabeth slowed to look for Rigel but there was no one to be seen. *Dammit,* she told herself, *you didn't find out diddly. Polaris said Cletus hadn't been here recently, but—*

She decided to drive up the left fork and see what the rest of the community looked like. *There's no sign saying not to,* she argued, and swung her car around.

The left fork led upward, zigzagging across a steep wooded hillside. The road was narrow and if she were to meet a car, she realized, there would be no room to pass. Elizabeth cursed her impulsive decision. Briefly she considered backing down, but quickly saw that it would be very difficult, if not impossible. She glanced at the abrupt drop-off, mere inches from her right tires, and doggedly drove on, praying that she would soon find a place to turn around.

The road grew even steeper; she shifted into low four-wheel drive. Old trees pressed in closer, the road grew narrower, and it began to seem as if she were caught in some endless nightmare. Higher and higher the jeep climbed. She was near the top of the mountain when at last a small clearing appeared to the left. A windowless building occupied most of the space with—*joy of joys*—a graveled area in front of it. There was just room to back her car in beside the shiny black pickup truck parked there and turn around.

As she was executing this maneuver, a door in the end of the building opened and two burly men emerged, both carrying rifles. They wore jeans and black T-shirts, and their eyes were hidden behind wraparound sunglasses.

"I got lost," she said ingenuously, when the larger of the two men stepped to her open window. He leaned down and peered suspiciously into the interior of the jeep, then at her.

"Just some batty old broad," she could hear him saying to his companion as he motioned her down the road.

"And I thought," she said aloud, "that they shunned the futile weapons of the world." Ollie's words, *They's a sight of mean people back in some of these hollers,* ran through her mind as she wound back down the steep road, one eye on the rearview mirror.

Near the entrance, her thoughts were interrupted by a piercing whistle and a shout. "Hey, ma'am! Can I get a ride out of here?"

A tall, thin man in his early twenties was jogging toward her from the woods. Like Rigel, he wore overalls. He had a bulging knapsack slung over one shoulder. Elizabeth stopped her jeep and, without waiting for an answer, the young man opened the door and jumped into the backseat, crouching down low.

"Please, just take me as far as the bridge. I can hitch from there. I've got to get out of this place."

Elizabeth turned to study her strange passenger. Long red hair, pulled back in an untidy ponytail, a complicated tattoo like a Celtic knot on his left arm, a wispy little goatee, and pleading gray eyes—"Okay," she said, quickly making up her mind, "I'll take you to the bridge if you'll answer some questions for me."

"Whatever. Could we just get going?" The voice was agitated but not threatening and Elizabeth started the car. As she drove through the entranceway, she was surprised to see a sleek BMW coming up the road. She pulled over as far to the right as she could and the shiny black car rushed by her and through the gate. The driver wore dark glasses and did not even acknowledge her presence with a nod. Looking in her rearview mirror she saw that the car had an out-of-state license plate. New Jersey, she thought, but couldn't be sure.

"We don't see many BMWs out this way," she remarked conversationally to her hidden companion as they continued down the road and past the junky trailers. The sofa was still smoldering on the fire; the goat in pajamas now stood on the roof of a car without wheels. All the children had disappeared and the clawfoot tub was tipped on its side, revealing a rust red interior.

"A Beemer?" the reply came from the backseat. "Black with real dark windows? Probably Mr. Dimato. He comes up every couple of months, him and his girlfriend. He's a real creepy guy but he's some kind of buddy of Polaris."

Her rider seemed more at ease now as they turned onto the pavement and started down the road to the bridge across the river. He unfolded himself and sat up. "I'm Dabih—shit, what am I saying? I'm Trent Woodbern. Sorry about jumping into your car like that but I didn't know when I'd get another chance to get out."

"Couldn't you just walk out?" Elizabeth asked, amused at the drama of the situation. "It's only a few miles to the bridge."

"Yeah, I know, but they don't make it easy if you want to leave. They kind of surround you and talk about stuff; I think they kind of brainwash you. A few months ago when I told them I was thinking about going back to college, the Pleiades Cluster showed up and by the next morning I was calling my trustee asking for more money to put into the community."

"What's a cluster?" asked Elizabeth, intrigued, remembering Polaris's words, *I have a cluster to orient,* as the young women had entered the dome.

"Well, the members of the community are divided into groups. When you first evolve, you're assigned to a constellation; I was in Capricornus. Everybody in a constellation lives together and works together and evolves mostly at the same time. But sometimes those who evolve faster get assigned to a cluster. Like the Pleiades; they're all super-evolved and totally close to Polaris."

Trent informed Elizabeth that he had worked as a river guide the previous summer, and when fall had come he had decided to live at the Starshine Community. "I just wanted a place to stay and there were all these fine honeys; besides, I wasn't ready to go back to school yet."

He was fairly vague about the inner workings of the community, saying only that he hadn't evolved far enough to be told everything. "I got as far as the rebirthing pool, that was okay, but then some things started to seem a little sketchy, like there are whole forbidden areas that only the most highly evolved can visit. And I'm pretty sure they monitored my phone calls. A couple of times when I was telling someone on the outside about some of the stuff that was going on, the phone would cut off and I wouldn't be able to call out again. We aren't allowed to have cell phones."

"Trent, do you remember—did a local man, in his forties, carrying a shotgun, visit the community recently?" Elizabeth asked.

"Are you talking about Cletus?" he replied promptly. "Everyone knew Cletus. He'd just come walking down that road from the top of the mountain with that gun over his shoulder and that big grin on his face. Only the highest-evolved are allowed up to the top and no outsiders ever, but Polaris didn't ever seem to mind about Cletus. He always made this big deal over Cletus's 'aboriginal wisdom' and something he called 'lateral evolution.' "

"I think I just drove up that road to the top," Elizabeth told her passenger. "There was a building without windows and two men with rifles."

"That might have been where they took me for occultation," the young man said. "I was blindfolded but I could tell we were going up. But I don't know anything about guys with rifles."

Trent explained that he didn't know whether or not Cletus had been at the community at any time during the weeks that had preceded his death. "I'd been put into total occultation. That's like being put in solitary for a month. Anyway, it's what you have to do before evolving another step; it gives you time to meditate and all. But it just made me realize that those guys are a bunch of Looney Tunes."

By the time they reached the bridge, Elizabeth's curiosity was fully engaged and she offered to drive Trent on into Ransom, hoping to learn more about the Starshine Community. He was about to accept when he spotted a van in the parking lot beside the bridge. "Oh, great! You can let me out here. That's a River Runners van. You know, the rafting company I used to work for; I can get a ride with them."

He was out of the jeep and loping toward the van with a hurried thank-you called back to Elizabeth. She watched as he was greeted enthusiastically by the van's driver and as he climbed into the passenger-side front seat. Wishing she could have heard more of his story, she turned back toward Ridley Branch.

Back at home after checking on Miss Birdie, who had gotten a cousin to come stay the night, Elizabeth sat on the front porch with a predinner gin and tonic and wondered what, if anything, she was accomplishing. *At least I'm learning more about who lives around here,* she mused. *I'd heard about the so-called hippie commune but sure didn't imagine anything like Polaris! My god! I've lived here twenty years and still don't know what's on the other side of the mountain. But Cletus did.*

As she rocked and sipped her drink, Elizabeth reflected on just how much Cletus must have known about the nearby coves and hollows. Though unable to read books, he was an intuitive weather forecaster and naturalist. In a city he would have probably ended up portioning out fries in a fast-food restaurant, but here, on the mountain and in the woods, he was fully competent.

"Damn!" Elizabeth said, gazing out at the ever-changing, ever-beautiful view where the evening star hung in the pale sky above the violet mountains. Suddenly she knew, knew with a growing conviction that Miss Birdie was right. There was no way that Cletus would have tried to cross the railroad trestle in the darkness or, indeed, at any other time. Not with his lifelong fear of water. She had seen how strong his phobia was the time he refused to help Ben reset the rocks around the shallow goldfish pool. *No, it wasn't an accident,* she decided. *Therefore, he must have been killed somewhere else. I've got to help Birdie find out what happened. We can't let it be like the Little Sylvie story—just something that happened and it doesn't matter now what the truth is. The truth does matter.*

The image of Phillip Hawkins insinuated itself into her thoughts. Kind, competent, an experienced detective, and he had time on his hands just now. She groaned and shook her head. *Why the hell didn't I accept his invitation to dinner? I could tell him about the Starshine Community and get his opinion about all of this. I bet he would have helped. But now I don't even have his phone number. Oh, hell, Elizabeth!*

Feeling frustrated, she tossed the remainder of her drink into the bushes and headed for the kitchen to find some leftovers for her supper. As she was opening the refrigerator door, a business card stuck under a flamingo magnet caught her eye. *Of course!* she thought, *Sallie Kate will know about the Starshine people.*

Her friend Sallie Kate McCrady was a successful real estate broker who specialized in mountain farms and getaways. Sallie Kate could always be relied upon to know who had bought or was about to sell what property. She and her husband lived far back in a remote hollow, in an old house that they had been renovating for years. Having been one herself, Sallie Kate was particularly attuned to the needs and desires of idealistic young people moving to the mountains for the so-called simple life.

Elizabeth put aside the idea of supper for the moment and dialed Sallie Kate's office. Though it was after six, there was a good chance her friend would still be there. The phone was picked up on the first ring and a cheerful Southern voice said, "Country Manors, this is Sallie Kate."

After explaining briefly the reason for her interest, Elizabeth asked, "Sallie Kate, what do you know about a Starshine Community up on Hog Run?"

"Oh, yeah, the trustafarians." Sallie Kate chuckled. "A bunch of rich white kids with trust funds and dreadlocks.

I sold that place to them back in '98. Actually, I've sold that property twice. It was the old Metcalf place and it belonged to sixteen heirs. They couldn't agree on how to divide it among themselves, you know how it is, everyone wants the bottomland, so finally they listed it with me. They figured, at least the money would be easy to divide.

"Well, I first sold it, I think it was back in '95, to a group called the New Church of Transcendental Ontology. They had big plans: got that dome built for a meeting hall and put up some cabins. That was as far as they got before the founder of the church skipped out with their funds *and* his first apostle's wife. Things just kind of fell apart after that, and the ones who were left asked me to sell the place for them. It was all set up for a group rather than a single family and, lord, you wouldn't believe the wackos I showed it to! One group that did meditation retreats was real interested till their geomancer said the alignment of the property was unlucky.

"Then there were some guys that I'm pretty sure were fronts for some kind of right-wing militia group; you know—short, short haircuts and camo pants and big SUVs with whip antennas. They looked at the place but decided they wanted something more remote. As a matter of fact, that group ended up on Devil's Fork, you know, way up at the head of Bear Tree. And, no, I wasn't the one that handled that deal. The agency that brokered that sale is in Asheville. The little time that I spent with the camo boys was enough to convince me we didn't need *them* out here." Sallie Kate's throaty laugh filled the phone. "I don't mind dealing with crazies, honey, but I draw the line at dangerous antisocial types.

"But anyway, you were wanting to know about the Hog Run place. It just sat there for a few years and I was

real relieved when this guy came along looking for a se-
cluded place to start a community. He seemed to have
very deep pockets; didn't as much as blink at the asking
price. He even liked the dome; the other potential buyers had said they'd probably want to tear it down."

"Sallie Kate, about the buyer—was he a guy with a
young face and pure white hair and a white beard?"
Elizabeth asked. "I met him out there today. He seemed
to be the leader and his name was Polaris."

At the other end of the line Sallie Kate snorted. "He
may call himself Polaris now but the name on the deed
was Ernie Hemick. Odd-looking fellow; I wouldn't forget that young face and pure-white hair. And those eyes!
Whew!" Elizabeth could almost see Sallie Kate fanning
herself. "I think I remember he was from New Jersey,
though he didn't have one of those Yankee accents. But,
Elizabeth, what's this I hear about you and Miss Birdie
going to that snake-handling church? Are you getting
weird on me, honey?"

III–May 1901

I was up in my room puttin on the fancy dress of white lawn that Mister Tomlin had brung me from Asheville when Aetha come in and stood by the window there at the foot of Clytie's bed.

Folks is a-comin by the wagon load, she said, a-lookin at me and smilin in that sweet way that makes her look like the picture of Mommy we have up on our mantelpiece. They heard as how Mister Tomlin had laid out money to butcher a hog and they're lookin to have a good time at yore weddin.

I turned my back to Aetha and she done up the little buttons that run down the back of that dress. Then she grabbed the new silver-backed brush Mister Tomlin had give me and set in to brushin my hair. Do you want me to fix your hair up like mine? she asked. You still look like a young un.

I was namin to put hit up, I told her, but Mister Tomlin give me a pretty white ribbon and said I should just tie back the sides and let the rest hang down. That's the way he wants hit.

Aetha went on brushin and atter a time she said, Hit's been most a year since you first got yore monthlies, ain't hit? I nodded yes and leaned to look out the window. Down in the yard I could see Clytie a-prissin around and makin eyes at all the men. There was a gang of young uns runnin back and forth on the foot log and I could see Romarie headin toward them, all red in the face and commencin to holler.

The big table we'd set out early in the day was fillin up fast with all kinds of good things for the infare and I seen Miz Johnson from over the mountain addin a pie to the stack. There must have been five or six pies there already and she put hers on the top, real careful. I seen three different cakes laid out as well, and I could smell the roasting hog meat and the sweet hickory smoke in the air.

Little Sylvie, said Aetha, I don't reckon no one's talked to you about what happens when you get married.

I shook my head no, for no one had. I figgered I knowed what she was talking about, atter all, I had growed up seein the bull go to the cows and the rooster atop the hens. Hit worried me some—oncet I seen two hounds get stuck together for the longest time but I guessed hit wouldn't matter so much if you was in bed when hit happened. You could always just go to sleep till you come loose, I thought.

Well, Aetha said, and then she stopped, kindly lookin for words. She kept on a-brushin the same place over and over and at last she said, Why, Little Sylvie, all you got to do is to keep in mind that hit's God's plan and as natural as can be. She smoothed my hair real soft-like and said, I don't doubt but you'll be just fine, for Mister Tomlin ain't no green boy to hurry things. He's a real gentleman and

I'm sure he'll be slow and easy with you. Just you remember that though at first hit might hurt a little and you'll likely bleed some, that's the way of it and atter a while you'll like hit just fine.

I turned and looked down at her big belly a-poochin out her skirt. I reckon, I said, and I grinned at her like one thing. She colored up bright as a rooster's comb then busted out laughin. Her and Fate Worley has been married seven years and they have themselves five young uns and one on the way. She laughed and hugged me tight and said, O Little Sylvie, yore a lucky girl! You'll have a fine man and a fine house.

He already bought me a sewin machine, I said. Hit's up in the little cabin. That little cabin where Mommy's brother had used to live was where we would go atter the marrying. Mister Tomlin had hired them Maitlands to haul up household plunder with their big sled. But when I had laid out to go up and see that the cabin was swept and cleaned some, Mister Tomlin had told me that he didn't want me goin up there till he had got hit fixed nice.

I wish that I had our house all built, he said, but I don't want to wait that long for you to be my bride, Little Sylvie. Howsomever I had kept a sharp watch and I seen the sewin machine on the sled and a fancy bedstead and all manner of big boxes and bundles.

Just then Romarie hollered up the stairs to say that preacher was come and was I goin to miss my own marryin to stay upstairs admirin of myself in the lookin glass. Me and Aetha come down the stairs and went out to the porch where they was all a-waitin. Brother Gosnell had his head to one side like he does and was just a-grinnin at Mister

Tomlin. O Mr. Tomlin! How fine-lookin he was! He had on a black frock coat and gray whipcord ridin britches with his tall boots that was as glossy as a new horse chestnut. He looked at me and smiled and I could see the Gentry girls and Clytie lookin pure green with envy. Mister Tomlin was the best-lookin man there and that's the truth.

Him and me stood there on the porch in front of the preacher. Folks was standin about down in the yard and I heared Granny Plemmons say Law, she's such a little thing; why she don't hardly reach to his breast. But then everone hushed up when Brother Gosnell begun to pray. He called on the Lord to bless me and Mister Tomlin and reminded the Lord how Mister Tomlin was seein to buildin Him a big new church house. Then he prayed that I would be an obedient wife and that I would abide by God's Word where hit says that the wife is subject to the husband.

When he was done with his prayin, Brother Gosnell joined our hands and spoke the marryin words. I promised to honor and obey like he said. Mister Tomlin's hand was a-tremblin as hit took holt of mine, but he said his words in a strong deep voice. And then he put the red stone ring on my finger. I felt like some queen in one of them old love songs, a-standin there in my fine new dress with ever eye upon me.

The preacher he left early on, so old man Owens pulled out his fiddle and struck up a reel. Folks formed up lines there on the clean swept dirt of the yard and Mister Tomlin led me out to the head of the line. We danced the Virginia Reel and Goin to Boston and when Mister Tomlin swung me round, he picked me clean off the ground and whirled me dizzy. Everone made over me and I felt that hit was a fine thing to be married.

Later, when the sun had dropped behind Pinnacle, the sky filled up with the prettiest colors—all pinks and oranges puttin me in mind of a big garden of roses and daylilies. Someday I'll have me a flower patch like that I said to Aetha. I was a-settin on the porch a-pickin at a plate of food she had brung me. Mister Tomlin was talkin to some men and had just sent one of the Gentry boys to bring him his horse from the barn. He said that hit was time for us to take our leave and head up the mountain to the little cabin. The food had mostly been all et and the women folk was gatherin up their young uns and tellin their men that hit was time to get home for the milkin. Some of the young fellers must have had some liquor hid somers for they kept slippin off and comin back actin the fool.

When Billie Gentry come back leadin the horse, Mister Tomlin sprung into the saddle then reined Nebuchadnezzar around to come up to the steps where I was waitin. Aetha hugged me real hard and whispered, Now, Little Sylvie, remember what I told you. I could see Clytie down by the foot log talkin to a feller and Daddy was showin some of his friends the English-made shotgun Mister Tomlin had give him that morning. Romarie weren't nowhere in sight; knowin her, she was makin a start on the dishes and feelin sorry for herself all the while.

Miz Tomlin, he says, and makes a bow from where he sets on his horse. I come to the top step and he reaches out his hand. Just set yore little foot atop of mine he says and I do and lo and behold, before I know it I'm settin afore him crostwise over Nebuchadnezzar's shiny withers. I worry that my pretty dress will be ruint, but I can see that Neb has been groomed till he's as clean as ary housecat. Mister Tomlin's arms are around me and he smells a little of whisky but I lean back against him and look at Aetha. She stands there on the porch a-wavin atter us as I ride up the road on a horse named for a king and a-leanin against my husband.

My husband. He lifted me down from Nebuchadnezzar and carried me up the steps and into the cabin as if I was but a babe. He set me down gentle on the bedstead and told me to sit quiet while he lit the lamps. They was all shiny new and the three of them filled the cabin with a fine golden light. I looked around, just a-marvelin at how nice it looked. When Uncle Lige had lived there, he had let hit get as dirty as a barn but now the floorboards had been swept and washed and there was a braided rug in the center of the room. The rocks of the fireplace had been new whitewashed and all the cobwebs and waspers nestes had been cleaned away. The new bedstead had one of the quilts I had pieced on it—the fancy red, green, and white pommygranate pattern that had taken me so long. Sewin all them little red circles on had near about kilt me, but seein it layin there, I was proud that I had made something so grand.

Under the window by the door was my new Singer sewin machine and I made to get off the bed and go see it close, but Mister Tomlin said, Now, Little Sylvie, there'll be time for that in the morning. I'm goin to go see to Nebuchadnezzar. You make yourself ready for bed.

He pointed to the new washstand and hangin on a hook by it was the fancy white nightshift Aetha had made me.

He picked up my hand and laid a kiss on the back of it. You are my own Little Sylvie now, he said, and he went out the door.

I could hear him leadin Neb around to the lean-to at the back of the cabin and I started to go and look at my new sewin machine. Then I thought about what Mister Tomlin had said and knowed that I wanted to get my clothes off and my nightshift on while he wasn't there to see. Hit weren't easy reachin all them little buttons down the back of my dress and me hurryin so but finally I had them loose. I pulled off my dress quick-like and got my nightshift over my head before I commenced to pullin off my camisole and petticoat. A thought come to me and I looked under the bed but there weren't no chamber there.

There never had been a little house up at this cabin, Uncle Lige bein content to squat in the woods. And though I've squatted in the woods myself many a time, I didn't much want to with Mister Tomlin out there. Then I remembered how the schoolteacher had things fixed at her place. So I looked in the bottom of the washstand and sure enough, they was a chamber—white china with pink flowers painted on it and a tight lid to it too. I made use of hit right quick and stuck it back behind the little door. Tomorrow morning, thinks I, I can dash it out in the branch.

There was a feather tick and two big feather pillows on the bed. I knowed that the linen sheets had been my Mommy's for Aetha had told me that she had give them to Mister Tomlin for our bed. I slipped between the sheets and lay there quiet, waitin for what might come. The ruby finger-ring glowed like fire when I held it afore my face with the light of the nearest lamp behind it.

Hit was a long time before Mister Tomlin come back in the cabin. I thought about the bull and the cows and how the ol bull would turn up his lip a-sniffin at their behinds afore he'd go to ridin them. I couldn't feature Mister Tomlin doin such as that but nor could I imagine just what would be the way of things. I looked at my sewin machine and thought that tomorrow I would set in to makin another quilt.

At last I heared Mister Tomlin comin to the door. I scootched down in the bed with the covers up to my chin. He come in quiet-like and said, Now, Little Sylvie, you needn't be afraid for I'll not harm you. I didn't say nothing, just lay there a-lookin at him. He blew out two of the lamps, but left burnin the one on the chest by the bed. Then he pulled off his coat and waistcoat and hung them on a hook. They was a bootjack by the hearth and he used that to get shed of his tall boots. He shucked off his britches right quick and I could hear the gold coins in the pockets just a-jinglin as he hung them britches on another hook. Then he set down in the straight back chair and pulled off his stockings. His feet was long and pale and hairy in the lamplight and his legs was thinner than what I had thought they would be.

Mister Tomlin blew out the last lamp and got into bed in just his shirt. The moon was near to full and a pale misty light lay over the bed. I could see the outline of his head there on the pillow beside me and hear his breathin comin fast like as if he'd been a-runnin. He didn't say nothing but reached his hand over and put hit up under my nightshift. He pulled me toward him and pushed his big whiskery face against mine. He commenced to kissin my lips and I begun to kiss back some.

Me and Clytie had practiced kissin on the backs of our own hands so we would know what to do when we got married but all them whiskers made it different. Then all at once he's tryin to put his tongue in my mouth. I had thought you was supposed to keep yore lips tight closed so as not to get spit on one another. But I remembered what Aetha had said and went on and opened my mouth.

All the while he's a-lickin around in my mouth, that hand under my nightshift is a-travelin around like one thing. My bosoms has just barely begun to show a little and I wondered was he lookin for them. Then he finds them and starts in to rubbin at my nipples till they're all hard and tender, like when the cold wind blows right through my dress. Next thing I know that hand starts down between my legs and I clench them together tight. He starts a-rubbin right there where the curly dark hairs is beginnin to grow, and just then there's a terrible racket right outside the cabin—the sound of whoopin and cowbells ringin and pie pans a-bangin together.

I reckon hit's a serenade, Mister Tomlin, I say as he jerks his hand away and sets up in bed. Them fellers always likes to cut a shine whenever they's a marryin. I could hear Billy Gentry hollerin, O Little Sylvie, give me a kiss and then someone else howled like an ol hound.

They was quite a few of them from the sound, mostly around the door. But I could hear laughin and someone cussin under his breath and I knowed that some of em must be climbin up on that big rock under the front window. That rock, hit's a great big thing most as wide as the cabin

but flat topped to where you can walk on it. On its down-
hill side it's only about a yard high but where it almost
touches the cabin a tall man could stand on it and look right
in the window. Used to my Daddy would throw out salt
for the cows on that rock and they would line up around
the edges like kittens around a pan of milk. I thought hit
would make a good place to dry apples come fall.

The sounds got closer and I pulled the covers up around
me. Mister Tomlin, I said, they'll not leave less you go out
and speak to them—maybe give them some money or a
drink of whisky. I hoped he could get rid of them right soon
for I was eager to know what was comin next between us
there in the bed. My nipples was still as hard as acorns and
I was beginnin to feel a kindly of a swimmie feelin down
there where he'd been a-rubbin.

Mister Tomlin didn't say nothing, just hauled out of bed
and pulled on his pants. He went to the door and opened
it and the noise stopped. I could see the lights from some
torches movin around and hear cowbells clankin. Boys, said
Mister Tomlin, I understand that it's the custom for me
to thank you for this ceremony of yours. I don't have any
liquor to offer you a drink but here's a double eagle for you.
I reckon that'll buy enough spirits for you all to drink my
health and my wife's several times over.

I heared a chink as his hand went into his pockets and
from the bed I could see the gold coin make a glitterin trail
in the torchlight as Mister Tomlin tossed it high to someone
standin there. They all set up a-whoopin again and ringin
them cowbells, but they begun to move away. We could
hear them hoorahin all down the mountain and at last

Mister Tomlin closed and bolted the door and come back to bed.

He pulled off his pants again and got in beside me. I was ready for some more kissin and I turned my face toward him. He reached for my hand and brought it down between his legs. I kindly knew what to expect and I took hold of hit like he seemed to want me to. He groaned out loud and said, O Little Sylvie, and he was breathin fast again.

I just lay there not knowing what should I do. But he has his notions and first it's one thing and then another and him a-gruntin like an old boar hog right along. Some of it seems plumb nasty to me but I think of what Aetha told me and how the preacher said the wife is subject to the husband and I do it.

Atter a time he kindly shudders and pulls me back up on the pillow beside him. Little Sylvie, he says, you'll be a fine wife, and he sets up and reaches over to a blue bottle a-settin on the windowsill. He pulls out the cork and takes him a big old swaller. I take my medicine every night, says he. It helps me to sleep. When he lay back down there was a heavy sweet smell on his breath. Good night, Little Sylvie, he says, and rolls over and begins to snore.

I lay there a-thinkin about what has just happened. Hadn't nothing hurt like Aetha had said hit would and I don't believe I'm bleedin nowhere, but except for some of the kissin and rubbin there at the first I weren't so sure what there was to like about hit. I get up and dip me some water from the bucket. Then I crawl back in the bed and lay there, a-listenin to Mister Tomlin snore and a-thinkin about my new sewin machine.

CHAPTER 8
THE EVIDENCE OF THE SANG
(THURSDAY)

PANAX QUINQUEFOLIUS, THE AMERICAN GINSENG, "... appears plentifully on the north exposure of the hill, growing out of the rich, mellow, humid earth, among the stones or fragments of rocks." William Bartram's words, written as he traveled through southeastern America in the late 1700s, were alluring, but as Elizabeth read on, turning the pages of *Foxfire 3* in search of more pertinent information, it became all too clear that ginseng was no longer common. While the once-common chestnut trees had been destroyed by disease, ginseng had been severely endangered by overhunting. The article went on to elucidate the various ways of hunting and growing ginseng, with an emphasis on the difficulty of finding it in the wild. Elizabeth sat at her dining table, reading as she ate her breakfast of grapefruit juice, coffee, and a thick slice of homemade bread topped with a scrape of olive oil and herbed goat cheese. Tracing the ginseng was the next step in her hunt for Cletus's shotgun.

The past two days had been a whirl of garden work. The tomato plants had been set out in their rows and the last of the peas had been picked. More broccoli had been added to the freezer, and the worst of the weeds in the flower borders had been ousted. The eternal battle to bring order out of chaos was in a momentary truce. Now she could devote a day or so to the task Miss Birdie had set her.

Elizabeth had decided that, rather than travel haphazardly from hollow to hollow asking for information about Cletus, she would "use the little grey cells" as Agatha Christie's Poirot had advised. Cletus's knapsack had contained ginseng; therefore, she reasoned, he must have gone somewhere ginseng could still be found.

She smiled at her own cleverness and read on. The *Foxfire* article was not particularly encouraging, pointing out that though "sang," as it was called in the mountains, usually grew on a north slope, large patches could sometimes be found on south slopes, planted in the wild by ginseng hunters. *Great,* she thought, *that really narrows it down.*

The buzz of the oven timer interrupted her reading. She pushed the book aside and gathered up her breakfast dishes. It was not yet eight o'clock and the morning air was still cool and misty. In the distance she could hear the plaintive calls of mourning doves and the clatter of a tractor bush-hogging a distant field. *Time to get going,* she thought. *Let's see what Birdie knows about ginseng.*

Twenty minutes later she was knocking on her neighbor's door. A paper bag containing a still-warm loaf of banana bread was in the basket she carried, as was her map of the Bear Tree Creek area.

Birdie did not come to the door in response to Elizabeth's knock, but called out from her recliner chair, "That you, Lizzie Beth? Come on in." The little woman looked pale and drawn, but she smiled up at Elizabeth. "I'm still down in the back, honey. Reckon they ought to take and shoot me. I kin just creep from the bed to my chair; that's 'bout all I'm good for."

Birdie's cousin hurried in from the kitchen, a dish towel in her hands. Dorothy was a stout, capable woman somewhere in her seventies. She had worked for years as a nurse assistant at a senior care center and, now that she had retired, delighted in looking after all of her elderly kin. "Why, look who's here! And look what she brung you!" Dorothy bubbled, taking a long sniff at the banana bread Elizabeth handed her.

"Birdie's been namin' to call you. We talked to the high sheriff last night and he says it could be another week before they do that autopsy."

"And he still don't think it were anything but an accident," Birdie fumed. "*And* they still ain't found that shotgun. Law, honey, I hate it that I can't travel about and ask where my boy was those weeks before . . . but I ain't able and that's a fact."

"Don't worry, Miss Birdie," Elizabeth assured her, "I'm going to go out looking today. I think it would be good for me to start by finding out where Cletus might have gotten the sang that was in the knapsack."

"I been studyin' on that, Lizzie Beth," Miss Birdie replied, hitching herself painfully up in her chair. "You know, spring ain't the time for diggin' the roots. Most folks can't even find the plants in the spring; them green leaves don't look any different from a lot of other weeds. It's in the fall when them leaves turns that yellowy gold and that big bunch of red berries jest hollers at you that folks digs the roots to sell."

She furrowed her brow and went on. "All's I can think is that Cletus must of been goin' to carry them

roots to a patch som'ers else. You mind they had a right
smart of dirt in with 'em. Likely he had a patch som'ers
back in one of them hollers. He allus did bring in a mess
of roots in the fall. Law, that boy was so proud to be
earnin' money. Last year he made 'most a thousand dollars and he told me that this year he'd have even more."

Birdie suddenly looked troubled. "You know, Cletus
kept that place a secret even from me 'cause he knows . . .
he knew . . . I'm bad to talk . . . and they's some would
rob ary sang patch they could. They's a lot of mean folks
wouldn't think twicet . . ." Her voice trailed off.

"Why don't she go over and talk to Raym Tyler?"
suggested Dorothy. "You know, up in Little Man Holler?
He raises tame sang and he buys the wild. Likely he
might know something."

"Raym Tyler!" Birdie spat. "Don't you name Raym
Tyler to me. Them Tylers is a rough bunch. Why, when
my man Luther was still livin' at his daddy's place, him
and Raym Tyler like to kilt one another, disputin' over
that line fence. No, she won't do no good talkin' to no
Tylers."

Though Birdie refused to discuss Raym Tyler further,
Dorothy was persistent. She was sure that Little Man
Holler would be the logical place for Elizabeth to start
her investigation into the source of the ginseng. "Raym
ain't so bad as Birdie makes out," she whispered as she
followed the departing Elizabeth to the front porch. As
she did so, Dorothy glanced furtively back at her cousin,
but Birdie's attention was fixed on the television set
where Oprah was participating in a demonstration of the
Heimlich maneuver.

"I know he's bought sang from Cletus and give him
a good price, too." Dorothy's voice was conspiratorial.
"Why, he even hired Cletus a time or two to help him

with those trout ponds he's got up there. Course Cletus knew not to say nothing to Birdie about it account of how she always took on so against Raym."

On her way up Bear Tree Creek once again, Elizabeth's attention was caught by a luridly painted old white Ford stopped at the foot of the road leading up to Walter and Ollie Johnson's place. The words "Prepare to meet thy God," as well as various Bible texts, were painted in foot-high letters along the sides of the aged vehicle. The trunk was open and a lean man in shiny dark trousers and a white shirt was lifting two bulging plastic grocery bags from its interior. As he hoisted them up, the flimsy material of one gave way and its contents spilled out, rolling into the road in front of Elizabeth's approaching car.

She braked immediately to avoid running over the cans of food that were scattered in front of her. The man gave her a brief nod and began picking up his groceries and setting them out of the road. *That must be the guy who's staying up in the old cabin,* thought Elizabeth. *The evangelist.* She cut the motor of her car and called out the window, "Excuse me, could you help me?"

The lean man glanced at her curiously, then, carefully setting the last can to the side of the road, walked over. Poverty-thin but wiry, he gave the impression of a man possessed by some inner tension that he had constantly to keep in check. He moved with the deliberate care of a martial artist, as if alert for a sudden defense. Elizabeth guessed that he was probably in his forties, though his pale blue eyes stared from a face as lined and careworn as that of a much older man, and his once-blond thatch of hair was stained with silver.

"Are you the one staying in the Johnsons' old cabin?"

she asked, wishing she could remember what they had said his name was. "They told me, that is, I was wondering if you had seen . . ."

He confirmed that he was indeed the one staying in the Johnson cabin and listened to her questions about Cletus without a change of expression. Finally he said brusquely, "Afraid I can't help you. At least he's in the Lord's hands now," and turned away to rummage in the back of his car, presumably for another bag to hold his groceries.

Abruptly dismissed, Elizabeth continued on her way. As she passed the little heap of cans and boxes the evangelist had piled by his car, she was puzzled to see, amid the cans of beef stew and baked beans, a box of sanitary napkins. *That's odd. Walter and Ollie didn't mention that he was married. What would* . . . Her thoughts were interrupted as a heavily loaded log truck came groaning around a curve toward her. It was straddling the centerline of the road, almost forcing her into the ditch. She prayed that the loose gravel and dirt of the shoulder would hold, and waited, without breathing, till the rumbling monster had passed. *Slagle,* she suddenly remembered, watching the hulking truck in her rearview mirror disappear around another curve. *That was the name. John the Baptizer Slagle.*

The turnoff to Little Man Holler was several miles past the two hollows she had visited earlier in the week; indeed, it was almost to the head of Bear Tree Creek. Straggling red letters on a weathered board shaped like a narrow fish said TROUT—1/4 MILE. The nose of the fish pointed up a rocky road that twisted and climbed through a dense rhododendron thicket. Elizabeth shifted into four-wheel drive and followed the road through the dark gnarled roots and contorted branches, finally emerging into a clearing where a stone chimney stood. Thick clumps of yellow flag and a huge lilac bush flourished among the weeds. At the edge of the clearing, crumpled green and red leaves of rhubarb and the green froth of asparagus fern were all that remained of some farmwife's garden.

Beyond the clearing, the road divided and a second fish-shaped sign pointed down the left fork. More rhododendrons shaded the road, suddenly giving way to rolling open land at the base of steep wooded slopes. The Tyler place had evidently once been a prosperous mountain farm, judging by the four large tobacco barns scattered over the cleared land, now mostly given over to pasture. One field, however, had many long beds of low-growing green plants covered with black shade cloth. *That must be the ginseng,* decided Elizabeth, noting that the field faced north.

The two-story frame house that sat at the end of the road was in dire need of paint, but otherwise was tidy. A small parking area lay next to a little pond and a series of flumes, doubtless the home of the trout-raising enterprise. Another red-lettered sign listed prices for trout and proclaimed TYLER'S TROUT AND GINSENG. OPEN ALL DAY, EVERY DAY BUT SUNDAY.

Elizabeth parked her car and got out. "Hello," she called toward the house. Mountain manners held that a stranger should make his presence known before approaching a house, so she waited a few minutes before calling again, this time a good bit louder. "Hello, Mr. Ty—"

From behind the house came an ominous barking and the rattle of a chain. Suddenly, a heavyset elderly man wearing a pair of grimy overalls burst out of the door. In one hand he gripped a stout cane, in the other, a double-barreled shotgun.

Elizabeth froze, her eyes riveted to the gun. The old man raised it to his shoulder.

"Goddammit, Dewey—" he bellowed, then he stopped short. He frowned at Elizabeth. "By God, I thought you was Dewey; he's got him a car just like that." Leaning the shotgun against the door frame, he limped down the worn wooden steps, making his way slowly to where Elizabeth stood. He pushed his face toward her and she could see the individual bristles of the gray stubble on his cheeks and smell the sour tang of his breath. Peering closely at her, his eyes narrowed behind his glasses as he demanded, "Be you kin to Dewey?"

For a moment Elizabeth was speechless; when she at last found her voice, it emerged as a ragged squeak. "No! I don't even know who Dewey is!" she stammered. Then, taking a breath and forcing her voice down to its usual pitch, she asked about Cletus and his shotgun. All the while she couldn't keep her eyes from going to the shotgun leaning against the door frame.

Tyler listened attentively to her questions. He shook his head thoughtfully when she finished. "Now that was the beatinest thing, to think of Cletus fallin' offen that trestle. Weren't like him atall to be up there. But, to answer yore question, I ain't seed Cletus since . . ." The gray-stubbled jaws worked pensively around the chunk of black chewing tobacco he had inserted at the beginning of Elizabeth's inquiries. "Lemme see . . . must of been back in March he come through here. I was lookin' for him long about now, though. He was gonna dig me some wild sang to put in my beds."

The bleary eyes behind the cheap black-rimmed glasses crinkled and Raym Tyler began to wheeze with laughter. "We got us a plan to fool them buyers and make our tame sang to look like the wild."

"There were sang plants in Cletus's knapsack. Maybe he had dug them for you," Elizabeth ventured. "Where might he have gone to dig them, do you think?"

The old man lowered a suspicious gaze on her and tightened his lips. She went on shamelessly, "Miss Birdie's cousin Dorothy told me you knew more about sang than anyone around."

"Could be. But them as knows, don't tell." Nonetheless his face softened slightly. "I will say that they's sang all around here. That's how come this to be called Little Man Holler; you know the bestest roots is forked and shaped like a little man." He scratched his ribs thoughtfully. "When I was able, I'd roam all these hollers and dig sang. But I allus planted the seed back, though sometimes I'd take and plant it in different places, just to fool them other sang hunters. I had me a big old patch way up on Devil's Fork that ort to be coming in good right now, and another . . . Well, just say, if nobody ain't found 'em and dug 'em, I had me beds in most of the hollers around here."

The old man's eyes roamed over the distant wooded slopes and he smiled grimly. "Course, now I can't get around so good; I can't make it up in the woods. That's why I went to growin' it down here. But Cletus, he could climb like a deer. And he could spot them ole sang plants like one thing. Anybody kin find 'em of a fall, but that Cletus he could find the bittiest little one-prong plant almost before its leaves would open. So we had us a deal; I'd tell him where my beds was, out in them other hollers, and he'd bring me roots and seed and we'd split 'em." Raym chuckled at some memory. "He was too simple to know how to cheat me and I allus did right by him."

A shrill whistle sounded from the far side of the field with the shaded beds. Raym Tyler turned, then raised his hand in reply. A tall man with a burlap sack in one leather-gloved hand and a long stick in the other was making his way toward them. As he drew closer Elizabeth felt an unexpected shock of recognition: It was the preacher from the snake-handling church.

"You do any good, Harice?" Raym Tyler asked, and without waiting for an answer, said to Elizabeth, "That there's my son; he's been a-huntin' serpents for his church."

Harice stared at Elizabeth and then one side of his mouth sketched a smile. "I know you this time," he told her quietly. He hefted the burlap sack toward his father and answered, "I done all right. Got me three big cop-perheads up there in that old rock pile where they den up." The rough brown sides of the bag undulated alarm-ingly.

Raym shook his head and stepped back. "You get ever one you can, boy. I'll be happy when they're all gone." He took another step back. "You didn't go over the ridge, now, did you?"

"Well, I was thinkin' on it. Over yon's the best place I know to find them old rattlers. But I figured to stop long of finding these three here." Again Harice gave the bag a little jerk; again his father took a backward step.

"Now, Harice, you listen to me. You best not go over the ridge no more. You know them new people up there has got posted signs ever'where you look. They're creepin' around them woods with machine guns and I don't know what all and I heared they ain't too particular about what they shoot at." A thought seemed to dawn on Raym Tyler and he looked at Elizabeth earnestly. "Ma'am, was you fixin' to go askin' questions about Cletus of them folks on Devil's Fork?"

"Well, I——" she began.

"Ma'am, you best stay away from them people. Or get you a man to go with you. Them folks are plumb dangerous. Won't even the law fool with 'em. I'm sorry I can't tell you no more about Cletus." The old man turned away and spat. Then he turned back toward Elizabeth and declared, "That Cletus was a good boy."

Harice Tyler stood unmoving, fixing Elizabeth with a sidelong gaze. She felt the same indistinct menace laced with attraction that had so unnerved her at the Holiness church five days earlier. "So you're follering Aunt Belvy's prophecy and seekin' in the dens and rocks of the mountains." It was not a question. Harice smiled that one-sided smile again but his eyes remained narrowed as he added quietly, "You want to be careful now; you may find yore answer or you may find a nest of serpents."

Realizing that she wasn't going to get any more useful information, Elizabeth thanked Raym Tyler for his help and headed for her jeep. Raym's son Harice watched her go with his unreadable expression.

"By the way, Mr. Tyler," called Elizabeth as she opened her car door, "who's Dewey?"

Raym Tyler leaned on his cane and began another bout of gasping laughter. "Harice, when this here lady come, I seen her car and thought it was that ole Dewey Shotwell. I come out of the house, namin' to set the dog on him." He elbowed his son and wheezed delightedly.

"But who is Dewey Shotwell and why were you going to——?"

"Ma'am, that ole Dewey's the worst sang hunter they is. That man'd dig yore sang even iffen hit was growin' in the floorboards of yore house. Dewey don't care where he hunts nor whose patch hit is; iffen he could he'd dig ever last root." The older man thumped his cane savagely on the ground. "I done warned him not to ever come up this way."

When she reached the hard road again, rather than turning to go back to Ridley Branch and the beckoning comforts of home, Elizabeth resolutely pulled out onto the pavement and headed farther up Bear Tree Creek. The poplars and maples, hickories and oaks of the mixed hardwood forest that clothed the lower slopes gave way to more and more dark evergreens: pines, firs, lacy hemlocks, and tall, mournful balsams with gray lichen on their trunks and branches. She was reminded of the primeval forest of fairy tales—the home of the witch in "Hansel and Gretel" or the lair of Little Red Riding Hood's wolf. Shivering in spite of the warmth of the day, she began to look for a place to turn around.

Maybe I'll ask Ben to come back with me tomorrow, she decided. But now the pavement was ending and there was a heavy metal gate, secured with a chain and padlock. A green county sign read DEVIL'S FORK—PRIVATE ROAD. The six-strand barbwire fence strung on either side of the gate boasted a no-trespassing notice on every post. A wooden shed to one side sheltered a call box and another written notice.

Elizabeth stopped her car in front of the gate and got out, intending to read the notice before she turned around. A rustling in the thick growth beyond the fence made her freeze: She looked up to find a lean man with a military buzz cut, mirrored sunglasses, and crisp camouflage fatigues watching her from the other side of the gate. "This is private property," he said suspiciously. "You looking for someone?"

With a growing sense of déjà vu, Elizabeth explained her business, describing Cletus once again and inquiring if he'd been seen there recently. The man rested his hand carelessly on the pistol in the holster hanging from his web belt. His mouth twisted as he replied, "That half-wit feller that roams around? Yeah, we seen him a couple or so months ago and sent him on his way. We got no use for defectives."

There was a sudden movement in the tree behind him. The man whirled, drawing his pistol and stiffening. There was a deafening boom and a red squirrel exploded in a bloody mist.

"That's how we handle varmints around here," the man told Elizabeth flatly, returning the pistol to its holster.

CHAPTER 9
ANGRY WHITE GUYS WITH GUNS
(THURSDAY AFTERNOON AND FRIDAY)

THE BOOM OF THE PISTOL STILL ECHOED AND throbbed in her ears as Elizabeth drove back down Bear Tree Creek toward the bridge. She had been stunned into silence by the wanton cruelty of the man at the Devil's Fork gate. *You should have said something,* she reproved herself. Yet at the same time, she kept hearing Raym Tyler's warning: *"Them folks are plumb dangerous."* Her heart was racing and she was gripping the steering wheel far too tightly. "Damn it all," she said out loud, "who *are* those people?"

She spent the afternoon in her garden, first furiously ripping out the old pea vines and then hoeing the rows of broccoli and cabbage with unnecessary speed. The image of the red squirrel on the branch disappearing into a gory haze kept replaying in her brain and she swiped her eyes and hoed harder. Dirt flew as she slashed at tiny weeds, leaning down to pick up small rocks and toss them into the road. A fresh crop of rocks seemed to surface every year: *Like evil,* she thought, *you can't ever get rid of it entirely.* The roar of the tractor coming up the road was a welcome distraction and she dropped her hoe and waved at Ben to stop.

"What's up, Aunt E? You want me to till where the peas were?" He had cut the tractor off and was looking curiously at the row of cabbages she had just hoed. "I thought you just did those last week. You entering some garden competition?"

Elizabeth looked back down the pristine row. "Just working off a little anger, I guess. I ran into a really awful person today when I was out asking about Cletus. If you'd like to have supper with me, I'll tell you about it then. I thought I'd make a stromboli tonight. And yes, I'd appreciate it if you'd do that tilling." She grinned up at Ben.

The stromboli—homemade pizza dough spread with last year's basil pesto and soft-dried tomatoes from the freezer, topped with thin slices of prosciutto and provolone, as well as grated Asiago—was rolled up and baked brown. The molten cheeses escaped from its fragrant interior as Elizabeth served out the portions. Ben sighed happily as he sipped a glass of red wine. "Thanks, Aunt E, this smells great. By the way, what were you so mad about earlier?"

"Let's just enjoy our meal. I'll tell you about it later." She filled the blue-rimmed bowls with tossed salad. "If I get started now, I'll just rant. Maybe I can be more rational once I've eaten."

They had finished their meal and were sipping coffee when Elizabeth asked, "Ben, do you know anything about the people living up at the end of Bear Tree

Creek—way up high on Devil's Fork? Raym Tyler, the guy I told you I visited today, was warning me about them."

"Do you mean those militia assholes? They are serious bad news." Ben shook his head and went on. "I ran into some of them when I was in Ransom with Julio on Monday. We'd picked up some fertilizer and parts for the tractor—did I tell you that the hydraulics went funky again?—and we stopped in at Sadie's Place for lunch. We got a booth and were chowing down on the meat-and-three special when the guys in the booth behind me started talking really ugly. I'd noticed them when they came in—three of them, all in camouflage fatigues and military boots. And those special drill instructor haircuts, you know—shaved all around and about a quarter of an inch of hair on top.

"I'd heard talk, it must have been almost a year ago, about some kind of militia group moving in up on Devil's Fork, and I hadn't paid a lot of attention but that's what I immediately thought of when I saw these three. Anyway, these jerks were saying stuff about the "mud races" being okay for farmwork but that they ought not to be allowed in restaurants where white men came to eat. I was getting pretty hot, but either Julio didn't hear them, or he just let it roll off. And then their food came and they quit talking."

Ben got up, went to the kitchen, and returned with the coffeepot. "So anyway, we finish and leave and don't say anything. We go out to the parking lot and there's this goddamn humvee, stupid gas-guzzling monster, and I know it has to belong to those creeps. It's near our truck, and as I go by it I notice this decal on the bumper." He indicated a five-inch length. "An American flag in the shape of the United States with a big cross growing out of the middle of it. And it says 'Adam's Sons in the Wilderness—God's People—God's Land.' "

Elizabeth waved away the proffered coffeepot. "So what does that mean?"

Ben poured himself another cup and sat back down. "When I was in my last year of college I did a paper on the ties between the militia movement and the religious right. That name 'Adam's Sons' rang a bell. So I rummaged around the Internet to see what I could find out. I came across the FBI's Megiddo report on domestic terrorism and it said that these militias think they've been chosen by God to fight during the coming Armageddon. They believe they'll be the last line of defense for the white race and Christian America."

Ben put both elbows on the table and leaned on them. "These creeps believe that the white race—whatever that is—descended from Adam and Eve, via Abel. They say that the Jews are descended from Cain, who, by the way, they claim was not the son of Adam, but of Satan, in the form of the serpent, and that old sinful Eve. And . . ." he raised a finger as Elizabeth tried to interrupt, "they believe that all the nonwhite races—they call them 'mud people'—don't have souls but were created by God along with the animals strictly to serve Adam's line."

"Sweet Jesus!" sputtered Elizabeth. "Where in God's name do they come up with this—this—idiotic—criminal—garbage?

"As you say, in God's name. Where else but the Bible? Their Web page cites chapter and verse for every one of these claims."

"But . . . but what are they doing here in Marshall County . . . on Bear Tree Creek?"

"Well, they really believe that the end of the world is near. It says in the Bible that before Jesus can come again there will be a huge battle between the forces of good and evil. Naturally," he smiled sourly, "they believe that the white race—the sons of Adam—are the good guys and they'll be fighting against the Jews and the nonwhite races."

"But, wait a minute," insisted Elizabeth. "Jesus was a Jew!"

"Not according to them, and they've got a whole pile of Bible verses they say prove it. Anyway, they're getting ready for this war they see coming, stockpiling guns and food and doing paramilitary training. Evidently, there're little groups of them all over the country."

"I can't believe this," Elizabeth said slowly. "Raym Tyler said they even have machine guns up there. Isn't that against the law?"

"For sure." Ben nodded vigorously. "But these Sons of Adam folks are protected as a religion. That makes the law, including the FBI, a little cautious in how they go about investigating them. Plus there's always plenty of politicians who don't want to do anything to piss off the Religious Right. And while these guys are admittedly on the far, far right, quite a few fundamentalist Christians agree with at least part of their agenda."

Ben stood up and stretched. "Don't get me started on those lunatics. Just looking at their Web site made me want to puke."

Elizabeth's first thought on awaking the next morning was of this hate group that had set up shop so close to her own beloved farm. *It's like knowing there's a nest of poisonous snakes out there,* she mused, then corrected herself. *No, it's not. I've always known the snakes were there and they're not evil—they're doing what they're supposed to do and it's up to me to stay out of their way. These guys are something else, something sinister.*

Again she saw the red squirrel exploding into nothingness before her eyes. Red, not gray. She had never seen a red squirrel in her woods or anywhere in the area. They were common on the other side of the county where the elevation was much higher. *But there were tufts of red fur on those squirrels in Cletus's knapsack,* she remembered. *And that horrible guy said Cletus had been there a couple of months ago. Could he have been there just before he died?*

Various scenarios, all unpleasant, ran through her mind. Finally she decided that it was time to talk to the sheriff in person. *At least I might find out if he's aware of the militia. And the results of the autopsy. And whether they're trying to look for Cletus's shotgun. And maybe I could mention the squirrels.*

Sheriff Blaine was scrupulously polite—as an elected official he was always mindful of his constituency—but he was not forthcoming. He welcomed Elizabeth into his office and offered her coffee, his shrewd brown eyes assessing and dismissing her as harmless. The folksy manner he used when talking with Miss Birdie had been replaced with a bland, official courtesy. Even the mountain accent was gone. No, the autopsy had not been performed as yet. Yes, he would notify Miss Birdie as soon as there was information. No, no sign of Cletus's shotgun; it was probably at the bottom of the river and resources didn't allow him to look for it. An accidental death, perfectly straightforward. Yes, he understood Miss Birdie was very upset, but he was certain that once the autopsy was done, the old woman could put her mind at ease. Sorry not to have been of more help.

Yes, he was aware of the group on Devil's Fork. They were a retreat center for a religious group called—he shuffled through some papers in a blue plastic folder—called *the Sons of Adam*. No, he hadn't had any complaints about them. Yes, machine guns were illegal but a perfectly legal semiautomatic was sometimes mistaken for a machine gun by a—he hesitated, looking for a polite word—by someone unfamiliar with weaponry. And as to the squirrels . . . he shrugged . . . well, he could hardly see . . .

Two lights were blinking on his desk phone and he looked pointedly at them as he stood, indicating that the interview was over. Elizabeth was closing the office door behind her when she heard him say into his telephone, "What's this about Dewey Shotwell? Where was he?"

As Elizabeth hesitated, her hand on the knob, she heard the sheriff's voice again, lower this time. "Hang on a minute." The desk chair squeaked, and the door was pushed firmly shut behind her.

Back on Center Avenue, Ransom's only street except for Cross Road, she remembered that she needed stamps and set off walking down the long block that comprised most of the business district of the small town. A knot of men stood talking excitedly in front of the county courthouse. One man in particular was gesticulating wildly, and she was so busy watching him that she didn't see the tall figure coming out of the hardware store until she bumped into him.

Harice Tyler was carrying a small bundle wrapped in brown paper and tied with string, the old-fashioned custom of Wakeman's Hardware. The Holiness preacher smiled when he saw the confusion on her face.

"Howdy, Miz Goodweather," he said quietly. "I had me a feelin' I was goin' to be seein' you again soon.

I believe the Lord wants you to come back to our church. I fleeced Him about you and now I've seen you two times in two days."

"Excuse me." Elizabeth frowned, flustered by this second unexpected encounter with Harice Tyler. "I don't understand. You did what?" Once again she found herself thinking that this man, under different circumstances, of course, could be extraordinarily attractive. *Bedroom eyes and a terrific smile,* she thought unwillingly.

Harice looked at her with gentle pity. "Hit's in the Word, Miz Goodweather. The place where the Lord sent an angel to tell Gideon that he had to deliver Israel from its enemies. But Gideon warn't sure if hit was really an angel, thought hit might of been a demon. So Gideon fleeced the Lord. He put out a sheepskin and said, 'If the Lord really wants me to do this thing, He'll make the ground all around the fleece be wet, but the wool, hit'll be dry.' And the next morning, that's just how it was."

He laughed briefly and continued, "But that ol' Gideon, he wanted to make certain sure. So the next night he put out another fleece and said, 'Lord, just so I know it's yore will, tonight let the wool be wet and the ground be dry.' And the next mornin' that's how hit was, and Gideon knew there weren't no getting away from what hit was the Lord wanted him to do."

He laughed again, a humorless sound. "Atter I seen you in church, Miz Goodweather, I kept thinkin' on you till I decided maybe the Lord was tryin' to tell me something. So I put a fleece before the Lord and said, 'Lord, if you want me to help that sinner woman, bring her before me.' And now I done seen you two days running."

"What do you mean, help me?" asked Elizabeth, bewildered. "Do you mean about Cletus?"

"Maybe help about Cletus, maybe help you your own

self." Harice Tyler looked at her more closely. "Didn't you hear the words what Aunt Belvy spoke to you when the Spirit was on her? She spoke of death and corruption within your gates."

He seemed to be looming toward her and Elizabeth took a backward step. His stern expression softened and he said gently, "But there's always hope for a sinner." He turned to go, calling back over his shoulder, "You bring Sister Gentry back to church and could be you uns'll find what yore seekin'."

"Mr. Tyler!" Elizabeth called out. "You could help me with one thing."

Harice Tyler turned slowly. "What might that be, Miz Goodweather?" He looked amused.

"Red squirrels," she replied, without thinking. "Are there red squirrels on your father's place?"

"Red squirrels?" Tyler frowned. "You mean them boomers? Now what for do you want to know about them? Boomers likes the high-up places where the firs and the balsams grow. Only red squirrels I know about on this end of the county is up on Devil's Fork and beyond."

As she continued on to the post office, Elizabeth's thoughts were racing. *Those squirrels must have come from the militia place. So Cletus was there before he died. And what the hell is Tyler up to? Does he have some information about Cletus? . . . Could he have seen him out in the woods up at his father's place? . . . So why doesn't he just tell me? . . . Why make all this mystery? And I hate being called a sinner, even when I know it's just a generic term for anyone not in their church.*

Engrossed in her thoughts, she had gone past the post

office door when she heard a familiar voice call, "Señora Elizabeta, can you help me, *por favor*?"

It was Manuel Cruz, the Mexican worker who had helped Ben and Julio earlier in the spring. Manuel had come to the States for many years during the growing season to earn money to send to his family but had never adapted as easily as had Julio. He missed his home in Chiapas desperately and had vowed to return for good at the end of this year when he would celebrate his fiftieth birthday. Manuel was short and powerfully built: His dark chiselled features could have come straight from a Mayan carving. He was motioning toward Elizabeth and holding out several forms.

They went into the post office together and Elizabeth helped him to deal with various money orders and payments. When that was accomplished, Manuel asked, "Señora, *puede usted* . . . can you give me a ride to the Ready-Mart? *Mis amigos* . . . my friends will pick me up there."

"I'll be glad to, Manuel, as long as you're not in a big hurry. I have to stop for chicken feed and for groceries on the way. And, please, not Señora. Elizabeta is fine. Unless you want me to call you Señor Cruz."

She bought her stamps and together she and Manuel walked back toward the other end of town where she had parked her car. She asked about the family that was waiting for him in Chiapas. His face glowed as he told her that he had sent home so much money over the years that his wife had been able to set up a store, *"una tienda grande, Señora—perdóname, Elizabeta—*and she is making money with it. I will soon be able to go home."

It was not until she arrived at her house and was opening the rear door of the jeep to pull out the bags of chicken feed that she saw the bright red sticker. Affixed crookedly below the back window, its bold, uncompromising letters shouted: RACE MIXING IS SIN. And in smaller print, *Joshua 23:12–13*. A twig from some thorny bush was trapped under the sticker.

CHAPTER 10
THE OTHER SIDE OF THE MOUNTAIN
(FRIDAY AFTERNOON)

S HE HAD UNLOADED THE GROCERIES AT TOP SPEED and shoved the milk and other perishables into the refrigerator willy-nilly. *The rest can wait,* she decided as she sat at her dining table, her grandmother's worn Bible before her. It was open to Joshua 23 and she read aloud: *". . . if ye do in any wise go back, and cleave unto the remnant of these nations, even these that remain among you, and shall make marriages with them, and go in unto them, and they to you: Know for a certainty that the Lord your God will no more drive out any of these nations from before you; but they shall be snares and traps unto you, and thorns in your eyes, until ye perish from off this good land which the Lord your God hath given you."*

The red sticker and the thorny twig lay on the smooth maple surface of the table. She felt a wave of nausea each time she looked at them. *They're like a voodoo doll,* she thought, and shivered involuntarily. Her first impulse was to burn them; somehow just throwing them in the garbage wasn't enough. She picked up the sticker and the bit of thorn and headed for the fireplace, then checked herself. *I'll show these to Ben,* she decided, and carried the offensive objects out to the porch where she stuck them down in a battered old watering can. Then she went to the kitchen and scrubbed her hands, irrationally trying to get rid of the sense of violation.

The bundle of mail she had tossed on the kitchen table caught her eye and she took it into the living room to look through. A *New Yorker,* the electric bill, a funny postcard from a friend, a reminder from the vet that Ursa was due for a rabies shot, and a lemon-yellow flyer, evidently hand-delivered, as there was no stamp on it.

The flyer announced a tent revival behind the BP station on the bypass. Brother John "the Baptizer" Slagle, "the prophet crying in the wilderness," would be calling souls to repentance for two weeks, culminating in a grand baptism in the "living waters" of the river. This announcement was followed by the words: *"BUT WHOSO-EVER DRINKETH OF THE WATER THAT I SHALL GIVE HIM SHALL NEVER THIRST; BUT THE WATER THAT I SHALL GIVE HIM SHALL BE IN HIM A WELL OF WATER SPRINGING UP INTO EVERLAST-ING LIFE. John 4:14"*

Below the text was a surprisingly well done drawing of a lake, divided down the middle by a stone wall. On one side of the wall, towering flames rose above the heads of the miserable wretches crowded into the burning pool. Tiny arms were flung up and tiny faces twisted in agony. Wiry little devils on the shore jabbed pitchforks at the few naked miserable souls who attempted to escape the inferno. On the other side of the wall, there were no flames, only gentle wavy lines of water. There were people here too, though not as many as on the fiery side. These wore flowing robes and radiant smiles and they held up their hands in praise and adoration to the shaft of light that shone down on them from a billowy cloud. At the bottom of the drawing in large block letters was the question: *"WHICH SIDE WILL* **YOU** *BE ON?"*

"Arrgh!" Elizabeth cried, startling the dog James out of the reverie he had been diligently pursuing on the end of the sofa. "They're everywhere!" She quickly folded the yellow sheet into a paper airplane and sailed it away from her. James jumped from the sofa and gave chase, but the yellow projectile looped and glided effortlessly to hang from the very top of the bookshelves at the end of the room. The little dog stood and barked at the tantalizing shape.

Elizabeth stared at the nose-diving airplane. *What is that reminding me of?* she wondered. *I had a thought just then—but it's gone. Damn these senior moments.* James continued to bark and dance about, then ran to the door and whined urgently. With one last look at the yellow plane, Elizabeth said firmly, "Come on, James, let's go for a walk."

She strolled along the path at the top of the pasture, James bouncing along at her side with occasional forays into fascinating clumps of weeds or pauses to sniff and mark a random rock. At the edge of the woods was a simple bench, a weathered oak plank nailed to two locust posts half buried in the ground amid clumps of yellow violets. It was one of five benches scattered along this path; Sam had made them as a birthday present for Elizabeth years ago, dubbing them the "stations of the walk."

She sat down and looked back at her house and its surrounding gardens and at the barns and sheds and the fields of herbs and flowers that stretched out below her, nestled in the wide lush hollow beneath Pinnacle Ridge. So many years to create this beauty, this safe haven, and now, suddenly, she felt as if it was all in danger.

The mountain rising in the west behind her house had always seemed like a silent sentry with its protecting arms wrapped around Full Circle Farm; today, it seemed alien and dangerous, for now she knew what lay on the other side.

It all started with Cletus's death, she mused. *So violent and inexplicable. And the more I look for answers, the more ugly things I find.*

She tried to imagine who could have wanted to hurt Cletus, how he could have been a threat to anyone. Could he in his wandering have seen something that made him dangerous to . . . *to who? A racist, hate-mongering militia, a bunch of weird people named after stars, an old guy ready to shoot someone for digging ginseng on his place, or his son who collects copperheads and rattlers to handle in church? Did one of these have a secret that Cletus stumbled on to? And how could I have known so little about what and who was over there just on the other side of the mountain?*

When she and Sam had first moved to the farm, they had made a point of getting to know their nearest neighbors on Ridley Branch. But, aside from a few friends living on Bear Tree Creek, all "newcomers" like themselves, the other side of the mountain might as well have been the other side of the state. And through the years many new people had come to the county, buying up the old mountain farms and trying to find a way to make a living. Some had not stayed long; some had become a vital part of the mountain community; and others, who had come in search of solitude, had kept a very low profile, happy to be no more than a name on a mailbox, if that. Elizabeth had realized some years ago that she no longer knew, as she had at one time, all the newcomers on Ridley Branch or Bear Tree Creek.

She let her eyes follow the outline of the ridge, thinking again how little she knew of her neighbors. *At least those militia creeps are five or six miles away,* she thought, then smiled. *And the closest ones are Walter and Ollie Johnson, just a little ways down the other side. They're good people, I'm sure of it.*

Once again she recollected how she and Sam had climbed the mountain and had found their cows in Walter and Ollie's pasture, next to the beautiful old cabin. Sam had admired that cabin, noting the great size of the carefully hewn chestnut logs that were its walls and the precision of the dovetail notches that joined these logs. *But that's all changed,* she thought. *Sam is dead. Walter and Ollie live in a trailer farther down the mountain now, and that revival preacher on the flyer, John the Baptizer, that's who's staying in their beautiful old cabin. Who knows how many fanatics live just over the ridge? Cletus probably did. Cletus could have visited all of them, did visit most of the ones I know about.*

The thought depressed her even more and she stood up to resume her walk. James began barking fiercely as Molly and Ursa emerged from the trees, trotting along the path toward her, on their way back to the house after an adventure of some sort. The two dogs ignored James but greeted Elizabeth in a businesslike fashion and continued on their way, no doubt ready for food and a nap.

The second bench was set a little way into the woods, facing northeast. Here she looked across treetops down into the valley of the river. Below her was a pasture where some of her red cows were lying in the shade at the wood's edge, chewing their cuds and staring at nothing in particular.

They look so peaceful, thought Elizabeth. *They don't*

worry about things like people do. It's that old question, Is it better to be a happy pig or an unhappy philosopher?

She sat on the second bench and pondered. *Some people say it doesn't matter what you believe as long as you believe in something. But those militia people believe horrible things. And even my neighbors, with their faith in the Bible as the literal Word of God . . .* She remembered clearly how at some point she had known that the religion of her childhood held more questions than answers for her. Reading about the slaughters resulting from the Crusades and the Inquisition was, for her, the beginning of a deepening distrust of organized religion of any kind. And subsequent history: Northern Ireland, the Middle East, Bosnia, and, most recently, the destruction of the World Trade Center in New York—*right here, in our country!*—all this brutality fueled by religion—had done nothing to change her mind.

It's dangerous when people believe that they possess the only truth and that God is on their side, she argued with an invisible opponent. *It can allow them to treat nonbelievers as inferior or even nonhuman. Look how some religions—even Christianity—have justified slavery. And treating women as inferior to men, don't get me started on that one.*

It was time to move on. At her side, James stiffened and, once more, sent forth an alarming peal of barks. The dog was staring anxiously down at the gravel road that wound past her garden and up to the house. Through the trees she could see a familiar red-headed figure emerge from the barn. Alerted by James's barking, her daughter Laurel looked toward the woods and waved, then continued on up the road. Elizabeth smiled and started back to the house, pleased, as always, to see her younger daughter and, again, as always, slightly apprehensive. *What new adventure?* Sam used to say when Laurel would burst into a room, as she so often did, calling out "Pa! Mum! You'll *never* guess what I'm going to do!"

Laurel was a perpetual source of delight mixed with concern. Wildly independent, she had always insisted on what she called her own "space." Elizabeth had, as they grew older, tried very hard to stay out of her daughters' private business, usually waiting to be told rather than asking. She had, however, tried just as hard to let her two girls know that she was always willing to listen and that her love was unconditional.

When, during her senior year of college, Laurel had become romantically entangled with a visiting art professor, Elizabeth had offered a quiet warning and then shut up when Laurel had explained the timeless nature of the passion she shared with her Aristides. And though Elizabeth had agonized privately as the affair wound down and the charismatic older man had left her daughter for another young woman, she had done her best to support Laurel's careful portrayal of a free spirit, unfazed by love's betrayal. Time had healed that wound, but Elizabeth was painfully aware that she would always be a little uneasy about what life had in store for her strong-willed younger child.

Laurel's backpack, a wild medley of solid reds and oranges, mixed with a marbleized fabric of turquoise and yellow, lay open on one of the porch rockers. Her sandals had been kicked off at the door and Laurel herself was at the kitchen sink getting a glass of water.

"God, it's good to have some decent water," she gasped, draining a glass at a gulp and immediately refilling it. "That city water is so incredibly bad. I think I'll start taking jugs of water back with me. Hi, Mum," she added as an afterthought.

Laurel was tall and slender, almost six feet tall, with

the bony features of the true redhead. Her bright copper-colored hair, which she wore, to Elizabeth's mute dismay, in fat dreadlocks, was pulled back and confined by a wide purple band. She had on baggy white pants that were spattered with every imaginable hue of paint and a tight knit top of flaming scarlet. She was almost beautiful and she was definitely memorable.

"Hi, sweetie," said Elizabeth, hugging her daughter hard. "What's up?"

"Not much. I don't work tonight so I thought I'd come out for a while. I saw Ben at the bridge; he said to tell you he was heading into Asheville to meet some friends. Oh, and he told me about Cletus! That's so awful. He was a really sweet guy. You know I still have that little wooden pig he carved for me. How is Miss Birdie doing? Ben said she was kind of freaking out."

Elizabeth explained the situation briefly, but already Laurel's attention was wandering. "So you're just driving around the area finding out where Cletus went before he tried to cross the river. Why does it matter to Miss Birdie?" Laurel asked, her head in the refrigerator as she scouted for leftovers. She emerged with a container of pasta and continued. "But anyway, I was looking in the barn for that old aquarium we used to have. I've got an idea for an installation."

They went into the living room, Laurel talking a mile a minute about her upcoming show. ". . . And they like all my great goddess paintings, so I thought—" She broke off, then with a burst of laughter, she hopped up on the step stool that sat at the foot of the bookshelves and retrieved the bright yellow paper airplane snagged high among the books. "What's this, Mum? Are you lapsing into a second childhood?" Without waiting for an answer she launched the plane toward Elizabeth.

"Remember how Rosemary and I used to sail planes from the top of the stairs? There were always some caught up on those bookshelves. There're probably hundreds down behind the books."

Laurel retrieved the glider from the corner of the sofa where it had landed, then, noticing the lurid drawing on the wings, unfolded the sheet and smoothed it out. She gazed intently at the picture and then squealed, "John the Baptizer! I can't believe it! Mum, he's coming here! On the bypass! Oh, this is so cool; you *have* to go with me."

Openmouthed, Elizabeth stared at her daughter. Finally she managed a feeble "Do what?"

"Mum, he's an outsider artist. You know, like Howard Finster or . . . or Minnie Evans. Self-taught, but look at the raw power in this drawing." Her long fingers traced the outline of the flames. "Just a few people know about him so far. He only sells his paintings at the end of his revival services and he's never had a show in a gallery. One of my professors was a real fan of his and she said that this guy was an untutored Van Gogh. But this could be a chance . . ." Laurel was pacing up and down the room in excitement. "If I could talk to him and get him to agree to a show, the folks at the co-op gallery might let me curate it. They would be so thrilled . . . I mean, talk about a coup . . . they'd probably give me a one-man show later on. The revival starts next week, it says. Oh, Mum, I've got to go! Please come with me!"

When Laurel set off back down the road three hours later, her knapsack was swollen by several books, a container of Elizabeth's frozen tomato-and-herb sauce, and a loaf of homemade oatmeal bread. She had also extracted from Elizabeth a reluctant promise to consider attending the tent revival.

Elizabeth dreamed often—always in full color, sometimes only mundane, sometimes truly exciting. She had little faith in the idea that her nighttime adventures actually meant anything, seeing them merely as the product of her busy mind churning over recent events. Occasionally the dreams were truly frightening and she would jolt awake, happy to have escaped whatever terrors her subconscious had arranged for her.

She was wandering in the woods. Brilliantly colored birds fluttered all around her, and wherever she turned, pools of water appeared at her feet. In each pool stood a figure that looked like Cletus. Then the pools all merged into one pool and the water turned to fire and Laurel was in the flames, laughing with pleasure. Elizabeth saw herself standing there with Harice Tyler before her, offering her a huge rattlesnake, but as she tentatively put out her hand for it, the viper turned into a thorny branch. Harice smiled at her and scolded softly, You just got to have faith, Elizabeth Goodweather.

She awoke gasping, then lay still, trying to trace the sources of the vivid images her sleeping brain had conjured up. *All those pools of water were like the wood between the worlds in that Narnia book* The Magician's Nephew. *But then the fire, that was straight from that flyer about the revival. And Laurel . . . of course because I worry about her . . . And the thorny stick was because of that thing stuck on my car,* she thought sleepily. *And Cletus, who drowned . . .* Her thoughts rambled on to that little pool by Walter and Ollie's old house that she and Sam had gone skinny-dipping in so long ago. She remembered how later Ollie had shown her the hidden natural shelf at the edge of the water where butter and milk stayed cool behind a fringe of ferns.

She yawned and thought again of the Harice Tyler in her dream. *What did he say? "You just got to have faith." Wasn't that what Dessie told me too?* Elizabeth lay there in the dark, rethinking the dream and remembering the sticker with its ugly message that had been slapped on her car. Suddenly she was no longer sleepy. Switching on her bedside light, she reached for the telephone and dialed information. In reply to the automated voice, she answered "Asheville," and to the nasal voice of a live operator, she said firmly: "Janie Hawkins."

IV-June 1901

Hit was wash day and I was haulin water from the spring when Levy Johnson come down the mountain. My fire was goin good but I needed me some more water for the rinsin. Levy was on his way to help Daddy with plowin the corn and he was ridin a big sorrel mare, all geared up, but when he saw me he slid down from the mare's back and said, I'll tote them heavy pails for you. His hair was the color of Mister Tomlin's gold pieces and his face was smooth and put me in mind of the ripe peaches on our red-leafed Cherokee peach tree. I smiled when I thought this for just then the sun broke through the mornin mist and I could see fuzz just like a peach has all along Levy's jawbone.

Hit was then that I hated my Daddy for what he had done in tyin me to a smelly old man with whiskers on his face.

I had been a wife for over a month now but I had yet to find the part about likin it just fine. Mister Tomlin treated me well enough, I reckon, but he had his notions. Though he went off most days, he had said that he wanted me to stay close to home and not go runnin back down the mountain to gossip with Clytie and Rom. I had made me a little garden and had that to tend and I had planted me some orange lilies and a slip of the old pink rose from down at the homeplace. Aetha had come to visit and showed me how to use my sewin machine. She had brung me some patterns traced on newspaper and I was makin a shirt for Mister Tomlin. Aetha had brung me a basket of scraps too and I was startin to piece a Lone Star quilt. But hit was tiresome to be by myself all day and when I saw Levy something inside me just seemed to bust loose.

My washtubs was set near to the branch and the clothes was soakin. I watched Levy pour the water into the rinse tub and thought how strong his arms looked and how sweet was his smile. He seen me lookin at him and he said, Well, Miz Tomlin, I best be gettin on. Yore daddy'll be lookin fer me.

Hit felt awful queer him callin me Miz Tomlin and him some four or five years older than me. I'd knowed Levy and his kin all my life. Though he went to school and to church over on Bear Tree Creek, while I went to the Ridley Branch ones, we had seen one another at shuckins and log rollins and the like. And at a play party last winter when we was all playin Tap Hands, ever time Levy was It, hit was my hands he'd tap. Clytie had been bad to tease me about him atter that but I hadn't seen him since.

How come you not to be at my marryin? I asked. I seen the rest of yore family that day.

He turned and walked over to where he'd hitched the mare. I don't know, he said, reckon I was too busy with work to go loaferin around. He stepped on a rock and swung himself up on the big mare's back. I got to get on, he said, and headed off down the hill.

I watched him out of sight but he didn't look around, not once. I thought again how pretty he looked with his yellow hair a-shinin in the sun. Then I went back to my washin.

Though Mister Tomlin had talked big about his wife not havin to lift her little finger to work, there was still the washin to do. And the cleanin and cookin. Mister Tomlin said that when we got into that house he was going to build, I'd have someone to help me. But hit didn't much matter to me for I had to have something to do all the day whilst he was off buyin up timber and makin arrangements for his sawmill. He traveled all around and sometimes, like this mornin, he would say, Don't look for me till nightfall, Little Sylvie, for I've business in Ransom with Lawyer Bailey.

I got my rub board and began to scrub at the dirty clothes. The sun was full up now and atter I rinsed the clothes in two waters and wrung them good, I stretched them out to dry over the big boxwoods that grow there by the branch. Then I dipped some of the wash water into a bucket and took it and the lye soap to wash the cabin floor. Not that hit was in much need of cleanin but I knowed Mister Tomlin set a great store by things bein just so.

Like I said, he had his notions. The least little smell of sweat just provoked him something fierce and he'd tell me to go wash myself afore I got into the bed. He said that when our house was built, hit'd have gravity water and a room with a bathtub all set up where I could take a bath ever night of the week. I never heared of such.

*But what I can't understand is the part that goes on be-
tween us in bed. Hit don't never take very long, and they's
not much to it. I have puzzled about hit some and I still
can't see what makes Aetha like this foolishness so much.
But then her man Fate is a young man.*

The sun was droppin behind the mountain when Levy and
his mare come back up the road. I was settin on the cabin
steps brushin my hair that I'd just washed. Levy looked at
me and nodded and made as if to keep on goin but I called
out, Light and set a spell, Levy Johnson. You can give me
some news of yore family.

He looked at me funny-like but pulled right up and set
there atop that big old sorrel mare. My family's fine, Miz
Tomlin, he said, like the words was coin he didn't want to
spend.

Don't be hateful, I said. You call me Little Sylvie like
you always done.

Well, hit took a time but at long last he clumb down
and come and set beside me. He told me all the news from
Bear Tree—Sim Shotwell was courtin Noveenie, the
youngest of the Johnson girls, and the Davis cow dropped
twin heifers that they named Hattie and Mattie. We was
a-laughin about some silly something or other when all of
a sudden, here comes Mister Tomlin a-trottin up the road
on Neb.

Levy stood up quick but a hank of my hair was caught
somehows on his shirt button and he had to stop to tug hit
loose afore he could go down the steps. Mister Tomlin set
there in the saddle and watched but didn't say nothin, even

when Levy called out, Evenin, Mister Tomlin, I was just givin Miz Tomlin the news of my family but I got to be gettin on. Then Levy clumb up on his horse and said, Evenin, Miz Tomlin, I'll tell them you asked atter them.

He pulled the mare's head around but before he could take her up the road, Mister Tomlin spurred Neb to block the way. He looked hard at Levy and said, I'll thank you to stay clear of my wife from now on.

He had his hand on his pistol when he said it and for a mercy, Levy didn't say nothing back, just kindly shrugged his shoulders and kicked the mare with his heels to send her on up the road. Mister Tomlin watched them go then turned to me and said, Get in the cabin, Little Sylvie, and get me some supper.

He didn't say nothing more whilst we et our supper but atter I had washed the dishes and was gettin ready for bed, he called me over to him where he sat in the big hickory-backed armchair.

Little Sylvie, he says, real soft but kindly eager like, do you know what Paul says about women? His eyes glittered like a cat watchin a baby bird and he pulled me close to where I was standin between his legs. The ruby ring felt heavy on my finger and I said No, sir, I don't guess that I do.

Paul says to the Ephesians, Women, submit yourselves unto your own husbands as unto the Lord. Didn't you hear the preacher say that back on our wedding day? He pulled me closer and his breath was comin fast. Little Sylvie, says he, I'm going to have to punish you for whoring after that Johnson boy.

I started to speak up for I wanted to say that he hadn't

ought to use that ugly word about me when all I done was talk to Levy but then he goes on, It says in the Book that committing adultery in your heart is just as bad as if you'd laid down with him.

Mr. Tomlin, I never—I start to say but he clamps his hand over my mouth. Don't speak another word, Little Sylvie. Just you go over there and lay facedown on the bed.

His eyes was wild-lookin and I was afeared of what he might do iffen I talked back so I went and laid on the bed like he told me. My heart was poundin as he took off his coat and vest and undid his belt. I figured I knowed what was comin and wasn't none too surprised when he come over and flung my skirts up. Then he commenced to pullin down my drawers and I closed my eyes and thought, well, maybe if we do it back to belly like the animals do, hit'll work better.

When the belt strap hit my rump I hollered like one thing and tried to jump up but he grabbed aholt of my shoulders and pushed me back down. Little Sylvie, you got to learn who is the master here, he said. You got five more coming, then we'll say no more about it.

Well, he give me five more licks and I bit my lip hard as I could to keep from hollerin again. That old belt burned like fire but I was set on not lettin him know how much hit hurt. Then when he was done, he unbuttoned his pants and went at it, his big old rough hands a-grabbin at my pore scalded bottom. I could feel that his old thing had gotten harder and this time he almost done it.

CHAPTER II
HUMBLE PIE WITH PINEAPPLE SALSA
(SATURDAY)

ELIZABETH AWAKENED AS THE ROOM GREW LIGHT AND sat up, as she usually did, to watch the sunrise. Her bed faced three large uncurtained windows that looked due east, and she loved the endless variety of sunrises that greeted her from day to day. Growing up in Florida and in the suburbs, she had never realized how the sun paced back and forth through the year, like a restless dog on a tether. During the winter it rose far to the southeast and skulked along the ridgeline, disappearing in mid-afternoon. But now it was rising a little past due east, on its way to the northeast where it would achieve the summer solstice, then begin the slow day-by-day journey back to the winter solstice. Watching the sunrise, with its reminder of the endless and inevitable cycles of life, was, she thought, her version of religion.

She waited till nine to dial the number the operator had given her. At some point in the night she had decided to swallow her pride and get in touch with Phillip Hawkins— partly because he was a friend of Sam's and a nice man

who deserved better treatment than she had given him—
and partly because he was a police detective and might be
willing to give more advice on how to proceed in answering the growing questions about Cletus's death. An
answering machine picked up almost immediately, and
Elizabeth began awkwardly to explain to the mechani-
cal voice that she needed to get in touch with Phillip
Hawkins. She was giving her phone number, enunciating
slowly and carefully, when a sleepy and rather grumpy fe-
male voice broke in: "Who is this anyway?"

Taken aback, Elizabeth stammered, "Ah—is this
Janie?"

"I asked you first," retorted the voice at the other end.
"Who are you and why do you want to talk to my—to
Phillip Hawkins?" A huge yawn echoed in Elizabeth's
ear. "And what time is it anyway?"

Remembering her own daughters' tendency to sleep
till noon on weekends, Elizabeth felt a twinge of guilt for
having called at an hour which was obviously far too
early to suit Janie, if this was indeed Janie. Trying to collect her thoughts, she replied gently, "I'm sorry if I woke
you. My name is Elizabeth Goodweather. Phillip Hawkins
is—was a friend of my late husband, and he came out to
my farm last Sunday for lunch. I need to talk to him and
don't have his phone number. I was hoping you could
give it to me. And it's nine o'clock."

Silence at the other end greeted her words. Elizabeth
began to wonder if Janie, if it was Janie, had gone back to
sleep. Then there was another long yawn. "I don't think
I should give out his phone number but I'll tell him you
want him to call. You already gave your number to the
machine. So I'll tell him, okay?"

There was a click and Elizabeth said "Thank you" to
a dead line.

Dammit, Elizabeth, she thought wearily, *this could have been avoided if you hadn't acted like a . . . like an idiot. You could have gone out to dinner with that nice man in a perfectly civilized manner; you could have asked for advice about Cletus; you could have had a nice, rational, mature person, a police detective yet, to discuss this with. But, oh, no, Elizabeth, you had to—*

The portable telephone, still in her hand, shrilled, cutting off her inner diatribe.

"Lizzie Beth, honey." Miss Birdie's voice trembled. "The sheriff done called. He says that hit's for certain sure that Cletus drownded." She paused, as if gathering strength. "They done that 'topsy and that's what hit showed. But I still ain't believin' he went for to cross that trestle. Something ain't right here and I'm a-countin' on you to help me find out what did happen. Lizzie Beth, honey, we got to go back to that Holiness church and see what else Belvy can tell us."

In the background Elizabeth could hear Dorothy twittering away. "Now, Birdie, you lay back down and let me talk to her." And then Dorothy was on the phone. "Lizzie Beth, she's takin' on right much about this. I told her you'd help her ever way you can, for she's that set on believin' that this weren't no accident."

Dorothy went on to say that Cletus's funeral was planned for the following Wednesday "with the viewin' Tuesday night. And Pastor Briggs says he's goin' to ask that revival preacher, that John the Baptizer, to give a message at the graveside."

"Tell Birdie I'll be there," Elizabeth assured Dorothy, "and tell her that I'll go with her back to the Holiness church." She sighed as she put down the phone. For all of the twenty-some years she had lived on Ridley Branch, she had never visited the local churches, knowing that she was not a believer and being afraid of giving offense if she went once and did not return. But now it looked as if she was in for a big dose of the emotional preaching so beloved by her mountain neighbors.

She glanced at the clock and considered her options. The flower beds needed weeding; the house needed vacuuming. "And I need someone to talk to," she said aloud. As if in response to her wish, the phone rang again.

"Ms. Goodweather," began a somewhat cautious voice, "this is Phillip Hawkins. My daughter said you wanted me to call."

She hadn't actually thought about what she would say if he called and it all tumbled out. "Phillip, I want to apologize—I don't know—that is, I didn't mean—oh, hell! What I'm trying to say is that I would very much like to have dinner with you. Sometime."

There was a silence and to her horror she heard herself babbling into the void. "That is . . . if you still . . . I mean, you did suggest it last Sunday and I—"

A warm chuckle put a merciful end to her faltering explanation. "That would be great, Elizabeth. What about tonight?"

Though her first impulse was to suggest another night—*all the restaurants will be crowded on Saturday night; my hair needs washing; I'll miss* Prairie Home Companion—she bit her tongue and replied, "That sounds fine. Where shall I meet you?"

"Where would you like to eat? There seem to be restaurants all over downtown Asheville. Janie told me about some place called Dapas—or something—that she really likes."

"Oh, Tapas. Good choice! I ate there a few months ago and the food's terrific. Pretty spicy and incredibly creative. It's very popular, though; we might need to call ahead."

Phillip said he would make a reservation for seven o'clock, and they agreed to meet at the restaurant. Elizabeth hung up the phone, feeling a mixture of apprehension and anticipation. She was glad she had talked to Phillip Hawkins—he was a link with Sam in some indefinable way. Sam had always spoken of his navy buddy as "a guy you can count on—totally rational and down-to-earth." *Rational would be good,* she told herself, thinking unwillingly of Harice Tyler and the dream of the night before. *And maybe he can suggest something for me to tell Miss Birdie. Or tell me what else I can do to find that damn shotgun.*

As she walked from the parking garage to the restaurant, she realized that she was early, so she slowed and began to look in shop windows. A cluttered display in an antique shop claimed her attention and she whiled away a few minutes examining the pricy blue-and-white transfer ware and the faded quilts that seemed to be a specialty. A movement caught her eye and she found herself gazing at her own reflection in a streaky old mirror propped at the back of the window.

She had made some effort with her appearance tonight: her hair, instead of hanging in a single braid down her back, was twisted into a soft knot at the nape of her neck. No makeup—*I got over that, years ago,* she thought—but her eyebrows were still dark enough to give definition to her features, and her blue eyes and silver-shot dark hair were a striking contrast to the golden tan of her face. As a further nod to the occasion she had abandoned her small gold hoops for larger earrings in the graceful shape of ginkgo leaves. A long flaring black linen skirt, a periwinkle-blue knit shell, and an unlined black linen blazer seemed very dressy after her usual jeans and work shirts. Flat-heeled black sandals completed her outfit.

I feel too dressed up, she thought dubiously, *but this is the kind of thing a lot of women wear every day.* She peered at the mirror with a slight sense of disbelief. *I do look pretty good . . . in a dim light and an old mirror.* With a parting grin at her reflected image, she turned toward the restaurant. A discarded newspaper flapping on a bench seemed about to blow into the street and she stopped to gather it up. As she was beginning to push it into a nearby trash receptacle, a name caught her eye.

The article was on one of the back pages, just a few lines. The body of Dewey Shotwell, Marshall County resident and locally famous ginseng hunter, had been found in the river below Ransom. Accidental drowning was the presumed cause of death.

Quickly she tore out the article, folded it, and slipped it into her jacket pocket. After cramming the rest of the newspaper into the trash container, she hurried on to Tapas. *Okay, this can't be a coincidence. Two bodies in the river in a month. And Dewey Shotwell was a sang hunter like Cletus. Could that old man, Mr. Tyler . . . ? But he acted as if he liked Cletus . . . And he said there was lots of sang up on Devil's Fork . . .*

Phillip Hawkins stood waiting for her in front of the restaurant. His khaki slacks and crisp sport shirt were unexceptional, but his face was freshly shaved and the faint aroma of shaving cologne indicated that he too had gone the extra mile in getting ready for this meeting. He greeted her with a smile and his eyes seemed to study her appearance in appreciative detail. "Ready to go on in?" he asked. "I checked, and our table is ready."

When they had been seated and had given the waitress their orders, there was an awkward silence. Elizabeth shook out her napkin and spread it across her lap, straightened her knife and fork, took a cautious sip of her water, and said, "So, did you find an apartment?"

"A house. I rented a house in Weaverville," Phillip replied. "It's someone's vacation cottage and I have it for a year." He straightened *his* knife and fork and went on, "It's okay. It doesn't have much of a view and it does have a little too much cutesy country stuff for my taste, but once I put away some of the teddy bears and ruffled pillows it'll be fine." He caught himself and looked at her, saying hastily, "Nothing against teddy bears and ruffled pillows, I just—"

"I know what you mean." Elizabeth laughed. "Duck decoys with bows around their necks and lots of soft blues and dusty pinks. It's a look that a lot of people like, but—"

Somehow their shared lack of appreciation for ruffled pillows had broken the ice. Phillip relaxed visibly and smiled. "You know," he said, "I'm glad you called. I was thinking about you the other day and wondering what had ever happened about that neighbor of yours. The one they found in the river? Has the autopsy been done?"

"It has, and it showed that he drowned—"

"So you're off the hook." Phillip pushed the basket of bread toward her as the waiter arrived with their wine. "You won't have to help his mother find out what happened. I was a little concerned when you said she was wanting you to go all around looking for a murderer—"

"But that's just it," Elizabeth broke in. "Miss Birdie is still convinced that someone killed Cletus. I don't know whether she just doesn't trust the autopsy or what, but she's dead set on our going back to the snake-handling church to see if the prophetess can tell her more."

She dipped her bread into the bowl of golden-green olive oil on the table between them, and continued thoughtfully, "I don't know, maybe I'm just humoring her, hoping she'll get over this notion she's taken. And I have to admit that I find the Holiness church absolutely fascinating—I mean, I was brought up an Episcopalian, one of 'God's frozen people' they used to call us. A service at the Holiness church is so far at the other end of the religion spectrum that I feel like I'm in a different world."

She fell silent, remembering the intensely visceral response she'd felt during the noisy, emotional meeting, the ecstatic state of the worshippers, the calm certainty of Harice Tyler's preaching, his compelling—*Stop it right now, Elizabeth,* she warned herself.

"And then, there's another odd thing." She pulled the folded piece of newspaper from her jacket pocket and spread it out before her dinner companion. "I just saw this article—this Dewey Shotwell who drowned—I think there has to be some connection with Cletus."

Phillip glanced at the article briefly, then said, "Another drowning? Could be a coincidence, but . . ." He didn't finish his sentence. Frowning, he said, "What do you know about this Shotwell?"

Elizabeth explained about the ginseng, telling Hawkins how Raym Tyler had made threats against Dewey Shotwell. "And the thing is, both Cletus and Dewey Shotwell were known to hunt for ginseng in the same area, there around Little Man Holler and up on Devil's Fork."

"Devil's Fork?" Hawkins said sharply. Elizabeth's eyes widened at his peremptory tone, and he continued quickly, "Unusual name. Where's this Devil's Fork located?"

"It's up at the end of Bear Tree Creek," she explained. "Some horrible militia group owns a lot of property up there. Supposedly they have a lot of weapons and I'm pretty sure they would be capable of . . . of almost anything. And there's the thing about the red squirrels."

She had just finished explaining the squirrel connection when their food arrived, large plates heaped high with grilled fish, black beans and rice, fried plantains, and several spicy salsas. One salsa in particular captured Elizabeth's attention. *What's in this?* she asked herself. *I want to make it at home. Red onions, garlic, hot peppers, probably jalapenos, cilantro, and pineapple.* But the pineapple was different, almost caramelized in places. Finally she decided it must have been grilled before being chopped up.

Phillip was saying something, she realized, forcing herself to abandon her analysis of the salsa. ". . . Those militia groups are unpredictable." His voice was low and serious. "Some of them are only big boys playing with big toys . . . though they can cause plenty of trouble just by being too macho. Then there're others with a serious political agenda. Those guys aren't afraid to break the law in pursuit of what they believe is right. And some of them probably have some legitimate gripes with the government." He paused and sipped his Rioja. "But whoever it is you've got up there on Devil's Fork, I'd suggest you give them a wide berth, red squirrels or not."

After dinner they walked slowly toward the parking garage where Elizabeth had left her car. Phillip was interested in all she told him about her visits to the different hollows and coves of Bear Tree Creek. "That's some collection of neighbors you've got," he said with a laugh when she told him about the trailer park of the damned. "That's what my ex-wife thought all of this area was like; she never would come with me to visit my folks over in Shut In." But his brows contracted into a frown when she began to describe the Starshine Community. "*That's* near you?" he asked. "What do you know about those people?"

Puzzled by the intensity of his question, Elizabeth began to retell her experience with Polaris and with the young man whom she had given a ride out of the community. "It was a very well kept place; there was obviously money behind it all, and everyone I saw looked healthy and clean, but—I don't know, it seemed a little weird. And there—"

"Weird!" Phillip exploded, "It would be! Goddammit!" He swung around and slammed his fist into the unyielding side of the brick building they were passing, then yelped in pain. Elizabeth took an involuntary step backward.

"Goddammit to hell!" He looked at his scraped knuckles, then up at Elizabeth, who was staring at him, openmouthed. Suddenly shamefaced, he said, "I'm sorry, I didn't mean to . . . oh, hell, the thing is . . . I can't believe this . . . the thing is, Janie told me just this morning that she wants to drop out of school and join this . . . this Starshine place. She says it's all part of her higher destiny."

CHAPTER 12
A LITTLE RATIONAL QUID PRO QUO
(SATURDAY)

GODDAMMIT," PHILLIP HAWKINS SAID ONCE more. "Higher density's more like it." The anger in his voice had been replaced by a great weariness, and he looked around him slowly as if searching for something. "Elizabeth, could we sit on that bench over there for a minute? I'd like to tell you a little about Janie. Maybe you can give me some insights about daughters—I'm really outta my depth here."

Elizabeth hesitated. Hawkins's startling outburst had alarmed her and she thought that it might be nice just to say good night quickly and get away from this unpredictable man. "I don't know—" she began.

He smiled and said quietly, "Elizabeth, please. I'm really sorry about losing my temper like that. I just get so damned frustrated trying to deal with Janie." He ran his hand over his bald scalp. "Tell me, did your girls ever act so unreasonable that you just couldn't talk to them?"

Elizabeth relaxed slightly and sat down on the bench, which was, she noted, in a well-lighted area near a popular coffee shop. *If he gets really angry again . . .* she thought, and then she remembered when Rosemary, the so-called "sensible one" of her two girls, had called home from school during her junior year to announce that she had decided to drop out. Drop out and go to Thailand and join a community of neohumanist yogic nuns. "Yes, as a matter of fact, I think I know how you feel," she told Hawkins. "But, fortunately, the girls have gotten more reasonable, and I've probably gotten more accepting."

She smiled, remembering how she and Sam had agonized over Rosemary's plan but had never actually told her what a dreadful idea they thought it was. Just when they had decided that they must do something, *anything,* to stop her, Rosemary had called and in an offhand tone had mentioned that the nun thing was off and she'd decided to stay in school and work for her doctorate. And, by the way, she'd gotten a fellowship.

"The thing about Janie is she's so gullible," Hawkins was saying. "And she doesn't seem to be able to think for herself; it's always all about what her friends are doing." He dropped heavily onto the bench beside Elizabeth and turned to face her. "Are you sure you have time for this? I hate bothering you with family stuff, but . . ."

"Really, it's okay," Elizabeth assured him. "Do you think she was serious about dropping out?"

"Yes, I do." His voice was resigned. "She's not happy in school; her grades are falling; she's switched her major twice; her boyfriend broke up with her. I think she's desperate for some sort of change."

"What about her mother? Will she go along with—"

"Her mother will pitch a fit and then blame me. You see, when we got divorced—about twelve years ago— Sandy wanted full custody of the kids. Well, I didn't like it but it made sense; it was my job—you know, long, unpredictable hours—that caused her to get fed up with me and with our marriage in the first place. So anyway, for years I was pretty much a hands-off dad. Oh, I had the

kids with me on a lot of weekends and we took trips now
and then in the summer. But all the decisions were hers.
If I ever tried to suggest that I wasn't happy with something the kids were or weren't doing, she'd remind me
that I wasn't able to be the full-time parent that she
was—" Hawkins stopped abruptly.

"Don't get me wrong," he said. "For the most part
Sandy did a great job. Our son Seth has turned out really
fine; he's in his senior year at ECU—got a full scholar-
ship—no worries there. And Janie was a real sweetheart
till about seven years ago. It was when she hit thirteen,
all of a sudden she and my wife, my ex-wife, I mean,
butted heads on everything under the sun. Sandy had
Janie on track to be a cheerleader, an A student, Miss
Congeniality—the whole nine yards. And Janie could
have done it; she's a smart girl and pretty, too—takes after
her mom—blond and petite. And she had always been
so . . . so . . ."—he struggled for the right word—". . . so
biddable. Whatever Sandy suggested—this hairdo, these
clothes, those friends—Janie would just say, 'Sure, Mom,'
and go along with the program. Actually, it worried me
a little; it didn't seem like Janie had a mind of her own.
She was a little Sandy-clone.

"But then all of a sudden, Janie's dropping out of her
extracurricular activities, she's dressing all in black, she
chops her hair off short and dyes it black, she puts a safety
pin through her eyebrow, and there's not a mother-
loving thing that Sandy can do about it." At the memory,
he grinned.

"Well, it tore me up to see Janie making herself look
ugly and acting like some street punk. But if I said anything to Sandy about it, she'd claim I was 'attacking her
parenting skills.'" Hawkins's voice was sarcastic as he
curved two fingers of each hand to indicate the quote.

"I even talked to a shrink I know; he works with the department sometimes. He went on about low self-esteem and broken homes. But at least Janie's grades stayed okay and she didn't act depressed. No eating disorders or anything like that. She just turned into a mouthy little somebody with a bunch of friends Sandy couldn't stand. She was staying out late too many nights and probably was involved with marijuana and alcohol, but she still pulled at least Bs in her courses. Finally she managed to scrape her way into college but when she announced that she was going to UNCA and nowhere else and that she'd be moving in with her boyfriend, Sandy said that she'd had enough—I could be the parent in charge."

"So Janie's, what, a junior? At least she's made it this far."

"Yeah, but we've averaged about a crisis per semester. Recently she's been skipping classes and hanging out with the street kids downtown. She informed me that panhandling gives her deep insights into the frivolity of our society." His voice grew pained. "I worry about her a lot—that's part of why I took this extended leave, so I could be around. She's not as antagonistic toward me as she is to Sandy, but I'm afraid if I start doing the heavy father routine I'll lose what little influence I do have. . . ." He looked at Elizabeth. "So what do you think?"

"What do you mean? About Janie?"

"About this Starshine place—Is it just something she needs to get out of her system? Will she go back to school?" He shrugged. "Maybe I'm more like Sandy than I thought. I just don't know what the hell to do, Elizabeth. I guess I'm asking you because of what Sam used to say."

"What did Sam used to say?"

"He said—I can't remember exactly how he put it—it was something like you had a mind like a man—logical, but you also had insights like women are supposed to have." Hawkins smiled sheepishly, "Oops. I guess that's a sexist statement, but old Sam really put a lot of faith in your opinions."

Elizabeth sat quietly for a moment, thinking of Sam. Then she said slowly, "I hate to give advice, especially when I don't know Janie, but I guess if it was one of my daughters I'd try to find out more about the Starshine Community before making a big deal of it. As you say, it might be fine; she might live there a while and then go back to school, but . . ." She paused, remembering the group of young women circling around Polaris. And the two men with rifles. "You know, Phillip, there were some things about that place that made me uneasy."

She told him, a little reluctantly, about her unauthorized drive up the narrow road and the armed men at the windowless building. "And the young guy who got a ride out with me. He acted almost like an escaping prisoner, but he may have just been dramatizing the whole thing for my benefit. There's probably a simple explanation—"

Hawkins groaned. "I'll start looking into it, but I'll have to do it without involving Janie. I guess I could—"

"They have a Web site," Elizabeth offered. "At least, that Polaris guy *said* they did. And I'll ask my daughter Laurel if she knows anything about it. She's usually up on all the stuff going on in this area."

"Well, that's a start," Hawkins said. "I really appreciate your listening to me. It helps just to talk to someone rational."

Elizabeth smiled, remembering that having someone rational to talk to had been part of her reason for calling Phillip Hawkins. But where she had hoped to get advice, she had ended up giving it.

A noisy group of young people burst out of the coffee shop and congregated near the bench. All immediately lit cigarettes. As the smoke drifted toward them, Elizabeth and Hawkins looked at each other and, with silent accord, rose and resumed their stroll toward the parking garage.

"I got so wrapped up in my own stuff we got off the subject of your neighbor." Hawkins looked at Elizabeth quizzically as he ambled along at her side. "You told me you were tracing Cletus's movements the week before he was found. So now that the autopsy has shown that he drowned, are you going to continue to humor your friend . . . Miss Birdie, is it?"

"You know, I've been thinking about that. I did say that maybe I was just humoring her but there's really more to it. You see, I've known Miss Birdie for years and I respect her a lot. She's a very smart woman—not educated but very smart. And if she knows anything, she knows about her son. If she says he wouldn't have crossed that bridge, well, I think she's probably right. I knew Cletus too and he was scared to death of water and stubborn as a mule. Once he'd made his mind up, nothing could change it." She sighed heavily and they both stopped walking. Her eyes rose to meet Phillip's gaze. "The only thing is . . . the autopsy result. How did he come to drown in the river if he didn't fall off the bridge?"

"Well, let's consider the possibilities. He could have been taken to the river by someone else and pushed in. Hell, he could have been drowned somewhere else and his body dumped in the river. Of course you would expect the autopsy to reveal signs of a struggle. He could have been drugged . . . but the autopsy would show if that—"

"I think they said his body was pretty beaten up from

falling on the rocks; couldn't that have covered up injuries caused by a struggle?"

Hawkins ran his hand over his shiny bald scalp again. "I don't know. Medical examiners are pretty sharp. But if there was no reason to expect foul play, and they were in a hurry—" He broke off, then began again, his eyes bright with excitement, "Where did they do the autopsy, anyway?"

Elizabeth closed her eyes, trying to remember what Sheriff Blaine had said. "I think he said that the medical examiner was in Chapel Hill."

"Hot damn!" Hawkins chortled. "We're in luck."

"Oh?" said Elizabeth, surprised by his glee. "What do you mean?"

"One of my best friends, R. L. Levine, was medical examiner down in Greeneville for years. Two years ago R.L. moved to Chapel Hill and was made chief ME there. If I call tonight, I'll bet I can get the inside scoop on that autopsy."

Elizabeth hesitated, a little surprised but thoroughly delighted at Hawkins's enthusiasm for what she had come to think of as her problem. "Will they—the medical examiner, I mean—do that? Give you that information?"

"No problem." He laughed. "This one will. I have a few markers I can call in."

He had insisted on seeing her to her car—"parking garages can be dangerous places at night"—and he'd promised her that he would be in touch as soon as he had talked to the medical examiner. Scribbling his phone number on a scrap of paper, he had handed it to her and said, "They just installed it at my new place. Call me if your daughter can tell you anything about those star people." She had thanked him for the dinner and they had said good night.

As she drove back to Marshall County, Elizabeth thought about the evening. *It went really well. It wasn't like going out on a date, just having dinner with a friend. He's a nice person and easy to talk to. I felt comfortable with him and, God knows, he seemed to feel comfortable with me— telling me all that about his daughter. I had a feeling she was trouble, just from talking to her on the phone—poor guy, trying to deal with that all the time.*

She shuddered at the thought of having a petulant twenty-year-old on her hands and shoved a cassette into the tape deck. Sheila Kay Adams's strong, pure voice filled the car, singing of love and death in a ballad that had been handed down in her family for seven generations.

> *. . . She steppèd up to Little Mathey Groves,*
> *Her eyes cast on the ground.*
> *Said, Please, o please come with me stay*
> *As you pass through this town, town,*
> *As you pass through this town.*
>
> *I cannot stay; I dare not stay.*
> *I fear 'twill cost my life.*
> *For I can tell by your finger-ring*
> *That you are Lord Daniel's wife, wife,*
> *That you are Lord Daniel's wife.*
>
> *Lord Daniel's in some distant land;*
> *He's left me for to roam.*
> *He's taken all his merry men*
> *And I am quite alone, lone,*
> *And I am quite alone.*

O please, o please come with me stay,
I'll hide thee out of sight.
I'll pleasure you beyond compare
And sleep with you all night, night,
And sleep with you all night.

It was nearly midnight when she pulled up in her driveway. She'd forgotten to leave on the outside lights and the batteries were dead in the little flashlight she kept in her purse. She picked her way carefully along the rock pathway, James leaping and barking in front of her. Molly and Ursa were nowhere to be seen. The sliver of new moon that hung low in the east over the dark mountains provided only faint illumination.

Suddenly she was aware of the unmistakable reek of skunk. The heavy, burning garlicky odor grew stronger as she climbed the steps to her porch. James's barking was frantic now and she could see the dark lump lying across her doormat. "Oh, shit," said Elizabeth.

The lump didn't move, but she was unwilling to step over it in the dark, so she retreated back down the steps and entered the house through the greenhouse door. After turning on the porch lights she cautiously opened the front door. The skunk was very dead; its head was partially gone, but there was little blood. The choking smell drifted through the doorway and James continued to bark.

She shut the door and went to change out of her good clothes before disposing of the little corpse. This body on the porch puzzled her: Molly and Ursa had been known to tangle with skunks before, but, to her knowledge, they had never killed one. And James was a known coward when it came to any animal larger than a mouse. *Oh, well,* she thought, *back to your rags, Cinderella,* and pulled on her oldest work clothes.

She found a flashlight, turned on all the outside lights, and headed for the toolshed. Armed with a long-handled shovel, she went to the edge of the garden. She swept the strong beam of the flashlight all around her. *If whatever killed this skunk is still around . . . or whoever . . .* Finally, reassured that she was alone, she set the light on the ground, still shining, and began to dig. James stayed close to her, barking and growling at some creature, real or imagined, on the mountainside. *He always barks at nothing,* she reminded herself, after stopping for the third time to shine the light in the direction James was looking.

When the hole seemed large enough, she got a pitchfork and gingerly transported the skunk to its grave, clumsily tucking the flashlight under her arm. She noticed how clean the dead creature's pelt was, not dirty and messy as it would have been if the dogs had dragged it home. *Curiouser and curiouser,* she thought, returning for the doormat, which she knew would never lose that skunk odor. James's barking grew more urgent and up on the mountainside she could hear Molly and Ursa baying.

She was very uneasy now as she picked up the doormat on the prongs of the pitchfork. A white oblong lying on the porch floor came into view. Leaning down to look at it, she saw that it was a postcard, blank side up. She was about to reach for the card when, high on the mountain, the baying turned into furious barking. The dogs had killed a raccoon once while she had watched helplessly and this sounded like the same sort of thing— angry growling and snarling as the dogs snapped at the cornered beast.

What if it isn't a raccoon? What if it's . . . She didn't finish the sentence, not even in her thoughts. Quickly she went into the house and grabbed Sam's big pistol from the drawer in her bedroom. *It's a Colt Python .357 Magnum,* he had told her. *I want you to learn how to use it.* She knew it was loaded. *Most people would be intimidated just seeing this gun in the hands of a wild-eyed woman,* Sam had said, *but in case that's not enough, we'll keep it loaded. I worry about you and the girls out here when I have to be away.*

"You're away for good, aren't you, Sam? But thanks for making me learn to use this thing." *Cold comfort,* she thought resentfully.

Turning off the outside lights, she hurried back to the porch and fired the gun into the air. *That will bring the dogs back,* she thought. *They're terrified of thunder and gunfire. And if it's a person instead of a coon out there, well, at least they'll know I'm armed.*

Her ears were ringing and she couldn't hear anything. But then she began to make out the sound of dogs running full tilt toward the house. Ursa and Molly bounded up the steps, panting heavily, tongues lolling out the sides of their slavering jaws. Keeping the gun behind her back and away from their gaze, she sniffed at each dog carefully, but neither carried the telltale skunk aroma.

"Okay, you girls, what's going on here?" she asked. They wagged noncommittally, whined, and nosed desperately at the front door. Elizabeth opened it for them and they crowded in, leaving muddy paw prints on the white card that lay in front of the doorway. Not even stopping to investigate their food bowls, they hurried toward the bedroom where, she knew, they would take refuge under the bed until the memory of the gunshot faded.

Still carrying the heavy gun, muzzle-up, Elizabeth returned to the porch and moved quietly to the far end where she could have an unobstructed view of the mountainside. Nothing but the usual night sounds met her ears, but high on the southern end of the ridge—*about where we border with Walter and Ollie,* she thought, the glow of a powerful flashlight swept briefly down the mountain then winked out.

She waited but the light didn't reappear. Finally, she went on with the task of burying the doormat. This time, she took the gun with her. She returned to the porch after one last careful perusal of the ridgeline. No sound. No lights.

Was it just a few hours ago that I was all dressed up and eating at Tapas? she wondered. She had almost forgotten the postcard, but as she opened the front door the light from within illuminated it. With a weary groan she picked it up and turned it over.

The picture was a reproduction of what looked like a colored woodcut. In the upper left-hand corner was the number 27. The image was a gruesomely realistic human heart on a yellow background. It was pierced by an arrow and blood dripped from the wound.

V-JULY 1901

*I don't know if hit was Mister Tomlin's treatin me so ill
that set my mind toward Levy. Maybe I'd already begun
to think about him that way when first I seen the sun
a-shinin on his golden hair. After that whippin, I didn't
talk with Levy no more and he quit comin down the road
that ran near our cabin, bringin the mare down the far ridge
instead. But I sometimes could have sight of him and hear
him whistlin a song as he went. Hit were always the same
one, Little Mathey Groves, that old love song about a
young wife who lays up with Little Mathey while her
man's away.*

*There hadn't been no more whippins for I had been
careful to do just like Mister Tomlin said, but seemed like
he was just bidin his time. Sometimes at night, when he'd
pull his belt off, he'd run it between his hands, feelin of it
and lookin at me. One time, when he was tryin to do it
again, he had me on my knees before him while he ran that
old belt real slow all over me. Hit didn't hurt but hit felt
nasty and put me in mind of a snake. He done other things
too and there come a time when I knowed that I didn't*

want to be his wife no more. Just the sound of him jinglin of them gold coins in his pockets like he always done was enough to make me bow up and want nothing to do with him.

I wished that I could talk to Aetha but she was gettin near her time and couldn't climb the hill to come to see me no more. And I couldn't go see her for Mister Tomlin had forbid me from goin anywhere but down to the homeplace ever mornin to fetch some milk. I knowed it weren't no good to say nothing to Romarie; she'd likely just tell me that I'd made my bed and now must lie in hit. I could just see how she'd look when she said it too and knowed I wouldn't never tell her about how Mister Tomlin done me with the belt. Not just the whippin but the other.

I studied on hit some and the next day when Mister Tomlin had gone off about his business, I walked down the hill to find my daddy. He was a-leanin on the wooden gate that opens into the little pasture just above the chicken house and he was a-watchin a great red bull with a ring in his nose. What went with old Abraham? I asked, and Daddy smiled and said, Got rid of him. This is a fine pure-blooded Hereford bull. I marveled that my daddy would have laid out the money for such an animal but didn't say nothing for I had been noticin just the past little bit that he was spendin money like one thing. Rom and Clytie both had wore new dresses to church last Sunday and Rom was talkin big about how Daddy had ordered a Buncombe Beauty Buggy all the way from T. S. Morrison's in Asheville.

Hit took me a time but at last I told my daddy that I found Mister Tomlin hateful and that he whipped me with his belt for the least thing. I told my daddy that I didn't *want to be married no more, but he just laughed and said I'd been bought and paid for and that I had ought to get back home and mind my husband or he'd take a strap to me hisself.*

Little Sylvie, says he, don't you know hit's the law that you got to stay with yore husband? Now get what you come for and get on back home.

Hit was some days atter this that Mister Tomlin set off up-river on a timber-buyin trip. I had been studyin on what my daddy had said about the law. I minded two years back when Daddy and the Paynes couldn't agree about the line fence, Daddy went to Ransom and talked to Lawyer Platt to find out the right of hit. So I laid out to do the same. Though I had never been to Ransom, I knowed that the train stopped at Gudger's Stand around seven of a mornin. You could get on and ride to Ransom and they was a train you could ride back in the evenin. I hadn't been to Gudger's Stand but only a few times, when Daddy would take us girls. Hit was reckoned to be a rough place with fights and drinkin goin on most nights but I figgered to be well away afore nightfall.

I rose in the black dark and dressed in my Sunday clothes. I took a basket with some biscuits and a jar of water and set out down the road. They was a half moon and I could feel my way along pretty good, but when I got near Daddy's house I had to leave the path and make my way through the fields so that the house dogs wouldn't hear me and set up a commotion. Some cows and the new bull was grazin nearby and as I seen the shape of that big creature, movin quiet in the moonlight, it come to me for the first time that, along with that fine English shotgun, Mister Tomlin had give Daddy the money that had bought the pureblood bull and my sisters' new dresses and the new buggy. It come to me that my daddy hadn't sold nare land nor timber to Mister Tomlin; what he had sold was me and neither him nor Rom nor Clytie was like to want to give that money back. Bought and paid for was what he had said.

Hit was three miles to Gudger's Stand and the sky was beginnin to lighten as I followed along the wagon road that runs by Ridley Branch down to the river. About halfway to the bridge is the road to Fate and Aetha's place. Up on the hillside I seen a light in their cabin and thought should I go talk to Aetha. But I couldn't tell my story afore Fate and all them young uns and I knowed if I tarried much longer I'd miss the train to Ransom.

When I come to the bridge I could see that the train hadn't got in yet. They was a little gang of people waitin there and I dreaded that someone amongst them might know me and ask what was I about. So I set my basket down and tarried on the bridge, lookin over the rail and tryin to decide what I would say. Standin in the water below me was a great tall gray bird with a long sharp beak. He was as still as if he was carved out of wood, just a-watchin the water at his feet. Then all to once he darted out that cruel beak and I seen a flash of silver as he brung up a fish and swallered it.

I looked at the river, runnin so fast there beneath the bridge. Teacher had showed us on a great map how a flatboat could go down this same river into Tennessee, on to

Alabama, back to Tennessee and Kentucky all the way to the Ohio River and from there to the mighty Mississippi and right smack down to New Orleans. And in New Orleans, she told us, you can get on a ship that can take you right around this world.

It seemed a marvel to me that this same water I was lookin at would travel so far while I stayed put. I thought how I would like to go on one of them boats and see all them places. Just then I heared the train whistle blowin and seen the locomotive roundin the bend. I quit my loaferin and grabbed up my basket to run to where the people was waitin.

For a mercy, didn't none of em know me and I watched how they did as they got on the train. I had taken some coins from Mister Tomlin's box where he keeps papers and such and I gave mine to the man in the black suit just like I seen the others doin. I set down by a woman with double chins who smiled friendly-like at me and I put my basket on my knee. The fat woman asked where I lived and who were my people and I told her but I didn't mention no husband. I had taken off the ruby finger-ring and left it wrapped in a rag and stuck in a little hole in the feather tick, for I had come to purely hate the feel of that thing on my hand.

When the train got goin I was some scared for it ran so fast and took the curves so quick that I was fearful of a crash but Miz Honeycutt (for that was the name of the fat woman) seemed just as calm and didn't even hold on.

So atter a time I begun to enjoy myself and was sorry when the train pulled up at the depot in Ransom. Miz Honeycutt told me she had come in to have a tooth pulled at the dentist and that she would see me on the trip back. *Iffen I live*, she said, but she laughed and winked when she said it.

I walked along with her down the street into Ransom. I have never seen so many people and horses and mules and wagons. They was buildings two and three stories high down both sides of the street. Between two of the buildings was a narrow stairway and a sign shaped like a big tooth hung out over it. The words on hit said *Dr. Adams: Painless Extractions*. Miz Honeycutt said that was where she was bound for and bid me stay clear of the far end of town. *That's where them old whisky wagons come*, she said, and a lot of no account rascals.

I walked on down the street, lookin in the windows of the stores and just marvelin at all the things they was for sale. One store had a sign tellin about Snuffles, the famous catarrh cure, and there was another sign for Thedford's Black Draught. I knowed about that for Rom use to make me and Clytie swaller that nasty-tastin stuff for a tonic every spring. They was some bolts of cloth too and one was the prettiest gray satin-striped dimity you ever seen. They was ladies' capes and fascinators and a big travelin trunk.

Then I saw in gold letters on the glass of an upstairs window: *James Vance Platt: Law Office*. There was another narrow stairway and an arrow on the wall sayin *Law Office*. I took a real deep breath and begun to climb the stairs.

Lawyer Platt knowed who I was right off when I named my daddy. When I told him that I was married and didn't want to be, he looked surprised. *How old are you, Miz . . . ?* he asked.

Hit's Tomlin, I said, and I'm thirteen. Lawyer Platt pressed his lips together and leaned back in his funny wooden chair. Hit was on little wheels and he could rock back and forth and turn hit ever whichaway. He just set there in front of his big wooden desk that was all heaped with papers and rocked back and forth in that chair.

Hit squeaked awful bad and I was about to ask had he tried puttin a little lard on hit when he said, Miz Tomlin, the law says you're old enough to marry if your father agrees to it. What makes you think that you want a divorce?

Because I don't like bein married to him, I said, and because he whupped me with his belt. Hit didn't seem fitten to tell him the other reasons—all the nasty ways Mister Tomlin had. Seemed to me not likin him ought to be enough.

Lawyer Platt straightened up in his chair and reached for a big black book he had on a shelf by his desk. Miz Tomlin, says he, do you know what Paul says about wives being subject to their husbands?

Back at the depot I was setting on a bench and lookin at a sign across the way that said Wanted, Country Produce of All Kinds. Poultry, Eggs, Corn, & Wheat. Top Prices for Roots & Herbs when Properly Dried. Then what do I see a-comin along the street, hangin on a man's arm but Miz Honeycutt. She kindly sags and staggers as she walks and I think maybe she's been at them whisky wagons she warned me about. But the man who's helpin her along don't look drunk and he steers her over to where I'm a-settin. Miz

Honeycutt's eyes is half-closed and her face is all swole up on one side.

Are you the young lady who sat with Miz Honeycutt on the train? the man asks real polite and I say that I am. I'm Doc Adams, says he. I gave Miz Honeycutt some laudanum to help her bear the pain of the extraction but she's slow to shake off the effects. Her husband's meeting her at Gudger's Stand. Would you be so good as to sit with her and make sure she gets off there? I'm fearful she'll sleep all the way to Tennessee.

Miz Honeycutt did sleep most of the way back with her head right there on my shoulder. She snored some and there was a kind of sweet smell on her breath, but something sweeter than whisky. Hit put me in mind of Mister Tomlin and that I weren't no closer to gettin shed of him. I thought about that old Paul too, and wondered how hit was that he'd come to be a saint.

Mister Honeycutt was waitin at Gudger's Stand and me and the man in the black suit helped Miz Honeycutt down off the train. Her husband thanked us and wrapped one arm around his wife, helpin her up into their wagon just as gentle as if she was made of glass. He even give her a kiss on the side of her face that weren't all swole up.

They drove off up toward Dewell Hill and I thought how happy that they looked. Then I took up my basket and started for the bridge. Hit were near six but hit don't get dark afore nine so I weren't lookin to have no trouble gettin home. I was the onliest one of the folks off the train to be headin across the bridge for the rest was all goin in the stores there at Gudger's Stand or up the road the Honeycutts took.

Under the near part of the bridge I see they's three fellers all huddled up together and passin around a fruit jar. I don't know none of them and they look kindly rough, but I hurry on and start across the bridge. I try to walk quiet but my boots on the bridge planks makes a hollow noise and by the time I get to the middle of the bridge I look back to see them followin atter me.

I walk a little faster and they speed up too. I hear them laughin and sayin things like, I'd sure like me some of that, boys. I think about turnin back and headin for the stores where there's other people, but I don't see how I'd get past these three. I think I'll hurry on to the other side. Once off this bridge, thinks I, I'll find some rocks and rock them offen me.

I get to the other side while they are still laughin and punchin at one another. I quick step down to the water's edge where they's a world of smooth river rocks and I fill my basket with as many as it'll hold. Good-sized ones, as big as my fist.

Before I get but a little ways down the branch I hear them comin. They're half runnin and they're not laughin now. I seen her first, hollers one. Shitfire, calls another, hit'll be who catches her first that counts. They was comin up on me fast and they had that look that dogs get when they gang up on something small and helpless. The one who was in front was well ahead of the others and when he got in range I let fly.

The rock hit him on his ear and he let out a great howl but he kept a-comin. You'll pay dear for that, you bitch, he hollers. I flung another and hit went wide but the next one caught him on the knee and he went down. The others kept comin and spread apart on the road to where when I threw a rock at one, the other would slip closer. They was better at dodgin than their friend had been and I was down to but one rock.

When they grabbed me and flung me down, I kept aholt of that rock. I meant to mash the nose of at least one of them but all a sudden they's the sound of a big horse cloppin along and I look up to see Levy. He's got a pistol in his hand and he says, Boys, you best get on out of here, right quick.

They pull me up and step back to their friend who's still a-settin in the road, holdin his knee and a-moanin. We was just funnin with her, says one. No harm done, says t'other, and they haul their friend offen the ground and make for the bridge.

Levy set there atop that great mare a-lookin down at me. What are you doin here, Little Sylvie? he asks me.

I been to Ransom, says I.

He looked at my basket, empty but for the water jar. Where's your husband? says he.

Off buyin timber, says I. He'll not be home for three days.

Levy set there like as if he was makin up his mind about something. Then he says, I'm on my way to your daddy's place anyhow. I'm workin for him these next few days—sleepin in his barn and eatin at his table. I best take you home. He reached out his hand and I grabbed hit with my left and heisted my skirts a little with the other. Then I set my left foot atop hisn and he swung me up behind him. There weren't no saddle and I had to wrap my arms tight around him to keep from slippin offen the mare's broad back.

Levy clicked his tongue and the mare set off at a walk up the branch. I was breathin fast and my heart was beatin so hard that I thought Levy must feel hit against his back. His shirt was damp with the sweat of a July day but hit smelled sweet to me. I laid my cheek against his back and felt his muscles tighten up. Little Sylvie, he said in a voice that sounded kindly strangled like, Little Sylvie, what are you doin?

Them fellers scared me bad, Levy, I said. I feel all swimmie-headed.

He didn't say nothing more for a time and we rode on. We didn't see nary a soul for at that time of day most folks was havin their supper or tendin to their stock. I pressed up close to Levy and I could feel his heart thumpin almost like mine. The mare's back rubbed between my legs and my knees begun to feel as weak as water. I wished that hit was a hundred miles we had to travel instead of just two.

He let me off before we come to Daddy's house so as I could slip along the path through the woods. But by the time I unwrapped my arms from around his waist and got down from off the mare, I was on fire for Levy Johnson. And when hit was black dark and I was settin out on the big rock in front of the cabin, a-listenin to the crickets callin and watchin the lightnin bugs risin above the meadow, hit didn't surprise me none to see a black shape come a-walkin quiet and careful the same path I'd followed. He's a-whistlin that Little Mathey Groves song and I says, Hey, Levy Johnson. Hey.

CHAPTER 13
Déjà Vu All Over Again
(Sunday)

The NEXT MORNING ELIZABETH SAT AT HER DIN-
ing table looking at the ugly red and yellow
postcard, which she had propped against a pot
of deep purple African violets. She was sipping
her coffee and pondering the possible significance of the
card and its lurid image when she heard Ben clattering
up the basement stairs, the shortest route into her house
from his cabin.

"Morning, Aunt E. Any coffee left?" Without waiting
for an answer he headed into the kitchen, calling back
over his shoulder, "So how was your date last night?"

"Not a date, Ben," she replied serenely. "Dinner with
a friend. And it was . . . interesting. He may be able to
give me some help with the Cletus thing."

Ben reappeared, a coffee mug in one hand and a heap-
ing bowl of granola in the other. He started for his usual
place at the other end of the table. "A late valentine?" he
asked. "A little gruesome for my tender young taste
but, hey—"

"I was hoping you knew something about it," Elizabeth
said. "I found it under the doormat last night. No telling
when it was put there, though probably not too long ago

because it was fairly clean until the dogs walked on it." She picked the postcard up by its corner and showed Ben the blank side. "There's no message written on it. I thought maybe you might have dropped it."

"Not me," said Ben, deeply involved with his granola. "Must have come from one of your admirers."

"There was also," she continued, ignoring his remark, "a dead skunk on top of the doormat. And I'm reasonably sure the dogs didn't put it there because they didn't have any skunk smell on them. Were you around last night? Did you hear anything unusual—anything at all?"

Ben paused, a spoonful of granola halfway to his mouth. "I thought I caught a whiff of skunk when I came over this morning but last night, no, I didn't notice anything out of the ordinary. I was in bed with earphones on and I had the music on pretty loud, you know."

She knew. When Ben played his favorite bluegrass music, it was generally so loud that he'd likely be unaware of anything short of a tank crashing through the walls of his cabin. He obviously hadn't heard the gunshot that had brought her dogs back to the house.

"I think someone was creeping around in the woods," she said, and went on to describe the events of the previous night, ending with ". . . and there was a light up at the ridgeline."

"Man, that's weird," Ben said. "I guess it could have been someone hunting out of season, but that doesn't explain the skunk or this thing." He nodded at the postcard.

A thought occurred to Elizabeth. "I didn't show you what I found on my car Friday," she said, leaving the table and stepping out onto the front porch. She retrieved the red bumper sticker and thorny twig from the old watering can and brought them to the table.

"I was walking through town with Manuel," she explained, "and we were obviously friendly. Then I gave him a ride. We stopped for groceries and went in the store together. That has to be when someone stuck this . . . this thing on the back of my car. I must have shoved the groceries in the side door, because I didn't see it till I got home."

Ben poked at the sticker with a disdainful finger. "What's the quote? I'm sure you looked it up."

"Oh, just angry old Bible stuff about going in to other nations and snares and traps and perishing off the land and thorns in the eyes. It makes me furious. I assume it's the work of those militia creeps we were talking about."

"Probably," Ben said, looking from the bumper sticker to the bleeding heart on the postcard. "So, are you thinking that the skunk and the heart are from them, too? That maybe it was them up on the ridge?"

"I don't know. It seems like a lot of trouble to go to just because I gave a Mexican guy a ride. There must be some other explanation. . . . I just don't know what it is right now. And another thing, what do you know about a Starshine Community over on Bear Tree?"

"That bunch of New Age wackos? Not much. They're supposed to be heavy into organic farming, but when our local growers group approached them about joining, they said they weren't interested. They never show up at any of the regional farmers' markets—I don't have any idea what they're up to. Maybe growing organic weed." Ben laughed as he took his empty bowl and cup into the kitchen. He whistled the theme from *The Twilight Zone* as he rinsed his dishes and headed out the front door.

Elizabeth cleared away her own breakfast dishes and went into the little office where the computer was. Investigations into Cletus's death were on hold till Hawkins had talked to the medical examiner. Right now, she thought, she would find out more about the Starshine Community. She planned to call Laurel around noon when her daughter was likely to be getting up after a late night of tending bar. Laurel, with her wide range of acquaintances in Asheville as well as Marshall County, would probably know something about the star children. Till then Elizabeth decided to check out the Starshine Community's Web page and see what that might reveal.

The page opened with a solid black screen. A many-colored starburst appeared in the center, small at first, then blossoming into myriads of tiny lights that swirled hypnotically before resolving into a menu. Elizabeth chose an option that would add sound, clicked on *About Starshine Community,* and sat back to watch and listen.

Another starburst and Polaris's head, with riveting turquoise eyes and flowing white hair, appeared at its center. Ethereal sounds, of the type she had heard called "space music," began to drift from two speakers, and Polaris's voice, resonant and enthralling, began. *"Welcome, starchild. Welcome, seeker. The heavens in their circuits have brought you to us. Endlessly evolving, endlessly revolving—"* Here Polaris's face vanished and the starburst began to form an eddying vortex. Elizabeth found herself staring fixedly into it as the music swelled all around her. The voice continued, *"This is the first step in your long journey to your primogenesis. . . ."*

The screen dissolved to a busy street scene, crowded sidewalks and scowling faces. One figure, a young woman, stood a little apart with a look of bewilderment on her face. She was surrounded by a barely visible silver aura.

"Many of you have felt the signs—a feeling of alienation, a sense of déjà vu. *Many of you, as children, have wondered if your parents* were *your parents, so unlike them you were."*

The urban scene dissolved to an idyllic country setting. A beautiful orchard, trees heavy with pink and white blossoms, lush green grass sprinkled with tiny white starlike flowers, and a group of young women sitting in a circle, hands cupped palm over palm, eyes closed in meditation. With a shock of recognition Elizabeth realized that she was looking at the same orchard she had driven by only a few days ago, possibly even the same young women, though not so obviously pregnant. *Like the man said, déjà vu all over again,* she thought and waited for the voice-over.

"If you seek to discover your true place in the universe, if you would reclaim your true heritage among the numberless stars, if you would rejoin the sidereal family and seize your birthright . . ."

Here the pastoral image changed to a shot of the night sky, but a night sky rarely seen by modern man. This was the pure sky, unsullied by man-made light, the sky that one might see in the middle of the ocean or a vast desert, a sky crowded with stars like a thick scattering of sand. Phosphorescent yellow-orange letters swooped across the screen and lined up to read "Come home to Starshine Community," just as Polaris's voice offered the same invitation. The glowing screen changed to a businesslike list of addresses and phone numbers and other contact information.

Elizabeth clicked her way back to the menu. *Starshine Retreats; Informational Weekend Workships; The Farm; The Studios; The Crèche.* Methodically working her way through the information she learned that Starshine Community offered weeklong retreats for "those starchildren who must, for a time, remain in the world." These retreats were offered "as refreshment for the spirit and as a chance for the starchild to continue his or her evolution." The weekend workshops for "seekers" were "a time for the sincere seeker to evaluate his or her place in the cosmos and to determine his or her current stage of evolution."

Ah, mused Elizabeth, *in just one short weekend, you too can know your place in the cosmos. Quick workers, these star people. I wonder what Cletus thought about them. Polaris talked as if he'd been there often.* She noted, as the prices for a weekend workshop scrolled into view, that enlightenment was not cheap. Six hundred and seventy-five dollars, even with organic vegetarian meals and a "rotation" with Polaris, whatever that was, seemed high. *Could Janie afford something like that?* she wondered. *What do they charge to* live *at the community?*

She clicked impatiently through the rest of the menu. There was the organic farm "with growing times attuned to the sidereal calendar"; the studios, which produced, it appeared, a wealth of airbrushed "otherworldly" art, all for sale; and the crèche, which was not a day-care center, as she had assumed, but rather, what used to be called a home for unwed mothers. *A little something for everyone,* she thought. *But what's the attraction for Janie?*

She glanced at the clock on the wall, noting that it wasn't quite time to call Laurel. A thought struck her: If she could get in touch with, what was his name, a yuppie-sounding name—Trey, no, Trent Woodsomething—the young man she'd given a ride out of the Starshine Community, maybe he could tell her more. She grabbed the phone book and quickly found the number for River Runners.

After a short wait, she was speaking with Debbie, one of the co-owners of the popular local rafting company. Elizabeth explained who she was and what she wanted.

Debbie paused a minute then said, "You're Ben's aunt,

the lady with the herb farm, up on Ridley Branch, right?" then without waiting for more information went on, "Trent Woodbern isn't here anymore. He was planning to stay through the summer—one of our guides broke a leg rock climbing and Trent was going to fill in. Anyway, Trent did a couple of trips, and then some weird guys came in . . . let me see . . . I think it was Thursday . . . asking about him. Trent saw their car pull up and told me to say he wasn't here. He ducked into the back room and stayed there till the guys left. It was too weird. As soon as they drove away, he came out and he was seriously freaked—shaking all over. He told me he was sorry but he couldn't finish out the season; he would have to leave immediately."

"Do you know where he went? Can you tell me how to get in touch with him?" Elizabeth asked.

"He left me his e-mail address, that's all. Said something about no one could trace him by that." Debbie hesitated, then said, "I guess it wouldn't hurt to let you have that. I mean, I know who you are and everything. Your daughter Rosemary used to babysit my kids when she was in high school."

"That's right, I remember now. It's been a while. But back to Trent, Debbie, do you remember what kind of car they were driving—those people who scared him so?"

"I sure do. It was a brand-new silver Navigator. Wretched thing took up almost two places in our parking lot. I don't know why they don't make those monster SUVs illegal."

Elizabeth scribbled down the e-mail address that Debbie gave her, thanked her for the information, and hung up. She glanced at the clock—still not noon. She punched the computer On button and went to the e-mail page. With a feeling of optimistic doubt she typed a brief message: *Trent, I'm the woman who gave you a ride out of the Starshine Community. Debbie at River Runners knows who I am and gave me your e-mail address. I have some questions to ask about the community, as the daughter of a friend is planning to join. Please reply. Elizabeth Goodweather.*

She keyed Send, hopefully flinging the message out into cyberspace. *Like throwing a coin in a wishing well,* she thought, *or a message in a bottle into the ocean.*

Just as she turned off the computer, the telephone at her elbow rang. "Hi, Mum, 'sme."

"Hey, Laurel, I was getting ready to call you. Tell me, do you know anything about a place on Bear Tree called the Starshine Community?"

"The baby place?" Laurel asked. "I've just heard that it's a really awesome place to have a baby—they do that underwater birthing thing and they have midwives and they're real supportive for single women. Why do you want to know? *You're* not, oh, that's silly, I mean, you couldn't be . . ."

"No, dear," Elizabeth replied. "That *would* be a miracle on several levels. It's about the daughter of a friend . . ." It took a few minutes to explain about Phillip Hawkins and his daughter Janie, and by the time Elizabeth had finished Laurel's attention was fully engaged.

"So what does this guy look like, Mum, this cop?"

"Ah . . ." Elizabeth considered the question. "Danny DeVito, but tall? Or at least taller than me. But pay attention, Laurel, I don't know that his daughter is pregnant—I think she just wants to join the community."

"Weird," intoned Laurel. "I know I've seen literature about that place somewhere . . . the women's center maybe. Anyway, a guy I know said that his ex-girlfriend had moved to Starshine almost a year ago. He was really bitter, claimed she'd been seduced by the head guru or whatever out there." There was a pause. "I don't think he meant that literally but—"

"Laurel, could you find out more about that girl? I'd really like to know if she's still there."

"I'll try, Mum. Rolf has a studio down on the river. I'll see what I can find out. But what I called about was the revival. I've got to see John the Baptizer! Did I tell you—he does his paintings *during* the revival meetings—while he's preaching? That's why they have that terrific spontaneity. The first one's Wednesday; will you go with me?"

"Oh, sweetie, Wednesday is Cletus's funeral. I don't think I can handle a funeral *and* a revival in the same day. But, listen, Birdie's cousin told me that this John the Baptizer was going to speak at the graveside—why don't you come with me to the service? It's at two. And Birdie would really appreciate it," Elizabeth added shamelessly.

"Well," said Laurel slowly, "I guess I should. For Birdie and for Cletus. But then you come with me to the revival on Thursday—no, Friday. I have to work Thursday night." There was a pause and she added in a serious tone, "Maybe I'll get saved," and waited a beat for Elizabeth's reaction. When there was none, she tried again, "Or maybe you will. Like it used to say on that barn—'Get Right with God.'"

The rest of the day was spent in pleasant garden tasks—a little light weeding, deadheading spent daffodils, setting out annuals. Elizabeth planted a lavish display of crimson, coral, and shell-pink impatiens among a lush swath of soft green ferns that stretched out under an old pear tree. *Instant gratification,* she thought, and after watering the plants well, hauled the hose down to her herb garden. Here she tucked in bright yellow and orange marigolds next to purple basil, standing back to admire the gaudy effect. Between the gray-green shapes of the budding lavender, self-sown raspberry-tinted foxgloves were already throwing up their elegant spires.

She always kept the Sabbath in this way—no loud weed-eater or mower, only those bits of gardening that allowed her plenty of time to pause and appreciate the beauty of her surroundings. Sitting on the east-facing slope that was part of her front yard, she imagined, as she had often before, that she could feel the world turning—that she was sitting in the front car of some immense roller coaster whose tracks ran along the earth's latitudes. She closed her eyes and felt herself rushing eastward in a precipitous descent. Then she concentrated on the warm ground beneath her, feeling that invisible roots were holding her in place against the dizzying spin and that she was drawing up strength through those same roots.

"And if you don't sound as New Age as the worst of them," she said aloud, emerging from her reverie and getting slowly to her feet. "You'll be journeying in your astral body if you don't watch it, Elizabeth Goodweather."

It was after nine when Phillip Hawkins called. He spoke with ill-contained excitement as he apologized for calling so late. "I just now heard from R.L.—you remember, my buddy the medical examiner in Chapel Hill? Looks like your Miss Birdie may be right. They took another look at the lung tissue and . . . are you ready for this? There's a lot of pathology jargon, but what it boils down to is that the water in the lungs is not entirely consistent with the residual water in the mouth and ears. In other words, maybe Cletus didn't drown in the river."

CHAPTER 14
WHISTLING IN THE DARK
(SUNDAY AND THEN WEDNESDAY)

S O THE SHERIFF'LL HAVE TO START INVESTIGATING,"
Elizabeth exclaimed. "If this proves that he didn't
drown in the river—"

"Hold on," Hawkins interrupted. "R.L. was
very careful to say that this didn't *prove* anything. It
was—how'd the report go? Anomalous something or
other . . . borderline findings well within certain para-
meters. Anyway, the sheriff's office already has the information and it's up to them how or even *if* they want to
act on it. What R.L. said comes down to this: there isn't
definite proof that Cletus drowned somewhere else, but
it isn't totally impossible. And by the way, they'll be taking a look at that other guy who was just pulled out of
the river, what was his name, Dewey something? If his
case shows the same anomalies, Blaine'll have to get his
ass in gear."

Elizabeth chewed on this information for several days. A
phone conversation with the sheriff was as frustrating as
her visit to his office. Yes, he was aware of the findings
of the medical examiner. Was Mrs. Goodweather aware

that medical examiners weren't always the wonder-workers portrayed in certain popular detective fiction? And how, by the way, did Mrs. Goodweather come to be so familiar with the medical examiner's report?

As she was unwilling to explain about Hawkins and his buddy R.L., Elizabeth thanked Sheriff Blaine for his time and hung up. She pondered her next move—Should she tell Birdie about this and get her to demand a more thorough autopsy? *No, Miss Birdie's had to wait long enough for the funeral. The facts, such as they are, are there; if I can find Cletus's shotgun and it's not in the river, maybe that'll convince Blaine to take this seriously.*

A line from a Dorothy L. Sayers book came to mind: "When you know how, you know who." *Okay, if Cletus was drowned somewhere else, where might that have been? Most of the branches in the mountains are way too shallow to drown a man in, and little pools like that one at Walter and Ollie's are uncommon. I wonder if there's water on the militia place?* Suddenly she pictured the flumes and pond of the trout farm in Little Man Holler and again saw the wild figure of old man Tyler bursting out of his door with his shotgun, calling out the name of the now deceased Dewey Shotwell.

Elizabeth, Ben, and Laurel sat in a pew toward the back of the funeral home's chapel. Miss Birdie's friends and relations from all over the county as well as a few from out of state had filled the room to overflowing. At the front of the room, surrounded by what the florist had called "floral tributes," was the metallic bronze casket containing the mortal remains of Cletus Gentry. The grim gray profile of his head was just visible, surrounded by silky white padding. A somber melody wafted from a hidden organ, and out of an adjoining room came a dark-suited, sleek-haired man who could have been nothing but a funeral director. He was ushering Miss Birdie, supported on her other side by Dorothy, to her seat in the front pew.

Miss Birdie, in a dark blue dress, was trembling and dabbing at her eyes with a crumpled pink tissue. All the matter-of-fact acceptance of her son's death that she had previously exhibited was gone. *It's almost as if a show of grief is part of the ritual,* Elizabeth thought. *Not like the funerals back home; a stiff upper lip, that's the formula that I grew up with.* Elizabeth had allowed herself no public tears at Sam's memorial service, only a lump in her throat that had made speech almost impossible. *And at least there was just the plain wooden box with his ashes—not a body.*

Elizabeth had carefully avoided "viewing the body" on the previous night. After a quick word with Miss Birdie and Dorothy, she had signed the visitation book and made her escape. But most of the friends and neighbors who were there had gathered in convivial little groups around the casket, gazing at Cletus and chatting with one another. The comment "Don't he look natural?" had been heard over and over. Elizabeth had doubted that he looked anything of the sort.

"Mum," Laurel murmured now in her ear, "is that him . . . on the far right?" Four solemn-faced men had taken their seats in the chairs on the raised platform. One was very young and wore cowboy boots with his ill-fitting new blue suit. Two were men in their late seventies; one had on an aged black suit that had been fashionable when Eisenhower was President; the other wore black trousers and a long-sleeved white shirt. After a moment Elizabeth recognized him as Pastor Briggs.

The fourth man, the one on the far right, was the man she had last seen at the foot of Walter and Ollie Johnson's road, the evangelist who called himself John the Baptizer. He, too, wore black trousers and a white shirt.

"That's the one," Elizabeth whispered to her daughter.

One by one, the first three preachers gave their "messages." It was always the same. Believe, and you go to heaven; doubt, and you go to hell. Each assured the congregation that Cletus was in heaven and warned their listeners that "we know not when we too may be called." Behind the pulpit, a man and a woman harmonized in a song that told of golden streets in glory.

Finally the funeral director came forward and signaled for the congregation to rise. Laurel tugged at her mother's sleeve and whispered urgently, "Mum, John the Baptizer hasn't spoken! I thought you said—"

"At the graveside," hissed Elizabeth. Pew by pew, the congregation was being directed to file to the front and past the open casket. She noted that the four preachers had lined up just beyond the casket, in a kind of receiving line, and were shaking hands with the mourners as they passed by on their way back to their pews. *When in Rome* . . . thought Elizabeth and filed up to the front, following Ben and Laurel.

Cletus was dressed in a white shirt and new overalls and his hands were folded over a Bible. His face was a waxen mask. Elizabeth tried to think of the living Cletus, whose shy smile and twinkling eyes had delighted her and her family for so many years. Then she was past the casket, and shaking hands with the preachers. "Thank you for the message," she could hear an elderly woman ahead of them saying, and "Thank you for the message," Laurel was saying to the young preacher. Elizabeth contented herself with a nod and a soft thank-you and followed the others back to the pew.

Now that the congregation was seated again, the fu-

neral director moved to the pew where Birdie and
Dorothy were sitting with Birdie's two ancient sisters-in-
law. The two old ladies, Cletus's maiden aunts, painfully
made their way to the casket, supported by the funeral
director. As they stood looking down on their nephew's
corpse, one of them uttered a low wail, a kind of whooping sound. The other joined in on a higher note and then
both turned away, wiping their eyes and keening softly.

And then the sleek funeral director was bending over
Miss Birdie, offering her his arm. She got up slowly and,
with Dorothy at her side, was escorted to the open casket. She stood there quietly for a moment, then reached
out a trembling hand and cried, "Oh, Cletus, I should of
gone first! Hit weren't right!" She began to make the
same whooping sound her sisters-in-law had and continued to call out, "Cletus, Cletus, I can't go on without you!"

Birdie sagged against her cousin; only Dorothy's stout
arm held her up. The oldest preacher stepped up, laid a
hand on Birdie's shoulder, and said, "Now, Sister Gentry,
hit'll not be long till you're with your boy again," and at
that it seemed to Elizabeth that Birdie's whoops grew
louder.

"I thought you said Miss Birdie wasn't taking Cletus's
death that hard," commented Ben as he turned their car
to join the motor procession to the little cemetery on a
hill overlooking the river. "Didn't you say she had been
worried about what would happen to him if she died
first?"

Elizabeth was jolted out of her reverie. The chant,
"When you know how, you know who," had been running nonstop in her mind. She considered briefly, then

said, "Birdie was upset at the thought that his death might not have been an accident, but, yes, she did say that it might have been best that he went first." She thought a moment and added, "I know Birdie misses Cletus and I guess she feels that this is the time and place for her to show it."

Laurel stretched restlessly and began to fiddle with the black scarf that confined her coppery bright dreadlocks into a semidiscreet ponytail. "Doesn't John the Baptizer have mysterious eyes?" she said dreamily. "I can't wait to hear him speak."

The pallbearers inched their way up the hill to the open grave, followed by the mourners in straggling twos and threes. Miss Birdie and her family members took their places on the chairs under the dark green canopy at the graveside, and John the Baptizer began reciting the Twenty-third Psalm in a low voice. The familiar words washed over them and Elizabeth felt the answering prickle of tears.

When he came to the end, "and I will dwell in the house of the Lord forever," John the Baptizer studied the casket, now mercifully closed, and repeated the words, "He leadeth me beside the still waters." His pale gaze swept the crowd and his voice grew louder as he began to speak in the hypnotic preacher's chant with the catch of breath at the end of each phrase. *"And Cletus walked beside the living water and it was the water of life . . . He went down to death but he will rise again . . . . will rise to glory incorruptible. Yea, I say unto you that every valley shall be filled . . . and every mountain and hill shall be brought low . . . yea, all flesh shall see the salvation of God. And all by the grace of the living God and the living water. . . ."*

The heads of the assembled people were beginning to nod in unison, and the pale-eyed preacher continued, mesmerizing them all with his eerily compelling gaze. *"And I saw an angel with great wings of mother-of-pearl . . . and the feathers of the wings were tipped with the deep blue of the sea and the fiery golden red of the sun. . . . And the angel came down and lifted up the soul and carried it away like a tiny sleeping child . . . And the mother shall weep for her child. . . ."*

And Miss Birdie *was* weeping, but the cleansing tears rolled down a face that was lifted up and shining with a transcendent peace. John the Baptizer approached her and, laying his strong hands on her shoulders, said, *"The revelator tells us 'They shall hunger no more, neither thirst anymore . . . for the Lamb which is in the midst of the throne shall feed them . . . and shall lead them unto living fountains of water . . . and God shall wipe away all tears from their eyes.' . . . Bless His powerful, wonderful, lovely Name."*

"That was some funeral!" exclaimed Ben as he and Elizabeth and Laurel sat down to an early supper of bread and soup back at Full Circle Farm. "Did you see how Miss Birdie looked, there at the end of the graveside service? She was joyful, almost . . ." he sought for the word, ". . . almost exuberant."

Elizabeth was thinking of the dull pain that she had nursed since Sam's death, but she smiled and said, "There's something to be said for an unquestioning, simple faith, I guess."

Laurel cut another slice of bread and buttered it lavishly. "So according to them, Cletus is in heaven because he was baptized. Not because he was a good person but just because of being baptized, right?"

"I think that's the belief," said Elizabeth, "but—"

"But Cletus wasn't baptized," objected Laurel. "He told me so a long time ago. One of my friends at school had gotten baptized and I was asking him and Miss Birdie about it. He said he was scared to go under the water and Birdie told him that he didn't have to because he was one of God's innocents, or something like that."

"Poor guy," said Ben. "He *was* that. But what I want to know, Aunt E, is who would have wanted Cletus dead? I mean, if Miss Birdie's right and that medical examiner's results are right, someone must have drowned him somewhere else and thrown his body in the river. Who would have anything against Cletus? Unless . . ." he put down his soup spoon with a splash, ". . . unless it *was* an accident and somebody got scared—"

"Or Cletus saw something he shouldn't have," Laurel chimed in enthusiastically. "Like maybe at that militia place."

"Oh, yeah." Ben nodded. "There're lots of stories floating around about those guys. I've been asking different people, Aunt E, and I found out that they're supposed to have something they call 'night games.' Something like hide-and-seek but the one who's It is . . . ah . . . expendable. Probably that's just a rumor, though," he added, seeing Elizabeth's horrified expression.

"Or maybe Miss Birdie did it," said Laurel quietly.

"Laurel!" snapped Elizabeth. "How can you say—"

"Oh, Mum, I'm not really serious. But look at it this way. Miss Birdie was worried about what would happen to Cletus when she was gone. And now, by her beliefs anyway, he's gone to the best place there is."

"Give me a break, Laur," groaned Ben. "Even if she

would do something like that, do you think she's physi-
cally capable of hauling a body to the bridge and dump-
ing it? No, what I think is that he saw something he
shouldn't have while he was roaming around. And what
about this Dewey Shotwell that was found dead? Wasn't
he the one that ginseng-growing guy was threatening to
shoot?"

The speculations continued noisily, growing ever
more far-fetched. Finally Elizabeth said sharply, "You
know, you two, this isn't a joke." She rose, wondering if
it had been a mistake to tell them about her so-called investigations. She had been caught off-guard by the emotions roused during the service and, while riding home,
had found herself telling her daughter and her nephew all
she knew or surmised of Cletus's travels in the days before his death.

Laurel and Ben, subdued now, came into the kitchen
with the dirty dishes.

"Mum, we know it's serious. I guess we're just being
silly in reaction to all the seriousness of the funeral."

"Yeah," agreed Ben. "Common reaction. Whistling
in the dark to keep from being afraid of the unknown."

Laurel and Ben said good night and left; Laurel for her
apartment in Asheville, Ben for his cabin. Elizabeth went
to the computer to check her e-mail. Still nothing from
Trent Woodbern, the Starshine dropout. She'd probably
never hear from him. And something Laurel had said, in
her usual offhand way just as she was leaving, had made
Elizabeth wonder even more about the odd community
on Hog Run Branch.

"By the way, Mum, I finally talked to Rolf about his
ex-girlfriend, you know, the one who joined that star

place. Well, he said that she was still there. He also told me that she was pregnant when they broke up and that he thinks that's why she went to the community."

"So what happened to the child?" Elizabeth had asked.

"Oh, she had it and gave it up for adoption," Laurel had replied breezily. "The folks at Starshine apparently arranged it all. But what really freaked Rolf out was this. He got to thinking about what a great model she had been and so went out there to see her recently, kind of wanting to get back together with her. So anyway, after going through this whole long thing with a guy at the gate, they finally let him in."

"And he got to see her?" Elizabeth asked, intrigued.

"Absolutely, and she told him that she would never leave the community. She also told him that she was pregnant again."

VI—OCTOBER 1901

The onliest time that me and Levy had a bed for our lovin was them first two nights while Mister Tomlin was gone. Atter that we had to make do with the hard ground back up the mountain until Levy found a little cave back under some big old rocks. The dirt there was soft and dry and Levy brung along an old quilt for us to lay down on and another to put over us when the weather begun to cool. I have said that Clytie was like a she-cat in season around the men and now I understand that hungerin. Many a day and night would go by before Levy and me would have the chance to slip off together and many a day and night I'd feel that hungerin risin up in me. I would've sent great cat yowls echoin all along the ridges and through the hollers if-fen hit would have brought him to me.

For now I knew what Aetha was sayin when she told me that atter a while I'd like hit just fine. Though, with Levy, there weren't no atter a while to hit; I liked hit all to oncet. That first night when he come to the cabin, we both knowed what we was about the minute he clumb up on that big rock and stood there by me.

I held my hand up to him without sayin nothin and he raised me up and pulled me to him. He started to say something but I wrapped my arms around him and kissed him hard. Hit weren't no time atall afore I stood there naked in the starlight and both of us a-tryin to get his overhauls offen him as fast as ever we could.

Atterwards, when we was in the cabin layin on the bed, he seen the blood on my legs. Little Sylvie, he says, ain't you and him ever . . . and then he got quiet. I told him something of how it had been and how my daddy weren't no help and then I told him why I'd gone to Ransom that day.

Mister Tomlin ain't no husband to me, I told Levy, and if the law won't help me get shed of him, I reckon I'll just have to run away.

Hit was some time later and we was just layin on the bed watchin the moon begin to rise. We'd fallen off to sleep atter the second time but Levy knowed he couldn't stay with me the whole night. If he weren't down in my daddy's barn when the house began to stir, folks might begin to suspicion something. Levy was a-restin his head on my breast and I was a-twinin my fingers in his hair that in the moonlight looked silver instead of gold. Will you come back tomorrow night? I asked him. Mister Tomlin won't be back till the next evenin, if then.

I'll come back if nothing don't happen, he told me. But, Little Sylvie, we got to be careful and think about how to get you free. Was you just to leave and take up with me, we'd both be churched, at the very least, and most likely Tomlin and yore daddy they'd lay out to kill me. We got to be real careful and think what to do.

But seemed like all we could think of doin that summer was to lay down with each other ever chance we got. We did make a plan where if he could meet me up in the woods, he'd put a little white stone atop an old stump that was near our spring. Whenever I seen the white stone, I'd know he'd be waitin for me that night in a certain little holler up the mountain. And later on, like I said, he fixed us a place in the cave under the big rocks.

Levy was careful to stay clear of the cabin and I was right sure Mister Tomlin didn't know nothing about what Levy and me was doin. Mister Tomlin had me to do those same things to him sometimes at night but he still couldn't do no good atall. And he would still bring out that hateful old belt and kindly worry at me with it. But hit got to where most nights he'd just drink some of his medicine and fall asleep. I had seen that when he took that medicine he didn't never wake till the sun was full up so I knowed at those times that I could be with Levy for part of the night at least.

Hit seemed like to me that when I was with Mister Tomlin, I was like a plant just swivellin up for lack of water. And when I was with Levy, well, hit put me in mind of when me and Clytie used to play boats in the branch atter a big rain. We'd take us each a little stick and call hit a boat. Then we'd drop our boats into the rushin water and see how they did. Those little sticks would get caught in the swirlin, racin water and tumble over and over. Me and Clytie'd foller along on the bank of the branch just a-watchin the sticks bein swept along on their way to the river. When I was with Levy, I was like one of them sticks, pulled along

and tossed to and fro by love. I was drownin in love and I
didn't want no one to pull me out.

I reckon I could have talked to Aetha but she had
enough troubles on her along of her new baby. Hit had
been what Romarie had called a blue baby and when I had
asked her about hit, Rom had squeezed her mouth in a
tight straight line and said, Something's wrong with hit's
heart. Aetha'll not raise that one. And then the babe had
took the bloody flux, what they call the summer complaint,
and Aetha was lookin so tired and worn herself, the few
times I seen her, that I purely hated to lay any more worries
on her. I had almost spoke, one September day when Mister
Tomlin took me to see her atter church. Him and Fate was
down at the barn lookin at Fate's team of Belgians and I
was settin with Aetha while she nursed little Louammia.
Afore I could begin my tale, she looked at me and said,
Little Sylvie, hit eases my heart to see you lookin so
bloomin. I got most all I can bear with this babe for doctor
says she likely won't see year's end.

The tears was makin tracks down her face and she
hugged the baby closer. I had seen first thing that hit didn't
look right atall for hit's skin was grayish-like, not pink, and
hit didn't seem to have the strength to suck but a little bit at
the time.

So I just smiled and told Aetha I was right happy and
told her about the quilt I was piecin.

By October I was most sure that I was in the family way.
My monthlies hadn't come since July and my breasts was
tender and startin to poke out. My belly was poochin out
just a little and Mister Tomlin began to be ill with me.

You're eatin too much, Little Sylvie, he said. Do you want to look like a fat old milk cow? And he would count the biscuits when we'd et our breakfast. I'll know if you sneak and eat any afore dinner, he would say. I want you to stay like you were when we married.

I knowed that the time would come when he would see that hit was more than biscuits got me this way and I set in to thinkin out a plan. I had seen a notice in one of the newspaper pieces that Aetha had give me for dress patterns and it had talked of cheap land and good jobs in Texas. A one-way ticket on the Southern Railway was eight dollars and fifty cents.

Next time we was able to meet I told Levy about this. I offered to take the money from Mister Tomlin's pocketful of double eagles whilst he was asleep but Levy wouldn't have none of it. *Don't you see, Little Sylvie, he said, hit's bad enough me stealin you. Iffen I steal his money too, what kind of a man am I?*

Levy said that he had it in mind to take a job in one of Mister Tomlin's loggin camps. That would be the fastest way he could earn enough to give us our new start in Texas. He said he'd likely be workin a ways off and wouldn't be able to get back to see me but ever now and again. I hadn't yet told Levy that I was likely carryin his child and I thought to wait yet another month to be certain sure.

Hit was a few days later that I went to the spring hopin to see the little white rock that meant Levy would be waitin for me that night. The rock weren't in its place but Levy hisself was standin there.

What are you doin? says I, Mister Tomlin's just down the road a-talkin to my daddy.

I had to see you afore I left, says he. I have to be on my way to the camp in Tennessee to start work tomorrow. If I'm not there, they'll hire someone else.

I wanted to bawl like a baby and I ached to hold him and tell him not to leave me. Levy seen it in my face and said, Now, Little Sylvie, don't take on. Hit'll not be long afore I earn enough to take us to Texas. He reached his hand in the pocket of his overhauls and brought out something all balled up in his fist. Close yore eyes, Little Sylvie, he told me real soft like and I could feel his hands brushin down on either side of my head. I opened my eyes and looked down. He had put the prettiest little gold heart on a glittery thin chain around my neck and was holdin out another one to me. I bought these off a drummer in Ransom, he said. Now you put this un on me to show that I am yore own true love. That way when I've gone off to the lumber camp you'll have something to put you in mind of me.

He bowed his head down to where I could reach to put the other necklace on him. I put my arms up around his neck and held him down so's I could kiss him. Then I took his hand and laid hit on my belly. I got plenty to put me in mind of you, Levy Johnson, I said. But I like us both wearin our little hearts for hit shows that we're a family.

Just then I heared the sound of coins a-jinglin and I jumped back from Levy. Right quick like I tucked the locket under my dress where it lay between my bosoms. I picked up the pails of water and said, Thank you kindly, but I can tote these just fine. Mister Tomlin just then come around the curve in the path and seen us there. He cut his eyes over at me real chill like. Get on with yore work, Little Sylvie, he said.

CHAPTER 15
WHO CAN UNDERSTAND?
(THURSDAY)

WHY THE HELL CAN'T HE GET AN ANSWERING machine?" Elizabeth muttered as she dialed Hawkins's number yet again. She had tried unsuccessfully to reach him several times on the previous night. What Laurel had said about the twice-pregnant girlfriend had set off modest little warning bells, and she wanted Hawkins to know about it. Hawkins had told her when they spoke on Sunday that Janie had promised to finish the semester before joining the Starshine Community, so there was no hurry, she reminded herself. But she also wanted to tell him about the trout flumes and pond up in Little Man Holler. Could Cletus have been drowned there? *Dammit . . .* she thought, as the phone rang for the sixth time, *it would be nice if—*

"Hawkins." The voice in her ear startled her and, for a moment, she forgot the reason for her call.

"Phillip," she managed to say, after an awkward pause, "this is Elizabeth Goodweather. I talked to my daughter about that community . . ."

Hawkins listened without comment to the story of the ex-girlfriend. When Elizabeth concluded, somewhat lamely, "I guess I just thought it was strange that she would go there, have a baby, give it up for adoption, and then get pregnant again right away."

"Yeah, that is pretty crazy," Hawkins agreed, "but who can understand women, especially at that age?" He laughed humorlessly. "At least I'm almost sure Janie's not pregnant. Sandy got her started on birth control way back. I didn't actually approve, but what're you gonna do?" Elizabeth could almost see his shoulders shrug.

"I did some checking around," he went on, "the Internet, like you said, and some other places. The Starshine Community is actually pretty highly regarded in some circles—mainly people looking to adopt a healthy Caucasian infant. Evidently quite a few young women who go there to have their babies give them up for adoption." He paused. "I don't blame them; the babies end up with two eager parents instead of one reluctant one, and the parents are always well-to-do. Do you know what it costs to adopt a baby these days?"

The conversation slid into generalities. Elizabeth told Hawkins about Cletus's funeral and her suspicions about the trout farm. Hawkins was disappointingly unimpressed by this revelation. Finally she mentioned Trent Woodbern, acknowledging that she had not yet heard from the young man. "But in case I do and if it's anything you ought to know, I'll call you right away."

"Ah . . ." Hawkins said after a pause, "I may not be around much for the next few days . . . Maybe you could—"

"Oh, I'd forgotten," said Elizabeth, "You've probably got to see about your aunt."

There was a puzzled silence, "My aunt . . . ?" Hawkins said tentatively.

"Your aunt who lives in Shut In—the one you said

you were here to see about . . . to see if she could manage living alone? Remember, you told me about her back when you first called? I forgot all about her till just now."

There was another pause and then Hawkins replied in cheerful tones, "Oh, Aunt Omie? I didn't remember mentioning her to you. Yeah, I went to see her and she about ran me off the place when I started talking about assisted living. At first I wasn't sure she even knew who I was, but she remembered me all right *and* remembered the time, I must have been around fifteen, that I had tried to ride her milk cow. That old cow jumped over a barbwire fence and left me tangled up in it. Aunt Omie remembered it down to the day of the week: 'Now, let me see, hit were a Tuesday fer I was churnin' when I heared the commotion.' "

He had slipped effortlessly and fondly into the mountain dialect, before returning to his own more educated and only slightly Southern accent. "Nah, she doesn't need any assisted living; that old lady could beat bears with switches. Maybe you'd go with me to see her some day. I think that you two would get along; you have a lot in common."

"Thanks, I guess," said Elizabeth.

An odd conversation, she decided as she hung up. Almost like talking to two different people. Hawkins had seemed unusually distant, not like the eagerly confiding person he had been on the night that they had dinner. *He's probably sorry he told me all that personal stuff and feels like he has to back off,* she decided. He had mentioned that he would be out of town for a few days and had said something vague about getting together when he returned. *Who can understand men,* she thought, *especially at that age?*

After the strangely unsatisfactory conversation with Hawkins, Elizabeth decided to go in to Asheville for some much overdue shopping. She drove from store to store, checking off the items on the list in her head. *Stop here, find a birthday present for Sallie Kate; stop there, pick up some batting for that quilt top you've been meaning to finish.* Several hours went by and, after one last stop to buy far too many esoteric household products for the spring cleaning that she had been vowing to accomplish for the past two months, she was done.

Except for groceries on the way home. But now I think I deserve a little treat. She found a parking place near her favorite used bookstore and told herself that she really shouldn't buy more than two books, as her shelves at home were already overflowing. *I'll just go look,* she decided, *maybe get a paperback to read while I eat lunch.* Glancing past the bookstore she could see that the little Japanese restaurant that had been a favorite of Sam's was still busy.

I'll take my time browsing, she thought. *The lunch crowd should thin out before long.*

Thirty minutes later, Elizabeth emerged triumphantly from the bookstore, clutching a vintage Vita Sackville-West gardening book and two scruffy-looking but still quite readable Tony Hillerman mysteries. She was smiling to herself in double anticipation of a good meal—*I wonder if they still have that garlic-seared tuna*—and three books to read. *Now if there will just be an empty table . . .*

Through the window she could see that there were indeed several small tables standing empty. Then, something about the couple sitting just on the other side of the window caught her attention. The woman, tiny, dark, and very beautiful, was speaking rapidly and evidently unhappily, if the expression on her perfectly made-up features was any guide. The man's back was to her, but Elizabeth instantly recognized the broad shoulders and shiny brown bald head of Phillip Hawkins. When Hawkins reached out to pat the woman's hand, Elizabeth turned and walked back to her jeep.

"Well, that was stupid," she muttered as she sat in her car in the parking lot of Back Yard Burgers with a Grazi burger and a lemonade. *But that place is so little, I'd probably have ended up sitting next to them and he might have thought . . . well, what would it matter what he thought? But who the hell was that he was with? Not good old Aunt Omie, that's for sure. And he said he didn't know anyone around here who was over twenty. Shut up, Elizabeth—so he makes friends fast.*

She took a bite of her sandwich and the sauce from the burger ran down her arm and dripped on her shirt.

Elizabeth swung onto the bridge that crossed the French Broad River and led to Bear Tree Creek and Ridley Branch, happy, as always, to be nearly home. On seeing a truck stopped up ahead, she slowed to a more moderate pace. The black farm truck was pulled over to one side and a tall dark-haired man was leaning casually on the railing of the bridge. There was nothing unusual in this: the bridge was not heavily traveled and often there would be a car or truck parked to one side, its passengers fishing or watching the rafters and kayakers negotiate the rapids. Elizabeth herself had stopped many times to take photographs of the river, sometimes with the mists rising off it in the morning, sometimes of the great blue heron that haunted its shallows.

The man leaning against the railing straightened and

casually stepped toward Elizabeth's oncoming car, holding up his hand for her to stop. As she braked reflexively, her inner, catty self purred, *Taller than Hawkins, much better-looking,* and *he has a full head of hair.*

"Would you care to give me a jump, Miz Goodweather?" drawled Harice Tyler. "I been thinkin' you might come along. You know, they say three's a charm."

Without waiting for her answer, the preacher produced jumper cables and opened the hood of his truck, calling to her, "If you don't care, just pull over a little and pop that hood, Miz Goodweather."

She wordlessly did as he said and he soon had the two batteries connected. Then he climbed into the cab of his truck and turned the key; the truck started without hesitation. Harice's white smile flashed at her as he emerged from the pickup and sauntered toward her. "I thank you kindly, Miz Goodweather."

Leaving the cables in place, he unhurriedly leaned down to her window. "When are you and Miss Birdie coming back to church?" he asked. "I told you there's always hope. We're meeting Saturday night; could be Aunt Belvy'll have another message for you."

He was so close that she could smell him—a not unpleasant combination of sweat and something pungent like black pepper and cloves. He wore dirty work clothes and today there was no hair cream on the dark brown wavy hair that fell in a stray lock across his forehead. He was looking at her very intently, clearly waiting for an answer.

"Saturday? I don't know . . ." she hedged. "I'll have to see what Birdie—"

"You come, with or without Miss Birdie," he insisted urgently. "You want, you can ride over with me."

"With you?" she echoed in surprise. "Don't you live over in Tennessee?"

"Used to I did, but when my wife died last year, I come back over to Bear Tree to give my daddy a hand on the farm. My kids is all married and on their own and Daddy ain't able to do like he used to—"

"Your father," Elizabeth interrupted. "I was wondering what your father thought about Dewey Shotwell's death?"

Tyler's eyes narrowed. "Now, Miz Goodweather, you hadn't ought to make nothing out of the way Daddy was carryin' on. Hit was just a game between him and Dewey, each one tryin' to do the other down. He didn't mean nothing by it."

He smiled widely and went on, "Everyone knows the Shotwells is bad to drink. Could be ol' Dewey took his liquor down to the river to get away from his woman. There's a bunch of sinners like to go down to the bridge to do their drinkin'."

His dark eyes surveyed the interior of her jeep. "Looks like you been grocery shoppin'."

Elizabeth started, suddenly anxious that no chance passerby see her loitering here on the bridge with Harice Tyler, their vehicles joined like copulating insects. "Yes, I have, and I have some stuff that needs to get home and into the refrigerator. So if you don't mind—"

Harice Tyler smiled and straightened up. "All right, Miz Goodweather." He removed the cables, gently shut the hood of her car, and stood aside, still smiling. "Saturday night, you remember now," he called as she pulled away from him.

A thought hit her and she stopped her car and reversed. "I have another question for you," she said. "Is there a pond up on Devil's Fork?"

Tyler laughed. "You're mighty interested in that place, ain't you? First the boomers, now you want to know about a pond. Now, it ain't what you'd rightly call a pond but they got kindly of a pit filled with water that they use in their training exercises. That what you was wondering about, Miz Goodweather?"

As she turned up Ridley Branch she could still see him in the rearview mirror, leaning on his truck and staring after her. She was mystified by Harice Tyler's apparent interest in her and not a little bewildered and annoyed by her own involuntary response to his sensual good looks and insinuating smile. *It almost seemed as if he was . . . was lying in wait for me; what did he say—'Three's a charm'?"*

She was just in front of Miss Birdie's house now, and with sudden resolution she braked and drove across the plank bridge to the cabin. The cars and trucks of family who had come to yesterday's funeral were gone now; only Miss Birdie's old pickup and Dorothy's ancient Fairlane were in sight. The monotonous murmur of the television could be heard from the house.

"Come right on in and get you a chair," Miss Birdie called out. She and Dorothy were in the kitchen, evidently turning out and rearranging the cabinets. Or, rather, Birdie was sitting at the kitchen table directing Dorothy, who stood on a straight-backed chair pulling old medicine bottles and mason jars of various murky liquids out of the cabinet over the refrigerator.

"Me and Dor'thy lit into the kitchen first thing this mornin'," Birdie explained cheerfully. "Oncet all them folks had left, just seemed like we had to get busy." She looked up, her bright eyes glittering. "Come hug my neck, Lizzie Beth."

"Miss Birdie, it was a beautiful service yesterday."

Elizabeth bent to touch her lips to the old woman's wrinkled cheek. "I wish Rosemary could have gotten home for it; she dearly loved Cletus, too."

"Birdie had her a beautiful letter from yore Rosemary," interjected Dorothy from her perch, scowling at the label on a brown bottle half full of some clear liquid. "She surely writes a good hand; she's a teacher, ain't she?" Without a pause she continued, "Whatever is this mess, Birdie? It looks like 'Pare—' something but the label is all faded."

"Hit don't matter," Birdie answered, "just throw it in the trash. No tellin' how long some of that medicine's been up there. Reckon there's some from when Luther was took so bad; might even be some older than that. Throw it all out, Dor'thy, I ain't got no need for any of it now."

Dorothy obediently loaded the assortment of jars and bottles into a heavy garbage bag and placed it by the back door with several others. "Well, there's a job done," she announced with satisfaction. "Now let's have us a glass of ice tea."

As they sipped their tea, Dorothy leaned across the table to Elizabeth. "Birdie said you was askin' about that Little Sylvie Baker. Now my brother's wife was a Baker and I one time asked her right out about Little Sylvie. What she said was that Little Sylvie took up with Levy Johnson and them two took the baby and a bag of gold from Little Sylvie's husband and run off to Texas. She said that Little Sylvie's father crossed her name out of the family Bible."

"What about Sylvie's husband?" asked Elizabeth. "Did he go after them?"

Dorothy frowned. "Now, I don't know as I ever did hear about that. He was the one built the church house;

they got his name wrote on the cornerstone—it's Tomlin, I believe. But I don't rightly know what did become of him."

"Weren't he the one got swept away in the big flood of nineteen and sixteen?" Birdie asked Dorothy. "That was when the sawmill got washed away—"

The cousins began trading flood stories: the bull that was found dead, tangled in the branches of a tree, the calf that was found alive on a rock in midstream two days after it had been swept away from its pasture beside the river, the mud two feet deep in the Gentry homeplace, the giant catfish "still alive and floppin' on the hearthstones," when the water went down and Miss Birdie's grandmother had returned to her flood-stricken home. "And how the place did smell!" Dorothy wrinkled her nose. "They couldn't never get the smell outen the beddin', what with the water and the mildew and the dead things."

It might have been last year rather than almost a hundred years ago, thought Elizabeth. *That flood is as real to them as anything. I guess when their generation was growing up with no television and not much in the way of radio or books, sitting around telling stories was the main entertainment.*

Finally Elizabeth said, "I have to be going; I've got groceries in the car I need to put away. But, Miss Birdie, I wondered if you—"

"Saturday night, that's when I want to go back to that Holiness church," Birdie said firmly. "Belvy called and said she'd likely have another message for me. And that nice Brother Harice, he come by to pay his respects. He ast about you, Lizzie Beth, and he said he'd be lookin' for us."

———

Ben was outside when she pulled up and he helped her unload the car. "Laurel called, Aunt E.," he announced, plopping two more bags on the kitchen table. "She said to remind you that you promised to go to the revival with her tomorrow night. She was going on and on about that John the Baptizer." He grinned. "You've sure been getting a big dose of mountain religion recently."

"So I have," groaned Elizabeth. "It's fascinating, but . . . I don't know . . . a little scary. It's just that these people are so sure they're right. At least, not just that, but they're also sure that everybody else is wrong. And if you believe that, then you can justify almost anything you do . . . you know, 'God on our side.' That's what scares me. Like that militia."

"Or the Germans, back when—*Gott mit uns*—or however they said it," Ben intoned, stiffening his arm in the Fascist salute. Elizabeth shuddered.

Late that night, just before going to bed, Elizabeth went to the front porch to call Molly and Ursa. James was already curled up on his pillow in her bedroom but the other two dogs were not home yet, had not been home for dinner. In fact, she realized that she had not seen the pair since that morning. *Probably off on an adventure,* she thought. It wasn't unusual for the two to spend the night barking up a tree on the mountain at a possum or raccoon, and then come home in the morning, starving, exhausted, bristling with burrs, and thoroughly happy.

She called and whistled to no avail. The night air was still, but cool and sweetly fragrant. Across the valley, lights twinkled from a scattering of homes. She could hear the distant rumble of a freight train on the tracks that ran along the river, and the lonesome cry of its whistle. On the mountain above the house, an owl hooted and another replied on a lower note. *So beautiful, so peaceful,* she thought and, with one last unanswered call for the dogs, went inside.

CHAPTER 16
JOHN THE BAPTIZER
(FRIDAY NIGHT)

THERE WAS HARDLY A PARKING SPACE LEFT WHEN Elizabeth and Laurel arrived at John the Baptizer's big revival tent behind the BP gas station. The lurid yellow flyers, as well as daily announcements on the local radio station, had done their work; cars and trucks crowded the recently bush-hogged field. An old Winnebago painted with bright apocalyptic scenes and Bible verses sat at a little distance from the tent, its generator humming. From within the tent, children's voices could be heard singing. Laurel gave her mother a disgruntled look. "I told you we should have left earlier; we'll be lucky to get a seat. But look at that incredible camper! I'll have to come back in the daytime to get pictures of it!"

Elizabeth had insisted on waiting till after seven, when the meeting was scheduled to begin, hoping to slip in unnoticed and sit well toward the back. As she and Laurel took their seats in the last row, a group of teenagers was introduced as "the Holy Ghost Singers from the Sycamore Cove Fellowship." They shuffled onto the platform at the front of the tent and fiddled with the two microphones before breaking into a ragged version of "I

Am Clinging to the Rock," accompanied by an older man with a battered acoustic guitar and a blonde young woman at a portable organ. By the time they reached the chorus, their shyness had disappeared and they sang in parts, the boys elaborating on the soprano line with a confident booming bass. Elizabeth leaned back in her chair and began to be glad that she had come. It would be nice to think about something other than Cletus for a while.

As the singers launched into the second verse, Laurel whispered in her ear, "I wish we could have sat up close, but at least he hasn't started painting yet." She nodded toward the half-dozen white panels that leaned against a table on the platform. "I've heard that he can do anywhere from three to six paintings a night, depending on how inspired he feels." Laurel twisted in her seat and peered all around. Then she whispered again, directing Elizabeth's attention to a row of completed panels, brilliantly a-swirl with color, that were propped up over to one side of the tent, "Those are probably the ones he's done on the previous nights. He doesn't sell them till the revival's over. They say he almost gives them away." She sighed deeply. "God, what a show it would be to have just two weeks' worth of his work. I've got to talk to him about that. But I don't see him anywhere, do you?"

The singers had paused and the guitarist was executing an exuberant finger-picking solo. Elizabeth was just about to tell her daughter to be quiet when, through the open tent flap, she saw the lean form of the evangelist stepping out of the Winnebago. He was dressed as he had been at Cletus's funeral, and, as before, gave the impression that some interior tightly coiled spring was quivering on the verge of release. Elizabeth's thoughts flashed to Harice Tyler, comparing his warm, dark eyes and easy way of moving to the remote, icy stare and rigidly controlled posture of this forbidding man. She watched John the Baptizer come quietly into the tent and stand at the back, nodding in time as the Holy Ghost Singers triumphantly concluded their song in rich four-part harmony.

The singers and the guitarist filed off the stage, but John the Baptizer remained at the back of the tent. Only the muffled tread of the singers' feet broke the silence. The congregation sat, hushed and expectant, all heads turned to the rear, waiting for John the Baptizer. A baby began to wail and was quickly quieted. The entire gathering seemed to be holding its breath, waiting . . .

"There was a man sent forth from God, whose name was John."

Speaking in a low tone that nonetheless filled the tent, the evangelist began to walk down the aisle between the rows of folding chairs toward the platform. A woman sitting at the end of a row grasped at his hand as he passed, but he brushed by her and stepped up onto the platform, turning slowly to face the congregation. The young woman at the organ played a few soft chords.

"The same came for a witness, to bear witness of the Light, that all men through him might believe."

His voice was louder now, though superbly restrained. He picked up one of the white panels and set it on a rough easel that stood by the table. Now Elizabeth could see that many jars of different hues of paint, each with its own brush, were neatly laid out on the table. John the Baptizer raised his hands over them in a gesture of blessing. He lifted his head, shaking back the thatch of silver-sandy hair.

"Send down the Holy Spirit to Your servant, who is but a voice, crying in the wilderness."

His eyes seemed fixed on a point high in the air as his hand picked up a brush and plunged it into a pot of deep blue paint. The organ music thrilled, then sank to a low accompanying undertone. Now words were pouring out of the preacher in a torrent, sometimes recognizable Bible verses, sometimes an incomprehensible babble. He spoke of seven angels with seven trumpets while with confident brushstrokes he sketched a picture to illustrate his message. Colors whirled and resolved into images on the panels before him and the words "present at the creation" came into Elizabeth's mind as, mesmerized, she watched the painting take shape.

" 'And the third angel sounded and there fell a great star from heaven, burning as it were a lamp, and it fell upon the third part of the rivers and upon the fountains of waters.' "

The voice of John the Baptizer rang through the packed tent and he flourished two brushes in one hand, slashing down a great stroke of orange and yellow across the paint-bedaubed panel as the organ chords crashed around him. Laurel let out her breath with an audible sound of pleasure. Craning her neck for a better view, she rose slightly from her folding chair.

Elizabeth gave her daughter's skirt a gentle tug and Laurel settled back down, quivering with excitement. Elizabeth looked at her sharply but Laurel was totally caught up in the moment, gazing at John the Baptizer with undisguised awe. The evangelist continued to preach from Revelations, warning of the coming apocalypse, punctuating his harangue with a repeated "Can somebody say amen?" At some point, evidently judging that his first panel was complete, he thrust it aside and began another. Nothing stemmed his overpowering flood of Scripture and prophecy. Throughout the tent the congregation was shouting out answering amens; some were

standing, many were weeping, and in a cleared area to
the side, a chubby young man was executing a little
hopping dance and throwing up his arms with a hearty
"Praise Him!" at every pause in the exhortation.

Elizabeth sat transfixed, partly by the flood of half-
unintelligible but oddly compelling language, and partly
by the contagious energy building all around her. She remembered Birdie saying that Cletus loved a revival, and
she felt a pang of sorrow that he had missed this one.
*Birdie said he loved bright things; he would definitely have liked
these paintings,* she thought. An idea nagged at her, *bright
things,* but then it was gone, swept away in a deluge of
words and images.

Laurel's eyes were shining and she was breathing
quickly as she watched a second painting take shape.

*"Church! The end times are coming near. Only the living
waters can save you from the eternal fire of His wrath; only the
living waters that flow from the crystal throne of the Lamb can
bring you to the Lamb. Say amen!"*

The rapid brush delineated a pale blue throne at the
top of the panel. The brilliant Presence that sat on the
throne was human in outline, but the bands of rainbow
color that shimmered around it obscured any precise features. From the base of the throne a whirling cataract of
waters poured down the panel, sapphire and emerald. At
the very bottom of the picture was a lake of fire, similar
to the one that Elizabeth had seen on the flyer announc-
ing the revival. But this was in color: blazing tongues of
ruby and topaz lapped around the little pink and brown
sinners whose arms were thrown up in entreaty and
whose mouths were all opened in haunting black Os of
suffering. The slashing brush dragged the blue waters
closer and closer to the fire, forming swirls that reached

down to touch and surround the suppliants. The music of the organ throbbed in sweet yearning.

"Church! I have seen the wonders spoken of in the Holy Word of God and I say to you again the time is near. For the woman and her child dwell in the wilderness and when her days are accomplished there shall be war in heaven."

The panel with the fiery lake was set aside and John the Baptizer began to create a Madonna. A young woman in draperies of deep rose and cerulean blue filled the center of the piece. Her head, blonde rather than the usual brunette, Elizabeth noted, was bowed over the swaddled child cradled in her arms. A halo of twelve stars blazed above her and her bare feet were set on a crescent moon. All around her slender form were the deep greens and browns of a forest inhabited by a multitude of birds sketched in bright colors with swift angular strokes. Above the forest rose rocky hills and cliffs of gray and black, reaching up to a billowing sky of livid purple and yellow.

Elizabeth frowned. *What is this reminding me of? It's something about Cletus, something—*

"That's the most traditional so far," whispered Laurel. "That sky is so El Greco. He must use some really fast-drying medium . . ." Her voice trailed off as she once more became absorbed in watching. Elizabeth sighed. The elusive thought had dissolved.

Setting aside the Madonna, John the Baptizer reached for another panel, then hesitated. He pulled a big white handkerchief from his pocket and wiped his face, then took a drink of water from a paper cup. The organ went quiet, the hungering clamor in the tent that had accompanied his preaching and painting died, and those who had been standing sat once more.

"The Lord tells me that's enough preaching for now.

We still got us more'n a week before the baptizing. Plenty of time to call home the sinners." The ecstatic frenzy that had sustained him through ninety minutes of preaching and painting had vanished. His voice was at a normal speaking level, but such was the stillness in the tent that Elizabeth could easily hear him.

"The Lord's telling me to walk amongst you now and pray with you. He's telling me to open myself and to make myself a vessel for His Holy Spirit so that in His precious Name, sin and disease, fear and sorrow, can be rebuked and cast out."

Elizabeth shifted uneasily in her seat. The folding metal chair set on uneven ground was becoming more and more uncomfortable. She glanced at Laurel, raised her eyebrows, and looked toward the exit. Laurel narrowed her eyes and silently mouthed *No way!*

Up on the platform a woman was singing "Tell the Blessed Story" while John the Baptizer drank another cup of water and equipped himself with a handheld microphone on a long cord. Elizabeth tried to gauge whether the cord would reach all the way to the back row where she and Laurel sat. She hoped not.

Laurel was whispering urgently at her, "Mum, I have to stay till it's over. I want to talk to him about lending the paintings for a show. Don't you see how incredible he is?"

"Okay, sweetie," Elizabeth whispered back. "It's just that my rear end is tired of this chair."

John the Baptizer began to move through the tent, pausing now and again to rest his hand lightly on a head or a shoulder and to pray. Sometimes he would speak quietly to the person he was touching and, on hearing a reply, shift his hand to another place on the body.

Elizabeth watched intently as the microphone cord stretched ever longer.

Finally the pale-eyed evangelist was praying with the thin young woman sitting directly in front of Laurel. Elizabeth could just catch some of the words: "Bless our sister and free her from the fears and terrors in the night. In the sweet Name of Jesus, I rebuke those fears!"

The outstretched hand clamped around the young woman's forehead and she staggered back, then raised her hands and cried out, "Thank you, Jesus!"

Elizabeth had been diligently avoiding eye contact with the preacher; now she breathed a long sigh of relief when he turned and walked back to the front. A sad-looking woman in a faded housedress was making her way up to him. Stringy hair hung on either side of her doughy face and her eyes were dull with mute suffering. A wiry little old woman who was holding the sad woman's arm whispered in the ear of the evangelist. He bowed his head for a moment, then made a signal with his hand.

The young woman who had been playing the organ stepped forward with a small bottle of olive oil. Elizabeth recognized the familiar tapered shape and blue label. John the Baptizer made another gesture, and suddenly half a dozen people were surrounding him and the sad woman, all reaching out to touch her, all praying aloud. The congregation rose as one, swaying toward the little knot of people at the front of the tent. A low hum of many voices filled the air, like the buzzing of an aroused hornet's nest.

Suddenly Elizabeth became aware that someone was closing the tent flap behind her, and without conscious thought, she grabbed Laurel's elbow, stood up, and propelled her startled daughter out of the tent.

"Mum," squealed Laurel. "What are you doing? I told you—"

"Sweetie," gasped Elizabeth, "I'm sorry. I couldn't stay in there a second longer. I never had claustrophobia before, but when that guy shut the tent flap, I just had to get out of there." She realized that she was trembling. "I felt like we were in danger . . . *you* were in danger and I had to get you out, too." Contritely, she smiled at her indignant daughter. "I'm sorry, that was silly of me. They were probably just closing the flap because the night air's getting cooler. If you want to go back in, I'll go with you."

Laurel looked back at the tent and then at her mother. "Mum, it's not like you to freak out like that. Are you okay?" When Elizabeth nodded, she shrugged. "No big deal. I have tomorrow off so I'll spend the night at the farm and come back in the morning and get pictures of the camper and try to talk to him then." She looked more closely at Elizabeth, then commanded, "Give me the keys. I'll drive home."

Ben was still up working at the computer when they arrived. He listened with a grin to Laurel's enthusiastic account of the revival and broke into a loud laugh when she told of Elizabeth's precipitous flight from the tent. "I thought you might OD on religion, Aunt E," he chortled. "But just think, if you'd stayed maybe he could have rebuked the demons out of your folding chair and healed your aching butt."

His face grew suddenly serious as he said, "By the way, Molly came back around nine. I heard her howling out on the porch. She's okay," he added hastily, "just all scratched and her pads are bleeding in a few spots. She was really hungry, so I fed her and then put peroxide and ointment on the torn places. She went right in to your bedroom after she ate and she's zonked out under your bed. But there's no sign of Ursa."

VII-DECEMBER 1901

*All the hillsides was gray and bare when we buried little
Louammia. Hit was mistin a light rain and Aetha couldn't
stop cryin. Hit didn't make no difference how much the
preacher and folks talked about Louammia bein the newest
little angel, Aetha just looked like there weren't nothing on
this earth would bring her any comfort. She leaned against
Fate who had tears runnin down his face too. He didn't
even try to wipe them away, just put his arm around Aetha
and together they walked over to thank the preacher and
the men who dug the grave. Then Fate led Aetha down
the hill and they headed back to their house where Miz
Gentry was watchin over the children.*

*I was grieved for Fate and Aetha and for their loss but,
like my daddy says, them as has can lose. And they still
had each other and five healthy young uns. And I didn't
doubt but what Aetha's skirt'd be poochin out again before
too many months went by.*

*Like mine was now. I hadn't said nothing to no one and
I had took to wearin a shawl most all the time to cover it. If
it hadn't been for Aetha's trouble, I might of told her but I*

don't know. Mister Tomlin hadn't said nothing, even when he'd seen me with the mornin sickness. He kept on a-plaguin me about gettin fat and not lettin me eat much. At first hit didn't make no difference for any food like to turn my stomach. But then the sickness passed and I was hungry all the time. There was days I'd slip down to Daddy's house and steal biscuits or cornbread out of the crock in the kitchen. One time Rom was there and I couldn't get at the crock without her askin questions that I didn't want to answer. That was the day I had went out to the barn and ate up ever bit of the old stale cornbread Daddy keeps in a lard can to feed his hounds.

Atter they burried Louammia I stood by the big white rock that marks my mommy's grave and I wished more than I ever had before that I could talk to her and she could tell me what should I do. Mister Tomlin and my daddy had been talkin to some of the men and then they left off and come over to stand beside me. Mister Tomlin took my arm and his fingers was pressin hard into my flesh. My daddy's lookin all mournful-like and I can see from the way he's studyin the little stones next to the one for my mommy that he's thinkin about the little boys him and her had lost.

Well, sir, says Mister Tomlin, I'm sorry for your loss of a grandchild. His bony old fingers bit into my arm. I'd hoped for a happier time to tell you our news but maybe it'd hearten you some to know that Little Sylvie's carrying another grandbaby for you.

Mister Tomlin had acted just as proud as anyone could be when he told my daddy about the baby. But when we got on Neb to go back up to the cabin, I seen that his eyes was as cold as the ground where Aetha's babe was layin. As we rode up the hill, he talked in a low voice that set the chill bumps to raisin on my arms. Little Sylvie, he says, I don't doubt that the brat in your belly belongs to that Johnson boy. But it doesn't suit me to be made a laughingstock for folk and so I'll let it be thought that this is my child.

Mister Tomlin, I says, why don't you let me go? Me and Levy'll go off and—

Oh, no, you'll not, he says, for I've sent Levy to do some business for me in Kentucky. He won't return anytime soon, for the roads are dangerous this time of year. Anything could happen.

CHAPTER 17
THE EZEKIEL VERSE
(SATURDAY)

ELIZABETH HAD SLEPT BADLY, SLEPT "WITH ONE EAR open" as she told Ben and Laurel at breakfast. "I kept thinking I heard Ursa thumping up onto the porch and I'd get up and go open the door and call and whistle, but she wasn't there."

"Sounds like the agnostic, dyslexic insomniac," said Ben, looking up from the magazine he had in front of him. "You know, the one who lies awake all night wondering if there is a dog."

Elizabeth gave her nephew a sour smile and stared gloomily into her coffee. "I'll call the animal shelter as soon as they open just in case . . ."

"That's not a bad idea," said Ben, "but haven't Molly and Ursa done this sort of thing before—gone off up the mountain hunting and stayed gone a couple of days?"

"They have . . . but not for this long. And they generally stick together. That's what worries me. I'll call around and ask if anyone has seen Ursa." A small chill ran over Elizabeth, that "rabbit running over your grave" feeling again. This was too much like her search for information about Cletus. Her unsuccessful search, she reminded herself, with a sigh.

"What about the radio station?" Laurel spooned last year's blackberry jam abundantly onto her toast. "You know, the local one—WRSM. Do they still do that show at noon—*The Trading Post?* There always used to be lost-and-found announcements on that. And I bet a lot of the folks out here listen to it."

When Laurel had left to return to the revival tent in search of an interview with the painting preacher and Ben had gone with Julio into town to get building supplies for some repairs on the tenant house, Elizabeth sat at the table and reviewed her options. She had wanted to go with Laurel but her daughter would have none of it. "Mum!" she'd said indignantly. "I'm not a child! This is business and I don't need a chaperone. Besides, what do you think he's going to do—seduce me behind the BP station?"

It's more likely to be the other way round, Elizabeth thought gloomily, remembering the brief but intense infatuation that Laurel had acted out with the aging hippie Aristides. Well, if she couldn't go with Laurel, what she wanted to do was to start walking up the mountain looking for her missing dog. But reason told her that this was not likely to yield results. There were hundreds of acres of woods and pasture, some of it so covered in briars and brambles that it was impenetrable to anything larger than a rabbit or a very determined dog. *And I have to go with Birdie tonight to that church in Tennessee. What I need to do first is make those calls: animal shelter, radio station, neighbors down on Ridley, though the dogs probably didn't go that way, and Walter and Ollie Johnson. Their place is the nearest on the other side of the mountain.*

Several hours later her telephoning had produced nothing helpful. Molly had awakened to make a brief, limping, necessary trip outside, had eaten ravenously, and then headed back to Elizabeth's bedroom, where she was once again fast asleep on the rug beside the bed. "Big help you are," grumbled Elizabeth, gazing at the lean red hound. "If you were Lassie you wouldn't rest till you'd led me to wherever Ursa is." Molly opened one yellow eye, regarded Elizabeth briefly, then shut it again with a profound sigh.

Well, hell, I can't just sit around, Elizabeth told herself. *I'll check my e-mail, then drive up Bear Tree Creek. Maybe if Ursa's over there she might hear the car . . .* She resolutely thrust aside the image of a shaggy black dog lying dead on the road and, trying to ignore the inward ache that had been steadily growing, went to her computer. Her older daughter usually sent a long, chatty e-mail on the weekend, bringing Elizabeth up-to-date with her busy life in Chapel Hill. But the only message in the In box was from Trent Woodbern—the runaway from the Starshine Community. It was brief and puzzling.

Tell your friend not to let his daughter join Starshine unless he never wants to see her again. All those women belong to Polaris. And they never keep their babies.

Elizabeth immediately sent a return message. *Trent: thank you for the information. I'll warn my friend right away but could you explain a little more? Are you saying that Polaris is actually holding these young women against their will? If so, shouldn't we get the law involved?*

She clicked on Send and sat rereading Trent's short message. Then she reached for the phone and dialed Hawkins's number. Eight, nine, ten rings. Still no answer and still no answering machine. *Probably out having lunch with that pretty little thing he was with on Thursday,* she thought bitterly, as she hung up. *But I really need to warn him—*

The abrupt ring of the telephone under her hand

broke into her thoughts. "Miz Goodweather? This is Harice Tyler. I heard on *The Trading Post* just now you had a dog missing." He went on to say that a few days ago two dogs had come through his daddy's place on the track of something. "A big black shaggy dog, could of had on an orange collar like it said on the radio, and a red hound with a green collar. They was atter something or other and was heading up into the woods 'tween us and that militia place."

"Thank you so much for calling," Elizabeth said. "Do you know if those militia people have a phone or how they would be listed? I'll call right away and—"

"They ain't got no regular phone, just them cell phones. My daddy was trying to get up with them back of this and he never could do no good. Finally had to go talk to the feller at the gate and—"

"That's what I'll do then," interrupted Elizabeth. "Thank you again for telling me about the dogs. I'll go up there right now."

"Miz Goodweather, you don't want to go up there today." There was real concern in Harice Tyler's voice. "They always have a bunch of people there on Saturdays, some big meeting and all. They just lock that gate and can't nobody get in. And Saturday's when they do what they call their 'live-fire' exercises. No, ma'am, don't you do that. And you hadn't ought to go up there nohow without a man goes with you."

"I'll get my nephew to—" She stopped in midsentence, remembering that Ben and Julio would be gone most of the day.

"No, Miz Goodweather, them folks wouldn't pay you no mind. But they know me. I've talked to a few of them one time and another and we get along all right. They foller Scripture just like I do, so we can agree on that."

Harice chuckled. "Course, we don't always foller it the same, but I reckon we both agree on what Paul says about the woman is subject to the man."

He ignored Elizabeth's indignant sputter and continued, "What I'm tellin' you is, was I to go over there with you, I believe you'd stand a better chance of findin' out about yore dog."

Reluctantly Elizabeth had agreed that she would wait till the next day to visit the militia compound. She would meet Harice Tyler at the entrance to his father's place so that he could go with her and "do the talkin'." Against her every inclination she yielded to Harice's insistence that entering the property today or alone would be dangerous.

"Besides, you're comin' to church tonight, ain't you? Aunt Belvy done told yore Miss Birdie she'd likely have a message for her." The preacher's voice grew smooth, almost wheedling. "And I been prayin' for an anointin' to handle ever since I got them copperheads that day you was up to Daddy's place."

When the conversation ended, Elizabeth felt strangely unsettled. She had turned down Harice Tyler's offer to drive her and Miss Birdie to the church in Tennessee that night. But she *had* told him that she would be there, and a thrill of anticipation had surged unbidden through her body as he promised, "You'll see what the Lord has for you tonight, Miz Goodweather."

Calm down, Elizabeth, you're just curious about snake-handling, that's all. Nothing to do with old bedroom-eyes Harice. Lunchtime was long past, so she made a quick cheese sandwich and got the book on the Holiness signs-followers and snake-handlers that Ben had brought her from the library. "You might like a little background on this church you're going to," Ben had said as he had held it out to her, opened to a photograph of a young woman, eyes closed in painful ecstasy. A fat rattlesnake, head pulled back as if to strike, was clutched in her hands.

As Elizabeth leafed through the pages, she found a section dealing with the rules of dress followed by church members and noted that women were supposed to keep their hair long, and to dress modestly, and to wear no jewelry. *Paul again,* she sniffed. *I think that the way I dress is modest, but evidently jeans are out. And earrings. But my hair is long, though thinking of that old curmudgeon Paul makes me want to get a crew cut.*

She was deep in the book when the phone rang. This time it was Miss Birdie's cousin Dorothy, in a state of great agitation. "Lizzie Beth, honey. You got to come over here right now! Birdie's nose is a-bleedin' like one thing. You got to come read the verses. Hit's supposed to be someone what ain't related."

"Verses? What verses? Have you had her put her head back and . . ." Elizabeth searched her brain for remedies, ". . . and . . . and hold a cold wet washrag to her nose? That might help."

"Honey, we done tried that but hit's just a-gushin'. They's a verse in Ezekiel that'll stop a nosebleed, but hit's got to be someone what ain't kin that reads it. You come right now!"

"Dorothy, I'm on my way, but . . . I'm probably not the one to do this. You see, I don't believe—"

"Honey, hit don't matter." Dorothy's reply was terse. "You just come do the readin'. Me and Birdie and the Lord'll do the believin'."

As her jeep bumped down the road, Elizabeth's mind was racing. *I wonder what caused Birdie's nose to start bleeding. Dorothy didn't mention a fall or anything. Verses! What's that all about? At least I can take Birdie into the emergency care center if we can't get the bleeding stopped. . . .*

She frowned as she neared Birdie's bridge. *Okay, Elizabeth, don't just assume that you know everything. Let's give Dorothy's way a fair chance—you can still take Birdie to the doctor if it doesn't work. Like Dorothy said, you don't have to do the believin'; just try not to stand in the way.*

Something John the Baptizer had said the night before swam into her mind. "He's telling me to open myself and to make myself a vessel for His Holy Spirit." With an effort that was almost a physical wrench, Elizabeth concentrated: *I have to try to believe that I can help. Open myself and help Birdie. In her way, not mine.* She cleared her mind of the words "superstitious nonsense" and tried to think of nothing but letting her own strength and health flow into her little neighbor. *Help Birdie. Help Birdie.*

She was still inwardly repeating that mantra when she entered Birdie's cabin. Birdie was sitting on the sofa, head leaned far back, and the dishrag that Dorothy was pressing to her nose was ominously red. A small pile of similarly stained cloths lay heaped on the linoleum at her feet.

"Birdie, honey, you keep this rag up to yore nose while I show Lizzie Beth the place in the Book," Dorothy directed her cousin. She reached for the worn black Bible that sat on a crocheted doily in the center of a low table littered with sympathy cards, copies of *The Progressive Farmer,* and a red-capped plastic peanut butter jar full of lemon drops.

"Hit's in Ezekiel, chapter 16." Dorothy's capable hands opened the book to a marker and she ran a finger down the page. "Right here, verse six. You put yore hand on her head and you read the verse, only where it says 'thee,' you say Birdie."

The verse was brief and Elizabeth sat down by Birdie and did as Dorothy had said, changing the *thou*s and *thine*s to *she*s and *her*s. She tried to project a certainty she did not feel as she read, "And when I passed by Birdie and saw Birdie polluted in her own blood, I said unto Birdie when she was in her blood, Live; yea, I said unto Birdie when she was in her blood, Live."

Beneath her hand Birdie's small head felt skull-like. Elizabeth squeezed her eyes shut and once again silently pleaded, *Please help me to help Birdie. Please.* Her hand on Birdie's head felt warm and tingling, almost as if an electrical current was passing from her body into the little form leaning back beside her on the low sofa.

There was a long quiet moment, then Miss Birdie said quietly, "I believe hit's done stopped." Elizabeth opened her eyes to see her little neighbor wiping the last smears of blood from her pale face. "Thank you kindly, Lizzie Beth."

Elizabeth realized that she was trembling as she removed her hand from Birdie's head. "Miss Birdie, are you all right?"

"Ay law," Birdie replied, "you stopped it just fine, Lizzie Beth." She smiled weakly as she lay back on the vinyl-covered sofa. "I knowed you could do it."

"Birdie," Elizabeth said, "You're not going to feel like going over to Tennessee tonight. In fact, why don't you let me take you in to the clinic? You look—"

"Naw, I can't hardly make it. Maybe hit don't matter." Birdie closed her eyes wearily. "About Cletus, I mean. Let my boy rest in peace."

"Birdie, honey, you just lay back and take you a little nap." Dorothy was pulling at Elizabeth's sleeve and nodding urgently toward the door. Taking a last look at Birdie, who seemed in these past few weeks to have become so much smaller and frailer, Elizabeth followed Dorothy outside.

"Dorothy," she exclaimed, once the house door had been closed behind them, "we really need to get Birdie to the doctor! She looks terrible . . . she's lost so much weight—"

Dorothy pursed her lips and glanced toward the house. "She didn't want nobody to know but she finally had to tell *me*. I seen something weren't right and I got it out of her." She paused, as if gathering strength. "The doctor done told her more'n a month ago that she's got cancer in the blood. You know, that leukemia. That's how come her to have these old nosebleeds. Mostly I can stop them with the wet towel, but this one today—well, it's a mercy you was there to read the words."

"But, Dorothy," persisted Elizabeth, horrified at this sudden revelation, "there's got to be something we can do—"

Dorothy shook her head. "We've done ever last thing the doctor said and it ain't done no good. And first thing this mornin' she called me in to her room. Said she was going to crack the Bible and see what the Lord could tell her. So I handed her the Book and she closed her eyes and opened it up. She kept her eyes shut and stabbed her finger right down at the bottom of a page. 'Read it out to me, Dor'thy,' she tells me, her eyes still squinched tight. 'Read it out.' So I looked where her finger's a-restin' and read it to her. Hit was in red for hit was Jesus's own words and hit said, 'Father, into thy hands I commend my spirit.' "

Dorothy's voice trembled, then broke. She cleared her throat. "Well, Birdie opened up her eyes and just looked so peaceful. All she done said was, 'Well, then, I reckon I can do like my Savior.' "

Elizabeth had more questions, but it soon became apparent that Dorothy was doing everything that could be done. "And I'll stay here long as she needs me. Birdie and me always has got along good."

A jumble of thoughts assailed Elizabeth as she drove home. Why hadn't she been aware of Miss Birdie's illness? Surely she should have noticed *something.* "They started her on chemo and blood transfusions and she was holdin' up real good and didn't want to tell nobody," Dorothy had said, "but ever since Cletus's funeral she's been goin' down. I believe she likely ain't got but a few months left."

And then there was the amazing effect of the Ezekiel verse. *My hand was warm and tingling and then the bleeding stopped,* she marveled, as she reviewed the events of the past hour. *It was amazing to me, but not to Birdie and Dorothy. They knew it would work; it was just an everyday folk remedy to them. Was it just the power of suggestion on Birdie's unquestioning faith? That's what Ben would say. But why did my hand have that feeling, that current running through it?*

A glance at the clock told her that she had just enough time to get something to eat and change clothes if she still planned to go to the service at the Holiness Church that night. *Birdie said that it didn't matter about Cletus; to let it be. My poor little Birdie! She's worn out from the disease and the chemo——! But even if she thinks she doesn't care anymore, I need to know the truth. I owe it to her and to Cletus. Maybe it doesn't matter, but I told Harice Tyler I'd be there and be there I will. I want to hear the praying and singing and Aunt Belvy's message and I want to see them handling snakes. And after the Ezekiel verse . . . well . . .*

Her hasty supper done, Elizabeth changed into a suitably modest long-sleeved blouse and long denim skirt. While she was brushing her teeth, the golden glint of her little earrings in the mirror caught her eye. She rinsed her toothbrush, considered for a moment, then quickly took the gold hoops from her earlobes and laid them by the sink. She studied herself, her deep blue eyes reflecting levelly back. Suddenly she undid the elastic band that secured her thick braid, letting the silver-streaked waves of dark hair ripple halfway down her back. She stared into the mirror, remembering that most of the women, young and old at the Holiness church had worn their hair long and loose-flowing. Harice Tyler's words, *"I can tell you ain't no Holiness woman,"* rang in her ears.

For a few seconds longer she contemplated her reflection. Then, remembering the time, she swiftly rebraided her hair. Again she studied the mirror. Finally she threaded the gold hoops back into her earlobes and left.

CHAPTER 18
A DEEP ANOINTING
(SATURDAY NIGHT)

THE LIGHT OF THE BALMY SPRING EVENING WAS fading and Elizabeth's resolution wavered as she approached the little white building that was the Holiness Church of Jesus Love Anointed with Signs Following. She pulled into the crowded parking lot and sat there a minute, motor still running. *What the hell are you doing here, Elizabeth? It was different when you were coming with Miss Birdie. Did you drive all the way over here to find out more about Cletus? Or was it to see Harice Tyler again? Are you just ignoring the possibility; no, the probability that Cletus was drowned in the Tylers' trout flumes? And, you know, if that's true, Harice would have had to be involved. His old daddy couldn't have carried a body off to dump it in the river.*

Light poured from the church door and windows and children chased one another up and down the concrete block steps. A family in a rumbling truck pulled up beside her and clambered out, Bibles in hand. They nodded and smiled at her, then walked eagerly toward the plain little building. She watched them, thinking how happy they all looked. The two little girls in pretty old-fashioned dresses skipped ahead of their parents, who were greeting friends on every side. Her eyes followed them to the steps and then she saw him.

He was standing in the open door looking up and down the parking area, no more than a black shape against the yellow light of the interior, but she recognized him instantly. At the same moment, he caught sight of her jeep and started down the steps. A giggling cluster of teenage girls accosted him at the foot of the steps but he waved them off and continued. Elizabeth cut off the motor and headlights and hastily removed her earrings, dropping them into her purse.

"Evening, Sister Goodweather," Harice Tyler said as he opened her door. "Aunt Belvy told me that Miss Birdie couldn't come so I wanted to make you welcome myself."

Escorting her into the church, he introduced her to a large, friendly-looking woman sitting on a bench near the front with a gaggle of small children. "Sister Morris, this here's Sister Goodweather from over to Ransom. She's here to see what this church is about." The woman smiled widely and slid over to give Elizabeth the seat on the aisle.

"We think a lot of Brother Tyler," Sister Morris said in an undertone, her eyes on Harice as he mounted the dais to exchange greetings with several other men. She pulled a squirming child into her lap and gave it a paper fan to play with. "He's been right lonely since his wife went to be with Jesus."

Elizabeth wondered if Harice Tyler's wife had died of snakebite. But she just smiled and asked, "Is all this good-looking bunch yours?" nodding toward the five young children who were ranged on the bench beyond Sister Morris.

"My grandbabies," the plump woman acknowledged

with a proud smile. "I got fourteen, but these is the least uns. They love to go to church with Mamaw."

A squabble between the boy and girl sitting nearest the wall demanded the grandmother's attention, so Elizabeth watched the congregation as they prepared for the services. Now the men on the dais were embracing one another. She had been surprised, on her first visit, to see these rugged country men kissing one another on the cheek, but her reading had explained that this had been prescribed by Paul in his epistle to the Romans, "Salute one another with an holy kiss."

Women were hugging women and settling their children along the benches. Aunt Belvy swept in, tall and imposing, and sat a little apart in a front pew, leaning back against a cushion that must have been placed there especially for her. Two young women whom Elizabeth remembered from her previous visit hurried into seats near the front, giving her strangely unfriendly sidelong glances as they passed. Harice and five other men took their places on chairs and benches behind the pulpit. Beneath the table to the side were three flat snake boxes.

The service began with a burst of spontaneous prayer. The men at the front knelt on the floor, leaning over their chairs or benches while the rest of the congregation hunched over the back of the benches in front of them or leaned down, covering their faces with their hands. The noise of loud individual prayer that had so startled Elizabeth on her first visit now took on a different aspect. *Not really cacophony,* she thought, *more like an avant-garde symphony.*

She had bowed her head in respect for the beliefs of this church where she was a guest, but she watched those around her through her half-closed eyes. To her right Sister Morris seemed to be running through a litany of names, asking blessings on each one and occasionally noting special problems. "Jesus, please help Angie Lee. It's her first baby and she's scared. Please put your arms around her and comfort her . . ." and across the aisle a very old man was praying for "them that's wanderin' and lost, Lord. Gather in yore sheep to yore heavenly fold."

As the service continued with singing accompanied by an electric guitar, an organ, and several tambourines, Elizabeth was struck by the unselfconscious ease with which the congregation filled the sanctuary with their faith. *This,* she thought, *this is what it means to "Make a joyful noise before the Lord."* The simple little building seemed to rock with fellowship, freely given and received. The invisible barrier that Elizabeth had deliberately erected around herself on her previous visit dissolved and she felt not so much an observer as a participant in the service. She enjoyed singing the emotional gospel songs—"Prayer Bells from Heaven," and a rousing rendition of "He Will Set Your Fields on Fire"—happy that her unmusical croak was drowned out by the exuberant voices of those around her.

The guitar and organ quieted as the first man stood to speak, but the jingle of the tambourine continued in a steady undertone, occasionally increasing in volume as the shouted responses of the congregation rang out. The preaching was predictable, as before, but this time she was able to focus on the consolation rather than the threat offered by the message. And when Sister Morris suddenly thrust a pudgy grandbaby into her lap and stood and shouted out, "Marema akailo, kareen a todai!" Elizabeth merely rocked the drowsy child and snuggled it till it fell asleep, gripping her shirtfront with a sticky hand. She felt very near tears, but a smile had spread itself across her face and she began to wish that she had a tambourine.

She became aware of a growing feeling of anticipation in the churchgoers assembled there listening to the preaching. The woman at the organ began to play quiet chords and the electric guitar occasionally wailed an instrumental amen to the speaker's message. The congregation rustled expectantly, longing for the visitation of spirit that would bring down a deep anointing on some of their number. At the front, Aunt Belvy had risen to her feet and was swaying back and forth. The tambourines and organ grew louder, beating out a quicker, more insistent rhythm, and each new speaker was greeted with shouts of "Tell it!"

A sweet-faced old man testified of his miraculous escape from illness—a bleeding ulcer that had been cured when the church members had laid hands on him. He was making his way back to the deacons' bench when Aunt Belvy threw up her right hand and shouted out, "Yea, I say unto the sinner, yea!" She wheeled and strode down the aisle to Elizabeth's side. Elizabeth found herself handing the dozing baby back to its grandmother and rising to meet the prophetess, just as Birdie had done. The two tall women faced each other; dark brown eyes locked with deep blue.

"You must persevere; seek in the rocks of the mountains and in the living waters. Two, there are two joined in blood and water. Two by the hand of the father, two by the false prophet." Aunt Belvy's deep voice had filled the little sanctuary, but suddenly she lowered it to a soft whisper, seemingly meant for Elizabeth's ears alone. "I say unto thee, thou shalt not deny the gift."

The dark eyes, so dilated that they seemed to be bottomless pools of midnight water, bored into Elizabeth's, then rolled back, leaving only the whites showing, and, as before, Aunt Belvy slumped in a near faint. And, as before, she was caught by two men and helped back to her seat.

The guitar and organ fell silent. Elizabeth felt the combined gaze of the congregation on her and hurriedly sat down as Harice Tyler stepped to the pulpit. For a long heartbeat or two he stood looking approvingly at her. Then, in a low voice that grew steadily in volume and intensity, he began to preach. "Brother Eldon was speakin' just now of being healed by this church. We know that it's one of the Lord's gifts to some of his children: Some have prophecy—" He glanced at Aunt Belvy, who was rocking back and forth where she sat. She nodded her head and put up a shaking hand. "Some have discernment." He gestured toward someone in the back of the room who called out "Praise His Name" as a tambourine was rattled vigorously.

"Some have the gift of tongues, like Sister Morris." A sharp bang on the skin of the tambourine and a steady jingle followed these words.

Elizabeth's neighbor on the bench smiled and said in a conversational tone, "Bless Him."

"What do we make of a sinner who's been given one of the gifts? A sinner who can lay a hand on an old woman and stop her bleedin'? A sinner who says she don't believe? Well, I tell you this: God is mighty. He can work through a sinner but at the same time He's a-callin' that sinner, He's a-showin' what he can offer, and He's waiting for that sinner to come home."

Harice Tyler was not looking at Elizabeth, nor were those around her, but she felt her face glowing red. The sermon moved on to God's mysterious ways and became too loud and too quickly spoken for Elizabeth to follow easily. The organ and guitar now kept pace with the preacher's impassioned words. As the momentum picked up, many of the people in the room rose, swaying and dancing in place. The music grew louder still and the baby on Sister Morris's lap wakened and put out its arms to Elizabeth, wiggling its fingers and demanding, "Hold you?" She took the toddler back in her lap, grateful for the distraction.

Elizabeth had closed her eyes and bent her head to inhale the sweet fragrance of baby shampoo and to consider what Aunt Belvy's message might have meant . . . *if I believed that sort of thing. A false prophet and two joined in blood and water. Water again* . . . when she became aware of a subtle shift in the atmosphere of the room. The *amens* and *hallelujahs* that had punctuated Harice Tyler's sermon had become louder, and the jingle of the tambourines was being answered by a dry buzzing sound.

She opened her eyes to see a heavy young man dancing in front of the pulpit. A black timber rattler was draped around his neck, its tail a blur of motion. A few feet away Harice was lifting two brilliant copperheads in his right hand and bringing them close to his face, so close that their slender forked tongues flicked delicately at his lips. His eyes were squeezed tight and his head was thrown back. On his face was a look of rapt exaltation.

Across the aisle from Elizabeth, one of the young women who had given her such an unpleasant look. Buxom and dark-haired, she was wearing a modest blue-flowered dress with a wide lace collar. Her pretty face was shining with happiness and her lips were moving constantly as she approached the man with the rattler and held out both hands. He paused in his dancing, slid the serpent from his shoulders, and laid it across her open palms. She raised the heavy snake above her head and began to turn in graceful circles, her long dark hair fanning out around her.

Elizabeth realized that amidst the loud music and shouted exhortations there was a quiet bustle of movement in her pew. All the small children were being shepherded to the back of the church, away from the handlers on the raised dais. Sister Morris and her brood were squeezing past her, the children gaping at the serpents and reluctant to move. As Sister Morris plucked the sleepy baby from Elizabeth's lap, she leaned over to say with a sweet, gap-toothed smile, "You stay here, Sister Goodweather, and see what faith in the Lord can do. I believe this deep anointin's been sent because you're here."

Elizabeth watched, spellbound, as the snakes were passed from one to another of those who felt the call to handle. She had read that believers were sometimes bitten, and that, of these, some died, though many lived to handle again. The library book had quoted a handler from Kentucky: "Some folks say the snakes is doped up or their fangs is pulled but I'm here to tell you, buddy, this thing is real."

This thing is *real,* she thought, seeing the snakes being handled casually, even roughly. These ordinary people, these farmers, factory hands, mothers and fathers were in a mystical state as genuine as that of any whirling Sufi, any meditating Zen monk awaiting *satori,* as any person of any faith seeking to attain oneness with God by abandoning reason and trusting to spirit. The danger was real, the snakes were real, and the faith was real. The handlers all seemed to be in a deep ecstasy, beyond disbelief, beyond doubt, beyond fear.

Harice Tyler had passed over his two copperheads to a waiting deacon who clasped one in each hand and hopped across the dais, calling out in unintelligible staccato syllables. Tyler watched him and then, glancing toward Elizabeth, reached into the third snake box. He lifted up a fat yellow rattler and held it out to the congregation like an offering. The snake lay placidly across his splayed fingers, its questing tongue daintily tasting the air. The guitar and organ that had been pounding out an earsplitting anthem, three parts gospel, one part rock and roll, grew softer. The insistent rhythm pulsed in a compelling beat as Harice Tyler held the big yellow rattler out and said, "This is for someone."

For a moment, caught up in the music and the mystery, Elizabeth thought, *I could do that.* She imagined holding the snake, silky and cool, strong and firm, in her hands and looking without fear into its slitted pupils. She had a momentary vision of herself dancing barefoot before the Lord, a copperhead in each hand, and Harice Tyler at her side. Harice Tyler was staring steadily at her now and holding out the big rattler, which lay unmoving in his hands.

She felt her body begin to tremble, and she shifted her weight forward as if to rise. Harice's eyes were locked with hers and seemed to be pulling her toward him. She hesitated, balanced there on the razor edge between reason and faith. Then, with a feeling of indefinable loss, she slid back in her seat and looked down. *No,* she thought, *no, not for me.*

It was almost midnight before she was on her way back over the mountain to North Carolina and home. Harice Tyler had escorted her to her car and promised to go with her the next day to the militia compound to ask about Ursa. He'd lingered beside her car and finally had said, "You hadn't ought to fight the Lord. I could see you was thinkin' about handlin' tonight. The Lord, He'll keep atter you iffen He wants you."

Then he'd stepped back abruptly and given her car a dismissive slap. "See you tomorrow, Miz Goodweather." As she drove off, Elizabeth had glimpsed the young woman who had danced with the snake, loitering purposefully by Harice Tyler's truck.

The road was dark and winding. Anonymous houses gave way to pitch-black fields and pastures, then the wooded slopes of the mountain road that would take her back to North Carolina. Elizabeth drove almost automatically while she struggled to make sense of the events of the evening. She was startled by her response to the service, her pleasure at being accepted so warmly by most of the congregation—*They called me Sister Goodweather!*—and her fleeting desire—*Where did that come from, Elizabeth?*—to take up a serpent.

"So what have I learned tonight?" she asked herself as she turned onto the road that would take her home. "Aside from the fact that I have fantasies about a snake-handling preacher with bedroom eyes." She slowed to let a possum amble across the road. "Aunt Belvy said to keep looking in the rocks and dens of the mountains, and I'm going to do that. And then there was all that stuff about two joined in blood and water. Could she have meant that Dewey Shotwell and Cletus were killed by the same person? And there was something about a false prophet—that could mean the militia people or . . . or Polaris . . . or . . ."

In bed at last, well after two, Elizabeth had trouble falling asleep, a rare thing for her. She had read till her eyes were burning with weariness and had finally turned out the light. She lay there exhausted, willing sleep to come so that she could stop reliving the events of the evening. *If only I had a sleeping pill or some—what was that stuff the doctor gave us when Rosemary was teething and would scream for hours? It would put her to sleep when nothing else would do.* She punched her pillows into a more comfortable lump and turned on her side.

Paregoric, that was it. Worked like a charm. But I think they had quit prescribing it by the time Laurel was born. Too dangerous in an overdose.

As she was sinking into sleep an image drifted through her mind—a brown bottle half full of a clear liquid. The torn and faded label had read "Pare—" and Miss Birdie had said, "Throw it out, Dor'thy. I ain't got no need for it now."

VIII–January 1902

The weather turned bitter cold and I spent my days sewin to make ready for my babe. Mister Tomlin had brung me a bundle of birdseye for hippins and some lengths of domestic and outing to make little gowns. Whilst I sewed I thought of Levy and wondered would I hear from him. I wondered did he even know I carried his child for I hadn't gotten a chance to tell him that last time we was together. I had been namin to when Mister Tomlin come up on us.

Atter I had finished with the gowns, I decided to piece a quilt for the baby. Aetha had give me a pattern called World Without End and I used my scraps to cut out the little pointy pieces in blue and white. I was gettin so big that hit pained my back to bend over the sewin machine for too long so I pieced my babe's quilt by hand. They was twenty five blocks to piece and I told myself that I would piece one every day and Levy would send word to me before I finished the twenty fifth.

Mister Tomlin didn't touch me no more. I believe that he was sickened by the sight of my belly. He stayed gone right much of the time and when he come home, he mostly et his supper and went to bed. He drunk that medicine most ever night now and snored till mornin. Now and again he would say something hateful, but he never offered to touch me.

When I had finished the twenty fifth block and still no word from Levy, I made up my mind to walk over the mountain and ask for news of him from his folks. I feared to wait much longer for I was swellin like one thing. Rom had said that my babe would likely come in April and Rom was generally right about such matters. She was reckoned to be a right good hand at catchin babies and had been with Aetha for all of hern, as well as helpin one and another of the women on the branch when their times had come.

Hit was a bright clear day and no wind. Mister Tomlin had gone to Ransom atter lamp oil and wicks and wouldn't be back til nigh dark. I dressed in my wool skirt and two outing petticoats and took a baccer stick to help me climb. The ground was hard froze with only a skift of snow on it but hit felt plumb good to be outside, walkin up the mountain past the places where me and Levy had laid down and swore to love one another true. I couldn't climb like I used to but before too very long I was a-standin on the top of the mountain and lookin down at the homeplace and over to the Gentrys' fields beyond. Down the other side I could see the Johnsons' cabin and barns. There was a woman makin her way to the spring, but I couldn't tell if hit were Levy's mother or one of his sisters.

Standin there under that clear blue sky and breathin in the clean cold air made me think Heaven must be like this.

I could see where Bear Tree Creek run and Ridley Branch and I could trace where the French Broad snaked through the valley at the foot of the Walnut Mountains. I could see the houses of Dewell Hill and far, far off to the southeast there was a smudge that Levy had told me was Asheville. I thought that my mother in Heaven was likely lookin down on the world in just this same way and I wondered if she knowed hit was me atop Pinnacle Mountain.

I looked up at that blue sky and said, Mommy, hit's yore Sylvie what you borned right afore you went up there. I wish you was here, you and my brothers. I'm in kindly of a fix just now but I reckon hit'll all come right in the end. Then I waved my hand and blowed some kisses up in the air. They weren't hardly a sound but for the bell on old Poll in the pasture behind the homeplace far below.

It come to me how foolish I must a looked so I quit my loaferin and slipped through the scuttle-hole there by the gap. I like to stuck in it what with my belly, but I squeezed through and hit the trail that the cows had made. While I went, I thought about what I would say to Levy's folks.

When I come to the spring I stopped and got me a drink with the dipper gourd that was hangin from a nail on the big oak just above the pool. They was a skim of ice atop the water but a place was broke out to one side where a path led down to the pool. The little stream that run out of the pool and down the hill was sparklin in the sun and ice was on the rocks like a thousand stars.

I seen someone lookin out a window in the house below me so I put the dipper back and hollered out, Hello, the house.

Atter a while the door opened and Levy's sister Mabel

called out for me to come in and warm. Thank you kindly, I said as I climbed the steps. I'd be grateful to set a spell.

Inside the house Miz Johnson was by the fire spinnin at her great wheel. She has a big loom out in a barn shed and she is the best weaver anyone ever seen. Well, Miz Tomlin, she says, what in the name of goodness be you doin out in this cold air and you with child? She reached for her spit jar then she said, I reckon you best pull off them things and come and warm. She didn't say no more but went back to her spinnin, that wheel a-creakin like a cricket with every round. I could see that Miz Johnson weren't none too pleased to see me and I wondered iffen she had suspicioned aught about me and Levy.

Why, says I, I was like to smother in that little cabin and I just took a notion that I'd like to go a-roamin for a piece. Likely hit'll be my last chance for some time. And then when I got up to the top of Pinnacle and seen your chimbly smoke I just thought I'd come pay a visit to you uns.

Miz Johnson didn't say nothing, just lifted her eyebrows and went on spinnin but Mabel spoke right up, Why, we are proud to see you, Little Sylvie. I don't reckon we've laid eyes on you since your marryin. Now, Levy said he seen you a time or two when he was workin for your daddy but—

How is Levy doin? I ask, not lookin at either of them but liftin my foot to the fire to warm. I believe Mister Tomlin said he went to Kentucky? Do you hear from him any?

We ain't heared nothing and don't look to, says Miz Johnson, sharp-like and spinnin right on. Levy's gone to work hard and better himself. Mister Tomlin said did Levy do a good job, he was namin to make Levy a boss and give

*him a house to live in. I reckon he'll find him a wife there
in Kentucky, says she, spinnin on. Ain't so many single
girls around here. And she cut her eyes over at me and I
seen that she knowed or maybe just guessed.*

*You warm yoreself, Miz Tomlin, says she, and then
you'd best hit for home. A married woman in your state
oughtn't to be a-wanderin the mountains. Yore husband'll
not thank you an you bring his babe to harm.*

*I felt my eyes fill up and I wondered would she have
been lovin to me had Mister Tomlin never come along and
had me and Levy courted and wed. I reckon she would
have. I think what made her so ill was fear for Levy. I believe that she was happy to have him well away from me
where she didn't have to worry about Mister Tomlin maybe
shootin him down as he rode along.*

*Thank you for the warmin, Miz Johnson. I'll just take
my leave now, I says, and I wrap my shawl back around
me. I quick make for the door afore I bust out a-cryin. That
wheel's a-creakin steady behind me and seems like I won't
never get its sound outten my head.*

*Mabel opens the door for me and steps out on the porch,
closin the door behind her. Little Sylvie, she says, Levy
talked some about you and—*

*Just then Miz Johnson hollers, Mabel, you come back
in the house! and Mabel gives me a tight hug and whispers,
He's in a place called White Oak. You be careful, Little
Sylvie.*

*The climb back up Pinnacle seemed steeper than I remem-
bered and I got to cryin so hard I couldn't hardly catch my*

breath. I kept thinkin on Levy in Kentucky and wonderin iffen he might be lovin some other girl. When I got to the mountaintop I was in deep despair and I thought to pull off my clothes and lay down under the sky and freeze to death. I was so crazy with wantin Levy that I pulled off my shawl and flung hit down and started in to undoin my shirtwaist. Then I saw that little gold heart he give me, glintin there between my breasts. I minded how he had said that he was my own true love. Just then the baby kicked like one thing and I knowed that I must bide till the babe was born and I was strong again. Iffen Levy hadn't sent word by then, I vowed, me and the baby would go to Kentucky and find him.

CHAPTER 19
SUNSHINE AND DOGHOBBLE
(SUNDAY)

ELIZABETH SPRANG OUT OF BED, REALIZING THAT SHE had slept far longer than usual and that she would have to hurry if she was to meet Harice Tyler at ten. *God, I hope we can find Ursa* ran through her mind, then she altered the thought to *Please, let us find Ursa.*

She dressed quickly in her usual jeans and work shirt and tried once again to reach Phillip Hawkins to tell him about the message from Trent Woodbern. Still no answer. She banged down the phone in frustration. *Okay, Elizabeth, if you ever do get hold of the man, will you also tell him about the bottle of medicine Dorothy threw out?*

She cut a thick slice of bread and microwaved a cup of tea, her mind busy with an unpleasant scenario. *They could have been in the truck and she could have given him enough paregoric to make him sleep really soundly—probably in a Pepsi. She told me how they'd always get a Pepsi as a treat when they went to town. She could have timed it so he was still asleep when it was good and dark and then driven to the trestle, driven out on it a little way and opened the door. She could have shoved him out . . .*

She shuddered and put down her tea and bread, untasted. *Birdie couldn't have done that, not to her only child,* she argued silently. But then she remembered how Birdie had shot her own beloved watchdog when it had been discovered killing a neighbor's lambs. "Couldn't you find another home for him away from here or keep him tied up?" Elizabeth had begged and Birdie had answered, tight-lipped and implacable, "What kind of life would he have tied up all the time? Naw, hit'll be quick and he'll not suffer and then I won't have to worry about how somebody else might do him."

And she knew she didn't have much longer and she knew Cletus couldn't be happy in an institution somewhere. That must be it. And all that getting me to drive her around and looking for his shotgun . . . was she just playing a part and now she's too tired and sick to keep it up? Dorothy said Birdie only has a few months to live. And as far as the sheriff's concerned it was an accident. So what would be the point of my saying anything about it to anyone? She felt a dull weariness as she prepared for her trip to Devil's Fork.

Harice Tyler was waiting, leaning against his truck when she reached the turnoff to Little Man Holler. "Naw, hit'd look better was you to ride with me," he said when she stopped to pick him up. "Just pull yore car up our road a piece. Won't nobody bother it."

She put up her windows and locked the jeep, then climbed into the cab of Tyler's pickup, after a hasty glance to confirm that there were no snake boxes and no suspicious burlap bags lurking inside. She realized that Tyler was watching her and saw an amused look come over his face. "You don't have to worry about ridin' with no snakes, Miz Goodweather. Don't nobody have to mess with serpents until they feel the Spirit move on them."

He got into the driver's seat and they started up Bear Tree Creek. "What did you think of the service last night?" he asked her.

She looked out the window of the truck, enjoying the brilliant sunshine slanting down into the narrow valley of Bear Tree Creek. The trees still wore the bright yellow-greens of spring and early summer and the air was scented with the heady smell of leucothoë blossoms—"doghobble," the mountain folks called it. Years ago she and Sam had decided that the doghobble bloom smelled like love-making and that its pungent fragrance was a signal for all wild things to come in heat.

"I liked it," she said, realizing that he was waiting for an answer. "I felt very . . . very welcomed." This seemed inadequate and she went on, "It was so different from the church I grew up in, and I don't mean just the snakes. The whole thing, how close everyone seems to God and to each other. It seemed so . . . real."

"Hit is real," he replied.

There was a guard at the gate to the militia compound, not the same man Elizabeth had encountered before. He seemed to know Tyler and the two chatted amiably for a few minutes. At last Harice told him, "I'd take it kindly was you to let me through. I need to talk to Colonel Flinn."

The guard shrugged, swung open the heavy metal gate, and waved them into the woods of Devil's Fork. Harice shifted his truck into four-wheel drive and eased it up the steep dirt and gravel road. "Looks like they'd shoot some of these big rocks," he commented as the truck crawled painfully over a half-buried boulder that resembled a small, basking whale. "A few sticks of dynamite'd make a big difference."

He grimaced as something on the underside of the truck scraped over a high rock. "Me and Daddy used t' come up here atter sang, but we allus come on foot or rode his plow mules."

Elizabeth's eyes were scanning the woods for any sign of Ursa. Just to make conversation, she asked, "Who lived here before these people bought it?"

"Ain't nobody ever lived here far as I know. Too steep and rocky fer baccer. And ain't many folks around here want to live in a place called Devil's Fork." Harice shook his head as his muffler scraped on another protruding rock. "Mostly when people from away buy land, first thing they do is put in a good road. I guess these old boys don't want much company."

The woods were thinning now and Elizabeth could see a small, relatively level clearing that seemed to have been set up as an obstacle course of some sort. There were climbing ropes dangling from a row of scaffolds made of locust trunks, a series of barricades made of the same unpeeled locust, and a high bridge consisting of slender logs laid end to end snaking its way over a large rectangular pool.

"They got ol' Clifford Webster and his backhole digger and bullnoser up here to dig that pit." Harice nodded toward the murky water as they made their way past the clearing. "Hit's dug eight foot deep. Clifford told Daddy that they use it for trainin'; make their men swim acrost it with all their clothes on and a big ol' pack and a rifle too. Just like the Marine Corps, he said. And then they make 'em run over them foot logs carryin' all that gear. Hit must be a sight on earth watchin' them ol' boys try to keep their balance. Them logs don't look to be more'n ten inches around."

They were approaching another level area, evidently the work of Clifford Webster and his bulldozer. Rough cuts in the mountain slope were almost covered in rampant grapevines, and a cluster of small buildings, crudely constructed of rough-sawn lumber, stood in a semicircle around a bare expanse of dirt. At the center a tall flagpole flew the American flag. The largest of the buildings was opposite the flagpole, and over its door Elizabeth saw the logo Ben had described to her—an American flag in the shape of the United States with a cross rising out of it. Beneath it were the capital letters *HQ*.

"Where are all the people?" asked Elizabeth, surprised at seeing only a pimply teenager in fatigues standing beside the headquarters door, his legs braced wide apart and his hands behind his back, sentry-style.

"Prob'ly up the mountain," answered Harice as he stopped the truck and cut the motor. "They get a lot of weekend fellers, ones what ain't quit their jobs but want to belong. They come out and Flinn and his buddies run 'em up and down all weekend. Even at night, what I hear."

The bright colors of the flag whipped and snapped against the clear blue sky as the young guard came around the truck to Harice's window. "State your business," he said curtly, with a scowl that was meant to be threatening.

Harice smiled easily and said, "Fine day, ain't it, son. You just tell Colonel Flinn that his neighbor over the hill's here to see him. He knows who I am."

The boy disappeared into the headquarters building. *That was easy,* Elizabeth thought. *So far, so good. Now if I can just keep my mouth shut and let Harice do the talking . . .*

The teenager reappeared at the doorway and beckoned to them. Harice opened his door and said, "Might be best was you just to wait in—"

Elizabeth shook her head. "No way. You can do the talking but I need to go in with you."

They were ushered in to a room containing a desk littered with papers and pamphlets. There were filing cabinets and a computer workstation, as well as a television and VCR on a stand. Behind the desk, the rough plank wall bore a large banner with the same flag-and-cross logo, this time with the words, *Adam's Sons in the Wilderness—God's People—God's Land*. A small man with thinning dark hair sat behind the desk. He was wearing camouflage fatigues and didn't look up from the sheaf of papers he was studying.

"What's the problem now, Tyler?" he growled at last, tossing the papers aside and leaning back in his swivel chair. He peered over the top of his wire-rimmed glasses with a sour gaze. "I warned the troops to stay off your land. We uphold the sanctity of a white man's property. Some of those new recruits—"

"Ain't nothing like that, Colonel," Harice drawled equably. "We ain't been bothered by yore boys since I put a load of rock salt into a couple of 'em. They must of thought couldn't nobody see 'em with their camo outfits and their painted-up faces. Naw, hit's about a dog. Miz Goodweather here's lost a big, black shaggy dog. I seen it go through my place back of this, a-headin' up yore way. Thought hit might be hangin' around here."

The colonel's sharp gray eyes rested on Elizabeth briefly. Without acknowledging her presence, he said curtly, "I wouldn't know anything about any dog." He picked up his papers again. "Ask Strickland about it on your way out."

Strickland, the young guard, seemed unsure. He might have seen a big black dog around, but not today. "Some of the men were trying to catch it, but—" He stopped short as if he'd said more than he'd meant to, then resumed his military stance by the door. His spotty face became a rigid, tight-lipped mask. There would be no more conversation about dogs, his expression said.

"Something's not right," muttered Elizabeth, and as Harice was preparing to climb back into the truck, she strode to the base of the flagpole and whistled shrilly. Then, in a deep, loud voice, she called: "Urrrsaa, Urrrsaaa!"

From the interior of the building farthest to the left came a frantic scrabbling and an answering bark. Elizabeth dashed to the door just as Ursa, trailing a short length of rope with a wetly frayed end, barreled around the building from the back. Seventy-five pounds of joy hurtled at Elizabeth, who sank to her knees to hug her dog.

"Once was lost but now she's found," commented Harice, opening the truck door for Elizabeth. Ursa, taking this as an invitation, leaped in.

"Let's just get out of here," said Elizabeth, seeing that young Stickland had gone back inside the headquarters building. "I've got her now and that's all I care about."

As they made their way back down the road, Elizabeth ran her hands over the dog in search of any wounds. Aside from being thinner than usual and covered with burrs and dried mud, Ursa seemed in good condition. Elizabeth felt under the long ruff of fur for the collar that carried her phone number, but it was missing. In its place was a tightly knotted rope, the end of which Ursa had evidently chewed through. Elizabeth worked at the knot patiently till at last it was loose. Her elation at finding Ursa was rapidly being replaced with anger at these people who had kept her dog tied up.

"There's some of them weekend fellers now," Harice commented as they passed the obstacle course. Twenty men in the inevitable camouflage fatigues were struggling up the long ropes or clambering over the high log barricades. To one side stood a burly figure, shouting at them in a deep, gravelly voice that would have done credit to any Parris Island drill instructor. Elizabeth stared in amazement as the man pulled off his cap and threw it to the ground in disgust at the seeming inability of one of the climbers to progress more than three feet up the rope. His back was to her, but the shiny, nut brown, bald head and the voice were unmistakable. Phillip Hawkins.

Suddenly he became aware of the truck passing and swung around. His eyes met Elizabeth's and for a moment he looked totally bewildered. Then, scooping up his cap, he slapped it back in place and swung back to his charges. "Come on, ladies, get your butts up those ropes!"

Elizabeth buried her face in Ursa's silky ruff. It smelled of the woods, of earth and leaves. She hugged the big animal and struggled to make sense of what she had just seen. At her side, Harice Tyler was saying, "They say a dog's man's best friend; looks like you must feel that way."

"You can trust a dog."

"I'm right proud you found her. I was afraid they might be havin' what they call a night hunt tonight. Those weekend fellers dearly love creepin' around the woods with their rifles and such. I had to talk to Flinn back of this; they was snoopin' all around my daddy's place and he don't hold with that. Flinn said they was just practicin' reconnaissance. I told him they could go practice it som'eres else."

As they passed through the gate and turned back onto Bear Tree Creek, Harice waved cheerfully at the guard.

"They ain't all bad. Some of 'em are just old boys who want to play soldier on the weekends. But they can be a little wild with them guns. Last time I seen that Cletus, he was talkin' about goin' over yon to transplant sang out of them beds Daddy planted back of this. Me and Daddy both told him to stay away from there, sang or no sang."

Elizabeth found it difficult to concentrate on Harice's words. The scene at the obstacle course replayed on an endless loop in her brain. *He was at my house . . . he knew Ursa was my dog . . . He was Sam's friend . . .* formed the sound track.

By the time they were back at the foot of Little Man Holler where her car was parked, Elizabeth had resolved to put Hawkins out of her mind . . . *and life. I'm not going to ruin the rest of this beautiful day worrying about that creep.*

She let Ursa out to nose around the roadside. She and Harice sat in his truck, talking of sang and dogs and springtime. The sun's pleasant warmth filled the cab; the urgent scent of leucothoë was strong in her nostrils.

"Thank you so much for going with me," she said finally, touching him lightly on the arm before she reached for the door handle. Immediately his other hand covered hers. She hesitated, feeling a surge of warmth and confusion. Then, delicately slipping free her hand, she continued, "They probably wouldn't have even let me in."

A small blue car came around the curve and pulled up beside Harice Tyler's truck. The dark-haired young woman who had danced with the snake the night before looked out of the driver's window with a melting smile. "Brother Tyler, I brought one of my special cakes for you and your daddy."

Elizabeth said a quick good-bye and drove back down the branch toward the bridge, Ursa happily asleep on the seat beside her. She fondled the dog's silky ears and Ursa awoke briefly to lick her hand. Black thoughts ran through Elizabeth's mind. *Is anyone what they seem? It's like the Little Sylvie story—did she abandon her baby or did she run off with it? Was she good or was she bad?*

Ahead she saw the sign to Lonesome Holler. Impulsively, she turned up the road. *Maybe Walter and Ollie can tell me more about Little Sylvie. That story just haunts me; it happened right on my place and Birdie and Dorothy only seem to know part of it. They said that the boy Sylvie ran off with was a Johnson and kin to Walter. Maybe Walter can tell me more of the story—if Ollie will let him.*

As before, Walter and Ollie were sitting on their porch. Elizabeth left the dozing Ursa in the car and greeted the couple. They were plainly delighted to have company and Ollie said, "How's our Birdie gettin' along? I know she must miss her boy. But it's good that she's got Dorothy to stay with her. That is the workinest woman. Have they found out any more about Cletus—how it happened?"

Elizabeth had already decided not to mention Miss Birdie's illness, since Dorothy had said that Birdie didn't want anyone to know. "Birdie's not feeling too well, but I know Dorothy's taking good care of her. And, no, they haven't found out anything yet." She went on quickly, "One reason I came by was to ask about a story Birdie and Dorothy were telling me. It was about Little Sylvie Baker, who used to live on my place. I thought maybe you all might . . ."

The look on Ollie's face would freeze water but Walter smiled broadly and leaned forward to speak.

"I know that story. It was my uncle she run off with."

"Well!" huffed Ollie, "I don't know why your family would even talk about such a thing! The idea—"

But this time Walter would not be denied. "My daddy

was the oldest of the children and Levy was his brother. It was Levy she went off with. My aunt Mabel was an old maid and she lived with us when I was growin' up. She loved to tell the story of how she had told Little Sylvie where Levy was when Mamaw Johnson didn't want her to know. She said that it was the most ro-mantic thing, how Levy had come back one day and hid out in the barn loft so wouldn't no one in the family know he was there. But when Mabel come out to do the milkin', he had called to her and told her that he was waitin' for evenin' then he was aimin' to go over the mountain and get Little Sylvie. Said he had train tickets to take them to Texas and he didn't expect they'd ever come back for he feared what Sylvie's husband might do."

Walter paused, glancing over at his wife. "You might as well tell it all," she said grudgingly.

"Well," he went on, having been given permission—"Aunt Mabel said she asked him did he know Little Sylvie had a baby and she always said that he had looked kindly surprised at that but said that he knew she was waitin' for him and the baby wouldn't need no ticket."

A thought occurred to him. "How'd you like to see a picture of Levy?"

He began to pull himself up from his chair but Ollie said, "Oh, for mercy's sake, Walter, I'll go get it," and bustled into the trailer.

Walter eased back with a satisfied smile. "He give Mabel a picture he'd had took when he was over to Kentucky. Said to give it to their mommy with his love and to tell her that he'd write."

"And did he write from Texas?" Elizabeth asked eagerly.

Walter frowned and scratched his head. "Now, I couldn't rightly say. Seems like I asked Aunt Mabel and

she said that if he ever had, Mamaw Johnson must have
tore the letters up like she done the picture. Aunt Mabel
said that Mamaw took on like one thing when Mabel
give her the picture and told her about Levy. Just tore
that picture in two and flung it to the ground. Wouldn't
never speak her son's name again. Of course Mabel, she
saved those two pieces of the picture and hid 'em."

Ollie returned to the porch with a yellowing envelope in her hand. "You have so much plunder in that top
drawer of yours I like to never found it."

Walter took the envelope and drew out a small sepia-
toned photograph. "Purty good-lookin' feller, don't you
think? All us Johnson boys was good-lookin' and bad to
court the ladies."

The photo had been torn horizontally and clumsily
put back together with Scotch tape that was brittle with
age. It showed a handsome young man with light hair
and a serious gaze. He wore a plaid shirt with its collar
undone and around his neck, on a thin chain, glinted a
tiny metal heart.

All the way home, down Bear Tree Creek, up Ridley
Branch, and up her own road, Elizabeth thought about
the young man in the picture. He'd remained true and
come back for his love, in spite of the danger. *But what
about the baby? Did they just abandon Sylvie's baby?* She
shook her head, trying to dislodge the ugly thoughts that
buzzed and settled in her brain. *A sweet story . . . except
the baby died. A nice friend of Sam's . . . except he's a member
of that militia. A wonderful husband . . . right up to the part
where he went for a stupid plane ride.*

At her side, Ursa sat up and put her shaggy head out
the window, happy to see familiar surroundings. James

and Molly ran barking to the car and sniffed Ursa from nose to tail before she could break away and bound toward the front door. Elizabeth followed the dogs, feeling suddenly exhausted. She let them in, fixed their bowls of dog chow, with an extra scoop for Ursa, then went to the phone to call the radio station and cancel her missing-dog announcement.

The stutter of the dial tone told her that there was a message on the voice mail. She punched in her number, and the same gravelly voice she'd heard shouting orders at the militia trainees said, *"Elizabeth, you got to trust—"* before it cut off in a wave of static.

CHAPTER 20
My Name Is Mary Cleophas
(Monday)

T HE MESSAGE ON THE VOICE MAIL MADE NO MORE sense the next morning than it had the night before. Elizabeth listened to it a third time, then erased it. Nothing made any sense to her now. She dragged through her routines—*make bed, fill bird feeder, fix breakfast*—her thoughts snarled into ugly and uncompromising patterns. *If Miss Birdie killed Cletus . . . If Hawkins is really a member of that godawful militia . . .* And she remembered the weight of Harice Tyler's hand on hers. *If I could believe . . .*

She shook off the confusion of thoughts and reached for the telephone. *At least I can check on Birdie, see if there's anything I can do. So much loss—Dessie, and Cletus, and now Miss Birdie.* She felt tears rising in her eyes and tried to quell the monotonous dirge that tolled unbidden in her mind: *And Sam, and Sam, and Sam.*

"She's a little low right now," Dorothy confided in answer to Elizabeth's question. "But I'm takin' her in to the doctor this mornin'. She's goin' to get a transfusion and that always seems to make her feel better for a time.

Pastor Briggs come by yesterday after church and prayed with us, and that friend of hers at the snake-handlin' church, that Belvy Guthrie, she called and talked to her the longest time. Birdie's gettin' ready to go the doctor now, but I'll tell her you called."

So much for that, thought Elizabeth, staring out her dining room window, oblivious to the bright sky and high scudding clouds that marked the beginning of a beautiful day. Ursa rubbed against her leg and she absently fondled the familiar shaggy head. In the distance she could hear the tractor—Ben already at work. She thought about telling him that the "nice guy" he had been so eager for her to go out with was a member of the Sons of Adam militia. There would be no pleasure in it, she decided, no pleasure in saying "See, I told you I didn't want a social life."

Without warning, the quiet of the spring day was shattered by the barking of all three dogs; the front door slammed and Laurel called out, "Let's go for a hike!"

"In here, Laurel," Elizabeth called, somewhat surprised that her daughter should be out at the farm so early in the morning. *And a hike? Not normal behavior for Laurel at all.*

Her daughter was bubbling over with excitement. "I talked to him, Mum. John the Baptizer has almost totally agreed to lend his paintings for a show. I told him about how they would reach so many more people that way and that we would have an opening and he could speak and share his message. And, no, he didn't try anything funny." Her deep blue eyes, so like Elizabeth's, sparkled as she pulled up a chair to the table. She was dressed in jeans and hiking boots, and her wild red dreadlocks were pulled back under a green bandanna.

"So anyway he told me to come back to see him at the

revival place when the revival was over and we'd talk more about the show *and . . .*" she paused dramatically, ". . . he wants to paint *me*!"

Elizabeth's heart sank. Laurel's disastrous affair with the visiting professor had begun in much the same way. Maybe this was the time for a small, carefully worded— but Laurel was chattering on.

"Did you know that he's staying in an old cabin up Lonesome Holler? That's just down the other side of the mountain, isn't it? Anyway, he told me that he's got a lot more paintings stored there. So I thought if I just showed up—I could say we were taking a hike—then maybe he'd let me see these other paintings. He said the revival might go on for another couple of weeks, depending on the Lord's will." She groaned and made a face. "No way I can wait that long!"

She jumped up and bounced out to the kitchen. "I had to work yesterday so I couldn't go then, but now I'm off till this evening," she called back. In a moment she returned with a cup of coffee and a piece of toast spread thickly with peanut butter. "He is just so . . . so intense! Those eyes! What a hottie! But a little scary. Anyway, I thought it might be good to have you come with me. Preacher or not, I don't want him thinking I'm some bimbo ready to pull off my clothes for the great artist. Not that I would actually mind—relax, Mum!"

Elizabeth had started to speak but Laurel went on in a mock-lofty tone, "I would only agree to that if it was as a model, a professional relationship . . . and only if the painting had redeeming social value."

She took a greedy bite of peanut butter and toast. "So, I thought it would be fun for us to walk over there; it's just down the other side of the mountain from us, isn't it? I think it must be where Ben and Rosemary and I ended up once years and years ago when we were exploring around. There was a sweet old couple living there and she talked all the time and gave us biscuits and buttermilk."

In the face of such enthusiasm Elizabeth was helpless. Her suggestion that they take the jeep, drive around to Bear Tree Creek, and walk up from Walter and Ollie's place was instantly vetoed. "Mum, look what a beautiful day it is! You know it'll be awesome up at the top of the mountain. And there'll be wildflowers! Anyway, I want it to seem kind of by accident that I'm there—you know, just out for a hike. You're always fussing at me for spending so much time indoors. I thought you'd enjoy a little mother-daughter walk in the woods!"

Mother-daughter trek is more like it, grumbled Elizabeth as, knapsack on her back, she toiled slowly up the steep zigzag way a bulldozer had cut some fifteen years before. Ben occasionally took a four-wheeler up this primitive road when he was carrying barb wire or posts to repair the line fence at the top of the mountain, but it was far too precipitous a trip on wheels for Elizabeth's taste. It would take them about twenty minutes to reach the top, with several stops along the way to admire the view, as well as to catch their breath.

As they climbed, Elizabeth pondered the irony of Laurel's being attracted to a mountain evangelist. *So much older than she, and such different backgrounds. Like that sleazy Aristides she got involved with. He was older, too. Is she looking for a father replacement?* Ahead of her on the trail Laurel was bouncing along with long effortless strides, obviously delighted to be on the track of John the Baptizer. *What would Sam have thought about this?* Elizabeth wondered with the usual surge of regret mixed with resentment.

The thought of Sam slowed her and she stopped to look back down at the sheet-metal roof, shining in the sun. Sam had built that house, and they had vowed that it was their last house—here they would grow old together. *Come to that, what would Sam think of me, lusting in my heart after a snake-handling preacher?* She could see Sam as if he was standing before her, big and comforting, with his lopsided grin. *If it's what you want, go for it, Liz; that's what he'd have said. After all, that's what he always did.*

Once at the summit she thought, as she had many times before, *I should do this every week.* The wind was brisk and welcome after the sweaty climb. The sun that was moving toward midday shone brilliantly—now and then obscured briefly by the flying clouds. The shadows of these same clouds raced over the farm stretched out below them, the intermittent sunny patches now highlighting one spot, now another. Full Circle Farm looked like a child's toy, with tiny barns and houses, minute trees and cows, and far, far down the mountain a minuscule tractor cultivating a pocket-handkerchief-sized field.

This is the way Levy would have traveled when he came to get Little Sylvie. I hope they got to Texas safely. I hope she took the baby. In her mind's eye she saw the handsome young man of the photograph walking resolutely down the mountain toward his lover and their child. *Was he glad about the baby? Or did he not want it? Who was the father, Levy or Little Sylvie's husband?*

"Come back, Mum," said Laurel. "You look like you're a million miles away."

"More like a hundred years," answered Elizabeth, shaking herself back into the here and now. "I'm glad we came," she said, giving her tall daughter an impromptu hug. "I always forget about this view."

Laurel returned the hug, then opened the knapsack she was carrying. "I'll take a few pictures before we start down the other side. I brought my camera so I can photograph John the Baptizer's work *in situ*."

As Laurel snapped one after another picture of the view on both sides of the mountain, Elizabeth walked a little way along the fence. The cattle were all in the lower pasture at this time of year, but soon they would be turned out on the mountain and she might as well see if this part of the fence was in need of repair. And down this way, near the edge of the woods, was where the pink lady slippers bloomed. If they were up, Laurel would surely want a picture of them. She strolled along happily, enjoying the easier walking after the arduous climb. The fence was in good shape, it seemed. Though a few strands could use tightening—

It was fluttering in the stiff breeze, a ragged strip of camouflage fabric, snagged on one of the barbs of the bottom strand of wire. She leaned down and angrily tore it off the barb and stuffed it in the pocket of her jeans. *Relax, Elizabeth,* she admonished herself. *Most of the hunters around here wear camouflage.* Turning back to where Laurel was waiting for her, she fingered the piece of cloth in her pocket. *But hunting season's been over for months. This fabric's stiff and new, probably never even washed. And this is where I saw that light when I was burying the skunk.* She thought unwillingly of the militia men at Devil's Fork, *every one of them in new camouflage fatigues . . . including Phillip Hawkins.*

Tears of anger and frustration stung her eyes and she wiped them impatiently away with the back of her hand. *Did he send those bastards over here? He knew I'd be in*

Asheville—having dinner with him. Oh, damn it all to hell! The wind was too cool now, and she dug the sweatshirt out of her knapsack.

They started down the other side, following an overgrown logging road down to Walter and Ollie's old cabin. While Elizabeth's side of the mountain was about evenly divided between woods and pasture, on this side the land, unpastured for years, was rapidly growing up in briars and young trees. The old path that wound down the mountain had patches of brambles or fallen trees that they had to skirt or scramble over as best they could. It was fully thirty minutes before they came to the clearing that Elizabeth remembered. Before them lay the huge oak tree and beneath it the beautiful little pool of water that she and Sam had refreshed themselves in so many years ago. Farther down the slope the rusted roof of the old cabin peeked through a grove of yellow-green young locust trees.

They knelt to scoop the cold water into their cupped hands. They were drinking deeply and thankfully when a quiet voice behind them said, "That there's livin' water; hit kin take you to glory."

Laurel scrambled to her feet; Elizabeth, painfully aware of her fifty-two-year-old knees, rose more cautiously. The thin young girl standing in front of them could have been an apparition from another time, except for the white plastic bucket dangling from her hand. She wore a shapeless dress of faded blue cotton. It clung to her full breasts, straining the buttons that closed it, brushed past her narrow hips, and ended a few inches above her slender bare feet. Her straight pale blond hair fell unconfined to well below her waist and her light blue eyes stared out of a countenance untouched by sun and innocent of makeup. It was a face Botticelli might have painted.

Laurel took a step toward the girl and blurted out, "You're the one in the picture—the Madonna!" Seeing Elizabeth's incredulous look she went on, "You remember, Mum, the one he painted at the revival?"

"Daddy paints a heap of pictures of me," the girl said placidly as she came forward to fill her bucket at the pool.

Elizabeth and Laurel watched her in silence, not knowing what to make of this unknown girl who seemed totally unconcerned at their sudden appearance out of the woods. *How old is she?* Elizabeth wondered. *She looks about twelve except for that bosom.* She wondered too if perhaps this girl was, like Cletus, a little simple. Something in those pale eyes, some emptiness—

"I was hoping your father might be here. I'm interested in seeing his paintings and he told me there were more at the cabin," Laurel was saying. "I'm Laurel Goodweather and this is my mother, Elizabeth. She has the farm on the other side of the mountain."

"Daddy ain't here just now," the girl said, lifting the bucket and starting down the path. "My name is Mary Cleophas. The pictures is this way."

They followed her in silence to the little cabin, its two rooms separated by a covered passageway, locally called a dogtrot. "The pictures is in here," she told them, opening a door. "You kin bring 'em outside to look at, hit's awful dark in there."

Laurel stepped in and Elizabeth heard her startled intake of breath: "There're dozens of them. Oh, Mum, this is awesome!"

In a few minutes Laurel and Elizabeth had brought out the painted panels—some thirty-three in all, Laurel counted—and leaned them against the sides of the cabin while Mary Cleophas watched tolerantly. A rainbow of color danced before them. The style was unmistakably that which they had seen at the revival, but these pictures had been painted with more detail and in more subtle colors.

"He told me that he works in tempera at the revivals because it dries faster, but he uses acrylic here," said Laurel, hastily snapping photographs of each piece. "These are so amazing! You know, he's totally untrained. He says the Lord guides his brushes."

One picture in particular fascinated Elizabeth. Like the Madonna painted at the revival, Mary Cleophas stood on a crescent moon, stars circling her head. But in this painting she was extremely pregnant and totally nude, and the background, rather than a forest, was an explosion of sunlight. Around the four sides of the painting scrolled the words: *"And there appeared a great wonder in heaven; a woman clothed with the sun and the moon under her feet and upon her head a crown of twelve stars."* The painting was full of a powerful beauty, and Elizabeth marveled at the delicacy with which the features had been painted. At the same time she felt surprised that the evangelist should use his own daughter as a nude model. And why had he depicted her as pregnant?

"I don't much like that one," said Mary Cleophas. "Hit don't seem right to be standin' there nekkid like that. But Daddy said hit was in fulfillment of God's Word, so I done it. God talks to Daddy and tells him things," she added matter-of-factly.

As Laurel was moving paintings around in order to get each one into the best light for photographing, Elizabeth had a sudden thought. "Mary Cleophas, did a man called

Cletus come up this way recently? It would have been a few weeks ago. He was in his forties and had—"

"I know Cletus," said Mary Cleophas, a slow smile illuminating her features. "He's awful nice." Her brow furrowed. "But I can't remember when hit was he come here. Seems like hit weren't too long ago but I can't rightly say."

A thin cry, like the mewing of a cat, interrupted Elizabeth's next question. Mary Cleophas looked toward the door of the other room, then down at the front of her dress. Two damp patches were spreading around her breasts. "Funny, ain't it, how the milk lets down when they cry?"

She turned to enter the dim room and Elizabeth followed her. Laurel, absorbed in her photography, didn't look up. In the room were two cots covered by faded quilts, a table with two straight-backed chairs, two kerosene lamps, and a large Bible. Several cardboard boxes stacked in the unused fireplace held canned food, loaves of bread in plastic wrappers, and bags of dried fruit. Dangling from threads fixed to the ceiling were dozens of folded paper cranes, pink, blue, green, and yellow. Beside the cot under one of the two windows was a wicker laundry basket lined with blankets. Mary Cleophas leaned over it and picked up a whimpering swaddled form.

"Mary Cleophas," said Elizabeth, shocked at the bare poverty of this little room, "are you all alone up here, just you and your father? Isn't there some woman to help—Where's your mother?"

"I never knowed my momma. Hit's always been just me and Daddy." The girl hugged the fretting baby to her with one arm and began to undo the buttons of her dress. "Since he got the call, him and me, we travel around in the camper, and Daddy preaches revivals everwhere he can. Use to, I would play the organ and sing, but when my belly got to growin', Daddy he was feared for what people would say and he brung me up here by night. Said I had best keep me close to the cabin and away from the eye of man. He said hit was in the Word."

Her face took on a look, almost of slyness. "But you and yore girl ain't men, so I reckon it ain't against the Word. And I do get awful lonely."

Elizabeth looked around the little room again. "How . . . didn't you go to the hospital . . . I mean, when you had the baby?"

The girl shook her head. "Daddy didn't let me see no one, not a doctor nor even a granny woman to help me when the pains came on. Him and me, we birthed this baby together. Daddy said I would bring forth a man child who was to rule all nations with a rod of iron." Her voice faltered. "But when he saw how hit was . . ." and her thin hand partly pulled back the tattered quilt swaddling the baby.

The child of Mary Cleophas looked at Elizabeth with milky blue eyes. Its mouth opened as if to cry but there was no sound. The infant turned toward its mother, rootling for the breast, and as it did so Elizabeth gasped. At first she had thought that some strange rag doll was wrapped up with the child, but then Mary Cleophas laid her baby on the cot and removed the quilt entirely. "He's got a little brother just a-growin' out of his belly." The withered trunk and limbs of the child's incompletely separated twin dangled limply against his body.

The baby squirmed impatiently, and its little partial twin moved with it. A feeling of revulsion swept over Elizabeth at first, but as she saw how tenderly the mother handled the infant and how the light of unquestioning love shone in the girl's eyes, she realized, *It's just a baby,*

Elizabeth. These things happen. A parasitic twin, I think it's called. Just a simple surgery and that poor baby would be normal.

Mary Cleophas continued on unperturbed, rewrapping her child, then opening the front of her dress and guiding the baby to her nipple. "Daddy says hit's a Sign, but he ain't yet sure what it means. He's a-prayin' on it and waitin' for guidance. Daddy said I'd have to stay in the wilderness, like it says in the Book, for one thousand, two hundred, and threescore days."

She nodded toward the origami cranes dangling in the air. "I learnt how to make them birds when I was little, back in fifth grade. I been makin' one every day so I kin keep account and know when my time is up. Daddy gives me his leftover flyers to fold into birds and they's always such purty colors."

Elizabeth stared at the cranes. "And you gave one to Cletus when he was here . . ."

"Yessum, Cletus he thought they was real purty so I made him one. He said he'd shoot me some squirrels and cook 'em for me too. I get awful tired of cold bread and such. Daddy brings me food when he can, but it ain't every day he can get out here. That Cletus, when he come along and saw how things was, he said he'd get me some meat."

"He had a shotgun with him?" exclaimed Elizabeth. "Oh, please, Mary Cleophas, try to remember *when* he was here! I really need to know!"

The girl was smiling down at her baby and rocking gently back and forth. She lifted her pale eyes and gazed dreamily at the rough ceiling. "Hit might of been that day I broke the oil lamp. Daddy was awful ill with me when he got home and said I'd have to learn to do without. He locked me in here for a time till I'd repented proper." She shifted the swaddled infant to the other breast and continued, "That Cletus is a good somebody; I think he knows about bein' lonesome too. Hit seemed good just to have him to set with and talk to."

She looked toward the door. "He said he'd come back soon as he got some squirrels but I ain't seen him yet. I told him not to come iffen my Daddy was here; Daddy says no man must see the baby till he's sure about what the Sign means." She gave Elizabeth a faint smile. "I done went against Daddy about that Cletus and likely I'll have to be punished. But you and yore daughter . . . well, you ain't men. But still, I believe hit'd be best iffen Daddy didn't know about you uns comin' here."

"Mary Cleophas," Elizabeth asked carefully, "where's the father of your baby, your boyfriend? Doesn't he . . ."

Slowly the pale blue eyes raised to look at her interrogator. Mary Cleophas's smile was gentle and weary. "I ain't never had no boyfriend. This here baby is God's child. My daddy said hit was like when God the Father give Jesus to Mary."

IX–APRIL 1902

I woke up in the dark with a pain in my belly like as if I'd been eatin green apples. Mister Tomlin was a-snorin like one thing but I eased out of bed so as not to waken him for he hadn't took his medicine the night before. I made for the door, thinkin to do my business outside. Hit was dark yet but to the east the sky was pale and the risin quarter moon lay on her back just a-restin on the tops of the far mountains. She glowed as orange as new rust and you could see the dark part just as plain, like a big swollen belly. I wisht that hit was Levy and not Mister Tomlin layin there in the bed for then I'd waken him and call him to me and we'd watch the moon together and he'd say as how she looked like me and we'd laugh and then we'd get back in the bed together.

I stood and watched the moon liftin up and just then a gush of water run down my legs. My belly cramped again so hard I had to hold to the door frame and I let out a cry. Mister Tomlin sat up and called out, Who is it? I told him that I was a-painin bad and that I thought the baby was comin. He got outten the bed and lit a lamp. Then he just stood there, his skinny old legs hangin out from under his shirttail, and watched me.

You'll pay for your sinning now, Little Sylvie, he says with an ugly laugh. Ever since Eve and her sin, women must bear their children in pain. He comes over to me and jabs at my poor swoled up belly with his hateful old finger. Lots of women die, he says, and the words is like rank poison drippin out his old mouth. Like your own mother, he says, and jabs my belly again.

Mister Tomlin, I says, I know what I done was wrong. And I have offered to leave. But right now I have to birth this baby and I'd take hit kindly was you to fetch Romarie for me.

He goes back and stretches out on the bed with his hands behind his head and says, You'll not leave till I'm ready for you to leave, Little Sylvie, and I'll not fetch your sister till it suits me. For all I care you can crawl under the cabin and whelp your brat in the dirt like any other bitch. And he closed his eyes and made like he was a-sleepin.

I went and got me another shift and pulled off the wet one. I dried off my legs and put on the clean shift. Then I set down to wait. The pains came and went and between them I thought about Levy. I put my hand around the little gold heart that hung there between my big old titties and thought, Wherever you are, Levy, yore child's a-comin into the world. I miss you awful bad, Levy, and I need you now.

I stood up and begun to pace back and forth. Hit helped me to bear the pain and while I paced I sang the words to Little Mathey Groves in my head. At last, just as the sun was risin, Mister Tomlin spoke up. Well, says he, I can see

I'll get no sleep with you carrying on like that. You might as well fix me some breakfast while I go after your sister.

Thank you, Mister Tomlin, I said.

Like I have said, Rom had helped Aetha and a sight of others in birthin their babes and I knowed that she was reckoned to be near as good as any doctor, but I hated the thought of her sharp tongue. O Mommy, I said out loud, now's when I need you the worst of all.

The pains let up just when Mister Tomlin rode off and I went to mixin up some cornbread for breakfast. I was kindly scared and kindly excited and hit seemed like I wanted to do a hundred things all to once. I'll turn this in the pan and set it to cookin, I thought as I stirred, then I'll sweep out the cabin afore Romarie gets here.

Just then the pain came back like a hot knife stabbin in my belly and the tears ran down my face into the batter. I steadied myself against the table and took deep breaths. When the pain let up I looked at the batter and thought, Let hit be. Tears ain't nasty and they'll do for salt.

The cornbread was ready when they come back and Mister Tomlin got him a big piece. Romarie asked me how close the miseries was comin and when I told her she sniffed and said there'd be a ways to go yet. You might as well go on about your business, she said to Mister Tomlin. Hit'll be this evenin or later afore hit's born. Besides, menfolk ain't no use at a time like this.

Mister Tomlin said that he'd go on down to where they was buildin the mill. Take good care of my little wife, sister-in-law, he said. She's—and he brung his big old handkerchief up to his face like as if he was about to bust out cryin. He wiped his eyes and just shook his head like he couldn't talk and went out the door.

Romarie looked atter him as he went and said, Now that's a fine man, Little Sylvie. I hope that you deserve him. But a lovin husband ain't no good around a laborin woman. And most of them can't stand the blood and the noise of the birthin nohow. He's best out of the way.

Just about then another of them big pains like to doubled me over and Rom said, Let's get you in the bed. No need to wear yourself out; you got to save yore strength.

She was as gentle as my mommy might have been, helpin me into bed. She even brushed out my hair, sayin that knots or tangles could hold the baby back. She took a knife out of the basket she brung with her and put hit under the bedstead to cut the pain. Then she busied herself with makin some tea from dried raspberry leaves for she said that would help to make the birthin go easier.

The day passed like a dream that was part nightmare. Some of the time I was painin bad and some of the time I would doze off. But all through it, Romarie was there, holdin my hand, givin me sips of tea, helpin me to squat over the chamber, and tellin me that hit wouldn't be much longer. Hit almost seemed that for this one day I had my mommy back. It was the sweetest feeling.

Finally, the pains was all one big pain, red and roarin all over my body. I wanted to call out for Levy but knowed I mustn't speak his name. I begun to weep and Rom had me to lay back. I got to see what's what, she said, just as gentle, and she washed and oiled her hands good and felt up inside me. Hit'll not be long now, she says, for I can feel the head. Then she took some sweet oil and began to grease up the way for the baby to come. In a minute, she says, you're going to have to push this baby right out, Little Sylvie, for hit's ready to come into this world.

Rom helped me to sit up against the pillows and I started to grab aholt of the postes of the headboard to have something to pull against whilst I pushed but Rom grabbed my hands. Take aholt of me, Little Sylvie, she said, for was you to put yore hands above yore head hit could cause the cord to wrap around the baby's neck and strangle hit. My knees was up and far apart and Rom was holdin my hands. Bear down, Little Sylvie, she kept sayin, and I pulled on her hands and bore down. I could hear someone makin deep gruntin sounds. I almost looked around to see who was hit, then I knowed that hit was me. I bore down and pushed and bore down some more till I thought I would split in two. Rom kept tight hold of my hands all the time. Now push hard, she hollered, and I done like she said. All to once I could feel the baby startin to move and I cried out, Hit's a-comin! Rom turned loose my hands and reached down between my legs. I pushed like one thing and bellered like any heifer too as Rom helped the baby to slide out like a bloody little fish.

Romarie brought my baby to me and set hit at my breast. She's a beautiful little girl, Rom said, but she's got a birth-mark—a little red streak down the side of her face.

They say that comes on account of something the mother seen while she was carryin the babe—reckon you must have seen a snake or some such, Little Sylvie, Rom said. Reckon so, I said, or some such, and I was thinkin of Mister Tomlin's hateful old belt.

But don't worry none about hit, said Rom, for hit'll likely fade. Now let's us help her find the tit; her suckin'll help you to get the afterbirth out.

My breasts was hot and tender to the touch and at first hit hurt as she sucked. But hit felt good too and I lay there just a-worshippin that little babe while there was more pains and then the afterbirth come out. Rom cleaned me up and gave me some more tea and some of the cornbread too, for I was plumb empty feelin. What are you goin to call her? Rom asked, and I said right away, I'll call her Malindy atter our mommy.

Hit was nigh dark when Mister Tomlin come home. I was dozin and dreamin when I heared the sound of hoofbeats. I tried to set up, thinkin that it was Levy come atter me at last but then I heard Romarie say, Well, Mister Tomlin, yore wife and babe are both just fine.

She lifted Malindy from my side and held her out for him to see. He reached out and laid back the blanket she was wrapped in. Why, says he, it's a little girl, beautiful just like her mama.

CHAPTER 21
HAWKINS EXPLAINS
(MONDAY)

MUM, THE STUPID BATTERY'S DIED!" LAUREL appeared at the door, waving her digital camera in frustration. "Plus, we're going to have to head back; I'd forgotten that I have to stop by my apartment before I go in to work." As her eyes adjusted to the dim light, she registered the fact that Mary Cleophas was nursing a baby, "Oh, wow, I didn't realize—"

"You're right, Laurel," said Elizabeth. "It *is* getting late. I'll help you put the paintings back." She gave her daughter a meaningful look and motioned her outside. "Mary Cleophas, I could bring you some food, some hot food, and whatever—"

"I thank you kindly, ma'am," Mary Cleophas replied, bending her head to kiss her baby, "but Daddy'll be back later on and he allus brings us some fried chicken and taters from one of them places up on the highway." She smiled serenely at Elizabeth. "I'd be proud was you to come back in a few more days when Daddy ain't here. I get awful lonely sometimes."

Elizabeth started out the door, then turned back. The sun struggling through the grimy panes of glass in the little window lit up the form of the girl sitting on the old cot, turning her hair to a pale golden halo. The paper cranes seemed to flutter in the mazy air and the scene was suddenly heartbreakingly beautiful.

"Mary Cleophas," said Elizabeth. "What's your baby's name?"

The girl looked up. "The Lord ain't yet told my daddy what hit is. But for now I call him Ishmael cause him and me's in the wilderness, like Hagar and Ishmael in the Book."

Laurel was obviously bursting with questions as they returned the paintings to the little room, but she waited till they were on their way back up the mountain to ask them. Elizabeth hesitated when it came to describing the grotesque sight of the baby's naked body. "It's a . . . a correctable birth defect. The baby was meant to be twins but the second one never developed fully and never separated. It's the sort of thing that used to end up in a freak show but now surgery could fix it."

"Do you think Mary Cleophas knows that?" Laurel asked. "She seemed to me like she was pretty otherworldly. Or maybe just simple. Where's the baby's father anyway?"

Elizabeth drew a deep breath. "Well, she said she didn't have a boyfriend—that it was like when God the Father gave Jesus to Mary."

"A virgin birth? Oh, please!" Laurel snorted and strode ahead on the trail. "Do you think her father believed *that*?"

Climbing steadily behind her daughter, Elizabeth replied, "That's not what she told her father; it's what her father told her."

"I don't get it," said Laurel, stopping in the middle of the narrow path and swinging around to face her mother. "What are you trying to say?"

"I'm not sure," said Elizabeth, her mind racing over the possibilities. "Laur . . . maybe John the Baptizer is the father of the child."

"Oh, Mum!" Laurel cried. "Do you really think that her own father . . . ? Oh, that totally sucks!"

"It's just a feeling I have," admitted Elizabeth. "Mary Cleophas seems so innocent—not like a girl who would even *have* a boyfriend, much less lie about one. And she's evidently completely under her father's thumb . . . although she was willing to defy him and see Cletus . . . and us. And she may be a little simple. I just don't know . . . maybe we ought to talk to Social Services. . . ."

Laurel was silent for a moment. Then she said, "Could we wait just a little bit? I mean, she doesn't seem afraid of her father, it's not like she's in real danger. And what if he's not the father of the baby? She could have lied when she said she never had a boyfriend. We ought to find out for sure first. If we call Social Services, they'll roar in there, take away the baby, probably put John the Baptizer in jail, and Mary Cleophas in a juvenile home, *then* try to find out the truth. What if there's some other explanation? There's got to be a better way!"

Back at home Laurel grabbed some bread and cheese for her lunch and flew out the door, calling back to her mother not to do anything about Mary Cleophas and her baby just yet. "I'll be back out Wednesday and we can figure out what's best, how to help Mary Cleophas," she promised.

Elizabeth stared after her daughter, feeling lost. *What's*

the right thing to do? She found the telephone book and looked up the number for Social Services. She looked at it for a long time before dialing. When a recorded voice told her that the line was out of order, she hung up the phone with a feeling of guilty relief. *I'll figure out what to do later,* she told herself.

She sat by the telephone, thinking about Cletus and Mary Cleophas. *The squirrels in the knapsack were for her, but he never got to give them to her. She's still waiting and hoping to see him. He would have given them to her before going home. And the sang plants, were they for Harice's father? What if Cletus got both the sang and the squirrels up on Devil's Fork and then . . . that's where something happened. He dropped the knapsack and eventually Pup dragged it home.*

Devil's Fork. She dug into the pocket of her jeans and pulled out the strip of fabric she had found on the fence at the top of the mountain. Again she saw Hawkins, in the camouflage uniform of the militia, in charge of training a new cadre of bigots. *How could I have been so wrong about him? Have I been wrong about everything? And where does that leave the theory that Birdie killed Cletus? Nowhere, I sincerely hope. But what can I do about any of this?*

Elizabeth had always found that when she was faced with a problem, hard physical labor was the best way of clearing her mind so that a solution could eventually emerge. She spent the afternoon in her garden, weeding and hoeing, and planting several rows of sweet corn. Sweet corn was always problematical, she thought, as she covered the newly planted rows with old chicken wire, kept for that purpose. First you had to protect it from the crows that dearly loved to pull up the sprouting kernels by their first tender shoots. Once the corn was almost knee-high, the crows lost interest and the chicken wire could be removed. Then, often as not, a hungry cow would spot the delectable green leaves and push her way through the fence to mow down the corn, leaving behind just several satisfied cow plops. And if, by some miracle, the corn survived to make ears—then there were the raccoons and the corn worms, and the crows again.

"Why the hell do I plant corn anyway?" she asked herself as she carried a last rock from the road to anchor down the chicken wire. *Is it just because I always have? Or is it part of an ongoing battle against Fate? Do I put up with the aggravation of losing most of the time for the sheer joy of an occasional win?*

Elizabeth glanced up at a crow who had been watching her with considerable interest from its perch in a nearby pear tree. Striking a dramatic pose, she declaimed in a loud voice, " 'In the fell clutch of circumstance, I have not winced nor cried aloud.' Something, something, something . . . 'My head is bloody, but unbowed!' "

The crow flapped lazily away with a derisive caw and Elizabeth turned to see Ben, a basket of eggs in his hand, coming out of the chicken house just below the garden. He looked at her in amusement and called out, "Is that what an English major does when she's out standing in her field?"

She was sitting in a rocking chair on the porch with a pre-dinner glass of wine when Phillip Hawkins came walking up the road. Her three dogs were trotting alongside him in a companionable manner. Her first impulse was to go into the house and shut the door, but curiosity won out and she stayed where she was.

He was out of breath when he reached the porch, "Elizabeth, I need to talk to you; I know what you must be thinking but it's not like that—Could I please have a glass of water first?"

She brought him the water without saying anything, resumed her chair, and waited, rocking slightly. When he had drunk the water and caught his breath, he began. "I guess I should have told you from the start the real reason I moved to Asheville. Janie was part of it; I really did want to be around to keep an eye on her; she does have problems; that much was true. But there was another thing.

"That militia place has got your sheriff's office worried and they wanted to get someone inside. Obviously it couldn't be one of the local cops, so Sheriff Blaine contacted my boss—they went to school together—and Blaine thought it would be safe bringing in someone from the other side of the state. It was an informal arrangement; officially, I'm on leave. So I showed up one weekend at Devil's Fork claiming to be a cop who was fed up with the preferential treatment minorities were getting—a cop, in fact, who'd been fired for his rough handling of some well-connected African-American guy. And they bought it: They checked around, but we had done our homework and they found the answers we wanted them to find. Flinn put me to work training a batch of recruits. And that's when you showed up."

He looked at her to see what her reaction was but she kept her face still and said nothing. He went on. "I should have known when your dog showed up at Devil's Fork that you'd be after her before long. Some of the guys had caught her and thought they could use her in their night games." He looked apologetically at Elizabeth. "But I pulled rank and said I'd take charge of the dog. I tied her up and was going to sneak her out and bring her back here. I figured I'd let her out down at your lower place and get back to the compound."

"Why didn't you just call and tell me where she was so I could stop worrying?" Elizabeth asked in a frosty voice.

Hawkins ran a hand over his bald scalp. "I thought about it. But I didn't want to answer questions about where I was; I figured I could get her back to you almost before you missed her. That was dumb and I'm really sorry that I caused you to worry. But how the hell did you know she was there, anyway? I about had a heart attack when I looked up and saw you in that guy's truck, just staring at me with those blue eyes."

After almost half an hour of explanation on both sides, the chill around Elizabeth's heart began to subside and she invited Hawkins to stay for supper. As they sat at the table with their reheated leftovers—shrimp and andouille sausage jambalaya that she had pulled from the freezer—he seemed eager to tell her some of what he had learned about the militia. "You've trusted me and I'm going to trust you. But this is hush-hush stuff, Elizabeth. So please don't let it go any further."

His brown eyes bored into hers. "A lot of those guys are just fairly harmless macho types playing soldier, but the higher-ups—Flinn and those around him—are linked to another group out in Montana. I think they're expecting a big shipment of automatic weapons and other matériel that's illegal for civilians to possess. And when that shipment arrives"—he grinned widely—"they're busted, and Devil's Fork can grow up in weeds."

Hawkins told her that he had heard about the skunk left at her door. "Some of the eager beavers saw you in town with one of the Mexicans and decided it would be a fun little 'night mission' to leave you their calling card, some postcard they'd found that looked threatening.

One of the new recruits knew who you were and where you live, and it was his idea—"

"Phillip," she interrupted, "could these creeps have been responsible for Cletus's death? That pool where you were having the training exercises—"

"That was the other thing I wanted to tell you about," he broke in. "You remember I told you about my buddy the medical examiner? Well, R.L. was in town last week for a meeting and we had lunch—you ever been to that Japanese place on Broadway? Great food . . . anyway R.L. told me that she'd found the same anomalies in that Dewey guy's lung tissue as there were in Cletus's—"

"Wait a second." Elizabeth put down her fork. "Your buddy R.L. is a she?" An unexpected and unidentifiable emptiness assailed her heart. *What does it matter, Elizabeth?* she thought fiercely, remembering the attractive woman she'd seen lunching with Hawkins.

"Sure, Rhoda Liliane Levine, that's my buddy R.L. Like I said, R.L. and I go way back. Anyway, I took her to lunch at that Japanese place and she told me about the second autopsy. Then she got into telling me all her troubles—seems her girlfriend dumped her for some chick she met when she was running a marathon—"

"Wait another second . . ." her heart soared and she began to grin, *but why should it matter to me?*—"R.L., good old R.L., she's . . . she's *gay?*"

"Sure," he said, confused, "didn't I mention it? Anyway, here's what I've been doing . . ."

Hawkins went on to explain that he was trying to find out if the militia had been behind the deaths of Cletus and Dewey. He had taken a sample of the water from the militia's pool that he was sending off to R.L. to see if it was a match for the water found in the lungs of the drowned men. "I've been dropping hints and asking leading questions, but so far nothing. Flinn and his boys either don't know or they aren't saying. But if the water sample is a match . . ." He speared a piece of sausage and chewed it with greedy gusto.

Two cups of coffee later, Hawkins stretched luxuriously. "Man, it's been great to get away from those crazies for a while. But if I'm not back pretty soon they may start to wonder."

They walked together to the porch and Phillip put out his hand and said, "Thanks for believing me, Elizabeth. I would have hated it if—"

"Me, too," she said, and they shook hands solemnly. Hawkins suddenly slapped his breast pocket. "Let me give you my cell phone number; out here in the mountains and valleys it only works some of the time, but I'd like you to have it." He pulled out a little notepad and a pen and scribbled a number. Ripping out the page, he offered it to her. "I feel like Sam would want me to keep an eye out for you, and—"

She stared at the piece of paper, then slowly took it. "You know," she said, "I've pretty much learned to take care of myself, Phillip. I don't like having to depend on anyone else."

Hawkins looked at her. "I think I understand how you would feel that way . . . after losing Sam—"

"I didn't 'lose' him," Elizabeth snapped. "That would have been extremely careless on my part. He died in a fucking plane crash." She pronounced the obscenity with deliberate precision. "I'd say that if anyone was careless, it was Sam . . . going flying with a friend who'd just gotten his pilot's license and who never had any sense anyway—"

She stopped abruptly. Then she brushed her hand across her eyes and said softly, "God, I sound angry, don't

I? I guess the truth is that I just can't forgive Sam for dying. I've been so mad at him that I've never even been able to cry for him."

Hawkins said nothing; instead, he reached out and gave her shoulder a brief squeeze. She straightened and said, "Thank you for telling me all this . . . about the militia, I mean. I hope you all can close them down. It's awful knowing there are people like that, people so full of hate, nearby."

Grinning like a boy, he said, "I think I can promise you won't have that bunch of sickos for neighbors much longer."

She watched him as he descended the steps, then called, "Wait a minute, Phillip. What you said about Janie wanting to join the Starshine Community? Was that part true?"

He turned, smiling. "Unfortunately, it was. But it seems she's changed her mind. She's just started dating a guy who's learning to build sitars, and she's decided to apprentice alongside him. Starshine is out. Sitars are in. At least for this week. Isn't that wonderful?"

It was a little after seven when the phone rang. She picked it up thinking it might be Laurel, and was surprised to hear Harice Tyler's deep mountain voice.

"Howdy, Miz Goodweather. You all right?"

"I'm good, thank you. Listen, I really appreciated what you did yesterday."

"Glad I could help you. Sometimes a woman needs a man. You ever think about that?"

"Ah . . ." she stalled, "well, I'm lucky to have my nephew Ben working here, and Julio . . ."

"That ain't what I meant, Miz Goodweather. I been

thinkin' about you a lot. Fine woman like you. And though you're a sinner, I know you felt the spirit movin' at church the other night. I believe you felt called. I was hopin' maybe you might come to church with me regular-like."

Elizabeth hesitated. On one side was the memory of the flurry of warm emotions—the longings and the comfort, the feeling of belonging, of surrender—that she had experienced during the service at the Holiness church. On the other side was the cool, clear, astringent voice of reason. Finally she said gently, feeling very much like a character in a Victorian novel, "Mr. Tyler, I admire and respect you and the members of your church. And I *was* truly moved by the service and by the strength of your beliefs. But I don't believe in the same way that you do." *Though I wish I could,* whispered the voice of what might have been. "I'm not saying that you're wrong and I'm right. It's more like what's right for you would be wrong for me." She paused, struggling to articulate her feelings. "I guess I'd say we're walking different paths toward the same truth."

"Fancy words, Miz Goodweather," Tyler retorted. He sounded affronted. "But there'll come a time when you learn there's not but one way. You wait and see."

CHAPTER 22
POLARIS GOES NOVA
(TUESDAY)

ELIZABETH CAREFULLY WEDGED THE MUSHROOM quiche into the basket and covered it with a dish towel. Underneath it was a spinach salad with bits of mango and green onions. She had put in a little jar of homemade vinaigrette and a chilled bottle of white wine, as well as a thermos of coffee and some chocolate chip brownies. Today was Sallie Kate's fiftieth birthday, and Elizabeth had arranged to pick her friend up at her real estate office and take her for a picnic lunch down by the river. She grabbed the gaily wrapped package that contained the gardening book she had bought for her friend, picked up the laden basket, and headed for her jeep.

As the car crept down the bumpy road, slower than usual to prevent damage to the fragile quiche, she pondered the revelations of the day before. She was profoundly relieved to know that Hawkins was not a member of the militia; indeed, that he was part of an operation to shut them down. *And if the water sample checks out,* she thought, *he may find out who killed Cletus.*

She felt lighthearted at the prospect. *Of course Birdie couldn't have murdered her own son. And even if she had, then how would you account for Dewey Shotwell? As soon as Phillip's buddy R.L.*—and her face blossomed into a grin at the thought of R.L.—*as soon as she analyzes that water sample, maybe a lot more things will fall into place.*

She had reached the hard road now and, as she swung onto the pavement, she found that she was humming loudly—"Praise God from Whom All Blessings Flow"— the hymn called "Old Hundredth" she'd sung as a child. When Birdie's little house came into view, Elizabeth slowed and, seeing that Birdie's truck and Dorothy's car were both there, turned to cross the plank bridge. *Sallie Kate's not expecting me till noon—I'll just stop to say hi.* She hurried to the door, knocked, and without waiting for an answer, let herself in.

Miss Birdie was on the recliner, covered with a light blanket. The television flickered busily, but the sound was off and Miss Birdie's eyes were closed. Dorothy was evidently busy in the back of the house—vacuuming, Elizabeth decided, instantly identifying the loud roar emanating from the bedroom. She approached Birdie silently, noting with dismay how the once-plump cheeks were hollow and the busy pudgy hands were now thin and still.

"Lizzie Beth." Birdie's eyes opened and she held out her hand. "I ain't doin' no good atall."

Elizabeth took Birdie's hand and tried to speak but Birdie went on, "I heared you been back on Bear Tree. You find out anything about my boy?"

"Not really." Elizabeth was unwilling to mention the water sample from the militia pond and to raise what might be false hopes. "But I haven't given up."

"Well, I ain't either," said Miss Birdie in a firm tone. "Belvy Guthrie's bringin' the preacher, that Brother Tyler, and some of them other Holiness folks over here this evenin'. They're going to lay hands on me and pray for a healin'. I'm thinkin' there ain't nothin' else can help me now."

Back in her car and on her way to Sallie Kate's office, Elizabeth thought about Harice Tyler. She knew that she had made the right decision. *What do I have a brain for if I'm not supposed to listen to reason? I couldn't pretend that I believed in the Bible as the literal Word of God. And that's his whole life . . . No, it would never work.* She heaved a sigh at the memory of Harice's dark eyes and lazy smile.

The words from a melodramatic scene in *Auntie Mame,* favorite reading in her teenage years, broke from her lips, " 'I belong to one world, you to another. We might find happiness for one brief moment but then we'd hate ourselves—yes, and each other too, for what we'd done!' "

"Get a grip, Elizabeth." She laughed humorlessly as she pulled into the parking lot of Sallie Kate's office. She took a moment to blot away the tears that so unaccountably blurred her vision.

The birthday girl was at her cluttered desk, a phone captured between her ear and her shoulder while she sorted through a bulging file folder. Her curly blond hair was untidy as usual, and several pencils stuck out of it at picturesque angles. She motioned Elizabeth to a seat and went on talking. "Yes, I had the listing twice before. I'm real familiar with the property." She mouthed the words *in a minute* at Elizabeth and continued, "He did? When?" An agitated babble at the other end of the line escaped from the earpiece and Sallie Kate shook her head. "I could look at it this afternoon, I suppose. I guess there've been a lot of improvements since—" More babbling that elicited raised eyebrows from the realtor. "I'll do what I can to help with that; see you later this afternoon."

She put down the phone and jumped up to hug Elizabeth. "I've been looking forward to this; I didn't eat any breakfast on purpose!"

The picnic area by the river was empty, and Elizabeth spread a bright blue-and-yellow cloth over one of the tables. As they ate the quiche and sipped the wine, Sallie Kate said, "Funny thing, remember you called me to find out about that Starshine place up on Hog Run? Well, honey, that call I was on when you came in was about that same property. Seems like it's gonna be up for sale again. The head guy was arrested two days ago and the other owners want out."

"What!" cried Elizabeth. "I was over there just a couple of weeks ago. Was it Polaris who got arrested?" Sallie Kate, her mouth full of salad, nodded vigorously. "And that's where you're going this afternoon?" asked Elizabeth, full of curiosity about the sudden breakup of the New Age community.

"That's what I told them." Sallie Kate cut herself another slice of quiche. "You want to ride along? It might be interesting."

Elizabeth considered a moment then said, "Sure, I'd like to. It's pretty up there." She poured out coffee and uncovered the plate of brownies. "So what was Polaris arrested for?"

"Omigod, are those the ones with the chocolate chips?" cried Sallie Kate. "I think the guy on the phone said baby-farming. And don't ask what he meant, honey, because I haven't a clue."

As they drove up Bear Tree Creek in the realtor's sturdy little Subaru, Elizabeth told Sallie Kate about her recent investigations. "You remember I mentioned that Miss Birdie doesn't believe her son's death was an accident. She's had me trying to find out where Cletus was in those days before he died, and it looks like he was most likely over this way." Elizabeth smiled wryly. "I've learned more about my neighbors over the mountain in a week than I did in all the time Sam and I've lived here."

Sallie Kate nodded. "Things have changed a lot in the past few years. Used to be, a new family moving in was unusual and we all took notice. But now . . ." She turned up Hog Run Road. "God, this little squalor holler just gets worse and worse!" she exclaimed as they passed the wretched huddle of rusting trailers. Elizabeth noticed that the sofa that had been burning on a pile of tires had resisted the efforts of the fire. Its charred frame sat, faintly smoldering, in the middle of a circle of scorched and blackened earth.

The blue-and-gold sign that had read STARSHINE COMMU-NITY was missing, and the roadsides were weedy and untidy. A single sandal lay abandoned in the dusty road before them. At the fork, the Visitors sign hung askew.

"The guy I talked to told me to follow that sign," said Sallie Kate doubtfully, "but it's pointing straight down. Reckon that's some kind of message?"

"It was pointing to the right before," Elizabeth told her. "Maybe you're meeting him at the dome."

As they followed the right fork, Elizabeth was struck by the change that seemed to have come over this formerly idyllic place. It wasn't just that the grassy strips

along the road were unmown; everywhere she looked
she saw indications that the force that had held all this together was gone. The electric fence around the goat pasture was sagging to the ground and the goats were
roaming free. As they passed the apple orchard, with its
cluster of cabins and yurts, the change was even more
dramatic. At one cabin a middle-aged couple was stuffing
a car trunk with bags and boxes of clothing, evidently the
property of the very pregnant young girl who stood to
one side glumly watching. Another cabin stood deserted,
its door flung wide open; a white goat poised on the
threshold peered out inquisitively.

"'. . . The center cannot hold; mere anarchy is loosed
upon the world,'" Elizabeth said absently.

"What?" said Sallie Kate, "what's that?"

"A poem by Yeats—with Polaris gone, and he did
seem to be very much the center of this place—things
are truly falling apart."

They were met at the dome by three blond, worried-
looking young men who introduced themselves as Mor-
ton Banks, Robert Frye, and Eugene Findlater, co-owners
with Ernie Hemick, previously known as Polaris, of the
Starshine property. *No more star names,* Elizabeth realized,
glancing at the signs in front of the silver Navigators in
the parking lot. Algol, Altair, and Canopus were now just
Mort, Bob, and Gene.

"We just want a quick sale," Bob was telling Sallie
Kate. "We had no idea what Polaris—I mean Hemick—
was up to."

"I think he must have brainwashed us all," put in
Gene. "I sure hope I can recoup some of my investment.
My dad's going to go ballistic." Mort said nothing, just
glanced mournfully at his Rolex, reached in a pocket,
and pulled out a brown prescription bottle. He shook

out two green-and-white capsules and popped them into his mouth.

Elizabeth and Sallie Kate followed the young men into the dome. The central dais where Polaris had stood two weeks ago now leaned forlornly against the wall. Cardboard boxes overflowing with papers covered folding tables and were piled on the floor. The harsh light from two floor lamps on long extension cords revealed a mosaic of dirty bootprints on the once pristine blue carpet.

Gene looked around bitterly. "It was all so beautiful. It was just incredibly awesome to be a part of something so—so cosmic."

"What happened?" Elizabeth asked him.

"Well, when the cops came after Ernie, they were looking for records about the adoptions. And drugs."

The story unfolded in sad bits and pieces. Ernie Hemick, aka Polaris, had burst onto the New Age scene four years ago, proclaiming himself the emissary of a civilization from a distant galaxy. He had sought out disciples, first among the wealthy, then as he gained support, more and more among disaffected young men and women.

"The whole thing was that he said we were starchildren," explained Bob. "Carriers of the star gene. He said that we were some of a special few in the world today who were descended from a group of travelers from his galaxy. They landed here thousands of years ago."

"Yeah," put in Mort, "they built Atlantis and when it sank, a few survivors eventually interbred with ordinary humans. That's who we're descended from."

"And one of the ways he identified you was that you were all blond, blue-eyed hunks?" asked Sallie Kate innocently.

"Well," said Gene modestly, "he said that the star gene usually—"

"So what's the deal on the adoptions?" Sallie Kate interrupted impatiently.

"Oh, that was to spread the star gene more fully throughout society. Pol—I mean Ernie said that by the next generation we could put an end to war and—"

"And it just so happens that healthy blond babies are hardest to find if you're trying to adopt. So he was selling the babies? Is that what it was? Jesus!" Sallie Kate went on without waiting for an answer, "And none of the mothers ever objected?"

Bob looked down at the dusty carpet. "Well, mostly they were happy to be part of the greater plan. But once Ernie left and wasn't here to bless the food—he used to sprinkle something he called 'stardust' in every serving dish—well, that was when things got weird."

Got weird? thought Elizabeth.

As the young men told it, matters came to a head when one new mother was sick and unable to keep food down for several days. Suddenly she had become violently opposed to giving up her child at the end of the regulation six-week period.

"The babies always stayed with their mothers for six weeks," Mort explained, "before being reassigned to their new parents."

"Yeah," said Gene earnestly, "so they could be breast-fed and absorb all the star immunities. But this chick had a cell phone, which was like totally forbidden, and she called her daddy—"

"Who is some political big shot." Bob picked up the tale. "And the next day the cops were all over the place."

"Well, honey, her daddy must know all the right

people," said Sallie Kate. "This story hasn't made it into the news. Daddy must be protecting his little girl."

As the three men now admitted, investigation had shown that Polaris had kept the members of his community on a low-level dose of some euphoria-inducing drug which, coincidentally, kept them all in a highly suggestible state. "Man, it was like Paradise; we were all so happy and in tune with the cosmos. Then all of a sudden, here's this chick freaking out and totally destroying the vibe—"

"Yeah," exclaimed Mort, interrupting Bob, "we had to put her into occultation, but then the cops came. . . . And after they took Ernie away, it all fell apart."

Elizabeth listened to the account with growing disgust at the reckless credulity of the so-called starchildren. "Wasn't Polaris worried about this drug harming the babies?" she asked. "I can't believe someone would do something like that."

The three ex-stars looked at one another blankly. "Jeez," said Mort. "We just trusted that Polaris was doing the right thing. I mean, he was in tune with—"

"Ernie was doing the right thing for Ernie," Bob said with bitter emphasis. "We might as well face it. He took us for all he could."

Gene looked around again. His eyes were wet and his voice quavered as he said, "It was all so beautiful. How could it have been wrong?"

"So everyone's clearing out and you guys want to sell?" said Sallie Kate, making some brisk notes on her clipboard. "What about Hemick? He's a part owner, is he going to agree?"

"Oh, yeah." All three nodded seriously. "Ernie said to sell as fast as we could. He's going to need the money for his lawyers."

The three co-owners took them on a tour of the community. They visited the vast barnlike structure that housed the communal kitchen and dining room, the dormitories, the studios, and the crèche. Everywhere there was evidence of the hasty departure of the starchildren: pots and pans and dishes stacked unwashed in the kitchen, sheets and blankets trailing off the dormitory cots, drawers pulled out and emptied. Unfinished paintings lay on the huge tables in the studios and the airbrushes sat uncleaned, their mechanisms clogged with paint. The crèche, a small but well-equipped maternity hospital, was in total disarray, as if the police search had been particularly thorough here.

"I think that's about all there is to see," Bob told them. "There's a big building farther up that no one but Pol— Ernie and a few of his special disciples could go to. The police say they were manufacturing drugs up there. Ernie had some contact up north who would show up now and then in a big black Beemer. I think he's been arrested, too. But anyway, that building's padlocked and cordoned off till they get done collecting evidence."

"Let's show her the rebirthing pool." Gene's voice was eager. "That ought to add to the value of this place— God knows it cost enough."

The rebirthing pool was a very fancy custom-made swimming pool. With a black-painted interior and boulders lining its edges, it looked like a natural pond.

"Honey, you all didn't cut any corners, did you?" said Sallie Kate. "Why do you call it a rebirthing pool?"

The three young men looked at one another, then

Gene said, "It was to mark the first step in our evolution as starchildren, to wash away all earthly thought and—"

"Kind of like a baptism," explained Mort.

"No," argued Bob, "more than that. It could fix people who weren't right. Remember when that local guy showed up, that one with the funny name?" Elizabeth stiffened. Polaris had told her that Cletus had visited the community. . . .

"He ate dinner with us a couple of times," Bob continued, "and Polaris told us that this guy who wasn't quite all there, this guy could be transformed if he just underwent the rebirthing ceremony."

"Cletus, that was his name," Gene put in. "I remember because it sounded kind of like a star name already."

"Oh, yeah, I remember now," Mort agreed. "But then something changed and a few days later Pol—I mean Ernie—told us that what's-his-name had trespassed in the forbidden area and wouldn't be coming back. He was no longer welcome, Ernie said."

Sallie Kate and the three hunks, as Elizabeth now thought of them, turned to inspect the building nearby that housed changing rooms and pool-cleaning equipment. Sallie Kate was growing more and more enthusiastic about the property.

Elizabeth stood transfixed, staring at the smooth, dark surface of the pool, then with sudden decisiveness she scrabbled in her shoulder bag and found a small plastic bottle of ibuprofen. She dumped the pills out into her purse; then, with two swift steps, she was at the side of the pool. She knelt and swished the little container clean, filled it and replaced the cap. *The water in the lungs wasn't entirely consistent with the water in the mouth and ears. . . .*

As they drove back down Bear Tree Creek, Sallie Kate chattered cheerfully about the possibilities the Starshine Community could offer the right buyer. "A retreat, or a summer camp, or a school—it's all there and ready to go. If I can just get the owners to agree on a price . . ."

And Elizabeth was remembering Aunt Belvy's words: ". . . There are two joined in blood and water, two by the false prophet . . ."

Polaris . . . a false prophet.

X-MAY 1902

Hit was a mild day and I was settin on the cabin steps a-givin Malindy the breast. Though the sun felt warm, I had her wrapped up good with her cap pulled snug around her little ears. Hit was mostly still but ever now and then a breath of air would make the leaves in just one part of a tree to tremble. I watched how the breeze moved around and I was marvelin at how hit caught just one leaf of the young peach tree I'd planted there near the cabin steps.

I set there just a-watchin that little sickle-shaped leaf flippin back and forth in the breeze. Will you? Won't you? Will you? Won't you? kept a-runnin through my head.

The bleedin I'd had after Malindy was borned had quit now and I felt purt near as stout as I used to be. I'd been walkin about more and more, hopin to gain my strength back. And now that the days was warm I had made up my mind to take my babe and walk to Gudger's Stand. There I could get on the train and ride to Ransom and at the depot in Ransom, I knowed I could get me a ticket to Kentucky.

Mister Tomlin had been watchin me close and he had

took to doin a queer thing. Ever night, afore he drunk that medicine of hisn, he would haul the bedstead to where hit blocked the door. When I asked him why he done this, he said he didn't want me roamin around none. I didn't say nothing, though hit meant I had to use the chamber at night. I knowed that when the time come, I could get out the window onto the big rock whilst he was asleep.

I begun to make up a bundle of what I would be able to carry. I put in most all of Malindy's little gowns and as many hippins as I could. Aetha had brung me a little calico poke with a molesfoot in it to put round Malindy's neck when her teeth begun to come through and I put it in too. For myself, I just put in a change of linen for I knowed I couldn't carry more, far as I must travel. I hid the bundle up in the loft of the shed out back and bided my time.

At last hit seemed I must take the chance. Mister Tomlin was startin to be ill at Malindy whenever she cried. Shut her up, he'd say to me, or I'll take the belt to both of you. Hit was a Tuesday night and I knowed there was a train to Ransom first thing in the mornin. Mister Tomlin had come home with the smell of whisky on him and had et a big supper. He pulled the bed agin the door like he done ever night and then set there on hit in his nightshirt, smokin his cigar and a-starin at me as I gave Malindy the breast.

He kept starin and starin till hit raised chill bumps on me. At last he says, There'll be a reckoning, Little Sylvie. Sooner or later, there'll be a reckoning. Then he lay back on the bed and afore long was asleep. I went over and took the cigar from between his fingers and stobbed hit out. He was snorin like one thing and I figured that this was as good a chancet as would come.

I set up for some hours, wantin to make sure that he was deep asleep. I thought how I would do—get to Gudger's Stand just at dawn, then ride to Ransom. I had fixed a note tellin Mister Tomlin that I was takin Malindy and goin over the mountain to Levy's folks. I hoped that if he come atter me that he would go there first and that I would be on my way to Kentucky afore that he learned the truth.

Some time back of this I had greased the window shutter but even so hit squeaked something awful when I pushed hit open. Mister Tomlin give a kind of snort and rolled over facin the door. Quick as I could, I went to where his britches was hangin and put my hand in the pocket. The gold double eagles was warm and heavy in my hand and kindly greasy to the touch. I wrapped them in a rag so that they wouldn't make no noise. Then I thought about what Levy had said about stealin and I took off the ruby finger-ring and put hit in the pocket where the gold pieces had been. I had come to hate hit anyhow.

Malindy didn't stir one bit when I lifted her from her cradle and wrapped her in the World Without End quilt. I tucked the coins in the quilt with her and took her over to the window. The sill was wide enough to where I could lay her on hit so I rested her there, took one last look at my sewin machine, and clumb out the window. I had my feet on the log just above the big rock and was reachin up for my babe when all to oncet Mr. Tomlin was there at the window. He grabbed up Malindy and smiled at me. But hit were more like a dog a-barin hits teeth than a smile. And then it come to me that I hadn't seen him swaller his medicine afore he laid him down.

He held my babe up high and for a dreadful moment I was feared that he had taken a notion to dash her onto the big rock like some of them folks done in the Bible. I cried out and he stepped back and must of put her in her cradle. Then he come back and leaned outen the window. You go on, Little Sylvie, he says, you go on if you've a mind to. But this baby that you've let on to be mine, why I reckon I'll just keep her. And then he slammed the shutter tight shut.

I hollered and carried on and beat on the door but hit didn't do no good. He wouldn't give her to me and he wouldn't let me in. I heard her begin to cry but right quick she quietened down and there weren't no sound atall.

Daddy come to the door when I called out. Hit was black dark but I could make out the shotgun in his hands. He didn't even let me come up to the porch, just told me to go back to my man and not to bring more shame on my family. I walked across the foot log and stood there not knowin what to do. Then hit come to me that maybe Aetha would understand. I still hadn't never said nothing to her about Levy but I thought that her and Fate might take my side.

By the time I toiled up the road to Fate and Aetha's place hit was first light. They was smoke comin out of the chimbly and I could smell sausage cookin. When I hollered out, Fate come to the door. What are you doin here, Little Sylvie? he asks, but he stands aside and lets me in.

Aetha's at the cookstove stirrin some gravy, but she takes

one look at me and says, Fate, you see to this for a minute iffen you don't care, and pulls me back to the porch.

Her oldest, little Lafayette junior, hollers out, Where's yore baby at, Aunt Sylvie? but afore I can say aught, Aetha pushes the door to.

Little Sylvie, she says, whatever is the matter? You look plumb wild.

My skirts is all wet and draggled with dew and my hair is trailin down. A blackberry bramble had caught me across the cheek when I was cuttin through the fields on my way and I can feel the long mark hit's left just a-stingin. I start in to tell Aetha what's wrong and all of a sudden I go to bawlin and can't stop. Aetha hugs me and tidies my hair some then makes me set down.

Little Sylvie, she says, do you know I was just this way when I had Lafayette? Hit's a kind of madness sometimes happens atter a baby comes. It hits different ones different ways. Some women won't feed their own babes nor have nothing to do with them. With me hit was the other way round. I just loved little Lafayette but I started thinking that Fate, his own daddy, was a-tryin to kill him and me too. But that craziness, hit passed right soon.

Rom had said Aetha was took right bad back then but I hadn't been old enough to pay hit no mind, I reckon. Anyhow, I seen that most likely she'd not believe what I was namin to tell her. Inside the house her least un started to cry and all of a sudden my milk let down and began to soak the front of my dress. I was still bawlin like one thing but then Aetha reached out and touched the wet spot. Don't you want to go home and feed yore sweet babe? she said.

The sun was full up by the time I got back. Neb was still in the pasture and the door was bolted from the inside. I begged Mister Tomlin through the door to let me see my baby and feed her. I could hear Malindy a-cryin and I knowed she ain't had nothing but the sugar tit I give her when I wrapped her up and laid her on the windowsill. I told him that I'd come back and not sin no more but he said I was a harlot and didn't deserve no child. I hollered and beat on the door till my hands was bloody.

At long last he said I could feed the baby but that I couldn't touch her nor see her. I was most out of my mind, hearing Malindy cryin and her soundin weaker every minute so I said I'd do like he wanted. He come out with some pieces ripped from my good shirtwaist and first he tied my wrists together behind my back then he tied a blindfold round my head. How'm I gonna hold my baby girl? I said.

She doesn't need the pollution of your filthy touch, Mister Tomlin said and jerked me by the elbow up the steps and into the cabin. He pulled me over to the corner where he'd moved the bedstead and pushed me down on it. The front of my dress was all wet with my milk and my titties was tight as touch-me-not seed pods. His rough old hands pulled at the buttons and I could feel one breast poppin out in the air. Then I felt my baby's sweet mouth on my nipple and my tears soaked the blindfold and run down my face and onto my bosom. Malindy sucked hard and quick and I could hear her gulpin for air. She sounded like a little pig just a-rootin at the old sow.

I started to talk to my baby, to sing the little horsey song Aetha had sung to me when I was a little un but he slapped me acrost the face and told me to hold my tongue. Will you put her to the other breast, please, Mister Tomlin? Hit's awful tight, I asked as meek as I could. But I could feel that she was slackin off and probly fallin asleep. Malindy had near bout drained that one side and was just playin like with the nipple, bitin it and lettin it loose, and then bitin it again. I could smell the sweet milky smell of her and there was the rankness of her dirty hippins. I leaned down to try to press my lips to her little head but Mister Tomlin snatched her away. I could hear her sleepy, chirpin sounds as he laid her in the cradle at the foot of the bed.

Mister Tomlin, I begged, You got to pat her little back to bring the air up lest she get colicky. He didn't say nothing and I stayed quiet, hopin he would change his mind and let me see my baby. I could hear him movin around the cabin and startin to speak scripture the way he done them other times.

Then his whiskery old face was at my other breast and he was bitin and suckin my tit. My stomach heaved and I was like to puke but I thought of my baby and kept still, hopin he would let me see her.

When he was done he just pushed me out the door and I heard it bolted shut behind me. I stumbled down the steps and stood there in the yard with my titties hangin out, my eyes yet blindfolded and my hands yet tied behind me. I knowed it weren't no use to holler, for Mister Tomlin wouldn't care and my family was too far off to hear. And I'd not have them see me shamed like this. So I stood there for a time and worked my wrists thisaway and that till the cloth strips Mister Tomlin had tied me with seemed some looser. Atter a time I could wrench one hand free, then the other and I pulled off the hateful old cloth from around my eyes.

The window I'd clumb out of to run off was open now so I clambered onto the big rock and hoisted myself up, wantin bad to see could I get ary sight of my babe. I had to leap up to try to grab holt of the windowsill and, bein but small, I missed, leavin the clawmarks of my fingernails traced on the logs. When finally I did catch hold and got a toehold on a log as well, I could see the cradle and the fuzz of Malindy's little head.

But Mister Tomlin must of heard the noise I'd made a-tryin to reach the window for he roused himself from off the bedstead where he'd been layin. He staggered as he came for the window and he looked down at me with the awfullest look I'd yet seen him make and said, Cover yourself, harlot. He started to pull the shutter over the window then he leaned back out and said, You're no more to me than a cow, you huzzy, but you can come back at milking time and feed your bastard.

CHAPTER 23
THE SNAKE HANDLER
(WEDNESDAY)

M UM, I KEEP THINKING ABOUT THIS JOHN THE Baptizer thing. How can I mount a show for a child abuser? If that's what he is. We have to find out. His paintings are so awesome. Anyway, I've got to go to work now . . . I'll come out tomorrow. Why don't I meet you at the foot of Lonesome Holler and we can walk up together and talk to Mary Cleophas. Say ten-thirty. Or if I can I might try to get there earlier. In that case I'll see you up at the cabin. I'll make sure John the Baptizer's car is still at the tent place so we don't run into him. Okay. See you then."

The message on the voice mail the night before had reassured Elizabeth somewhat. At least Laurel was proceeding with caution in the matter of John the Baptizer. A shiver ran over her as she remembered Laurel saying "He wants to paint me!" and the image of the painting of the nude, pregnant Mary Cleophas rose up in her mind, followed by the memory of the strange infant with its undeveloped twin dangling against its belly.

She had gotten up early to fix some food to take to the girl: meat loaf, macaroni and cheese, green beans cooked with fatback—the sort of meal she thought Mary Cleophas would enjoy. The containers would all stay warm if she packed them in a cooler with towels for insulation. And there was still plenty of time to run to the grocery store and buy some things for the baby before driving up Bear Tree to meet Laurel.

The little pill bottle with water from the rebirthing pool sat on her desk. She had tried several times to contact Hawkins, but with no success. Her night had been restless, haunted by dreams of Cletus and the other drowned man, first at the militia compound, being hunted in the night by men in camouflage, wearing night-vision equipment. Then the dream shifted to the rebirthing pool, and Polaris and the three hunks were saying, "They've seen too much," as they held her and Sallie Kate under the water, oblivious to the flailing arms and terrified cries that came up in great liquid bubbles of sound.

On her way to the grocery store, she noticed that Dorothy's car was not at Birdie's house. *Probably a trip to the doctor,* she thought. *I hope that's all. I should have called this morning.* She wondered what the laying on of hands had been like, if it had brought Birdie any comfort. *Harice was there . . .* she thought, then abruptly stuck a tape in the player and tried to lose herself in *Dirk Gently's Holistic Detective Agency.*

The parking lot at the grocery was unexpectedly full. As she circled looking for a place, she was chilled by the sight of the camouflage-painted humvee that Ben had described. The decal on the bumper was unpleasantly familiar: the USA-shaped American flag, the cross, and the words: "Adam's Sons in the Wilderness."

Elizabeth parked as far away from the vehicle as she could and hurried into the store. She scanned the checkout stations, but saw no sign of any militia types.

Grabbing a buggy, she went straight to the baby food aisle and loaded up a selection of items for a very young baby. On her way to the checkout it occurred to her that Mary Cleophas might like some fresh fruit.

She was assembling a collection of oranges, apples, and bananas when she suddenly heard a familiar voice. Looking up, she saw that Harice Tyler and the buxom young woman who had brought his daddy one of her special cakes were standing by the potatoes. After saying something to the young woman, Harice came toward Elizabeth.

"Mornin', Miz Goodweather," he said. Behind him the pretty brunette made a disgusted face and flounced toward the front door, abandoning her shopping buggy where it stood.

"Miz Goodweather, I'm goin' to ask one last time, bein' as how the Lord has brought you afore me again: Will you come to church with me tonight and give the Lord a chance?" There was no sign today of the lazy smile, and the dark eyes were implacably hard, not soft.

Elizabeth met his gaze with equal resolve. "Thank you, Mr. Tyler, but no. I guess you could say that what I *don't* believe is just as strong as what you *do* believe. I'm sorry."

With a derisive snort he turned away from her. Elizabeth watched him go, then went back to her shopping. But she gave him a few minutes to leave in order to avoid yet another meeting in the parking lot.

The humvee was gone. She took a moment to walk around her car and make sure that no obnoxious sticker had been affixed to it this time. Breathing a sigh of relief on not finding any, she got in. She glanced at the clock and decided to drive the short distance down the road to John the Baptizer's tent and make sure that his car was still there.

A portable yellow sign near the road read, *"Baptizing at Gudger's Stand—Sunday 10 am—The One Way Trip to Glory!"* And there, beside the luridly decorated old camper, was John the Baptizer's equally old and gaudy Ford. Elizabeth smiled with satisfaction. She turned around at the nearby gas station and headed back up the road toward Bear Tree Creek. She was looking forward to giving Mary Cleophas a hot meal and talking with the girl about her father.

As Elizabeth neared the river she thought about the coming baptizing, picturing the sinners being led out into the water and then pushed under, to rise up saved. Laurel had mentioned that Cletus had never been baptized because he wouldn't go under the water. *I can understand that. But at the funeral, John the Baptizer seemed pretty sure Cletus was in heaven. Odd that other preacher didn't tell him that Cletus wasn't baptized. Maybe they're giving him the benefit of the doubt. Or maybe they're counting that final immersion as a baptism. . . .*

She pictured Mary Cleophas as she had first seen her, like an apparition by the little pool saying, "That there's livin' water; hit kin take you to glory." The girl was so beautiful and innocent. Was she, as Laurel had suggested, a little simple too? Did she even understand who her baby's father was? Mary Cleophas's description of the living water kept echoing in Elizabeth's brain. Where else had she heard those words? And then she remembered the open grave and John the Baptizer standing beside it saying, "And Cletus walked beside the living water and it was the water of life . . . the waters took him to glory incorruptible."

"Oh, my god!" she said aloud, pounding her fist on

the steering wheel. "What if John the Baptizer wasn't speaking figuratively? What if he was describing what happened?" Suddenly it all fell into place. *The squirrels in the knapsack . . . if Cletus was coming back with squirrels to cook for Mary Cleophas, and her father didn't want anyone to know about her and the baby . . . and the little pool in the clearing . . . how could I have been so stupid as to overlook that? And her father had locked her in the cabin, supposedly to punish her for breaking the lamp, so she couldn't have seen . . . And Aunt Belvy's prophecy . . . two joined in blood and water, two by the hand of the father, two by the false prophet . . . it fits, oh, my god, it all fits. Cletus and Dewey, Mary Cleophas and the baby, the baby itself, two joined in blood—Oh, shit!*

She instantly realized that all of her painstaking speculations about Birdie, about the starchildren, even about the militia, were ludicrous. *Motive and opportunity—the killer had both. And Cletus would have trusted him because he's a preacher. He's crazy, of course . . . all that about Mary Cleophas and her child having to stay hidden from the sight of man.*

Another certainty presented itself. *And by his twisted logic he could decide to father a child on his daughter like . . . what did Mary Cleophas say? . . . Like when God the Father gave Jesus to Mary. Oh, my god!*

She drove on. And as her thoughts swirled and coalesced, only to dissolve and form new patterns, she remembered her first visit to the Holiness church. Aunt Belvy had looked at her with sightless eyes—*Woe to the sinner, she said, and something about death and corruption . . .* then the words came to her: *Her child shall weep in the wilderness.*

"Laurel!" Suddenly Elizabeth was filled with the irrational but overwhelming conviction that Laurel was in danger. *She said she'd meet me at ten-thirty or earlier. I've got to get there and get her away before John the Baptizer decides to come along. And Mary Cleophas and the baby, too. Just get them away and we can sort it out later.*

She was on the bridge now and she pressed down on the accelerator, illegally passing a pickup truck driven by a very old man going twenty miles an hour. Once on Bear Tree Creek, passing was virtually impossible and she didn't want to be behind this truck all the way to Lonesome Holler. *I've got to get them out of there before John the Baptizer comes back. Something bad is about to happen . . .* She refused to let the words *or has happened* take shape, and concentrated instead on what she would say to convince Mary Cleophas to leave Lonesome Holler.

"If I'm wrong," she said between clenched teeth, "it'll be embarrassing. But if I'm right . . ." She stopped talking to herself and concentrated on driving as fast as she safely could on this narrow winding road, full of blind curves and precipitous drops along the side. She blared her horn at a nervous chicken that had been going to cross the road but quickly turned and retreated in a squawking feathered flurry.

Elizabeth had taken her foot off the accelerator to brake for a particularly sharp curve when she felt something heavy slide across her left foot.

She knew instantly what it was. The thick musky smell that had emanated from the snake boxes at the Holiness church seemed to fill the car, and the dry whisper of scales slipping over her hiking boot revealed what was riding with her . . . *she shall ride with death,* Aunt Belvy had said. Elizabeth felt the hair on her arms rise and a cold dew of sweat break out all over her body. Moving as little as possible she slowly, minutely, increased the pressure on the brake pedal, easing the car to the side of the road.

Only when the car had stopped did Elizabeth dare to look down. The rattler, only a medium-size one, if that mattered, was stretched across her left foot, moving its triangular head from side to side, as if looking for a way out. She sat there frozen, foot on brake, not even daring to breathe. The car was still running and she found herself hoping that possibly the vibration would be calming to the snake. The desperate thought almost made her laugh aloud.

No sudden moves, she told herself. *Maybe if I just stay still it'll crawl away.* She looked at the clock on the dashboard. Ten thirty-seven. Laurel was probably already at the foot of the road to Lonesome Holler. But John the Baptizer could be on his way at any minute. She knew that she had to get there and get her daughter and Mary Cleophas and the child away before the evangelist came. And somehow she was utterly certain that he would be coming.

Now the snake was moving. Elizabeth battled to control the shudder that threatened to send her body into a spasm as the rattler slid across her foot and into the little space leading to the backseat. With infinite care Elizabeth moved her hand slowly, excruciating inch by inch, to the door, expecting at any moment to feel the sharp fangs pierce her flesh. Her fingers touched the door and carefully, quietly, she felt for the lock. Holding her breath, she eased the lock toward the off position, hoping that it would disengage silently.

The loud click made her start, and from the backseat she heard the angry buzz of the snake's rattles. Sitting frozen, she waited for the sound to stop. As she began to gather her courage for a sudden leap from the car, she realized that first she must release her seat belt. And the latch was there between the seats—so terribly close to where the rattler must be.

She moved her hands gradually and fearfully—the left to hold the belt and prevent it from winding back with its usual clatter; the right toward the release bar on the latch. Her clothes were damp now with the clammy sweat of fear as she moved her hand closer to the buckle. *I have to do this,* she thought, imagining the double rush of burning venom into her hand. And then her fingertips touched the latch. Praying that it would release smoothly, she pushed the bar; the latch opened with a muffled click.

Immediately her right hand shoved the gearshift into park as her left pulled the belt free and opened the door all with one motion. She swung her legs from under the steering wheel and tumbled out. The next second she was standing on the pavement, breathing hard.

"Okay, now what?" she asked the empty road. It was another four or five miles to Lonesome Holler. Either a car would come along and she could get a ride or—*but what if the driver of the car is John the Baptizer? You need your car. You have to get that damn snake out of the jeep, Elizabeth.*

She edged nearer to the open back window, irrationally fearful that the reptile might leap out the window and sink its fangs into her face. *Snakes don't jump like that, you fool!* she assured herself. *Do they?*

Cautiously she brought her face nearer the window but she could see no sign of the rattler. *Unless I stuck my head right in . . . and I'm not about to do that . . .* Withdrawing a step, she thought furiously. *If only I had one of those snake-catching sticks like they use. Shit, Elizabeth, if only you had another car, if only Laurel weren't in danger, if only this weren't happening. Stop dithering and do something!*

Taking a deep breath, she resolutely grabbed the handle of the back door. As the door swung open, the coiled snake raised the tip of its tail in a warning rattle and lifted its menacing head. Elizabeth stumbled backward hastily. *Not good. If it sees me, it won't come out.*

She opened the doors on the other side of the car, then the back hatch. Inside, the snake had stretched out across the floor and was beginning to explore, its questing head trying various escape routes. It was entirely possible that hours could go by before a car would come along. A burning rage filled her, anger at her helplessness, anger at the person who had put this reptile in her car, fury at the mindless menace that held her at its mercy.

The snake was moving away from her now. It seemed to be making for the open door on the other side, but then it stopped and began to investigate the area under the driver's seat. *No, not there,* Elizabeth prayed silently. *Go out! Now!* As she watched intently, the rattler began to slide under the seat. *Out! I've got to get to Laurel!*

"Oh, no, you don't!" Without thinking about the consequences, Elizabeth grabbed the reptile firmly around its narrow neck and flung it out of the car and into the ditch. "Arghh!" she cried as she shook her hands madly to get rid of the feel of the snake, then watched, trembling with triumph and adrenaline, as it slithered away into the weeds and vanished.

She was still standing there when she heard the sputter and rattle of an ancient truck approaching. It was the same old man she had raced by on the bridge. Now he gave her and her car a contemptuous glare as he crept by and disappeared around the next curve.

Frantic with worry and desperate to get to Laurel, Elizabeth jogged a little way down the road, in the opposite direction from the snake, and found a long dead branch. Snapping off the twigs as she went, she hurried back to her car. She had to get to Lonesome Holler but she needed to be sure there weren't any more snakes in the jeep. The thought of more snakes made her feel weak all over and she wanted to sit down. *I can't believe I grabbed that rattler. I didn't decide to; I just did it.* Her heart was pounding and she bent over abruptly, putting her hands on her knees and hoping she wasn't going to faint.

In a moment she felt calmer and she approached the jeep, still idling there on the roadside. Through the open door she could see a rough edge of burlap protruding from under the driver's seat. She jumped back, trembling. Then, gingerly, she poked the branch at the material. Nothing happened. Slowly, she maneuvered the branch to drag the burlap bag out of its hiding place. It resisted her attempts at first, but she continued to manipulate the branch and tug at the burlap. At last she hooked the bag out of the car, leaping away from it as it sailed through the air. It landed a car's length away and lay there on the pavement, flat and empty.

A red fog of anger rose in her mind as she remembered that Harice Tyler had used a similar bag—*or this one!*—when she had first encountered him. "Goddammit!" she shouted, spooking a blue jay out of a tree. "Only then it was copperheads."

Somehow the anger cleared her head and she used the branch quickly, but thoroughly, to assure herself that there were no more snakes hiding in the car. Filled with a cold fury, she slammed shut all the doors, got in, and put the jeep in gear.

She was at the foot of Lonesome Holler in just over six minutes. Laurel's old green Subaru was pulled over to the side of the road and a piece of paper was flapping under one of the wipers.

Mum, I woke up real early this morning and decided to come right out. I wanted to get some pictures of MC in the first light. See you when you get here. XOX, L

XI–MAY 1902

I was like to drop, not havin had no sleep so I took myself up the hill to the little place in the woods where I used to lay down with Levy. I felt so crazy-like that I could almost believe Aetha was right and I was just a-dreamin all that had happened. The ground was dry by now and I lay down in the little hidden place and fell fast asleep.

When I woke the sun was droppin down toward Pinnacle and my breastes was tight full again. I made for the cabin but the door was still bolted. I called out, Mister Tomlin, I need to feed Malindy. I say it nice and soft, hopin he'll not make me have the blindfold again.

At first he don't answer. Then he says in a voice that sounds hoarse-like, Your brat's asleep; come back in a little while.

I can't hear a sound from Malindy and that don't seem right. So I go back to the rock and clamber up to the window again. My fingers is tore up from before and I leave bloody marks over the scratches on the logs but I manage to get to where I can just peer over the sill.

Mister Tomlin was layin on the bed and didn't have on

*nothing but his shirt. He had a bottle of whisky in his hand
and my baby was layin acrost his lap. Malindy didn't have on
no clothes nor nary a hippin. She was snorin awful loud and
didn't look natural somehow. Then I seen Mister Tomlin
take a big swaller from that bottle and lay it to one side.*

*I tried to hoist myself up through the window but he
come over and banged the shutter closed again. I heared
him latch it and then heared the bedstead creak as he lay
back down. I knocked on the shutter and called out, Mister
Tomlin, you let me see my baby, but he didn't answer nary
a word. I could hear his breath comin fast like it done those
other times and I called out, What are you doin to
Malindy?*

*I scrabbled until I could get me a purchase on one of the
logs and pull myself higher. They was a knothole in the
shutter and I could just make out to put my eye to it.
Mister Tomlin was layin there on the bed like before but
his head was flung back and his eyes was rolled up till
didn't but the whites show. He had my baby in his hands
and he was a-rubbin her up and down over his floppy old
thing. Hit won't do no good, you nasty old turdhead, I
hollered. You leave my baby alone.*

*I tried to push the shutter open but lost my grip and
slipped down the side of the cabin. I stood there on that big
rock, like to bust with hate for Mister Tomlin. Just then he
hollered out that hit was his baby and he could do with hit
like he wanted.*

*There weren't nothing for it but to run down to tell my
daddy about what Mister Tomlin was doin. I near flew
down the trail but when I got to the house they was all
gone. I tried to think where they might be and then it come*

to me that hit was Wednesday and they was all at the Wednesday night church meetin. I ran in the house to see had maybe Romarie stayed home but no one answered when I called up the stairs. So I turned to leave, thinking to run to the church house and tell ever one of them about the terrible things Mister Tomlin was doin to my baby.

Just above the door, restin on a pair of deer antlers, was the English shotgun Mister Tomlin had give my daddy. I pushed an old mule-eared chair up to the door and clumb up so's I could reach down that fine shiny double-barreled shotgun. I knowed hit would have a kick even harder than Daddy's old gun. That one had like to knock me down when I had kilt that old coon what got all the cockerels.

I went to where Daddy keeps his shotgun shells. There was birdshot, like he used to shoot dove, and number five, like he used for turkeys. I looked till I found the double ought buckshot. Daddy had showed me how there was twelve round balls in each shell and he had told me how they would fan out and knock down any big buck. I put two shells in the shotgun and some extry in my pocket. There was a great peace come over me for now I knowed there was a way.

I was climbin the road back to the cabin when I heared hoofbeats. I drawed back in the thick brush and hid. I could hear that hit was Mister Tomlin and he was a-singin as he rode, singin about bein washed in the blood of the lamb.

I drawed a bead on him just like my daddy had showed me. With my left eye shut I looked down the long barrel to the little nub stickin up there at the end, then I leveled the gun till that nub was restin on the ramp there at the back. I brung the gun around slow till that nub shown against

Mister Tomlin's whiskery face. I kept it trained on him as he rode and I could see them wattles of hisn, quiverin as he sung. I knowed that I had but to squeeze one trigger and he'd drop down as he went.

And I'd a done it too but it come to me that might not no one believe me about what he done to my baby. Like as not they'd arrest me, maybe even hang me. I knowed if that happened I'd likely never see Malindy again so I lowered the shotgun real slow and waited till he was good and gone and I couldn't hear his hateful singin no more.

Then I hightailed it back up the hill to our cabin. I thought to hear Malindy a-cryin but hit was quiet as could be. The shutter was still closed and he'd padlocked the cabin door. I didn't think twicet, just shot that padlock offen the door.

Hit didn't take but the one barrel to do it but that shotgun kicked like a mule. Hit would have knocked me plumb offen the porch hadn't I had my back mashed hard against one of them locust poles holdin up the porch roof. My ears was ringin so loud with the sound hit made I couldn't hear nothing else. I knowed the loud noise must of waked my baby and she was likely just a-screamin but I couldn't hear her. I pushed open the door and run across the room to the cradle. I was laughin and cryin and my dress front was wet with milk.

The cradle was empty, just the little rumpled sheets of domestic that I had hemmed so careful and the little quilt I had pieced when I was waitin for her. I put my hand on them and they was wet and cold.

Malindy, I called out and pulled back the covers of the

bed. Malindy! I'd watched Mister Tomlin go and I knowed he didn't have her with him.

She weren't in the bedstead nor nowhere in sight and, though the ringin had near bout quit, still I couldn't hear no sound of her. I tore into the boxes and baskets that was stacked in the corner, callin out her name.

When I found her at the bottom of Mister Tomlin's travelin valise, I knowed right off she were dead. She was still warm but her eyes couldn't see me and when I took her up she felt like an old rag doll without no stuffin. I opened my shirtwaist front and put her to my breast though I knowed hit weren't no use. I bent my head down to kiss her like I had wanted to before and I could smell the sickly sweet smell of Mister Tomlin's medicine on her little lips. The taste was bitter and I could see a sticky trail of the medicine runnin down her chest to between her legs.

I don't know how long hit was that I set there, just a-whisperin to her and callin her all the pretty names I had for her. I even sang her the horsey song but when she began to grow chill in my arms, I made up my mind. I'll not have you buried under his name, Malindy, I promised as I laid her on the bed. Then I tore one of the pages from out the account book Mister Tomlin kept and wrote down the truth of what had happened. I querled up the paper real small and put hit into the empty medicine bottle that was there by her cradle.

Your name is Malindy Johnson, I told my baby, and I washed her clean with the water that was there in the bucket and dressed her in the little white outing gown that I'd worked pink and purple thrift flowers on. I tucked the bottle with the paper in it under her gown next to her heart and I wrapped her tight in the blue and white World Without End quilt. She looked so natural hit was almost like she was just asleep.

I carried her outside the cabin and laid her beneath the plumy ferns nigh the branch. The ground was soft there and I thought she could have the music of the water rushin over the rocks for a lullaby. Then I took the grub hoe from the shed behind the cabin and commenced to dig. I sung the song about the angels as I labored.

The dirt was soft and she was so little. Hit didn't take no time to make a hole big enough and deep enough. I laid her down and covered her face with the quilt. Then I begun to put in the dirt, a handful at a time till she was all covered. My tears was rainin down on her but every handful of dirt took her farther away from me. When I couldn't see her no more, I finished fillin in the hole, rakin the dirt with the hoe. Then I kneeled down beside her grave and prayed that I would die too. Hit seemed that there weren't nothing left in this world for me. But when I closed my eyes I thought of Mister Tomlin, a widder man again and lookin for a young wife. I'd not have him do another girl this way, thinks I.

I got up from my knees and told Malindy goodby and I went back into the cabin. I took a shell from out my apron pocket and reloaded the shotgun Mister Tomlin had give my daddy for me. Hit wouldn't take but one barrel for what I was naming to do but I meant to be ready. Then I set down to wait. I knowed hit would be nigh dark afore he come back but there would be light aplenty. . . .

CHAPTER 24
BEHOLD HE COMETH
(WEDNESDAY)

ELIZABETH DROVE AT A RECKLESS SPEED, SQUEALED TO a stop by Walter and Ollie's trailer, and started sprinting up the road. Walter and Ollie came out onto their porch to see who it was, but she just called to them that she would stop by later and explain. As she rounded the first bend she could still hear Ollie chattering.

A huge poplar tree lay across the road, its tangle of still-living branches making passage almost impossible. As she crawled under the trunk near the root ball, Elizabeth could see that she was following a well-worn trail, the same path John the Baptizer must take when he came to visit his daughter and the child. *Calm down,* she thought, as she scrambled over another downed tree, a locust this time. *You got here before him and that's what counts.*

It was many fallen trees and at least forty minutes before the little cabin came into view. Elizabeth was panting with exhaustion as she opened the door of the room where Mary Cleophas and her baby had been. No one was there, but otherwise it looked just as it had two days ago—the neat cots, the boxes of food, the Bible on the table, the little paper cranes dangling on their threads.

Laurel's probably got her up by the pool taking pictures, Elizabeth thought, and hurried out the door and up the hill to the clearing in the woods.

It was as empty as the cabin. Elizabeth stood, hands on hips, under the big oak tree that grew by the side of the pool, wondering where her daughter and Mary Cleophas could have gone. She started to call Laurel's name, but her throat was dry and burning with thirst. Kneeling by the little pool, she bent to scoop the cool water in her cupped hands.

Mary Cleophas's pale blank eyes stared up at her through the clear water. Her mouth was open in a silent cry and her long blond hair wreathed around her and the swaddled child that she still clutched in her arms. Her body swayed in the water.

"My god, my god," Elizabeth whispered. Then: "Laurel!" she called frantically. "Laurel!"

The door to the room where the paintings were kept was shut; she pushed it open and called again, "Laurel!" The light here was dim, but against the far wall she saw the unruly tangle of red hair that was her daughter's most arresting feature. Elizabeth's cry of relief ended in a sob.

Half-concealed by a stack of canvases was a life-size portrait of Laurel's head and upper body, painted in John the Baptizer's ruthless style. White flowers twined through the flaming red hair, and she wore a purple-and-orange shirt that Elizabeth recognized. Elizabeth put out a tentative finger, but she already knew. The paint was still wet.

She burst back out the door, whispering her daughter's name. A muffled thumping a little way off caught her attention. It emanated from a tumbledown outbuilding so overgrown with wild grapevines that she hadn't noticed it in her first frenzied search of the place. A small high window, fringed by the remains of rusty chicken wire and screened by vigorous green vines, faced her. "Laurel?" she said softly, and the thumping grew more pronounced.

The door was on the other side of the little building, held shut by an old three-tined pitchfork run through two hasps. She pulled the pitchfork out and, holding it in her right hand, cautiously opened the door. Up against the wall beneath the window sat Laurel, her bright clothes and hair powdery with dirt and the dust of ancient chicken droppings. A faded red bandanna gagged her and a rope bound her arms behind her, wrapped around her slim waist, and snaked down to tie first her knees and then her ankles together. Withered wildflowers clung to her dreadlocks. Her eyes were wide and angry and she made impatient noises in her throat.

Elizabeth dropped the pitchfork and ran to her daughter's side. "Laurel, sweetie, are you all right? Has he hurt you?" She tugged at the bandanna, working at the knot with trembling fingers. At last it was loose and Laurel spat out the second wadded rag that had been in her mouth. "Mum," she whispered, "he's insane! He killed Mary Cleophas. He—"

"Where is he?" Elizabeth hissed urgently, her fingers busy with the knots that bound her daughter's wrists.

"He said he was going to the mountaintop to talk to God. But he's been gone a while. Oh, Mum, hurry! We have to get away."

The knots were many and tightly tied. As Elizabeth struggled to free her daughter, Laurel gave her a frantic account of the past few hours.

"I got here about seven and walked up. I'd made sure his car was back at the tent revival place, so I figured Mary Cleophas would be alone and I could talk to her about who the baby's father was, as well as getting some good pictures of her in the early light. When I got to the cabin, the door was open and I went in. No one was there so I figured maybe she'd gone outside to pee or something. I was just standing there looking around when all of a sudden this shape filled the door." She squirmed uncomfortably. "It feels like I could slip my wrists out if you can just loosen the ropes a little more."

Laurel's numbed hands fumbled ineffectively at the knots around her knees as she continued. "It was him, John the Baptizer, and he remembered me from the day I went to talk to him about the show. It was a little creepy, after what you'd said about him maybe being the baby's father, but I tried to act all calm. He said he'd gotten a ride with someone last night after the revival because his car wouldn't start and he had something important to do out here. All the time he kept staring at me with this funny hungry look and I was starting to get really weirded out. Mum, for God's sake, hurry! He could be back any minute!" Her voice took on an edge of hysteria.

"I swear I'll always carry a knife after this," Elizabeth muttered, and tackled the ropes at Laurel's ankles. "I've almost got them, sweetie. Just hold still." Elizabeth's fingers were bleeding now and most of her fingernails, short though they were, were torn.

"I saw Mary Cleophas and the baby in the pool," she whispered. "Why did he kill them?"

Laurel answered in a strangled whisper. "When I asked him where they were, he said God had revealed to him that the baby was the Antichrist and that he must put it to death. And Mary Cleophas, too, so that he could take a new bride."

She swallowed a sob. "Then he grabbed me and shoved that stinking rag in my mouth. He's incredibly strong, Mum; he got my hands behind my back and held my wrists with just one hand. All the time he was singing this creepy song about the flowers and birds and the voice of the turtle and shit like that. He tied my wrists and he made me walk up to the pool and he showed me what he'd done, like it was something he was proud of. He said he'd sent them to glory at dawn like God had told him. Oh, Mum, did you see them? Mary Cleophas was still holding that poor baby!"

The knots at the ankles were stubborn and Laurel's frantic attempts to help with her still numb fingers only slowed Elizabeth. Keeping her voice even, and hoping to distract her daughter, she asked, "What else did he say?"

"He said that God had sent me to be his spouse and that together we would have a child that would do something or other. Rule with a rod of iron, I think it was. Anyway, he started fumbling with my clothes and I told him I was having my period." She glared defiantly at her mother. "I know it sounds lame, but it worked. He backed off like I'd said I had AIDS and he said he couldn't go in unto me while I was unclean. So he tied me up to a tree and stuck flowers in my hair and did one of his damn paintings of me."

The last knots around Laurel's ankles were finally giving way when they heard a voice echoing in the stillness. *"Behold he cometh leaping upon the mountains, skipping upon the hills . . . Thou art all fair my love, there is no spot in thee . . . Thy lips, O my spouse, drop as the honeycomb: Honey and milk are under thy tongue; and the smell of thy garments is like the smell of Lebanon."*

John the Baptizer was approaching, singing in a joyous baritone.

CHAPTER 25
FIRE AND WATER
(WEDNESDAY)

ELIZABETH YANKED LAUREL TO HER FEET AND POINTED to the window. The singing was closer now. She whispered fiercely in her daughter's ear, "Get out the window as soon as he's at the door. Go as fast as you can down to Walter and Ollie's. Call nine-one-one." She bent her knees and locked her hands together. "Put your foot here and you can grab the sill."

"Rise up my fair one and come away," sang John the Baptizer.

"Mum, I can't leave you—"

"Just do it!" Elizabeth snarled. "I'm not the one he wants! Get out! *Now!*"

Laurel put a tentative foot in Elizabeth's locked hands and with a panic-driven explosion of energy, Elizabeth hurled her toward the window. Above her, Elizabeth heard Laurel's boots scrabble against the rough boards of the wall. Then she had a hold and was through the opening. Elizabeth grabbed up the pitchfork; at the same moment, the door was flung open. John the Baptizer stood there in a rusty black suit, a fading smile on his face and a bunch of wildflowers in his hand.

He stared uncomprehendingly at Elizabeth. She stood

frozen, holding the pitchfork in both hands. A breathless moment passed and suddenly the rustling and pounding footsteps of Laurel's escape could be heard. A light of understanding dawned on John the Baptizer's face and he swung back toward the door.

Gripping the pitchfork tightly, Elizabeth ran straight for the evangelist. John the Baptizer gave a startled yelp that turned to a howl of pain as three rusty tines sank into his side. His knees buckled and he fell to the ground, clutching the shaft of the pitchfork. Elizabeth let go of it and made a dash through the open door, but as she passed the writhing body, a hand shot out and caught her by the ankle. She kicked viciously at him with her free foot: his face, his crotch, anywhere to do damage. He bellowed with pain but the viselike grip grew stronger. Then, with a sudden, savage twist of her ankle, he brought her down. Her head hit the door frame and she crumpled to the dirt.

Someone was pouring water on her head and she brushed at her face to keep it out of her eyes. She had a terrible headache and something was wrong with her hands. Reluctantly she opened her eyes. She was lying under the big oak beside the still pool where Mary Cleophas and her baby were waiting. John the Baptizer stood over her, one hand pressing a bloody towel to his side, the other pouring water from a bright red-and-yellow Bojangles cup onto her head. "It's good you woke up," he told her conversationally. "You ought to be awake when you enter in to Glory."

A rope bit into her wrists; he had tied her hands together in a prayer position. *How long was I out?* she wondered desperately. Then she thought, *At least Laurel got away. Maybe she's already called for help and they'll be here soon. If I can just keep him talking . . .*

"Why did you kill Cletus and the other man?" she asked the preacher. "Cletus was just trying to help your daughter." She tried to sit up but he pushed her flat with his foot. A look of pain shot across his face as he did so.

"Just you lay still," he cautioned. "It'll not be long." He seemed to be listening for something, his head cocked to one side. "Mary Cleophas was supposed to stay hidden from the eye of man. It was a sign when the child was wrong, but I didn't understand it right off. The Lord had told me to keep her hid, so when those two come along and found her, I knew what must be done."

He looked at her happily and asked, "Have you been washed in the blood of the Lamb? It's just a quick thing and then you go to dwell in the house of the Lord forever. That's where I sent that feller with the squirrels and that's where I sent the one that come along a few days later, said he was following the first feller's trail 'cause that one always knew where the best sang was."

His eyes grew dreamy and he removed the bloody towel, glanced at it and turned it to a drier side, pressing it back against his wounds. "They was both baptized in the living waters, like it says in the Book. Living waters that flow from the rock and return to the sea. Course I couldn't leave their earthly husks here; both times I carried them out by night and took them to the river. The Lord give me the strength to do it. I'll not be able to carry the rest of you to the river. But it's fitten that Mary Cleophas and the child lay there. I put stones on 'em so they can't raise up and come after me."

His eyes brightened as if he had just heard a beloved voice. He threw his head back and looked at the sky. "I hear you, Lord," he cried in an exultant tone. Bending, he grasped Elizabeth's bound wrists and began to drag her over the grass. "It's time," he declared, and pushed her into the pool.

She sank down into the clear water, the breath driven out of her by the shock of its deathly cold. Her feet touched the rocky bottom and something brushed against her leg and she saw the long pale hair of the drowned girl wrap itself around her ankle. The dead infant's blanket was floating loose now and the tiny shriveled arms of its attached twin waved and beckoned to Elizabeth through the icy water. Shrieking, she floundered away from the silent forms swaying softly there beside her. Her head broke through the surface of the water into the sweet, sweet air and she gasped, filling her lungs greedily again and again. The sunlight dazzled her eyes. John the Baptizer, a black shadow shimmering against the sun, was standing at the edge of the pool, watching. Holding one hand outstretched over her, he broke into a rambling prayer.

Elizabeth fought madly to get a hold among the rocks and tree roots. The banks were slick, almost vertical, and she kept slipping back. John the Baptizer ignored her frenzied struggles and prayed on, his voice resounding throughout the clearing in a maniacal chant. Suddenly Elizabeth's bound hands slipped into a crevice just above the water line and her fingertips brushed a damp metal cylinder of some kind. As she ran her fingers over it and felt the metal change to wood at one end, she knew that she had at last found Cletus's shotgun.

John the Baptizer was speaking in tongues now, great ugly syllables rolling and slobbering out of his mouth like the death agonies of some horrible beast. He leaned over the pool, reaching out his hand for Elizabeth's head. She forced herself to stand motionless, waiting for him to get closer.

As he leaned nearer and nearer, drops of his spittle fell on her face. His pale eyes were rolling back in his head and his words were coming in gasps. She took one last breath, then, with all her strength, thrust the shotgun barrel straight up, smashing it into the nose and mouth of the praying man. A shriek that became a bloody gurgle formed in his shattered mouth and he tottered and fell.

Trembling with shock and cold, Elizabeth struggled out of the pool, her tied hands forcing her to slither like an ungainly seal. She gave the still body of the evangelist a wide berth and started running. Her bound hands made her clumsy and she was terrified she would fall. Only once did she pause briefly to look back. John the Baptizer had not moved. Then she ran, as fast as she could, oblivious to the messages of pain her body was sending her.

The road was steep and, with her hands bound, the many fallen trees were difficult to climb over. Twice she tripped over roots and was flung to the ground. Each time she staggered up, she was certain she heard dragging, relentless footsteps following her down the trail. Her heart was pounding and she gasped for breath. Her twisted ankle gave an excruciating twinge each time she put her foot down but still she pushed on.

She was wriggling under the big fallen poplar, inch by painful inch through the dirt, when her shirt snagged on the stub of a broken branch. It was just out of her reach and she could go neither forward nor backward. She pulled with all her strength but could not tear free. Then, like an animal in a trap, she lay there panting and exhausted, her face wet with tears of frustration. The thump of her heartbeat filled her ears, and at first she didn't hear the approaching footsteps.

Someone was hurrying toward her. Caught under the huge log, Elizabeth couldn't see the path but she could hear short gasps of breath as the footsteps grew closer. She gave one last desperate thrust to rip herself loose then two booted feet came to a halt inches from her face. The spatters of paint were unmistakable.

"Laurel! Thank God! Get me loose!"

Her daughter quickly unsnarled the snagged shirt and pulled Elizabeth from under the tree. She carried a twenty-two rifle and her face was filthy and grim.

"Mum, are you okay? I called nine-one-one but they haven't come yet. I was going crazy and finally Walter said he'd get his squirrel gun. Mum, are you hurt? Why are you wet?"

"I'm fine," Elizabeth said, ignoring the throbbing pain in her head and every muscle in her body. "Be quiet a minute."

They stood silently, mother and daughter clinging to each other as Elizabeth strained her ears for any sounds that might be the wounded evangelist. She heard only the usual small rustlings and chirpings of the undisturbed forest. At last, she sagged wearily against Laurel and murmured, "I don't know . . . maybe I killed the bastard. See if you can untie my hands. We need to get back down to the trailer."

She had swallowed two tall glasses of Ollie's super-sweet iced tea when she remembered that she had Hawkins's cell phone number in her wallet, which was locked in her car. Though they had called both 911 and the sheriff's office, as yet no help had arrived. *It's worth a try,* she told herself as she eased her aching body down the steep porch steps.

The phone rang, but there was no answer. There was a blur of static and Elizabeth was about to hang up when suddenly Hawkins's voice was loud in her ear. "Elizabeth—are you all right?"

"I need help," she replied wearily. "I think I've killed a man. We've called nine-one-one—"

"I'm with the sheriff right now," he said quickly. "We've just busted the militia and we're leaving the others to mop up. I'm riding with Blaine to answer some weird call up someplace called Lonesome Holler."

They were there almost before Elizabeth could hang up the phone. After hurried explanations from Elizabeth and Laurel, with background interjections from Ollie— "I knowed something weren't right and I said to Walter . . ."—the sheriff suggested, "Ms. Goodweather, why don't you and . . . uh . . . this young lady wait down here?"

Hawkins quickly said, "We might need them to show us how it happened." He hesitated, looking at Elizabeth. "That is, if you feel up to it."

Elizabeth smiled mirthlessly and gave Laurel a one-armed hug. "The Goodweather women," she told the two men, "are up to anything."

They circled around the little cabin, making straight for the pool where Mary Cleophas and her baby kept their silent watch. A faint odor of burning filled their nostrils and they quickened their pace. The smell grew stronger and as they came into the clearing, Elizabeth saw a great blaze of fire between them and the little pool. Panel after panel of John the Baptizer's strange, apocalyptic paintings were heaped in a roaring bonfire. She could see the bright fantastic figures writhing and twisting in the flames as they were consumed and turned to black ash. Laurel uttered a cry and lunged toward the fire, but Elizabeth pulled her back.

"Let them go," she said. Then it came to her. "Phillip," she said in horror, "he must still be alive! We have to—"

She looked at Hawkins and then at Blaine. Both men were holstering the guns they had drawn when approaching the cabin. And both were staring through and beyond the blaze at a dark shape that shimmered in midair.

The black-clad body of John the Baptizer twirled slowly at the end of a long manila rope hung from the old oak. His head drooped, and the bulging eyes above the crushed nose and mouth seemed to lock gazes with the pale eyes of Mary Cleophas and her infant child staring up from beneath the surface of the little pool.

XII—MAY 1902

Hit was near black inside the cabin afore I heared him comin. I stayed back from the window for I didn't want him to see me but I could hear him talkin to hisself and sayin scripture. He swore something awful when he seen the busted padlock and the hole in the door and then the door swung open. He weren't nothing but a black shape against the fadin light and I fired one barrel right at his heart. He pitched forward afore I could even make out his hateful face.

The kick from the gun flung me down for I had forgot to brace myself. I was pullin myself up off the floor, my ears a-ringin, when I heared Mister Tomlin say, like he was a long ways off, O Little Sylvie, I fear you've killed your own true love.

Then I heared the scratch of a Lucifer match and looked up to see Mister Tomlin lightin the oil lamp on the chimbly piece. He had his pistol in his other hand and was a-pointin hit at me.

The yellow lamplight come up and I seen that hit was Levy layin there on the floorboards. His arms was flung out towards me and his pretty golden hair was all spattered with his own heart's blood.

I screamed and started to throw myself down at his side but Mister Tomlin picked up the shotgun from where it lay. He put it to my breast and said, I found your fancy man coming for you, Little Sylvie, and I convinced him to walk along with me. Mister Tomlin's eyes was as icy blue as a winter sky and he whispered in my ear, Now your family can all be together, Little Sylvie.

CHAPTER 26
A QUESTION OF FAITH
(THURSDAY)

WHEN ELIZABETH FINALLY OPENED HER EYES, the sun was high overhead. She looked incredulously at the bedside clock—one-thirty in the afternoon. *I never sleep that long,* she thought, but then reflected that it had been late before they had finally returned home from giving statements at the sheriff's office. Evidently the exertion and shocks of the day before had taken their toll. When she gingerly forced herself out of bed in search of coffee, every inch of her body ached. Pulling on a T-shirt and a pair of scrubs, she glanced in the mirror. There was a nasty bruise on her right cheekbone and some reddened scratches below it, but otherwise she looked happier and more alive than she had in many years. She smiled cheerfully at her reflection and headed for the kitchen. The delicious aroma of French roast coffee filled the air.

It seemed unremarkable that Phillip Hawkins should be in the dining room sitting at the table with Ben and Laurel. He jumped to his feet on seeing her and held out both hands. "Are you feeling okay, Elizabeth? Laurel's been filling Ben in on the whole story. You both had a narrow escape."

"Mum was amazing," Laurel exclaimed. "She fought like a . . . a . . ."

"Like a mother defending her child?" said Elizabeth, grabbing Laurel's hand and squeezing it. "But, Phillip," she turned to Hawkins, who was still standing and watching her and Laurel with placid approval, "I thought I'd . . . well . . . I thought I'd killed John the Baptizer. I certainly tried to. Anything to get away. How could he have managed to . . . to hang himself?"

Hawkins poured another cup of coffee and handed it to her. As they both sat down, he said, "You did a lot of damage all right, but it looked worse than it really was. Besides, people in desperate situations sometimes have incredible reservoirs of strength." He took a sip from his cup and smiled at her through the steam. "As you should know.

"I talked to Blaine this morning," he went on. "He and his deputies were back out there at the scene early, looking around and trying to put all the pieces together. Blaine said it looked like John the Baptizer had tossed the rope around one of the lower branches of that oak and used it to walk himself up the trunk. Then he sat there on the branch and made the noose and—"

"But *why*?" Elizabeth interrupted. "If he thought he was doing what God told him . . . ?"

"Blaine thinks he found the answer to that one. He said they were going through the cabin and saw a Bible open on the table. Blaine said it looked like John the Baptizer had dragged himself in there and cracked the Bible. You know," he went on, seeing the puzzled look on Ben's face, "lots of folks around here use the Bible to answer questions—open it up and put your finger on a verse at random. Then you read the verse and take it as the answer to your question. Anyway, Blaine said the

Bible was open to Matthew twenty-seven and there was a bloody fingerprint smeared down the page starting at verse four."

Just like Birdie did, Elizabeth thought, and shivered.

Ben jumped up from the table and headed for the wall of books in the living room. Returning, he quickly leafed through the Bible he was holding. "It's about Judas . . . in verse four he says, 'I have sinned in that I have betrayed the innocent blood . . .' and then he goes and hangs himself."

"Oh, my god," said Laurel quietly. There seemed no more to say, and silence fell in the snug, little room. Ben closed the Bible gently and laid it on the table. Hawkins looked appraisingly at Elizabeth.

"What's this about a rattler in your car?" he asked. "You didn't tell Blaine about that yesterday."

"She didn't tell *me* till we were coming back home last night," said Laurel, sounding a little indignant.

The telephone rang and Ben answered it. "Just a moment," he said, handing the phone to Elizabeth with raised eyebrows and the beginning of a smirk.

"Miz Goodweather?" It was Harice Tyler. Elizabeth's eyes widened and she started to reply but Tyler continued evenly, "Miz Goodweather, I just found out about that serpent and I thank the Lord you wasn't harmed. I believe the Lord must have been with you. Now Sister Warren's here with me and she wants to ask your forgiveness."

There was a pause, then a woman's voice said, "Miz Goodweather, it was me put that serpent in yore car. When Harice—when Brother Tyler went to talk to you there at the grocery store, why, the demon of jealousy just grabbed ahold of me. I knowed Brother Tyler had a serpent in his truck; he'd told me about how he just caught it . . ."

She paused and in the background Elizabeth could hear Harice saying, "You got to go on, Sister Warren; you got to make it right."

"Miz Goodweather, I was just blind with the demon jealousy. You a sinner woman and a good man like Harice trailin' after you—" She stopped abruptly. There was a murmur in the background and she continued.

"I took that bag with the serpent in it out of Brother Tyler's truck and put it under yore front seat. I thought maybe it could be a kind of test to see was you worthy of Brother Tyler. I see now that I was wrong, that it was the Devil leadin' me and I'm askin' yore forgiveness, Miz Goodweather." There was an expectant pause.

Elizabeth thought about this. *Forgive you, you bitch? I'd like to rip your throat out. You almost kept me from getting to Laurel in time.* But she surprised herself by saying, "Okay, I forgive you."

There was a smothered giggle at the other end of the line. "That's real Christian of you, Miz Goodweather. I want you to know that me and Harice—me and Brother Tyler's fleecin' the Lord about what to do. Brother Tyler's goin' to pray with me regular to expel that demon of jealousy." There was another giggle and, with a soft sigh, Elizabeth hung up the phone.

"That explains the rattlesnake," she said. "Is there any more coffee?"

"Were you just talking to the person who put the snake in your car?" Hawkins looked puzzled. "Don't you want to press charges?"

"I don't know. After yesterday—after everything that happened—it's like I don't want to be angry anymore.

The person I just talked to . . . well . . . it was all a mis-understanding . . . a stupid mistake."

"That was that preacher, wasn't it?" asked Ben. "That one at the snake-handling church in Tennessee?" He laughed. "You know, at one time I thought you might be starting to believe all that stuff. When you came home over there you were kind of . . . kind of starry-eyed."

Elizabeth smiled. "There's a real appeal to blind faith. It would be comforting just to believe and not have to deal with the hard questions, but, to tell the truth, in the end it scares me. Look at those women who gave up their babies because they believed in Polaris—"

"Not to mention all the fools who believed in the white-supremacy line of the Sons of Adam," added Hawkins.

"And Mary Cleophas and John the Baptizer—they both believed he was doing God's will," said Laurel solemnly. "That kind of faith's scary."

The events of the previous day having been told and retold, Laurel had returned to Asheville and to her job. Ben was hard at work digging a new outhouse hole near his cabin, and Hawkins and Elizabeth were sitting on the porch. He was explaining that he was planning to stay on in the Asheville area for at least six more months. "I really am going to teach Criminal Justice at AB Tech next semester," he told her. "And try to get to know my daughter a little better." He stared out at the mountains, where the late sun was casting long blue shadows. "I'd like it if she could meet you and Laurel—"

The telephone rang and Elizabeth reached for the cordless phone that she'd brought out to the porch.

"Hit's a miracle!" Dorothy cried, in response to Elizabeth's guarded hello. "Lizzie Beth, I want you to know that some of them Holiness folks come to the house yesterday evenin', you know, them folks from that snake-handlin' church in Tennessee? Well, that Belvy Guthrie made 'em to come and they gathered all round Birdie and they was prayin' and callin' out and speakin' in tongues, oh, hit was a sight on earth! Then Brother Tyler anointed her with sweet oil and laid hands on her and when they was done, Birdie said all the pain had gone out of her vertables and she wanted her some biscuits and gravy to eat. She hadn't taken nary a bite of food in two days."

"Well, that's good," said Elizabeth, "I'm glad the praying made her feel better—"

"Honey, that ain't all hit done!" Dorothy almost sang the words. "When I took her back to the doctor this morning, he done that blood test they allus do and he said her count was plumb normal; said maybe him and the other doctors had been wrong all along, or hit was a spontaneous emission or some such words. Birdie's plumb cured, Lizzie Beth! And hit was her faith what done it!"

CHAPTER 27
WORLD WITHOUT END
(THURSDAY AND FRIDAY)

WHEN THE JOYFUL CONVERSATION ENDED, Elizabeth turned to Hawkins, grinning like a madwoman. "That was Miss Birdie's cousin calling to say that Miss Birdie's been cured of her cancer by prayer."

Hawkins's brow creased, but before he could speak, Elizabeth raised her hand. "And the doctor's blood tests confirm it, though *he* calls it spontaneous remission."

A door banged in the house and they heard the sound of hurrying footsteps. Ben burst onto the porch. "Aunt E! Aunt E, I think I've dug into a grave!"

They followed him to the site of his new outhouse, about fifty feet up the hill behind his cabin. There was a little flat-topped knoll and the beginning of an excavation. "I'd gotten down about three feet and all of a sudden I hit like a layer of rocks," he explained. "That was weird because there hadn't been but a few rocks till then. So I heaved them out and started digging again and I hit this." He pointed at the heap of red dirt piled around the excavation. Amidst the stones and clods was what looked like a dirt-stained bundle of rags. At one end of the bundle, the rags had fallen away to reveal a small, stained skull and the glitter of blue glass.

Elizabeth reached out to the bundle but Hawkins caught her arm. "We can't touch this. I'll call Blaine."

"Phillip," Elizabeth said, "these bones are really old—"

"Doesn't matter," said Hawkins. "The sheriff'll come out, cordon off the site, treat it like any crime scene. They'll collect the bones and try to find out who it was—"

"I think I know who it was," Elizabeth said somberly, kneeling beside the little bundle. She peered closely at the rags which, beneath the dirt stains, seemed to show faint triangles of blue and white. "It's a little quilt—the pattern called World Without End," she said softly.

Sheriff Blaine had been grimly humorous about this latest call. "What, Ms. Goodweather, another one?" His men had indeed cordoned off the area with yellow tape and, as they searched the excavation, they had quickly uncovered two more rag-clad skeletons, as well as a corroded shotgun. Ben had watched, fascinated, from the cabin steps, envious that Phillip was allowed a role in the investigation. Elizabeth sat beside him, a feeling of melancholy growing as the excavation proceeded. *Now I know how Sylvie's story ended. The baby died. And . . .*

"Man and woman, by the looks of what clothes are left," Blaine reported as the three black body bags were carried gently down the hill to the sheriff's waiting vehicle. "You might be interested to know this: I took a close look at all of them and both the adults have buckshot pellets buried in their sternums. If those two didn't die from point-blank blasts from that shotgun, I'll turn in my badge. Of course, the ME'll have to confirm it."

He looked closely at Elizabeth. "I know you haven't

lived here but twenty-something years and these remains are likely a lot older than that. But do you have any thoughts, any *intuitions,* about who it was buried back there?"

"I think that I do," said Elizabeth. "There's a story about a girl named Little Sylvie who used to live in this cabin—"

Blaine shook his head in disbelief. "I might as well show you this," he said, laying a clear plastic evidence bag on the steps. "This was in a bottle wrapped up with the baby. Ben here must have broke the bottle when he dug into it."

Through the plastic, they could see a yellowed piece of paper, crossed with faint blue and red lines. The faded writing was uneven but clear, and Elizabeth read it aloud.

This is my baby Malindy Johnson——Mister Tomlin kilt her with the Medcin in this bottle and I aim to make him Pay——Wrote by Sylvie Baker.

"So that's who the baby is. And the others are Little Sylvie . . . and . . . ?"

"Another thing." The sheriff pulled out two more evidence bags. "These were around the necks of the adults." In the bags were two dirt-encrusted gold chains. From each dangled a tiny golden heart.

Elizabeth put a finger against the plastic, feeling the outline of the heart. "The man is Levy Johnson," she said. "They didn't make it to Texas."

Back at her house Elizabeth made a quick phone call to the library, then fixed a fresh pot of coffee. She and Phillip and Ben sat on the porch and she told them the story of Little Sylvie as she had heard it from Birdie and Dorothy and from Walter. "It began with Dessie, though," she explained. "Dessie said there was something not right about the story that Little Sylvie had abandoned her baby. The day she died, Dessie told me she had dreamed of Little Sylvie lying dead with her baby in her arms. And that was true."

"Well, then, who killed them?" demanded Ben.

"Probably the husband," said Phillip. "Do you have any idea what happened to him?"

The portable phone Elizabeth had set on the railing rang and Elizabeth said, "I may in a minute." She answered the phone and listened intently for a few moments. "Thank you so much, Barb," she said. "I really appreciate it." She turned to the two listening men.

"Sylvie's husband, an Isaiah Tomlin, drowned in the great flood of 1916. Dorothy or Birdie had said that they thought that's what happened, so I asked a friend at the library to check on it. Tomlin was a wealthy and important man in the community and I felt sure there'd be a newspaper story about it."

"And since he was a wealthy and important man," mused Ben, "he could get away with murder. I guess everyone just took his word for it when he said that Little Sylvie had run off."

"Phillip," asked Elizabeth. "What will they do with the bones?"

"Well, once they're satisfied they've identified them, they'll release them to the families—if there still is family."

"Walter Johnson is Levy's nephew and Dorothy has some kind of connection to Sylvie," said Elizabeth, thinking hard. "Maybe I can get the families to agree and we can bury them all three together in the old Baker cemetery up on the hill near the road." Her eyes were misty as she added, "I want to make sure everyone knows the real story . . . all these years they've thought she was a heartless woman who left her baby to starve . . . now we know what really happened. And I want to plant flowers on their grave. There's a mass of orange daylilies and some ancient pink shrub roses over at Ben's cabin . . . maybe it was Sylvie herself who planted them. I'll transplant some of them for Little Sylvie."

She woke early the next morning just as the darkness in her room was fading. Her first thought was one of sheer joy—*Birdie's going to be all right! I don't have to lose her too!* The dog James was sleeping shoved tight against her knees. She disentangled herself and sat up to look out the three big windows just beyond the foot of her bed. Green security lights twinkled in the distance, and across the hidden river she could see the warm golden glow from a few houses with early-rising occupants. As she watched, more lights blinked on. She imagined families getting ready for the day, children, lunch boxes, coffee, sleepy greetings, hurried kisses.

She was still watching as the sky grew lighter and a narrow crimson line edged the mountaintops. The undersides of the scattered low-hanging clouds became tinged with pink, and suddenly the molten edge of the sun appeared over the tallest peak. As the day broke, filling the sky with glory and her room with sunshine, Elizabeth began to cry softly. Her tears were for Dessie, for Cletus, for Mary Cleophas and the child she had called Ishmael. And for Little Sylvie and her lover and their baby. And finally, at last, there were tears for Sam.

About the Author

VICKI LANE lives with her husband, two sons, and daughter-in-law on a mountain farm in North Carolina. She has completed her second Elizabeth Goodweather novel, *Art's Blood,* and is at work on the third.

If you enjoyed Vicki Lane's debut mystery, SIGNS IN THE BLOOD, you won't want to miss her next crime novel featuring Elizabeth Goodweather and set in the hills and hollows of Appalachia.

Read on for an exciting early look at ART'S BLOOD, the second Elizabeth Goodweather mystery, coming soon from Dell.

ART'S BLOOD

BY

VICKI LANE

ART'S BLOOD

Coming soon from Dell Books

PROLOGUE

FROM LILY GORDON'S JOURNAL—FIRST ENTRY

I still see the bed—its wide expanse floating like a snowy island on the deep pearly carpet—the creamy tufted silk coverlet neatly folded back—the heaped pillows, their pale lace soaked and stiff with her blood. Even the smells come back to me—Chanel No. 22, that sweet, spring-like fragrance she always wore—the scent of the white roses on the nightstand—and something else—a harsh, ugly, insistent smell—cloying and faintly metallic. And after all these years I still see her satin slippers beside the bed, placed neatly parallel to await a morning that never came—and the shadowy marks of her heels on the linings seem almost too much to bear.

On that day and until the day we buried her, he had seemed broken—weeping and bewildered, letting himself display a weakness none would have imagined. Was it genuine sorrow, I wonder now, or only a charade, as subsequent revelations would seem to suggest? And the child—so beautiful, so like her mother that it broke my heart to look at her—the child remained dry-eyed and quiet—already, I see now, beginning the long retreat that has transformed her into what she is today. And these are the scenes, the faces that haunt my nights.

It was at Dr. L's suggestion that I began this journal. Use it to record everything—doubts, fears, even confessions, he said. We all have our sins of omission as well as commission. If something troubles you, write it down. No one will ever read your journal; I want you to do it for yourself alone. Just write everything down and then let it go, he said. Burn the pages as soon as you finish them, if you like. I smiled grimly. A woman of my age had best keep the matches near to hand, I told him.

He patted my shoulder in that irritatingly patronizing manner of his and called me a wonder. With all you've weathered, he said, it's not surprising that you have bad dreams. He explained, as if to a child, that dreams are often caused by the mind's sifting through matters inadequately resolved in the waking hours—experiences, thoughts, emotions too unpleasant to be dealt with and so, repressed. Earlier, Dr. L had the effrontery to suggest that I see a psychiatrist, to work through some of these issues as he put it, but I dismissed that idea as preposterous. And so he proposed the journal.

If only you were a Roman Catholic, he chuckled. There's a lot to be said for a routine examination of conscience followed by confession and absolution. Clears the mind, so to speak. Many people blame themselves for trivialities when they've lost someone. They think If only I'd done this or hadn't done that . . . He helped me up and walked with me to the door where Buckley was waiting. Dr. L is a fool in many ways—there are things I would never speak of, even to a priest. But I think that he could be right in one thing. I believe that putting these memories down on paper, giving them a shape, however ephemeral (for I do intend to burn these pages), will help me to sleep.

So now I have my journal to keep me company through the interminable afternoons—the quiet, tedious times when the tick of the clock in the hall seems to slow and hang suspended like a dust mote in the fading light—the light that dims inexorably, all as if in rehearsal for the long night which soon must come. It's at these times that the past is most real, that the dead still live. And it is at these times that I see F as she was then, my mountain flower, my heart, my soul.

CHAPTER I
DON'T KNOW MUCH ABOUT ART, BUT . . .
(SATURDAY AND MONDAY)

FROM HER VANTAGE POINT AT THE TOP OF THE STEPS leading into the gallery, Elizabeth Goodweather regarded the pile of burnt match sticks with an expression that wavered between hilarity and disbelief. The heap of pale wooden slivers, some charred just slightly at one end, others little more than a fragile curl of carbon, sat in the exact middle of the room on a low pedestal covered with a sheet of thick red vinyl. The *assemblage* was about four feet in diameter and its peak was almost knee high. And it was growing.

The bare, bone-white walls of the gallery had been covered with a fine grid of narrow scarlet-lacquered shelves bearing red and blue boxes of kitchen matches in uniform stacks. As Elizabeth watched, one after another of the dinner-jacketed and evening-gowned throng of art patrons took boxes from the wall and began striking matches, extinguishing them, and adding them to the accumulation that was the focus of the evening's event.

Seemingly all of Asheville "society" had turned out to mark the late August opening of the Gordon Annex. The costly addition to the Asheville Museum of Art had been the gift of a single benefactor—Lily Gordon. This elegant little woman—*somewhere in her nineties,* whispered a woman to Elizabeth's left, had cut the crimson ribbon that stretched across the entrance to the annex and had said a few brief words in a voice that, though slightly cracked with age, was clear and carrying. Now she sat in a comfortable chair with the museum's director crouched on one side of her and the chairman of the board leaning down to catch her words.

She was wearing a simple but beautifully cut evening dress of black satin accented with white, *vintage Chanel,* Elizabeth's neighbor had informed a friend, and her arthritic fingers were covered with rings that glittered as she reached up to accept a glass of champagne from the chairman of the board. Behind her chair stood a tough looking, gray-haired man in a dark blue suit. His craggy face was expressionless and his eyes scanned the throng without stopping. *More like a secret service agent than an art lover,* Elizabeth thought.

Fascinated, she studied the little group, wondering what this very old woman made of the scene unfolding before her apparently amused gaze. *She's always been the museum's greatest patron,* someone behind her murmured, *absolutely millions of dollars. Her house is absolutely crammed with art—Picasso, Kandinsky, Pollock—just to name a few. She and her husband began collecting just after World War II. Of course—*

The voice moved away and Elizabeth smiled, wondering if she looked as out of place as she felt in this rarified crowd.

"You *are* coming in for the opening of the Gordon Annex at the Art Museum Saturday, aren't you?" Laurel, her younger daughter, had said on a visit out to the farm a few days earlier.

"Ah," Elizabeth had hedged, "Saturday. . . . Well, I . . ."

"*Mum,* this is a really important show! And you *know*

the artists—Kyra and Boz and Aidan. They're renting Dessie's house which makes them neighbors. So the least you can do . . ."

As an aspiring artist herself, Laurel was very much a part of the burgeoning art scene in Asheville and had done her best to develop Elizabeth's appreciation for the latest trends. Last year Laurel's passion had been outsider art; this year performance art was evidently the next new thing. While Laurel supported herself with a job tending bar at an upscale restaurant, she devoted most of her free time to constructing vast mixed media 'pieces', as Elizabeth had learned to call them. Recently, however, Laurel had begun to speak wistfully about the 'ephemeral beauty' of performance art and of the spiritual purity of a carefully choreographed presentation that would never be repeated.

Laurel had been relentless. "It's going to be something really special—the people attending the show will be part of the creation—" She had broken off, seeing Elizabeth's face, which unmistakably said *Oh, great.* "—if they choose to, I mean. And then Kyra and Boz and Aidan will be taking pictures during the piece and next month Carter Dixon's giving them another show at The Quer Y to display the photographs. *And*—" she had continued, with the air of someone producing a trump card, "there's going to be a really awesome twist to the whole thing that I can't tell you about now but it's going to generate some incredible publicity for those guys."

Elizabeth had at last agreed to meet Laurel at the Saturday night opening. Kyra and Boz and Aidan *were* neighbors and one did for neighbors whenever possible. *Even if it means going to some ridiculous performance and dressing up—evening clothes, my god!* Elizabeth had fumed, rummaging in her closet for something to wear. At last she found an ankle-length black skirt in a heavy polished cotton, something she had worn to some long ago event, and a white silk shirt, a Christmas present from her sister two years ago, still in its gift box. A narrow jewel-toned scarf, long forgotten in the back of a drawer, would work as a cummerbund. Suddenly her mood had improved. *They're just kids, after all, and to have a show at the Art Museum is a big deal for Kyra and Boz and Aidan.*

KyraandBozandAidan: one tended to think of them that way. Indeed, when they had first moved to the little house across the road from her farm, Elizabeth had assumed they were a *ménage a trois*. Laurel, however, had explained, with the careful patience of one speaking to the elderly and un-hip, that while at first Kyra and Aidan had been partners, when Boz had come on the scene they had briefly experimented with a three-way relationship; but eventually Kyra and Boz had excluded Aidan from the king-size futon that dominated the larger of the two bedrooms. However, no matter who slept with whom, the three still functioned artistically and domestically as a single entity and seemed to live in relative harmony.

After the death of her old neighbor Dessie, Elizabeth had been saddened to see the once neatly-kept yard growing up in weeds and had welcomed the news when one of Dessie's daughters called to say that the house was rented. "The said they was friends of Laurel and they seemed real nice, though they are awful hippies. They want to fix up the ol' barn fer a place to do their painting and such."

And the three young people had settled into the rural mountain community with uncommon ease. Boz and Aidan had been quick to offer help with simple carpentry and plumbing repairs for some of their older neighbors and were said to be "right good hands to work", while Kyra, whose nose ring and tattoos were the source of much head-shaking and tongue-clicking among the local women, had won hearts by joining in, friendly and competent, at a quilting bee held at the volunteer fire department. Elizabeth had taken her new neighbors some homemade bread and a basket of fresh herbs when they first moved in *was it February? Almost six months back.* But chores of the farm had kept her busy and beyond a quick chat on the few occasions she met one or another of the trio at the mailbox, Elizabeth had seen little of the three.

There had been the occasional encounter in Ransom, the nearby county seat, a somnolent country town which had only recently attained its second stoplight. She'd seen them recently in Wakeman's Hardware where she was purchasing hinges to repair a sagging door. They were clustered around a metal bin, evidently assessing the artistic potential of a mass of nails. Boz, at six five and in his customary red cowboy boots, towered over the other two. His frizzy brown mop of hair, wide crooked nose and acne-pitted face were unattractive, at best, but his deep confident voice and booming laugh seemed to mark him as the obvious leader of the trio.

Aidan was as handsome as Boz was ugly. *Beautiful rather than handsome,* Elizabeth had thought at the time. Slender, but well-muscled, Aidan stood not quite six feet tall with smooth tanned skin *except for that ugly burn scar on his arm,* and long blond hair that he usually wore in a sleek pony tail.

Kyra was tiny, barely reaching Aidan's shoulder. With her spiky hair dyed a jetty black, the nose ring, and the multiple tattoos, she was an incongruous sight amid the hardware and farm implements—yet in spite of all these affectations, Elizabeth had suddenly realized that Kyra was a very pretty young woman.

Elizabeth shook herself out of her reveries and tried to pay attention to the scene unfolding around her. *Strike on Box*—had been billed as "participatory performance art" and it was the first "piece" to be presented in the new modern wing of Asheville's art museum. Kyra and Boz and Aidan, billed simply as The 3—the name they signed to all their joint art works, were moving around the gallery, each armed with a digital camera. Kyra was flitting about the room with her camera, chatting easily with onlookers and encouraging their participation. Aidan's camera was focused on the growing pile of burnt matches and, as Elizabeth watched, Boz, snapping shot after shot, approached the chair where the old woman was sitting. He thrust the camera close to her unsmiling face and said something. An expression of distaste pulled down the old woman's thin lips but she did not reply. Instead she raised one hand slightly.

Instantly the blue-suited man came forward and motioned Boz to move away. Boz stared down in disbelief at the smaller man and laughed. The smaller man took a step forward and spoke briefly. After a moment's hesitation Boz shrugged his shoulders and moved on. The other man watched him go, then turned to the old woman whose displeased look had not wavered. She raised a finger and the man bent his head near to her mouth as she spoke a few words then resumed her aloof study of the evening's entertainment.

Elizabeth watched, bemused, as the flamboyant Boz moved through the crowd, seemingly unfazed by the recent rebuff. He moved to one wall where a voluptuous blonde, *trophy wife,* Elizabeth decided, was stretching up to retrieve a box of matches from the topmost grid. Boz crept up behind her, aimed the camera at her stiletto heels then slowly, lasciviously, shot the length of her tightly gowned body, lingering on her rounded buttocks then focusing on her cleavage when she turned around. Her squeal expressed surprised delight and a tanned, silver-haired man who had been wordlessly watching Boz, burst into a raucous guffaw. "He's immortalized that expensive ass of yours, Vanessa. Now *you're* a work of art."

Across the gallery a little knot of attendees burst into laughter. From their midst emerged a trim middle-aged man in beautifully tailored evening clothes. His head was completely bald and shone as if waxed. Diamond studs sparkled in his earlobes and a vest, lavishly embroidered in deep metallic blues and greens could be seen beneath his dinner jacket. A man's voice somewhere to Elizabeth's right said in a low tone to an unseen companion, "Carter Dixon's here to protect his little investment. I warned him that he was taking a chance with a loose cannon like Boz but, oh no, Carter knows best. He swears that the photographs from this performance will fly out the door, once he mounts the show at the QuerY."

"Carter sometimes likes them rough," sniffed the other man. "I, personally, don't care for the acne-pitted look. Now the other one . . . that blonde boy . . . quite delicious. Just like that gorgeous elf in the *Lord of the Rings* films."

Carter Dixon, owner of Asheville's newest gallery, had succeeded in gaining Boz's attention and was speaking urgently to him as the young artist continued his circuit of the gallery, seemingly intent on capturing images of all the attendees. After a few minutes, Boz turned the camera on Dixon, aiming first at his bald head then, as he had done with the shapely Vanessa, slowly panned down the length of Dixon's body, pausing at his crotch then crouching down to move around for a rear shot.

Dixon whirled, his face flaming, and melted back into the crowd. Pleased snickers erupted from the pair at Elizabeth's right and they moved away, trading delighted speculations as to whether or not *those* particular photographs would show up at the QuerY.

Elizabeth looked around the crowded room for Laurel who seemed to have disappeared. Standing on tiptoe, she tried to catch a glimpse of her daughter's fiery mop of dreadlocks somewhere among the careful coiffures of the society matrons who were giggling like teenagers as they struck match after match.

But Laurel was nowhere in sight. Elizabeth began edging toward the door that led to the smaller gallery where Rob Amberg's photographs of rural Appalachia were on display. She had seen these before, indeed, an autographed copy of his book graced her coffee table. *All this foolishness,* she thought, *I need to look at something real.*

As she wove her way between the chattering art patrons, feeling safely invisible in her anonymous black skirt and white shirt, Elizabeth realized that The 3 had suddenly left the gallery. She hesitated, wondering if a new phase of the performance was about to begin but the smell and smoke of hundreds of matches was becoming annoying. Deciding that she would risk missing whatever was coming next, Elizabeth resolutely shouldered her way between two brittle-faced women who were regaling each other with horror stories concerning the outrageous demands of their respective *au pairs.*

The smaller gallery was blessedly quiet and uncrowded. A few patrons were studying the large black and white photographs whose subjects were so like many of Elizabeth's neighbors. She went first to the picture of a sturdy white-haired woman in a house dress leaning down to milk a cow. *Just like Dessie,* she smiled, remembering her late neighbor. She was moving slowly around the gallery, working her way to her favorite picture—a shaggy workhorse being led down through a snowy barnyard toward a rude gate—when she heard the sound of familiar voices.

She paused to read the artist's statement, which was on an easel by the door. Beyond the door was a small hallway where restrooms and an elevator were located and looking out the door Elizabeth saw The 3 reflected in the glass of a large framed poster that hung beside the elevator. She was about to move away to avoid being caught skipping out on their performance piece when she heard Aidan say, "And you'll show up before they actually arrest me." In the reflection she could see him tossing his long straight yellow hair back in a strangely girlish gesture. "I sure as fuck don't want to end up in a cell with some big Bubba type who fancies me for his bitch."

She could see the mirrored Boz clap Aidan on the shoulder and hear the growl of his deep voice. "Don't worry, man; I'll be back in time to save your skinny ass."

Elizabeth strained to catch what Kyra was saying. The young woman's voice was pitched low and she sounded distressed, ". . . tell us where you'll be . . . danger . . ." That was all Elizabeth could hear before Boz's deep rumble cut off Kyra's murmurings.

"Naw, baby girl, it's better Aidan don't know where I'm at. They might want to give him a lie detector test and he'd spill his guts. Now you two get on back in there and we'll get this show on the road."

Hurriedly, Elizabeth moved away from the door and back to the main gallery and the pile of burnt matches. Without the presence of The 3 and their busy cameras, the attendee/participants seemed a little weary of the game now and many were ignoring the unopened match boxes still on the gridded wall. Most of the men seemed to be huddled in knots discussing financial matters or golf and the table at the side where champagne was being poured was doing a lively business. The ancient benefactress and her bodyguard were gone, but no one had presumed to sit in her chair. The director and chairman were deep in talk, each with an empty glass in hand.

"What do you think, Mum?" Laurel, her tall, slender frame clad in a long floating garment made of red-orange silk shot with gold threads, materialized suddenly at her mother's elbow, and waved her champagne glass at the pile of burnt matchsticks on the red circle. "Look at the composition that makes! And the grid on the walls—well, obviously it references Modrian, but the ongoing depletion speaks so clearly of a postmodern sensibility!" She nodded toward the dark lattice of shelving. It was mostly empty now, but for a few untouched matchboxes, and Elizabeth had to admit that it did have a certain. . . .

"Well," she ventured, "in the words of the philosopher, I don't know much about art, but—where did that outfit come from, Laurel? It looks expensive."

Laurel grinned and struck a pose. "It's an original—Lisa lent it to me. We did a trade; I'm going to model some stuff for—"

She broke off, seeing Kyra and Aidan re-enter the room and begin snapping pictures again. Elizabeth was amused to notice that many of the patrons who had been busy with their champagne and gossip were suddenly moved to resume the lighting and extinguishing of matches. Just as one particularly expensive-looking woman was elaborately placing her match at the very apex of the pile, there was a loud hissing sound. The gallery patrons stared, jaws agape, as Boz, wielding a big fire extinguisher, covered the woman and the pile of matches with white foam.

There was stunned silence and then Boz spoke. "Aidan, you pathetic shit, it's over." He dropped the fire extinguisher and walked calmly over to Aidan and Kyra. A woman behind Elizabeth hissed, "Isn't this exciting! I just love performance art! But I had no *idea* that Marilou was going to be part of it."

Marilou, evidently the woman who had been covered with foam, didn't act as if she had known either. She was wiping the foam from her face and making sputtering noises as she looked down at the ruin of her turquoise silk gown. The throng of guests made no move to assist her as they watched eagerly to see what would happen next.

Elizabeth was confused. Aidan and Kyra seemed to be cowering away from Boz as he approached them. His massive body, clad in the black slacks and black tee shirt that were the uniform of The 3, strode toward them, red cowboy boots resounding on the slick floor. Aidan and Kyra stood there dumbly while Boz reached out, snatched the cameras from their hands, and hurled them to the floor. With a sardonic grin he began to stamp on the cameras.

"Boz, you crazy fucker!" Aidan's anguished howl reverberated in the stunned silence as he dived for the cameras. "You're destroying the show!"

"You got it, little buddy," replied Boz. Satisfied that the cameras were ruined, he calmly walked over to the nearest wall and began pulling down the flimsy shelves. Kyra was crying helplessly and the woman who was standing behind Elizabeth whispered again, a little dubiously this time, "It's all part of the art, isn't it?"

is thick and glossy, and the current robin is blithe, busy with twigs and straw, eyeing me without rancor despite the weeks which have passed since I was last here.

The old gate creaks open and I frown. They are aware that they are not to follow me about unless I ask that they should. Except for the day of Colin's death, it has been many years since I last came here but nonetheless, they should know better. If it is Norah, fussing and tutting, I shall be short with her.

But it is not Norah. Squinting, I peer between the pink blossom and the white, between the trailing roses. Someone is coming toward me across the grass—and my heart leaps hard and strains beneath my clothes. If a thing is desired hard and long enough, can it achieve tangible substance? I would have thought not. Yet undeniably, my heart's desire, my longed-for love, approaches me.

"Dickon?" I say wonderingly. He is as he was when I first met him, a boy again. The only time I saw eyes bluer was when Richard's wife came.

"Hello," he says.

"Who are you?" I ask the question because now that he is closer I can see that it is not my long-ago Dickon, though remarkably like.

"Dickon," he says and I gasp. "Dickon Craven."

Such symmetry. Such synthesis. "And where are you from, Dickon Craven?" I ask him.

He takes a wooden pipe—yes, a pipe—from his pocket and gazes about him. "I'm here with my mother," he says. "And I know you're Miss Mary."

"That's right."

"Wasn't there someone here who could charm animals?" he asks. He blows on his pipe and at the sound of that low little call, the years drop away from me. The robin appears and lands importantly on a branch of a dwarf apple tree.

"There was indeed."

"I'd certainly like to have met him," this Dickon says. He plays again, a spray of crooked little notes and I swear that though I had never before seen rabbits in the secret garden, two of them now appear beside a bush of lavender and sit up, for all the world as if they were at a concert.

"I think," I say, "that he would like to have met you."

"Who was he?"

"He was your grandfather."

"My mother has told me all about him. And about you."

"Your mother being?"

"Amy. It means 'the loved one.' It's French, originally."

"And where is Amy, the loved one?"

"Up at the house, I think."

"What about your father, Dickon?"

"He's dead. He died at the end of the war." He looked puzzled. "But you know that."

"I just wanted to be sure."

For the first time in years, I remember the skipping rope which Dickon's mother bought for me. If I had it now, I would skip until I reached a hundred. Or more. A thousand. Ten thousand. Energy fizzes through my body. I stand. I hold out my hand and he takes it. Ah, the feel of those warm fingers. The trust they offer. My heart is flowering. I had imagined it to be a dried-up seed-pod, waiting for rain. And now it is being watered. The tender shoots of love are already springing. "I should really like to meet your mother, Dickon."

"Come on, then." He blows again on his pipe and the rabbits dash away. The robin puts its head on one side then flies before us to the gate which leads out into the world beyond the secret garden, where life awaits me.

For Everyone Held Spellbound By The Magic of
The Secret Garden and *Return to the Secret Garden* . . .

A LITTLE PRINCESS

Francis Hodgson Burnett

"An odd little child, with old-fashioned ways and strong feelings," ten-year-old Sara Crewe arrived at Miss Minchin's London boarding school like a little princess: with splendid clothes in velvet, lace and silk, beautiful dolls, furs, and even a French maid. But when a terrible misfortune leaves her penniless and alone, Sara's spirit never wanes. Here, in one of the best-loved stories in the world, we follow the adventures of the irrepressible Sara as she introduces us to a series of unforgettable characters, in a delightful tale as timeless as the dreams of children of all ages everywhere. **With an introduction by Lynn Sharon Schwartz.** (526228—$3.95)

*Prices slightly higher in Canada.

Ⓢ **SIGNET**

CLASSICS TO STIR THE IMAGINATION

☐ **THE PHANTOM OF THE OPERA by Gaston Leroux.** Filled with color and theatrical spectacle of the paris Opera House in the nineteenth century, and the ageless fascination of love transformed into murderous obsession, this classic work of mystery and suspense remains a riveting journey into the dark regions of the human heart. It continues to thrill audiences to this day as an unparalleled work of sheer entertainment. (524829—$4.95)

☐ **THE HUNCHBACK OF NOTRE DAME by Victor Hugo, with an Afterword by Andre Maurois.** Immensely popular from its original publication to the present day, Hugo's haunting love story of the monstrous, gentle Quasimodo, and the gypsy dancer Esmeralda, stands unsurpassed as an enduring and vivid historic and literary triumph. "Hugo's characters were to live . . . in the minds of men of all countries and all races . . . They are unforgettable because they possess the elemental grandeur of myths and epics."—Andre Maurois (522222—$4.95)

☐ **THE TURN OF THE SCREW and Other Short Novels by Henry James. With a new introduction by Perry Meisel.** Wonderfully readable and totally involving, the short novels of Henry James allow readers to experience the full range of his skill and vision. From his chilling masterpiece of phantoms of the mind, The Turn of the Screw to Daisy Miller, the classic story that established James' reputation, this anthology functions as a perfect James primer: an accessible route to the singular art and imagination of an author who profoundly influenced American writing for a century to come. (526066—$4.95)

Prices slightly higher in Canada.

Ⓢ SIGNET

TIMELESS TALES OF MYSTERY AND IMAGINATION

☐ **DRACULA by Bram Stoker. 100th Anniversary Edition, with an introduction by Leonard Wolf.** He sleeps in a lordly tomb in the vaults beneath his desolate castle. His stony eyes are open. His cheeks have the flush of life beneath their pallor. On his lips—a mocking, sensuous smile moist with scarlet-fresh blood. He has been dead for centuries, yet he may never die . . . Here begins the story of an evil ages old and forever knew—a story of those who feed a diabolic craving. The story of Count Dracula. (523377—$4.95)

☐ **FRANKENSTEIN by Mary Shelly.** The classic novel of steady mounting terror, written with a near-hallucinatory intensity by Shelly when she was only nineteen years old. An immediate sensation when it was first published in 1818, Shelly's Gothic masterpiece has been the source of inspiration for the flowering of the romantic— and feverish—imaginings of generations—both young and old alike.
(523369—$3.95)

☐ **DR. JEKYLL AND MR. HYDE by Robert Louis Stevenson.** Conceived in a nightmare, the tale of the scientist Dr. Jekyll and the mysterious drug that transforms hin into the fiendish Mr. Hyde, that loathsome and twisted reincarnation of pure evil, has retained the ability for over a hundred years to send the blood of its readers running cold. (523938—$3.95)

☐ **THE FALL OF THE HOUSE OF USHER, And Other Tales by Edgar Allen Poe, with a new introduction by Stephen Marlowe.** The celebrated master of the macabre, Edgar Allen Poe brought his nightmare visions to vivid dramatic life in his classic stories. Here are fourteen of his richest tales including *The Pit and the Pendulum, The Tell-Tale Heart, The Fall of the House of Usher, The Purloined Letter* and others. Lush, mysterious, poetic, and darkly romantic, these stories are Poe at his inspiring best. (524632—$5.95)

Prices slightly higher in Canada.